COLOURS
of DECEPTION

HEATHER L. WEBSTER

Published by WindSong Wines

Copyright © 2021

ISBN: 978-0-6452368-0-4 (paperback)

First edition, 2021

For book orders and enquiries, contact:
HeatherWebster4@bigpond.com

NATIONAL
LIBRARY
OF AUSTRALIA

A catalogue record for this
book is available from the
National Library of Australia

This book is dedicated to my family past and present who have contributed to my being, and to all the readers and writers who value imagination and creativity in all its forms.

Chapter 1

Robe, South Australia, 1990

Mac stood strong and solid as the pier as Costas manoeuvred the *Aphrodite* through the narrows and towards the dock.

'Good evening Captain,' he smiled with mock salute as he caught the mooring rope. 'I hope we have a profitable catch.'

'Bloody hard trip. Earn your keep and unload this lot. It's your turn to get wet and stink of fish guts.' Costas ran a hand through tangled hair, across his lined face.

Mac secured the boat, fastening the heavy ropes to the jetty, before backing up his truck. Seagulls squabbled and squawked. With the massive winch on the pier Mac hoisted the precious lobsters into the refrigerated crates on the back of the truck.

'How's prices?'

'Eighty dollars this week for a three-kilo lobster in Hong Kong if it's still wriggling,'

Costas grimaced. All the captains loved fishing but were suspicious of agents and flummoxed by paperwork. Big lobster money beckoned from Asia but most played safe and sold their catch locally.

'And wouldn't you like to wriggle that girl of yours to Hong Kong,' called David from the next boat. 'I don't know what she sees in you, you're smellier than the bait.'

'How would you know, you lazy bastard, you've never kept a woman for more than a night. One taste and they spit you out. Worse than an octopus, I've heard. All arms and suckers.'

Weary men hosed the decks, coiled ropes, refuelled and emptied storage tanks. Seagulls screamed as they quarrelled over the final scraps.

'Red sky at night, sailors' delight,' Costas smiled. 'I need a big red steak, a cold beer and a long sleep.'

His crew murmured agreement as they lugged duffle bags to their cars and headed home.

Mac drove to the cold store depot and deposited the catch as the last of the sun flashed on the white sand and circle of houses against Robe's hills.

At midnight, he drove back to the cold stores.

The sea was calm, no wind. Mac knew the piers and vessels like the back of his hand. He'd worked them during the lobster season for nearly fifteen years. The *Aphrodite* had been refuelled and greased winches turned without a sound. When the storage cache was full of lobster, he allowed himself a tense sigh of relief.

The sea looked solid. Smooth and black as oil. The deserted docks were a patchwork of grey sliding shadows. Surrounded by reassuring silence, he started the *Aphrodite's* engines.

Mac had chosen the *Aphrodite* with care. She had been one of his favourite boats ever since he was a skinny-legged kid with big ideas who learned to wash her down and stow her gear for a bit of pocket money. Since he was fifteen, he'd crewed for Costas when an extra hand was needed.

Safety dictated that a boat her size needed a crew of two, but Mac set off alone. Speed was essential. He had borrowed the boat before and knew that Costas would welcome the extra hire money. But Mac had not asked permission. He'd not even hinted about the trip to anyone. A night trip would need an explanation and he was a hopeless liar.

He cast off the heavy ropes and edged the *Aphrodite* out from the mooring just as he had done a hundred times before, then set his course. The calm weather augured well for a quick trip. Adrenalin pumped through his nervous body, banishing the cold and masking his fear. The rendezvous would be in the high seas – maritime law deemed that the ocean beyond any nation's territorial waters was 'high seas', not that sea surged higher there than anywhere else, he thought with a tight smile.

The night wrapped closely around him: deep dark with thick cirrus clouds shredded across the face of the moon. Fitful breezes began to pluck at his curly brown hair like the fingers of dead sailors. The change was forecast to come from the south about 4am. By that time Mac planned to be safely home in bed. His gut churned with anticipation as he sucked cool salt air to quell his queasiness. Guilt tightened his stomach. It crawled from a knot in his belly up his back and flamed his cheeks.

'Everything'll be all right,' Mac muttered. 'Costas'll be OK when he gets the money.' He repeated the mantra over and over in his head but felt no comfort. Mac knew these waters. The lobsters tucked safely in the holds below deck were not complaining. What could possibly go wrong? As soon as the boat reached deeper water away from prying eyes, Mac opened the throttle and the *Aphrodite* surged forward.

Mac banked on these few hours improving his life forever. Soon he'd have money, plenty of money. Catherine would love him even more. The boat cut through the water and he enjoyed the feeling of the familiar deck beneath his feet. The *Aphrodite* was solid, with good equipment and a new state-of-the-art GPS system. Navigating was easy. He had transferred plenty of fish at sea before. Nearing the specified coordinates, his heart pounded hard against his ribs. Tonight was a giant gamble and Mac didn't often gamble. Guy had made the plans and arranged the deal.

'One trip a year'll be all you need,' he'd said, time after time. 'Just one load, you know you can do it.'

He'd convinced Mac there was no chance of failure. The full cargo of lobster was a cinch. The skippers trusted him – he loaded and transported their lobsters every week. Guy had organised the buyers and the deal would be cash. No paperwork, no middlemen, and best of all, no tax. Mac would deliver the lobsters to the waiting boat, collect the money and be back in the harbour by two. He'd reimburse the skippers for their lobsters; pay Costas for the boat and pocket a juicy profit for his initiative. It was good for everyone. The taxman might lose but cheating him was fair game. Mac stood to clear $50,000. It would reduce his debt on his dream vineyard to a manageable level. Costas and the others would understand after Mac delivered the money. Tomorrow he would be *King of the Docks*.

As rendezvous time neared, his heart pounded and sweat dampened his armpits despite the cold. The sound of a powerful engine thrummed across the water and Mac exhaled with relief. He shook his arms to release some of the tension knotting his shoulders. The wind picked up and the surface of the sea ruffled into a small chop. With open ocean and the Antarctic to the south, forecasting was never precise. He frowned as he smelled ice on the wind and the cold reached deep in his lungs. The forecast change would arrive earlier than expected. Engines throbbed and a giant ship loomed out of the darkness. Mac's signal, short/long/short flashes as agreed, was acknowledged and the ship cut its speed. In a heartbeat, the trawler drew alongside the *Aphrodite*, and men peered down silhouetted against the floodlights.

Mac waved.

A winch swung over the side and three men in a wire cage descended to the deck of the *Aphrodite*.

''ello, 'ello' one of them said as he emerged from the basket-like cage and pumped Mac's hand. Mac was relieved. 'You fish for money tonight?' he joked, with a wide smile.

Conversation was not easy, but the smiling and backslapping felt right. Mac gestured to the hold, unlocked the hatches and locked the ladder into position. The men moved easily around the deck, familiar with the universal task of loading and unloading. They all wanted to complete the task and leave as fast as possible. As crates of lobster were hauled up, Mac tied off the tenders and climbed into the basket to be winched high above the decks of the *Aphrodite* past painted Asian characters and above the flaking letters spelling *Peking Star*.

So far so good. Just meet the captain, confirm the load and collect the money. As the night turned soot black, racing clouds masking the moon, three short men wearing yellow waterproofs, stepped into the harsh light. They shook hands with great enthusiasm as names were snatched away by the wind. Two of them ushered Mac down a short flight of stairs to the captain's cabin while the third scuttled off to check the lobsters. In their bulky gear, all the men looked similar. Only Mac's height marked him out.

'We like lobster in my country. Rich business,' said the captain as he and two others stood across the table from Mac in the low, crowded cabin. Mac flicked through the money as the Captain handed it over. Excitement quickened Mac's blood; he had never seen so much cash. He skimmed each stack and handed it to the second man who wrapped each wad in waterproof oilskin. The Captain talked a lot and Mac leaned in to catch his words. The third man sealed the packs and Mac slid them into zipped pockets inside his waterproofs and pants. The last bulky one wouldn't fit so he put it in the outside pocket of his jacket.

The workers on the *Aphrodite* loaded rhythmically, connected winching hooks to the crates, which swung up from the tiny boat onto the wide decks above. Amid the noise and bustle of activity, thumbs-up served as the universal signal for 'All Good'.

The huge vessel intrigued Mac. He'd never been on a modern factory ship before. Under the harsh floodlights he recognised equipment for many types of fishing – seine and drift nets, jigger lines for squid, reels to haul in the long lines that could be set for shark or tuna, even dive cages and scuba equipment. It was vast compared to the *Aphrodite*. The

multiple decks had massive storage capacity and it would be self-suffi-
cient for long journeys. The crew probably spent months, even years, at
sea. He wished he could explore further.

Soon enough, the deal was done, the lobsters counted, money transferred. Mac smiled as he slapped his hands against the bulky packages
of cash stowed in his pockets. Excitement replaced apprehension as he
realised the plan had worked. His heartbeat and breathing slowed as he
climbed into the last cage to be lowered to the *Aphrodite* and race home.
Cold wind rolled from the south, smelling of icebergs. The change had
arrived in full force, a good two hours early. The Chinese ship's engines
revved, ready to power away.

As Mac reached the deck, the cage jolted and, stepping out, he fell
as the deck lurched upward. With horror he realised that, as the weather
had deteriorated, the *Aphrodite* was knocking against the giant ship.
Under the shadow of the deck, the tenders were askew and as the ship
accelerated away, these David and Goliath vessels would collide. If a big
wave came, the *Aphrodite* would be damaged. Mac didn't want to waste
his profit fixing the boat.

'What the hell are you doing?' he yelled up toward the ship.

Mac saw the tension on the mooring line suddenly increase. In an
instant it was too tight for him to untie. He would need to chop the rope
to separate the boats. He ran across the sharply angled deck to grab the
axe but slipped and fell. His jacket snagged on a protruding lobster cage
and the outer pocket ripped open. The oilskin money package unrav-
elled, and a wad of notes spilled onto the wet deck. He grabbed the stack
and flicked the precious notes to shake off the water. In the uncertain
light his heart fell like a quarry stone. On board the ship he had seen
and counted the money – $400,000 had been in his hands. To his horror,
he realised the wet notes in his trembling hand were worthless rupiahs,
neatly sandwiched with Australian fifty-dollar notes on the outside. He
had been conned by the oldest trick in the book. He reached into his
pants and ripped open another package. They were the same. As the

second man had wrapped the wads of money in protective oilskin, he had switched the bundles of notes. Confused, then horrified, Mac felt his entire life collapse around him. Panic rose, gripping his throat. His legs buckled as he struggled to breathe.

Harsh sounds from timbers splintering under stress pulled him back to the danger on the boat. The gathering wind, the choppy sea and the huge difference in size between the vessels threatened the *Aphrodite*. As the large ship accelerated, it jerked the tiny boat into its side. This rendezvous location had been carefully chosen to be far away from usual shipping channels – no help would be around if his boat floundered.

Even if he was able to launch a lifeboat and avoid being crushed by this juggernaut of a ship, how could he explain the loss of the lobster, the damage to the *Aphrodite* or his presence in the Southern Ocean? Guy's great idea for making money evaporated like dry ice before his eyes.

'You fool, you stupid fool.' He punched the air. Even if he managed to save his life, he couldn't ask for help. His mind raced as he weighed up the dreadful options. The boat's location and the prevailing currents meant that a lifeboat would be swept toward Antarctica. That would mean freezing to death.

It is said that as you die, your life flashes before your eyes. But Mac imagined his future following this disaster. With the cash, he could have nursed the *Aphrodite* back to port, repaired the damage and paid for the lobsters. Without the money, his reputation would be in tatters, he would be in debt, if not in jail. No one would forgive him. Far from his dream of paying off the Langhorne Creek vineyard, his life would be destroyed. How could he have been so stupid? Catherine would never forgive him and what about his little girl? He beat his hand against his head and punched the railing. Too late he recognised he was a fool.

Every sensation, sight and sound, each pounding heartbeat took an age. Then Mac's will to survive surfaced and he leapt into action. Terrified by the breaking timbers and the danger posed by the freshening wind and choppy waves, he heard rushing water as it poured into the boat. His mind raced, grasping and discarding options. In a triumph of optimism over any form of sense, he decided to reboard the *Peking Star*. Cutting the *Aphrodite* adrift would prevent further damage. With luck and the trace from her distress signal, a salvage ship might find her in the morning.

Mac had seen long shark lines running from the transom. He would jump off the *Aphrodite* into the water, swim to the stern of the *Peking Star* and attach himself to one of the long lines, then climb on board and get his money. They'd have lifeboats. It was the only option he could see in a totally screwed situation.

The wind strengthened and crashed the boats together again. The *Aphrodite* listed; inrushing waves turning the surfaces slick and hazardous. Empty crates and unsecured equipment slid across the deck. The *Aphrodite* lurched in unpredictable ways. Wielding the emergency axe with the strength of a man possessed, Mac chopped the mooring rope and separated the two vessels. He kicked off his boots and shrugged off his bulky waterproof jacket and jumper. Reaching into the deck locker he grabbed a dark buoyancy vest and tied a length of cord around his waist, assessed the orientation of the two boats, the direction of the waves and the rising wind. Fear weighed like a stone in his gut as he jumped into the icy water.

Chapter 2

Ice from the South, 1990

One shocked breath after plunging into the freezing ocean, Mac was swimming. The roar of the engines was deafening. Damn, he hadn't considered the turbulence from the huge propellers. The water was calm one minute, surging the next. Buffeted one-way then another, as each wave surged, he lunged his head high in the hope of seeing the fluorescent floats on the long lines. Waves slapped his face and the wind howled across the dark and icy water. Numbing cold sapped his energy but, fuelled by fear and adrenaline, he powered with short choppy strokes across the twenty meters to the black shadow of the ship.

Every minute in the icy water sucked energy from him. Optimism dissolved into despair, and then he felt a snaking drag across his legs. Hoping desperately it was not a shark he lunged, grabbed and yowled with pain as a large hook snagged the palm of his left hand. He held the line tightly, pulled the hook loose, ripping a chunk of flesh from his palm, then, despite the pain, hauled on the line until he reached the main rope. He looped his arm over the line. Cold numbed the jagged wound but made it hard to attach a safety line.

Hand over painful hand he hauled his protesting body toward the ship. He knew he was shark bait. If not sharks, the cold would kill him soon.

The cloud parted and moonlight silhouetted a hull, black and as smooth as a medieval watch tower. The few lights on deck didn't reach down to the water. The net launching platform was his only chance. Mac edged himself close to the platform, gritted his teeth and summoned the last of his energy. As the next wave surged, he grabbed some trailing net and, drawing on strength built from years of working with cold heavy nets, dragged his numbed body onto the steep, slippery platform. He crawled up the slope, a clumsy spider on a tatty web. He shivered uncontrollably. The platform shuddered and creaked each time a wave surged below. The rough rope provided welcome grip. He climbed high to the net housing, and blind in the dark, stumbled over crates, ropes and nets.

Out of the wind, he beat his uninjured arm against his body, shook the streaming water from his tight curled hair and stamped his legs. In the water he had cursed the dragging weight of his clothes. Soon they might warm him. Gradually his shivering slowed, and his breathing returned to normal. Arms stretched forward like a blind man, he struggled through the dark feeling for a place to hide. When he tripped into a tangle of tarpaulins and rope, he burrowed deeper and there, cocooned between rough dry layers, fell into an exhausted sleep.

Soon he woke in agony. The jagged wound on his hand throbbed. Thirst raged, his tongue like a carpet ball in his salty mouth. The last of his energy had been depleted hauling his battered body on board. Physical pain was nothing compared to his mental anguish. Struggling in the swirling water behind the ship, Mac thought nothing could be worse than freezing to death in the inky black ocean, but the recognition that he had ruined his own life and that of the people he loved, hit like a brick. Fear for their future and loathing for his own gullibility consumed him. He cursed Guy. Had he planned the double cross from the beginning? Did he know Mac would not get his money? It had all been so slick. Mac had thought he'd made a friend, or at least a canny business partner and they would work well together for a long time.

But Guy would make more money if Mac was not paid. He must have known about the money switch. Mac pictured his handsome, confident face and suddenly saw a con man. He had been a fool to be so trusting.

With salt caked on his skin, he forced himself to crawl deeper into the hold in the dim light of early morning. He needed water then food.

It soon became a pattern. Each dawn, he scavenged crabs and small fish which had escaped or been discarded from the nets; he snatched mouthfuls of rainwater that gathered in depressions in the tarpaulins. A patina of salt covered his skin and matted his hair. His world reeked of fish and oily diesel. Never a fastidious eater, he was surprised by what he now considered edible.

On the nights when the crew did not fish, Mac emerged from his cocoon-like hiding places in cupboards and storage crates. His trousers grew loose around his waist and his back was bony against the hard floorboards, but the salt had helped heal his hand. He obsessed about the ease with which he was lured into this ridiculous scheme. He had been flattered by Guy's attention and relied on his experience to make this scheme work. It had seemed so simple. A good price, a good profit; no one would lose. Most of all he cursed himself for not considering the risks and the now obvious consequences.

On the rare nights when he ventured on deck for some welcome fresh air as most the crew slept and the night crew focussed on the passage ahead, he drew scant comfort from knowing that his family, which grew more distant with every passing day, were sleeping under the same stars. Below decks, his memories and dreams were vivid with pain. Mac lost hope faster than weight.

The ship steamed on. Large factory ships like this spent months, if not a year, at sea. Mac reasoned that taking fresh lobsters on board might signal that this journey was near an end. The ship seemed low in the water; he hoped the holds were full. Over many days and nights of careful creeping, Mac pieced together a mental map of the decks: the fishing gear, the way the ship operated and every lifeboat or object useful in an escape. Avoiding detection was easier than he expected because, while there were multiple decks and huge storage capacity, the crew was sparse. Every day he waited for an opportunity to find the captain's cabin and recover his money; every day he was thwarted. Mac prowled craftier than a fox on the hunt. Recovering his money was his sole hope. But as the days passed, staying alive dominated his thoughts. If he was discovered, he was sure the crew would kill him or throw him overboard. During the day, Mac tried to sleep, and skulked in corners silent as a rat. As he observed the crew's hard lives, he regretted the unappreciated luxury of his former life and cursed his greed.

Mac wasn't ready to die. Each day he searched for food to rebuild his strength. One day he scavenged some rice after a cooking pot had spilled on the deck and savoured the bland flavour and feeling of full-ness it brought to his belly. On the same day, deep below decks among the ballast, he found scores of plastic drums of freshwater. He greedily drank his fill. It was a relief after licking rain puddles. There was plenty to sluice his body clean. From that day, he hoped his luck was changing. Every night he drank as much as he wanted and flushed the salt out of his system. Salt had controlled the infection in his hands, but thirst had tormented him. Below deck, tonnes of fish of all types were packed or stacked in boxes and racks. He tasted them all. Raw, salted and dried fish tasted almost palatable now he had plenty of water. He explored, ate, found locations to hide, sleep or keep watch and slipped around the massive ship like a shadow.

After what seemed like weeks, Mac sensed changes in both speed and direction of the ship from the vibration of the engines through the fabric of the decks. The weather had warmed, so he knew they had travelled north. Fishing illegally in Australian waters, they would stay west, away from the major shipping channels. Mac scoured the horizon, scanned the sea, searched the stars, and sniffed the air for any scent of land. He wished an Australian coast guard patrol would intercept the vessel. What else could he hope for? As tough as it was on-board, he hated the thought of being in a lifeboat or going overboard again to take his chances in the sea without knowing people were close.

The northwest of Australia would be a lonely graveyard. He wouldn't stand a chance in that barren desert even if he made it to shore. He needed to wait until the ship reached Indonesia or Southeast Asia where there might be a chance of a landfall with drinking water and people. He would be a reverse refugee, an Australian catching a small boat to land without authority in Asia. If the ship docked at a port, he would face legal problems but that would be better than going overboard again. He didn't want to die on the desert shores of northern Australia, hundreds of miles from anyone.

Mac tracked the crew's movements and deciphered their activities by sound. When they drew in the nets or long lines, their attention was focussed outside the boat. The activity on deck drowned any noise he might make below. The most dangerous times were processing days. The monotony of splitting, scaling and salting thousands of fish made the crew restless and eager for distraction. On those days Mac explored deep among the cargo and ballast. He was lucky to be marooned on such a large vessel. If it had been smaller, the crew would have discovered him long ago. He learned to eat, drink and excrete without being detected but yearned for a hot shower, a clean set of clothes and a decent feed. As he identified dozens of boltholes, he grew bolder moving around. Recovering his money remained paramount and he imagined endless improbable ways to get even with the men who had stolen from him.

His frustration at failing to find his money was relieved by his interest in the cargo. Mac discovered caches of ocean treasures. Salted, dried, and fermented fish filled entire storerooms. One of the giant freezers was full of the rare but much sought-after Patagonian toothfish. Mac recognised the slender fish with ugly broad heads and knew they only lived in the cold waters of the far south. No wonder the ship had such strong long lines; some of these fish were two metres long.

The bulkheads housed an Aladdin's cave of small treasures. Boxes and boxes of delicately sliced dried abalone and shark fins would be worth a fortune. Dried and wizened fish bodies looked like they belonged in an old Pharaoh's tomb, rather than plate or medicine jar. Tray after tray of rare leafy sea horses had been dried and stored with care. Tiny equine heads topped bony bodies covered with leaf-like growths. Their camouflage had not been perfect enough. Everything about them was weird; prehensile tails and a pouch so the males could care for the eggs. There were racks of starfish, sea urchins and dried sea cucumbers. Mac presumed the shark's teeth and fish bones were valuable from the careful way they were packed; thousands of deaths paving a better life for others.

One evening as he slipped a big shark's tooth into his pocket, he heard footsteps and quickly shoved the tray back on the shelf and dived into the cupboard opposite, afraid to shut the door because of the noise it might make. One of the crew slammed the cupboard shut as he walked back along the corridor. Another moment and Mac would have been discovered. He was getting careless.

Checking for silence, Mac pushed the door but it stuck fast. After a solid shove, he almost fell into the corridor. The passageway was clear but fine sand from the trays dusted the floor and his big tell-tale footprints led straight to the cupboard. He scuffed his prints and scampered back down to the gloomy hold past giant jars of jellyfish bodies with tangled arms and cases packed with the rigid blue floats from Portuguese Man of War jellyfish. Perhaps they were destined for the traditional medicine market. This museum of sea life must deliver lucrative profits to justify the costs and the risks.

After days fishing with drift nets, the engines stopped, and the crew unpacked scuba gear. Would it be pearls? If only he could get his money or even pearls and get to Broome, he'd hitch his way back to South

Australia. If he got home, maybe he could find a way to repair things, but would the ship go anywhere near Broome? A ship this size couldn't sneak around undetected.

As the diving began, Mac heard captain and crew gathering on deck. This was his chance. He crept along the upper deck passageways. His heart beat faster. He raced to the captain's cabin door, pushed his shoulder against the lock and yanked down the handle. Much to his surprise the door lurched inward. With the door closed, he sucked in his breath. It was bigger than other cabins, but there was nowhere to hide. His big body could not fit in the packed wardrobe. As the noise receded, he sighed with relief and rifled through cupboards and drawers. The whisky was tempting. The small, sharp knife would be handy. His eyes were drawn to the maps on the table, but they gave no clue to their current location or destination. All the navigational charts would be in the wheel room. Mac cursed as he pulled back a curtain and spied the robust, locked safe built flush into the wall of heavy timber. The thought of his money so near was galling.

Turning back to the captain's desk he searched for money, gold, anything valuable. The printed material was indecipherable Asian script except for one letter on the desk in a more familiar alphabet if not language. He slipped it into his pocket with the knife. He crept out of the cabin, scuttled along the corridor, scrambled down the steps and eased into his familiar hiding place among the dried fish.

On deck, he heard the diving gear being packed away, the engines engaged and any chance to escape evaporated as the ship resumed its journey. Mac was shaken from his near miss. He'd risked much and gained little. He moved deeper into the hold to a more distant hiding place deep among the ballast and breathed a little easier. He couldn't make sense of the letter, so hid it away on top of some boxes. Later that night he saw the giant clams that the crew had hauled on board. They were like stone boulders.

Mac pieced together all the information he could remember about the west coast of Australia; it was precious little. From school he remembered that the coastline was very, very long, and almost uninhabited. Apart from fishing illegally, reefs and rocks were hazardous to all ships, especially a heavy one. Water of varying depths made currents move in unpredictable ways and the fine detail on the charts would be unreliable. Rocks, or worse still, coral, was dangerous because cuts are prone to rapid infection. Being knocked against the jagged skeletons of untold millions of coral polyps would be an excruciatingly painful way to die. Mac also remembered his Uncle Ben's vivid stories of shark fishing in these northern waters.

'Fishing rigs ripped out our hands. If we hung on, the shark would pull the boat,' he'd say. Memories of his little girl, Zoe, tormented Mac's dreams and he would wake dark with regret. His head pounded but he was determined to survive. He counted each day with a scratch on the back of a crate to keep track. Twenty-seven so far. Nearly Zoe's ninth birthday, another twist of the knife.

The more he saw of the storage areas, the more he was intrigued. Freezers and cold stores were full of precious lobsters and oysters. Mac knew fish, but he saw varieties that he had never even imagined. Stashed below deck were barrels of salted fish oozing fermenting juice, thousands of strings of aromatic dried fillets and rooms of whole smoked fish. He was no longer starving but his unrelenting diet of fish and water had lost all culinary appeal. It was survival rations. The salty, oily and fermenting smells sickened him. He craved fruit and bread and wondered how long it would take for him to get scurvy.

The pirate's bounty was packed in scrupulous order, including colour coding that reflected the value of the cargo. He explored during the day when there was sufficient light to see in the gloomy hold.

Down in a forward hold, there were crates of pale cream and green raw jade from Cowell on the west coast of South Australia he assumed. Mac admired the well-oiled operation. Most of the crew were hard men who toiled, hauled, and processed fish, then hauled more nets and gutted yet more fish. In the cold south they had all looked miserable in their drab, thin clothes. In the warmer north, even if they started work at dawn and laboured long, they played dice or cards in the evenings after eating their food. Strung up in their sleeping hammocks they looked like the dried fish they spent all their days preparing.

But, there were brains behind this operation. Guy would have planned the double cross from the beginning. The ship's captain just delivered the final blow – Mac had put his own neck deep in the noose.

Even in his most optimistic dreams Mac couldn't imagine how he could launch a lifeboat without detection. One by one he dismissed the options. At least he was well hydrated. He ate raw, dried or salted fish, drank water that tasted of plastic and slept fitfully on bare boards in a storage cupboard. He waited.

Chapter 3

The Stowaway

Mac lived on a steady diet of hunger, hatred and fear. Every day he cursed Guy afresh. Every day he tried to think of a way out. The temperature climbed and the rain increased so they had reached the tropics. On cloudy days, the ship drew a phantom line in a pale landscape where sea and sky merged into watery blue. Oppressive heat pressed close and left him limp with exhaustion. Nights, pale and grey enclosed him – a tight oyster of unreality.

Sometimes he lost hope. Tears fell as he thought of Catherine. Every breeze brushed him with shame as he imagined what people would be saying. Catherine would think he was dead. He had betrayed her trust. And his little girl Zoe – could he ever face her again? Mac had been so proud of his beautiful daughter and he had failed her. He would not be there to support her, protect her, or even to see her grow up. The shock of his disappearance would be coupled with the destruction of his reputation; he would be branded a crook, a failure.

He'd hurt friends too. His loyal workmates, Dave, Steve and Pedro had lost valuable lobsters. That was bad enough, but Costas had probably lost *The Aphrodite*, which was his life. Shame gnawed his gut. Every night he carried self-loathing to his rough bed on the bare boards of the hold or cramped in storage cupboards.

His father often said, 'Sometimes you just have to put one foot in front of the other and take the next step. Don't think how far your destination is, or how long it will take, simply take the first step and then the next one.' So, for now, he followed his father's advice.

He tried to imagine where the ship would refuel. Even the huge storage tanks could not last forever. Any landfall started to feel better than this endless journey. He fantasised about finding the islands he read about as a child like Hawaii with idyllic white beaches fringed with coconut palms and welcoming women in grass skirts. He knew precious little about Asia other than that Indonesia had millions of subsistence farmers. If he jumped ship and got to shore, he would never blend in. Tall and white, he would have no money, no passport and no legitimate cover story. Still, he had a better chance of staying alive on a South East Asian island than marooned on the deserts of the Western Australian coast or being discovered on board when the ship reached its destination. China or Hong Kong would be the likely markets for this valuable cargo; both were unsympathetic to stowaways. The further north he was carried the more difficult it would be to get back to Australia.

Mac thought about fishermen he knew who worked the waters north of Darwin. They had big boats and tall stories of the wild tropical waters that were home to marlin and game fish. If he ever got off this ship, perhaps he could work his way back to Australian waters. Maybe there would be a friend of a friend among the commercial fishing, cruising or charter boat operators of the north. That way he might be able to sneak back into the country without detection if he could hook up with a sympathetic crew in Bali or Papua New Guinea, he might be able to return to Australia.

One night, alone on deck in the dark, the breeze whispered a promise of green. Mac raised his head and sniffed like a tracker dog. He was not mistaken; in addition to the usual diesel and brine he detected moist, fruity smells. He filled his nose and mouth with the welcome scent as if it was his vineyard and its finest wine. He peered until his eyes hurt but could see nothing but shadows and clouds. As the dawn rose, he hid below nursing a kernel of hope. The usual pattern of travel and fish processing continued.

Next morning the pattern of activity on board changed. After hearing the crew shout, he also spied a speck of land on the horizon, and then another. The ship seemed to be travelling parallel to a coastline or chain of islands. Hope surged. If they docked at a major port he would be in trouble. If the ship stayed too far out from land, he would drown attempting to swim to shore.

Could the land be Borneo? His grandfather had been stationed in Borneo during World War II and told bloodthirsty stories of deadly kris blades, cannibals and fierce fighters. He thought the ship must already be further north than Timor. Mac's reliable geography petered out at the Australian coast. Papua might welcome a lost Australian sailor, but the ship must be further to the east, or was it west by now? Mac fumed with frustration.

He reasoned that he must take a chance soon. Small boats in the water suggested that fishing communities were close. The boats were too far away for him to guess the nationality of the people on board and he doubted his ability to know even if he could see them. An outrigger canoe implied small town rather than big city.

Mac gathered the letter – reasoning it must be important even though he couldn't read it, the knife he had stolen from the captain's cabin, and the few things he'd brought on-board. He wrapped the letter and a pack of mainly useless money in his waterproof pants and tied them around his waist under the buoyancy vest. He knotted a couple of short lengths of robust rope around the long board to make it easier to hold. He packed his pockets with several shark's teeth and a smooth, bright cowrie shell to remind him of South Australia He was as ready as he would ever be. All he needed was an opportunity.

Like a blind man, Mac sensed the progress of the ship through the engine noises and creaking hull. In the dead of night, he woke with a jolt as the ship groaned and lurched against the thrust of the engines. Mac heard a wave break against the ship, but there was no storm, no wind. He could hardly stop himself racing on deck. Whatever was happening was unusual. Rhythmic swells caught the ship broadside as the crew rushed to turn the ship into the waves. A siren sounded and the shouting became frantic. Mac's brain clicked into action. A Tsunami? If waves bottomed out on a shallower seabed they could lunge far inland. This may be his chance.

Mac crept to the back of the ship and slipped down onto the net platform. He looped one rope around his waist and attached it to the ropes knotted on the board. He prayed the waves were headed toward land, some land, any land, then, as the next wave surged, he jumped, like an ill prepared surfer, into the dark water.

As his head broke the surface, he heard the engines roaring high above him. The wave grew beneath him and he saw another gathering further away in the moonlight. He held tight to his plank and, as the water swept him along, angled his board away from the ship. The noise was deafening as he watched the waves pound the ship broadside. The engines strained to turn the bow into the waves.

Gradually the ship angled and pulled away. Mac felt powerless, bobbing in the water like a seedpod tethered to his wooden husk. He hooked his arms under the rope and as silence settled, felt desperately alone. He imagined vast depths and prowling sharks. As the bright moon curved across the sky, he could not see or hear any sign of land. Wave after wave surged but didn't break. He was pleased the water was warm as he held clutched his plank and conserved his flagging energy.

Then the noise began. Changing from smooth solid hills of energy, the waves crested and crashed. Wave energy transformed into wild turbulence as the bottom of the waves dragged ragged on an uneven seabed. The water boiled around him. He was pushed under the surface of the water and fought to snatch every breath. Pieces of wood, branches and vegetation churned in the water. Noise filled his nose, his ears, beat against his chest. He was buffeted back and forth. Then, he seemed to be dreaming. It was a wild and noisy dream filled with darkness and rushing water. Pounding water and crashing waves carried him through the blackness.

Chapter 4

London, Summer 2011

Zoe and Monica sat at the table in Zoe's top floor flat celebrating with a bottle of champagne.

'I can't believe I've done it,' said Zoe, grinning. 'My second serious exhibition opens tomorrow and everything is finished. Twenty-seven pieces. If they all sell, I'll be rich.'

'Well you've taken long enough.' Monica smiled 'More than two years since your last one.'

'You know, I think my father would have been pleased. I haven't thought about him for ages. He started all this. Used to buy me drawing books. He'd say *Sit quiet. Look hard. Everything looks different when you really get to know it, people, animals, even hills and stones.* I'd beg for bird books every Christmas and birthday. My mother would say John Gould reproductions were too old and serious for me, but good old Dad always delivered. Then after he disappeared, drawing was my best excuse not to talk.'

'Pity your Mum isn't here,' Monica said.

'You know she never believed the rumours and refused to believe Dad was dead even after all those years. She lived to keep Dad's dream alive.'

'It must have been hard.'

'Mmm. I wouldn't have the vineyard if Mum hadn't been so single minded. I appreciate that now I know how hard it is to earn a living.'

'Well, we're here now and I'm proud of you,' Monica said, giving her a quick hug to lighten the mood.

'You've always been good for me Monica. Ever since Uni – seems a lifetime ago. We were so young. How we loved being smart arses.'

'Yes, it was fun,' said Monica. 'Remember being scared in those old dark stacks that creaked in the basement of the Barr Smith Library?'

'And – what about those pathetic challenges we used to set? Who could track down the most esoteric fact, or invent the weirdest metaphor – all to impress our lecturers. God, we must have been painful,' said Zoe.

'I don't know. I thought the lace undies on the Chancellor's statue was quite fun. I always envied you being tall and slim and blonde,' said Monica as she leaned forward and topped up their glasses.

'I wanted your dark curly hair and flashing eyes. You were such a mess even then, always dropping books and trailing papers. But you were bold. Always got the boys. I loved that you'd argue about everything. With anyone.'

'You were too scared of making trouble.'

'You got me into trouble, and I learned it wasn't too bad.' Zoe laughed. 'Good lesson.'

'Why did you take that daggy job with the government after graduating,' said Monica. 'Your marks were better than that.'

'It paid the bills and gave me time to paint,' Zoe replied. 'That's what I wanted to do.'

'Well, I couldn't wait to leave Adelaide and dive into the hustle and bustle of political dramas and intrigues of a real city,' replied Monica.

'So much has happened in the seven years since I got here.' Zoe sighed. 'God I loved those first days in London. I remember wandering around with my eyes popping out: the Tate Modern, the National Gallery and the miraculous V&A. It was luscious.'

'I was terrified by Fleet Street at first. Thought I'd fail,' Monica said. 'Mum said Fleet Street might have enough stories to keep me busy. Out of her hair I think she meant. She hated me winkling out all the family secrets and embarrassing the oldies.'

'You always had a good nose for a story. But I think you only succeeded because of your questions. You were so brash. Everyone would have been too scared to lie to you.'

'But I've also been lucky getting good jobs. Right place. Right time. Don't forget, I never doubted your ability either. Knew you could swim fast in this big pond.'

'This is starting to sound like a three-bottle conversation. If my new works sell, I'll be ecstatic. I'm not sure my latest style will grab people, but I've done nothing but sketch and draw and paint, for months, years. It's all George's fault.'

'Where is he by the way?' asked Monica emptying her glass. 'He was supposed to be here an hour ago.'

As if on cue, the front door snapped open and George appeared in a stylish narrow lapelled suit, blue shirt and navy boots.

'It's dog eat dog in the art business,' he said. 'Sorry I'm late. Never thought I'd complain about enthusiastic buyers. Our publicity is working a treat.'

'Hello George. We were just talking about you,' Monica grinned as she gathered the slender man into a crushing hug.

'Sure, sure. I hope more portraits are in your plans Zoe. I've just had an interesting conversation about the fact that, despite digital cameras and the Internet, wealthy people are buying painted portraits. If you tap into that market, you'll make me rich too,' George grinned wolfishly.

'Drink, George?' Monica asked as she disappeared into the kitchen.

Zoe was delighted that her friends were so relaxed in her flat. She thought about the way portraits required her to study people in depth, but from a distance – it was safe. Over the past months, she caught herself watching people obsessively and imagining their lives. From the edges of crowds or social events, she sketched personalities in her head. She found herself lingering over coffee, studying faces as she waited for the tube or just sitting in the park. Young and old, ugly or beautiful she liked to think she saw the maps of life from wrinkles and laughter lines. She'd filled sketchbooks with mountains of noses, rolling hills of ears and eyes that radiated hope, despair, love, fear or the deep weariness of age or disappointment.

'Remember your first show?' asked George as he shut the fridge and joined them with a brimming glass. 'I've never done one for anyone who was so excited. 'Let's hope this one will be even better.' They clinked glasses in a happy toast and Zoe remembered that she'd met David after her first exhibition. How she wished he were here. Memory was like a cat, it crept up warm and furry and then bared needle-sharp teeth. He'd promised to be back in time for the opening.

Chapter 5

Monica Investigates

'Yes, yes, I've got him,' Monica shouted with triumph as she slammed down the phone. All the other staff had left the office. As she shifted her weight on the protesting chair she wondered if she could think without chewing. Liquorice was her current favourite, with fruit bars, mints, nuts and pencil ends all grist to her mill. She needed energy to power her ceaseless activity. She sat back and spotted Jacob. Tall and immaculate in his overall, he hovered in the doorway. He had emptied the bins, finished the vacuuming and stood, silently wringing his duster between nervous hands.

'Hello Jacob, how are you this week?' she asked softly.

Jacob pulled crumpled papers from his pocket.

'Please Miss Monica what means this?'

With patience that would have surprised her editor, she went through the papers, explained what he needed to do and helped Jacob fill in the forms. This sort of thing happened often when it was late and quiet. Someone would hover at her door waiting for a break in her furious typing or her voluble telephone calls before asking advice.

Monica knew the army of cleaners, porters and couriers who toiled silently and often forgotten in the building. She trusted in the power of truth and goodness and believed if she practiced it and encouraged others to do the same, then right would prevail. What seemed huge problems to them were often simple and she often cringed that they were treated with such distain.

As Jacob left, she was pleased that her earlier phone conversation had identified a potential source; it was just what she needed for an expose´. Feeling hungry and wanting company, she called George.

'Come and have a drink with me,' she wheedled. 'Zoe's busy. David's back. I don't trust that man.'

'I know that tone. I'm just second best. You're on a mission and I'm just your cover.'

'Ah, you know me too well. George please. I'm hungry. I'll buy. Come to the Duke with me.'

'Well, I was just thinking about dinner. See you there in 30 minutes.' George was willing to be pressured. He enjoyed hearing about her juicy investigations.

Monica gathered her things, locked the door and raced out of the building. Dark night, she thought. I know why I always choose strong colours – stops me getting run over. These bracelets are not made for running though. I sound like I could join a Jamaican steel band.

Rummaging among notes and books, cards, peppermints, a much-scribbled diary, tissues, money and keys, Monica applied rich burgundy lipstick and ruffled her black curls, which were forever in a tumble. As she surged into the warm pub, all curves and colours, the crowd parted like the Red Sea before Moses.

'George!' She wrapped her meaty arms around the elegant man. His fashionable cashmere was sprinkled with rain.

'Hello Monica. Wow. That handbag is huge. Are you off for a short holiday?'

'Give me a break. I need stuff. And this has got a dozen pockets. At least I can always find my phone.'

'No straight lines for you are there? That bag suits now you mention it.'

'Always the voluble, self-assured reporter, you know. My bag is like me. I'm not fat, I simply have thick skin. And like me, my bag is not huge, it is sufficient to support my needs.'

'So, who or what are we hunting tonight, Monica?' asked George after they found a seat at the side of the crowded pub. Monica was always chasing information that would make a good story. Better that she deflect attention, drill into others and uncover scandals, than let the dark worms of her own self-doubt and vulnerability be exposed.

'I'm having a bad week. My editor is hard work,' she said leaning forward. 'He's dripping with sarcasm. Said he admires my acerbic wit. Last week's article was a roaring success: wealthy family profiting from squalid tenements – a natural extension of their ancestor's success in the slave trade and tea production. But he's refused my article on the thefts and vicious deaths that have marred the history of famous jewels in Britain. He suggested a poke at royalty was a bridge too far for his conservative readers. Coward!' she huffed.

'How about a good sex scandal? Don't mind one myself.'

'Sex and the clergy have had a lot of coverage. But my current target, a bishop, appeals to me because he has made such a public display of condemning behaviour like adultery, child abuse, homosexuality and fraud, while practicing at least two of those in secret, if my information is correct,' Monica replied.

'Ooh, which ones? Is that why we're here tonight? I knew there'd be a reason for this particular pub.'

'Well, it started with just a few fragments, but I think I have a juicy kernel that might expose him,' she offered with a wink.

'And, I suppose, as usual, you want justice?'

'You know me. It's not enough to expose them. Victims need to be compensated. Slavery and serfdom may be illegal, but they still occur right under our noses every day. According to Home Office stats there are over 130,000 slaves in the UK today. Greed and exploitation are always worth tearing down.' Monica perused the menu.

The pub was warm but noisy and as the hubbub increased it was hard to have a quiet conversation.

'Surprisingly good food,' said George after tasting his fragrant steak and ale pie.

'I've not eaten here before.'

Plates removed, fresh drinks in hand and with the bar scramble quietening, Monica began.

'I have two current leads, one high up in the clergy and the other a self-made millionaire. I think the bishop is just a sleaze – clever, manipulative, or perhaps worse. The rich guy seems to have spent all his life defrauding people with such skill and frequency that he's now rich enough to look respectable and play with the big boys. If he devoted the same effort to something legal, he might have achieved great things. I can't decide which of these two I dislike most.'

A shadow flicked across George's face. 'I've come across some master manipulators in my time. They're all too common in the art world. I don't like fraud. Do you think the rich guy is fleecing people?'

'Not sure.'

'I think one of your greatest strengths, my friend, is your ability to swim through murk. You spot evasions in the flickering of an eye. I can rarely spot the inconsistencies,' said George.

'Well, I've had plenty of practice. On my dark days, I think I live in a seething morass of lies and deception. No wonder my crusader outfit gets a workout. I may need it for the bishop. Tonight's contact claims he's a victim. We'll see.'

Monica's description of her source was ambiguous: middle-aged man, brown thinning hair, glasses. He would contact her about 9 pm. Probably the guy with the twitching eye and the brown coat at the back of the room chewing his fingernails. Monica sensed he would bide his time until he felt brave enough to approach her.

'Years ago, finding information was like searching for grass in a desert. Now, the Internet's a teeming jungle, so more often than not, the information is there, but it's lost in the forest. And, there are plenty of false trails and lies camouflaged as facts,' Monica complained.

'It's a good thing you have so many contacts. You always find someone who knows someone...'

'George let's give this guy some space.'

'Sure. I'll call Zoe and tell her I've sold another of her works, then get a drink at the bar.'

'I wouldn't count on getting her. You know David likes all the attention,' Monica said rolling her eyes. 'No hurry.' Sure enough, as George left, the man with the tic sidled up to Monica. He introduced himself as Roger and began to ramble. Monica signalled for the waiter to bring him a drink.

'Tell me again how you know this,' she said after about ten minutes of uninterrupted diatribe. Monica was not convinced. The anger was there but the detail was lacking. 'To publish anything, I need names, dates, times.'

Monica glanced over to see George perched on a stool and chatting to the barman.

'Do you happen to know the man in the brown coat talking to my friend Monica, the large colourful woman at the table toward the back?' asked George jutting his chin in their direction.

'Sure, you don't have to worry about him. You're much better looking,' replied the barman.

'Thanks, but do you think he's reliable?'

'Old Roger is always complaining about something. It's hard to sort the wheat from the chaff,' the barman said over his shoulder as he moved to serve another customer.

After about half an hour of repetition and contradiction, Monica thanked the potential informant and, with little conviction, promised to keep in touch. As he shuffled off, she beckoned to George to return.

'Well, that story is a long way from being complete. If I go down that path, I'll need corroboration.'

'The barman thinks he's a lightweight, if not a troublemaker,' said George. 'Don't trust everything he says.'

'I may need to switch my attention to the businessman. My editor will be pleased. The Frenchman didn't look as juicy as the clergyman, but he might offer a better fit for the magazine.'

'Remember Balzac's quote – *Behind every great fortune is a great crime*; perhaps your rich man will be a better subject than he appears to be,' said George.

'I'll ask Richard what he knows about my lead. He knows everyone. Their paths may have crossed. Perhaps I could involve Zoe too. We've worked on a couple of jobs together in the past, and she might be perfect for this current line of enquiry. My target is known for being susceptible to a pretty face. That might work. Perhaps I can engineer a painting commission for Zoe. I like it when we work together. I know I can trust her.'

Following George's lead, Monica levered herself out of the creaking chair. They headed slowly to the door, reluctant to leave the warm pub and brave the cold night air.

'Good night George.' She kissed him on the cheek. 'Thanks for your support. Dinner with you is always a pleasure. I had a suspicion that all that vitriol would come to nothing.'

As Monica walked through the cold drizzle on her way to the tube, she was disappointed. I'll look at my next prospect tomorrow, she thought. Might've lost a bishop. Wonder if I have a knight or just another pawn. As long as he makes a good headline my editor will be happy – at least for a while.

Chapter 6

The Break-Up

Travelling to her appointment at George's Gallery, Zoe remembered her first meeting with David. Soft blond curls, irresistible blue eyes and very attentive. Just what a lonely girl craved. She liked his romantic Scottish accent. He shared her love of art, and they found plenty to talk about.

After a few months, they moved in together in a tiny flat on the top floor of a converted but slightly decrepit mansion in Wimbledon. It worked well. David's work as an architect demanded that he regularly spent time away from home, leaving Zoe plenty of time to work. Zoe was besotted. David always came first. She wanted to be with him, loved being with him, and adored being wanted.

Their first year together was a dream. Zoe relied on him for emotional as well as financial support as she painted with a passion. As the economy faltered, David spent longer periods of time away from home chasing work and became more critical about money at home. Zoe worried too.

She focussed on building a substantial body of work for her second exhibition. Being with David brought the peace of mind she needed to produce quality work.

'I still can't believe how successful the exhibition was George. Thanks for all your work and especially for getting the crowds along. David was pleased,' said Zoe as they shared a coffee.

'Well, you warmed to the occasion my lovely. And I have good news. I have enquiries about another commission for you.'

'Wow, that's great. That's three from the exhibition. All I need is one of them to translate into agreements and I'll be set. Are you happy to be my agent and do the negotiating? I hate all that contract stuff.'

'Of course. Usual fee plus the occasional lunch.' George laughed.

'Guess it's always better to have too much work than not enough.'

'This one is potentially very useful. The woman has influential connections.'

As he headed out of the door, Zoe wrapped her arms around her body and hugged herself. It was all coming together: her career, David, her friends. After the drama of moving to the other side of the world, all the uncertainty of being able to support herself doing what she loved for a living, and feeling so terribly alone, everything was working out. She decided to call David and share the good news. Usually, when he was away, she waited until he called just in case she interrupted a meeting or a presentation. She knew he hated distractions to his working day

'Hello David, it's me. Good news.'

'Oh, it's you Zoe. I'm in the middle of something.'

'Sorry, just wanted to share.' Zoe regretted the phone call.

'I'm busy. Was going to call and tell you I need to be away next weekend,' he said.

'Is anything wrong?' Zoe asked. They usually spent weekends together.

'No, I'm just worried about money and not getting this latest contract. Perhaps things will sort themselves out in time.' Then he was gone. No discussion. Little warmth. He hadn't asked about her good news. Zoe's shoulders drooped.

Thrown from her celebratory mood and unable to concentrate she wandered around the flat, folding up the shopping bags, hanging the coats and stacking shoes on the rack by the door. Since the Global Financial Crisis, David's work had dried up and competition was tough. She had hoped that after her successful exhibition and as more of her works sold, David would be pleased that some of their money worries had eased. She channelled her concerns into scrubbing the bath. Within an hour the entire flat was sparkling.

In a well-established pattern for subduing unwelcome thoughts, she plunged back into her work. In the tiny second bedroom, among the storage boxes, piles of spare clothes and an unused pair of David's skis, her first commissioned portrait stood on an easel. It was due for delivery in four days. She thought it was finished but decided the nose was not good enough. It would never be a beautiful nose; too bulbous for beauty, not strong enough for character, but at the moment it leered like a satire. Doubt flooded through her. She knew it was not good. She mixed colours, realigned the bridge, and flared his nostrils but it failed to convince. Zoe was almost relieved when the phone rang. Perhaps she would have a fresh perspective after a break.

'Zoe Macintosh?'

'Yes, that's me.'

'My name is Bronte. I'm the woman who is having an affair with David. It's been going on for nearly a year. I thought you should know.' Zoe couldn't breathe. Her heart pounded as if it would leap from her chest as her legs buckled as she crumpled onto some storage boxes.

'I know he is very good at denial, so this is my name, and this is my telephone number if you would like to check. I can assure you that I am real.' Each word ripped into Zoe like a wrecking ball. She couldn't speak.

Warming to the torture, the woman on the phone catalogued their regular meetings and trips together. Zoe reeled as her world was shredded and her self-esteem crushed.

He'd lied through his teeth. He'd betrayed her. Why didn't she see it coming? Clearly, she was so stupid that she couldn't even judge someone who was supposed to be close to her. She lay among the boxes as wave after wave of echoes of that soft voice drained hope from her world.

When David appeared, several hours later, she was still crumpled in a tangled heap on the spare bed.

'Get out,' she said sitting on the edge of the bed. 'I've had the call. I guess you know that. Too much of a coward to even tell me yourself.'

'I know. I'm sorry,' he said shrugging his shoulders. She didn't think he looked sorry. 'I'll just grab a few things,' he said, his face impassive.

After a few minutes, the door closed. Zoe felt as if all the air had been sucked out of the flat. She struggled to breathe.

Over the next week depression, relentless as a starving wolf pack, stalked Zoe and filled her consciousness. Black fog smothered each waking moment and tormented her dreams. The damp London sky and the evening twilight were stifling.

More than the destruction of her personal life, she couldn't work – how could she paint when she couldn't see? The success of her exhibition had evaporated. Her eyes were clouded.

She walked the streets numb with pain, cold and broken; and like a wounded animal sought refuge in a familiar place. Yearning for warmth and wide skies, she stumbled down to the travel agent and booked a flight to Australia.

Monica called but Zoe couldn't discuss how she felt. She offered to organise the practical things, deal with the landlord, and would help her pack.

George offered to deliver Zoe's completed commission.

'Work through it,' he said. 'Concentrate on some great new work.'

Easy for him to say, thought Zoe.

It was simple for Zoe to sever herself from life in London. No fuss, no fanfare. The mail: electronic and envelopes could pile up near the door of her flat; she would not care. She bid a tearful farewell to Monica, hefted her cases and boarded the Heathrow Express among tides of travellers, each hiding their own story.

She trusted the old house at Langhorne Creek to absorb her pain. It had once before. Zoe needed silence to heal, she couldn't bear to see friends or colleagues. The thought of their sympathy, or more daunting, their rueful acceptance was unbearable. Some of them had even warned her.

Chapter 7

Art Connections

'You see, I was right about David,' Monica complained as she shared coffee with George at their local a week later.

'Zoe's taken this really hard,' he responded.

'Hard – she's an absolute mess! Just when her confidence was high after the exhibition, he's destroyed her. It'll take her months to recover,' Monica sighed. 'I'm exhausted. It's tough at work at the moment. I've been following my millionaire but all I can get is gossip. Bad behaviour confirmed by some but denied by others. I've even applied my *front page of the newspaper* test to see if it's in the public interest to publish without proof, but I still can't decide.'

'You'll sort it out. Do what you think is right,' George replied.

'It's like the parable about the blind men and the elephant. I think you need to sit on your story for a while. Perhaps you can't see the whole elephant yet.'

'I know I've got something that smells though. Maybe it's the crap the elephant left behind,' laughed Monica. 'I need another story for next month though. How's your business, George? Any good gossip?' Monica knew George dressed and entertained as if he was rich but he was never ostentatious. Underneath his unruffled demeanour, he worked hard, and people often confided in him.

'Always interesting,' he said.

'That's a cop out. That damn word means nothing.' Monica had grown to know George well over the years and appreciated his sharp intellect. Few people knew he had a great brain for business as well as art. He was a canny trader and seemed to know which way the winds of business and fashion blew.

'You can always sus me out Monica. We could be a great double act.'

'Sure. In fact, we'd make a good couple if I was four inches shorter, a ton lighter and you weren't gay. Well, help me with my problems, and I'll find you buyers,' Monica offered. 'How about helping with my industry story? It's a bit outside my expertise. Not industrial espionage, trade secrets and all that, but it looks crooked. The bishop story's too messy.'

'Business stories aren't simple either,' warned George. 'Especially now with offshore tax havens and multiple ways of hiding ownership. There's often a lot of unravelling to be done. Sometimes I wish companies would *stick to their knitting*. It'd be a lot easier to keep track. But there's no such thing as core business now, everyone seems to be into everything. Your Montague is a classic example. The company used to be based in France. The French may not have won many wars, but they understand that money makes the world go around. France is rich in resources, but richer in ambition. And there aren't too many willing colonies these days. And of course, there is the innate superiority of both French technology and French people,' he sneered.

'Charm often opens the right doors,' Monica replied.

'*Montague Corp* has been an aggressive acquirer. People are prepared to pay big guilt money for their consumption. Their profitable paper and board recycling businesses grew from timber logging throughout South-east Asia and the Pacific and some suspect wood chipping businesses in Australia. It's a model performer in Europe and the elegant boardrooms of London and Paris; but I suspect different rules apply far from home. It's maintained high profits.'

'You know a lot,' said Monica. 'Maybe I'll just interview you.'

'The art world is not immune from dark and dirty deeds, but I've been aware of Montague for years. I hold them responsible for the loss of my father's job. Their callous behaviour did much to cripple my home region.'

Chapter 8

Tricky Business

A week later, looking her business best in flowing maroon silk and only four clanking bracelets, Monica sauntered into the elegant ballroom of the Park Royal. Among the advertising banners for yet another global investment company, drinks were being served before the networking dinner. After a dozen airy kisses and even more insincere handshakes, she spotted Richard Stirling across the room and her mood improved.

'Hello, hello,' she called. 'Thought you'd be here somewhere. Always keen to get in the social pages.'

Richard smiled down at her – a real smile which lit his lean face.

'The other day, I heard a rumour that you jog,' Monica joked as they stood together. 'Who can imagine sweat on that graceful brow.'

'I like to keep them guessing,' Richard responded as they stood comfortably together.

'I need you to introduce me to someone.'

'Always happy to trade. And, I might have a client for Zoe. One of my friends is having a special birthday and I suggested to his wife that she might have a portrait done,' he smiled.

'Might take a while. That bastard David has left her, and she's run back wounded to Langhorne Creek. She's not even painting at the moment.'

'Pity. She's got talent. And she's easy on the eye.'

They wandered casually to the balcony where luxuriant pots of fragrant jasmine, shaded nooks and private tables would have suited a romantic rendezvous.

Monica thought, not for the first time, how much she liked Richard. He exuded the calm assurance of a rich and attractive man. Well into his sixties, he radiated experience without any hint of slowing down. A silver fox, canny and cunning with a great gift for camouflage. She smiled to herself. Good at loping in and out of boardrooms, social circles and bedrooms.

'I need to find out about a Frenchman,' Monica said. 'It might save you from the boredom of Sudoku,' Monica goaded knowing he enjoyed her anecdotes, a stories or information. Both loved unravelling puzzles.

Monica studied his handsome face in the evening light. She had enjoyed her fair share of romps, but nothing serious. Richard was a friend. They looked an odd couple. Richard's tall slender figure, always neat and contained, was the opposite of Monica's colourful exuberance.

'Who's the latest target?' Richard replied with a smile.

'Yves Montreau and the *Montague Corp*. You may have come across him in your share trading.'

'Not share trading! Investing please,' he huffed.

Monica knew Richard maintained his wealth by trading shares, but *investor* did suit his more elegant approach. His long experience as a financial controller for a multinational oil company, equipped him for understanding money. He was married, of course, but did not consider that any impediment to enjoying life's many pleasures. All his activities were conducted with good taste. His clothes were no exception. Tonight, the suit was charcoal, a splendid foil for his silver hair and slightly rakish air. Most of all Monica admired his eyes. They were grey, sometimes hard as steel or soft as a nestling dove. They could change in an instant. Monica loved the gleam that would light up his eyes when they plotted.

'My investing provides a roof over my head and keeps me from being a burden on society. Tell me first about your interest in Montague and then I'll tell you about my latest project. We may not have enough time tonight for both,' he said as the waiters began to move guests into the dining room.

'I'm interested in Montreau because I think he's crooked. Illegal activities in faraway countries,' Monica explained.

'Ahh, I know of the Montague Corporation. But not well. I'll have a look. I think there is a take-over in the wind between Jobes Investments and the Witherspoons. Know anything?'

When Monica helped with information, she had learned that Richard was generous. There was nothing crass involving brown paper bags instead he would offer tickets to a show or an invitation to an excellent dinner at his expense. After one lucrative deal he suggested she might like a friend of his to manage some shares for her. When she laughed, saying she didn't have any, he gave her some for Christmas. Over the years their relationship had transformed Monica's life from one of financial struggle to comparative ease.

Over a shared drink, they would talk about people or a company. Richard had a good nose but was always impeccably polite. She may have something to offer. If not, she would ask around, find out who was dining with whom, and more often, who was sleeping with whom, meeting with unexpected people or behaving out of character. London was a big city, but few activities went unwitnessed. Picking up on the importance of small events, seemingly chance encounters, and following improbable hunches, was challenging and fun. Monica loved their last venture which proved price collusion, had started from noticing an unusual set of golfing partners playing a round when their businesses would normally have kept them apart.

It might need a little time and some skilful research, but Monica knew that Richard would help her uncover the secrets of Yves Montreau and *Montague Corporation*.

Chapter 9

The French Connection

Yves Montreau, principal of Montague Corporation, allowed himself a moment of uncharacteristic reflection. His wife, Adriana had always desired his money rather than his presence. His dark style and her blonde beauty made an eye-catching contrast. She had a penchant for slim black dresses teamed with large pieces of expensive jewellery. They shared a luxurious life and never asked each other inconvenient questions. Seen together on sufficient occasions, they were viewed as a stable couple. Both found this satisfactory in contrast to their first marriages that were altogether too dull, too full of recriminations and too demanding of time and emotions. Yves was pleased when their interests kept them apart.

It was unusual for her to call him at his office.

'Yves, I have just heard from Marco. He has had some wonderful pieces delivered from a new dig. I will head off to Verona tomorrow. I thought I should let you know I will be gone before you're scheduled to return.' Yves pictured her as she spoke. Tall and blonde, tanned to the exact shade required by high fashion, her slenderness verged on skeletal. Always impeccably dressed, coiffured and manicured, she would be far more interested in packing than his opinion.

'Of course,' Yves replied conscious that her current interest in Italian sculpture would make the trip costly. He was amused that she felt just enough guilt to ring.

'I'll meet you back in Rouen in a couple of weeks then. Good luck.'

'Switzerland later in the year?' she queried. He recognised the minute peace offering and grimaced at the thought of how much money she must have already spent.

'Perhaps,' he responded, dissatisfied with travel for pleasure. Adriana knew Switzerland was one place he still enjoyed: clean to the point of obsession and reliably tasteful. Yves admired impeccable manners and, in particular, the deference of his Swiss bankers. Their respect for discretion over many generations fuelled a banking system built on secrets. It was usually staffed by stolid older men with long experience and reliably closed mouths. Too many people these days held rigid views of right and wrong. Yves viewed this as an unnecessary constraint in business where the fast, the skilful, or those with the best lawyers won.

Yves pictured the soaring Swiss mountains, brisk air and the exhilaration of the ski slopes. It was as if, when the snow fell, it blanketed the deeds of the past year and with the thaw, inconveniences dissolved away like last year's dead leaves. He had travelled widely and had no desire to explore further. The volubility and loudness of the Italians irritated him. The Mediterranean provided a pleasant diversion in summer and could be enjoyed from France without having to suffer the neighbouring countries where so many things did not work. Each year he grew more elitist and less tolerant.

Yet, he craved new challenges, the next moneymaking venture, the next woman. As a young man he had pictured himself a modern-day Marco Polo, collecting curiosities, treasures and market opportunities in each location he lived or visited. He travelled extensively, becoming a master of creating opportunity. He was nimble. After reaping the profits, he rode the crest of the wave well ahead of any fallout.

He recalled his first days in French Polynesia with pleasure. He was fresh, and the women were beautiful. The trade goods were exotic and the people easy to seduce. It had been postcard heaven in New Caledonia: gentle, generous girls, wide, clean beaches and good profits from pearls and timber, even copra for a while. He saw himself a modern-day Gauguin, making not just art but profit from the native life.

His early passion for success grew. Tuna had been a good venture: big fish, strong demand. Simple to move on when inconvenient questions arose, and the correct paperwork did not. The Internet and regulation had spoiled that. Twenty years ago, the Pacific had a greater appeal to the French than their former African colonies or even Vietnam. Exotic products sold well. What he thought might be purgatory was softened by interesting wine, excellent seafood and solid profits.

Yves revelled in the expensive lifestyle he had crafted from his great financial successes through the skilful reinvention of his persona. He continued to increase his wealth by trading, buying companies, switching between fields of endeavour and, over the past ten years, playing the share market. He was a master at spotting weakness and ruthless at squeezing advantage from those under stress.

The French invented more than the word bureaucracy – they had raised it to an art form and spread through much of the civilized world. His complex schemes generated wealth but lately he was bored – bored and irritable. Money was no longer enough.

New technology, which seemed to be central to new business, depressed him. He had no patience with the latest crop of young social climbers who could barely mask their naked ambition. Most of all he was annoyed with the tell-tale evidence that his good looks were fading. He rallied back to the present as his secretary Monique, attractive but already conquered, offered the mail. His eyes followed her high heeled, elegant sway across his favourite room with quiet appreciation. All the colours and furnishings harmonised. The pale walls and cream ceiling decorated with delicate leaves and flowers complemented his elegant collection of Empire furniture. A few pieces, the side table for example, were well-crafted nineteenth century copies but sufficient to fool even some experts.

He gazed at the large gilt mirror to see his reflection against a classic Parisian vista. The most exquisite roofline of the most beautiful city in the world, he thought for the hundredth time. Each year it became harder to tempt him away from France.

Chapter 10

Reflections

Yves' investment in Alston, a robust pharmaceutical company, grew at over eight per cent annually and delivered strong dividends. The enterprise was large enough to have a diverse portfolio, and small enough for him to gain a Directorship with his significant shareholding. The prospect of big money excited him but, he sought something beyond that. He decided to travel to London and address the Board on his vision for accelerating company growth and profitability.

The spacious and ultra-modern Boardroom on the 23rd level had floor to ceiling windows, with panoramic views over the Thames and the financial district. Amid polite greetings and reserved handshakes, the eight Board members took their seats around the table. Yves asked the secretary to distribute a small dossier, and the business began.

When the Chair called his agenda item, Yves rose to speak.

'With improving health care, older people are increasing as a percentage of the population. Many are wealthy. I believe this company should make a major strategic investment in halting, if not reversing, the effects of ageing.'

The older board members sat a little straighter, and their eyes grew a little wider. He had captured their interest. Yves, the outsider, the newcomer, the Frenchman was rich and successful; those were the things that mattered around a Board table. His compelling presence exuded masculinity. There was nothing soft about Yves; he was a model of the future he sketched They stretched forward to hear what he had to say, to see if he could prove himself.

'Like all of us, men of our age generally keep fit,' he said, gaining their approval with a winning smile. 'People may use the words distinguished, but thousands like us, would pay handsomely to look and feel younger. Our challenge is to move Alston beyond the traditional medical model. I acknowledge modern medicine's success keeping people alive with the assistance of our medications. This has been the profit generator of this company for years. I am not proposing that we stop those product lines,' he added. The men around the table nodded in relief. 'This business sells many hydrating creams for men. We need to leapfrog these treatments and invest in products that deliver age resistance or reversal.' He paused for effect. The fine furnishings and exclusive location leant truth to his words.

'My plan promises to reverse the signs of aging. If I'm right, and I have evidence to suggest that I am,' he smiled with utter control. 'It would become our most valuable line. It will need significant investment. But, unlike mere cosmetic products, this project will deliver more than hope.' Yves continued with growing confidence as a slight frisson of interest rippled around the room.

'The shareholders will benefit, but just imagine what this development might deliver for each individual around this table.'

'Well, Yves, have you found the Elixir of Life?' one member challenged with a dismissive wave of his hand.

'Perhaps,' he responded with a glittering smile. 'Scientists always want significant additional testing. My proposal seeks to bring a promising young group into the company where we can secure the intellectual property. Expensive, yes – but think of the profits.'

Yves knew the other board members valued the company's research arm. He didn't give a damn about the science but the commercial and personal potential excited him. Scientists measured success by publication and the respect of their peers. Sometimes, sharing their discoveries with colleagues destroyed the possibilities for protecting the IP. Yves had already acquired some patents in secret. He would capitalise on those at a later date.

'Let me outline exactly how we can deliver this vision,' he explained with mounting enthusiasm. 'Details of the team are outlined in the dossier I have distributed. The target they have identified as an anti-aging agent would not require registration as a drug. Being derived from a natural plant extract there is an easier path to market.' Yves paused, savouring the excited looks. They were drawn, as he had been, to the seductive combination of profit and personal potential. He read it in their faces.

'Initially, I need your agreement to two things. Firstly, to employ the research team so we can keep them, and their research, tight in the company. Secondly, to fund them intensively so we can bring this product to market quickly. Both will be expensive but, I believe this strategy will deliver a solid outcome and exceptional returns.' Yves drew their attention to the dossier that contained the preliminary cost benefit analysis, ROI and NPV calculations for the next ten years.

'The timelines are tentative, but conservative,' he ended with a flourish.

The Board room buzzed. Questions flew around the table about the Intellectual Property protections, the research, the people involved, estimates of costs and time frames.

'The team is right here in London,' Yves explained, I have already talked with them. They are attracted to the prospect of good facilities and making themselves famous. They believe they can win a Nobel.'

The Directors considered, and then endorsed his strategy, including the necessary budget. Yves' mind flitted ahead. He wanted immediate action. Personal benefit. His reading of the research and the young, ambitious people was exciting. Being driven back to his apartment appreciating the new smell of the limousine, he reflected.

For millennia, people dreamed about the *Fountain of Youth* or the *Elixir of Life*. The universal dream could be a new frontier for medical research. It offered untold wealth if he could control this research at the ground level and keep its methodology secret. Just the thought of it made his pulse rate increase. It was such a sexy thought.

He left the Board meeting with everything he'd anticipated and more. This was the project he needed. Steel had amused him for a while. He enjoyed dealing with those mills in Sheffield. The factories had been full of old-fashioned, pompous English managers and antiquated work practices. The workforce resented the French ownership of their company. They did everything possible to thwart his new methods and fought to retain staff. It had given him great pleasure to close them down. Let them complain, it was better than winning the wars the English were always going on about.

Yves enjoyed winning. Sheffield might have seethed with resentment, but the workers and the town had been powerless to stop him. And such a dull place. The canals were metallic grey, brimming with sluggish water and lined with ragged vegetation beneath the factory walls blackened by decades of soot. The air had been full of smoke for decades. The cutler's guild and other craft associations still celebrated their history and innovations while their workers, like their buildings, stood like anachronistic museum exhibits.

Yves was relieved to sell; he had never been to an uglier city. Now, unemployed men skulked along the abandoned canals fishing in a desultory way among the weeds. The money he made had funded a stake in a Chinese manufacturing company, which could deliver much more product for a lower price than the stolid and resentful English. And after two years, he had sold that at an even bigger profit. Steel didn't match his style; too much engineering and too many technocrats who were far too good at logic and analysis.

Yves enjoyed his move into pharmaceuticals. Selling hope suited him. That was where his strength lay. He knew what motivated people, and how to manipulate their hopes and dreams. Yves was upmarket, skilful and experienced. It was a dangerous combination for those he dealt with. His greatest assets were charm and understanding human behaviour, especially the desire to make a quick profit. He allowed all to believe that he was the answer to their dreams. His ability to deliver the dream, if not the profit, relied on the confidence he drew from being an attractive and persuasive man.

Like it or not, beautiful people got a better deal in life; people wanted to be around them, trusted them. Yet gazing in the mirror every morning, he was forced to acknowledge that his best asset was fading. Last birthday, his fiftieth, people said he was looking distinguished, someone even called him a statesman – he was horrified.

He realised that, within a year or two, he would start to look old. And the more he worried about it, the worse it would get; laughter lines would become wrinkles. His confidence would falter. A solution hovered almost within his grasp.

He wondered for a moment if he should talk about the research with Adriana. Her skin was still beautiful. Some of her friends were looking plastic as they invested in more and more treatments.

Yves lived for the addictive rush of winning. It was pleasant having the houses, the money, the victor's trophies but he craved the thrill of defeating others. He did it with style of course; anything else would be boorish and distasteful. If there was anything worse than losing, it was losing without style.

He had made manipulation an art form. His schemes always resulted in personal profit, but never involved violence. If others lost money, he viewed it as the contemporary manifestation of the *survival of the fittest*.

Buoyed by the Board's acceptance of his funding proposal, he instructed his secretary to contact Nathan, the leader of the research team. He needed a meeting as soon as possible to seal the deal.

Chapter 11

New Research

Yves didn't flinch at the grungy clothes and dreads as he welcomed Nathan to *The Fire Stables* with a firm handshake. He believed that Alston's determined approach would pique any researcher's interest. Scientists didn't care about investors, shareholders and companies – only about winning money and working in teams that were on the path to sparkling publications.

'Welcome, I'm Yves Montreau.'

'Hi,' mumbled Nathan as he shrugged and his eyes slid to the corner of the room.

'We wish to keep this meeting confidential at this stage,' Yves began. 'Please, let's order, then we can talk. I believe my secretary mentioned our interest in a long-term arrangement if discussions go to plan.'

Nathan grunted over the top of the menu, then ordered with enthusiasm. Yves smiled.

'We understand your team works best together. We are offering five-year contracts to all four members. In addition, you will have state-of-the-art laboratory facilities and sufficient funds for the tests you need. The salaries will be fifty per cent higher than you currently receive at the University.' Nathan's eyes widened. 'We are prepared to negotiate on publishing. And we will consider contract extensions depending on performance.'

Nathan took a deep breath. His leg twitched and he fingered the edge of the starched blue tablecloth.

'I'd need to convince the whole team. We need the total skill set,' Nathan said. Yves sensed he was trying not to seem eager. 'It's not just the skills, but the way we spark. And we can put up with each other. Funds are crucial. Last month I spent the equivalent of a week writing reports for administrators who are incapable of understanding the first thing about this research. Total waste of time.'

'Yes, yes,' said Yves. 'I understand that competition for research grants is fierce, and you need more than the reputation of the University College – however excellent it may be.'

'It's my time and brainpower that gets wasted. Those bean counters don't realize this is my peak. Got to keep lateral before I lose the edge and get old.'

Yves recognised the impatience of youth and a driven personality.

'An entire week of my life lost forever. Imagine the work I could have done.' He sighed then wolfed down most of the Mediterranean platter.

'I'm interested in your assessment of the team,' Yves said.

'We're all different. James designs our experiments, a pedant. Drives me mad – always off on a tangent of his own. Sometimes I wish he'd see that making breakthroughs is more important than checking every result a hundred times. But he keeps us honest. Cheng is the innovator – maddening, intuitive, unorthodox and inspirational. She's off-beam with ideas that keep us fresh. Nick's the modeller. He can take a few key results and extrapolate trends that would otherwise take months to trial. Boring but essential. Keeps us from wasting time. He's more than a stats man, crunches solid new ways to test. Mostly we spark off each other – there's a real buzz. We're all pretty motivated.'

'But you haven't talked about money,' Yves asked. 'Do you know how much you need to do the additional experiments, to bring this thing to fruition? Why else would you be applying for grants?'

'Not sure. Plenty, of course,' responded Nathan. 'We're working damn hard. Long days, plenty of nights and most weekends but we desperately need money to speed it all up. Don't want some other team stealing the glory.'

'Just what I thought. Well, you have 48 hours to consider my offer. The details are all documented,' Yves said handing over a file. He looked directly into Nathan's eyes without even a hint of a smile. 'We've made a generous offer. After two days, it will lapse. The offer will be made to the Harvard team. This company won't be kept waiting.'

Opening the lab door, Nathan saw the team had gathered.

'You look smug,' said Cheng smiling. 'Tell all.'

'Lunch was delicious.' He teased them with a smile, and then perched on the bench. 'Seriously, you know how hard it is to get grants. And we've discussed the need to build our reputations while we're young. Tenure in positions at the universities doing the best work is virtually impossible. I don't want to chew energy thinking about the job.'

'We know that Nathan,' James shouted. 'Get on with it.'

'We've always said that private investment in medical research is risky, and that science can be compromised if it's associated with the private sector. But we know the frustration of living hand to mouth between grants and how our work is slow without money.' Nathan paused.

'Let's not underestimate the risks. How do we know what the company will do with our research? They could tie it up for years. I just know we need to keep the team together, run the tests and be sure the experimental designs are robust,' Nick said jumping to his feet.

'We can't afford to be tainted by commercialism. But we also need to concentrate without distraction for a couple of years. We can't waste time wondering if we'll have a job next month.' Nathan continued 'It seems a solid offer. The contracts are five years. The money's far better than here.'

Cheng leafed through the folder Nathan had slapped on the table and said,

'The facilities on offer are top shelf, far better than those here at the university. The work will be quicker.'

'I'm sick of being cramped in these old labs,' Nick said. 'Unlimited access to the NMR is appealing. Here we have to book analyses weeks in advance and prove we've got the funds.'

'We all know the telomere work is hot. We're competing against some of the best labs in the world. Since our first breakthrough, we know the major cause of ageing is damaged chromosome ends from DNA fraying on the telomere ends. We've known the race is on. It doesn't take much imagination to see that ways to slow or even stop the aging process would a giant scientific breakthrough and a bloody huge financial opportunity. But to get published, claim precedence, win the prizes, we have to show how the telomeres operate,' Nathan continued.

'Easy to say, bloody hard to do,' said Nick. 'We stand the best chance if we stick together.'

Cheng chipped in. 'If we can show what makes the telomeres unravel and then how that expresses as aging, we'll be famous. Re-binding telomeres is a wild idea. We can't test it on animals. We need experiments involving people, and we'll never get the money to achieve that here.'

Nathan laughed. 'We might get mice, or even fruit flies. But that's not enough. And we can't prove the theory if we can't do the tests.'

'The prizes are up for grabs. I reckon the Nobel is up for the right team,' said Nick.

'You'd expect commercial interest,' said Cheng.

'And today I read that Ceber is entering the market with extracts of that Chinese herb *Astragalus*. Their herbal solution must be posting results. But our ideas have greater traction for discovering the cause and the way it operates,' Cheng added. 'If we can find a way to turn genes on and off at the right time, we'll be famous, not just hopefuls. If the cellular treatments to turn hTERT back on works, we'll be heroes. How many plant extracts, egg and sperm cells, and specialized melanoma cells have we already have trialled? Hundreds. Everyone knows the problems of ageing begin when telomerase is switched off after adolescence. Our treatment already slows aging in cancer cells.'

'We're so close. We know the Harvard team can activate telomerase. If our treatment binds the telomeres longer and neater, we're there. It's the fraying that expresses as aging. But, if we can't move to human trials soon and prove the mechanism, it's all just theory,' James said.

'Well, I'm euphoric about the latest results and think that's a good omen' said Cheng. Negative results are useful and spur new thinking, but I reckon these positive results show we're on the right track.

'For scientists we are being very emotional about what should be a logical, rational decision,' James said.

'Well, it is about time you recognised that creativity can be intuitive as well as an intellectual exercise,' replied Cheng. 'Stop being so linear.'

'We're at a crossroads. I don't want to hesitate,' Nathan said.

'I'm all for the move,' said Cheng. 'No waiting, no nonsense, just get on. Extra lab space and brain space will give me precious thinking time. It's hard in this cramped lab. And I'm bloody sick of worrying about money.' Cheng echoed all their thoughts. She pirouetted around the lab with her arms waving.

'Calm down Cheng,' said Nick. 'You know my predilections. I'll calculate the probabilities and evaluate all the options. But I'm sure attracted to more money for a few years rather than living hand to mouth or grant-to-grant. Girls, beer and restaurant dinners all sound good.'

'You could have made plenty of money in finance,' said Nathan.

'Yeah, but it would bore me witless,' said Nick. 'Then I'd be no fun.'

All eyes gravitated to Nathan.

'OK but we keep the team together.'

James, as always, kept a straight face as he said, 'Tell me you are not serious. Sell out to a private company? Talk about joining the forces of darkness and prostituting ourselves. Who'll own the IP? What if they bury our work?'

'You might have done a major in philosophy, but don't fuck around and play devil's advocate. Tell us what you think,' said Nathan.

'I don't care one way or the other about the source of funds. But it's only logical to test the argument,' James shrugged. 'How many times have we discussed the pitfalls of going private? We know there's risks.'

'Yes, but we need to stay together.' Nathan knew that working with this team was the closest James had ever come to having a functional family.

'Well protect us James. Scrutinize the contracts and make sure we won't be sold out.'

'Let's sleep on it,' Nathan proposed. 'Read the stuff. Meet again in the morning to decide and let's get on with it.'

It was raining as they gathered in the laboratory the next morning. They were all subdued; a mood which reflected the cool, misty morning.

'Let's set the ground rules. First – it's all in or all out? We don't split the team.' They all nodded. 'If we refuse this offer, I'm not writing any more grant applications. I've had enough, someone else can do it,' Nathan said. Last night's euphoria had worn off.

'Miserable lot. You all look like you're hung-over,' said Cheng.

'Well, it's likely to be a life-changing decision,' said James.

'We might be brilliant scientists.' Cheng laughed. 'But I'm naïve about commercial arrangements. It's uncomfortable. The offer looks too good to be true. Money, security and great facilities. They even say publication rights.'

'With this set-up we'll have a fighting chance,' Nathan said. 'We can't let those Harvard bastards beat us.'

All the team wanted to accept the offer. They talked back and forth, chewing over old ground, making more coffee. Finally, Cheng said,

'I'm in.'

'Me too,' said James.

'Then I'm in,' said Nick. 'That settles it.'

'Yes, I think it's the right time,' said Nathan. 'I'll call Yves. Then let's stash the cultures and go to the pub for lunch.'

The documentation included a forty-page employment contract the company described as standard. It would bind them for five years. Nathan worried about the uneven battle of skilled commercial negotiators versus Team Novice.

Chapter 12

Flight to the Sun, October 2011

A deep sense of hopelessness shrouded Zoe like a cloak. She knew she would probably recover but could not imagine how. At Adelaide Airport the struggling taxi driver thought all his Christmases had come at once when she said,

'Will you drive me to Langhorne Creek?'

When they arrived, after the hour's trip, it was like stepping back in time. Her mother and father had dreamed about restoring and expanding the old stone cottage, but that dream faltered when he had disappeared all those years ago. Zoe and her mother Catherine had lived in the small house all through her time at school.

'Hello Mum,' she said to the air as the taxi disappeared back up the driveway. How ironic that this empty house is the closest thing I have to a home, she thought.

She retrieved the key from under the pot on the veranda and climbed the steps. She put her hands against the stones by the door. They felt more solid and dependable than anything she had felt for a month. The house had been built by hand from local limestone in the 1880s. While the walls were prone to salt damp, which wicked up through the mortar year by year, weakening the stone and crumbling the mortar, the structure would last another hundred years.

The heavy door creaked as she pushed it open, breaking the spider webs that tried to weld it to the wall. She walked up the hallway. High roofs, with lathe and plaster ceilings, kept the house cool in summer and held in the warmth of fires in winter. The house was sparsely furnished, and even though the paint was in poor condition, Zoe was thankful for the basic cleaning that had been done as part of the lease. She wandered through the echoing rooms and was pleased that spare bedding was still rolled up in the bottom of a wardrobe. Exhausted, she threw it on a bed, curled up, foetal, and cried herself to sleep.

Next morning, Zoe could feel her parents' presence in the corners; glimpse their dreams in the shadows. As she wandered from room to room, memories of her mother rose, she imagined her father in the vineyard.

Crumbled lavender in the bottom of the bedroom drawers made her cry, for the destruction of her relationship and with it, her self-confidence and for her long-suffering mother, snatched too young by an early death. She sobbed for her long-lost father too. Then she cried for all the lost opportunities of her childhood, which could have been so different if her father had not vanished.

Vivid dreams troubled her tormented nights. Her sense of failure saturated her days like creeping damp. She obsessively reiterated David's shocking admission. She heard his cold words over and over again like an insane recording of Ravel's Bolero, getting faster and faster, louder and louder.

Despite her isolation and the searing pain, Zoe knew it was right to return. She couldn't talk or work until she understood herself. Zoe slowly realised this was why she had been drawn back to this house. She needed to find herself.

Zoe felt close to her mother here. Endurance had been her lasting legacy. She also remembered her father's strength; *I'm your Mallee bull*, he would roar as she rode on his shoulders around the house. The memories grounded her like anchors. She felt a link with the land. There was a thread of belonging, of continuity. The stones for the house had been collected from nearby paddocks and, in time, they would tumble back into the soil but, for now, the walls sheltered her, a palpable reminder of her parent's love. The memories gave her strength. She hoped her isolation would grow into independence; her weakness into self-sufficiency.

Zoe spent hours wrapped in silence. She began to appreciate small things: the simplicity of the house, it's durability. She admired the high roof that collected precious water; the wide verandas which threw welcome shade in the summer and kept washing dry from winter rain.

She grew familiar again with the four main rooms that flanked a modest central hall lined with hooks, which once held hats and coats, jackets and scarves. Each room had a small fireplace. One chimney had been bricked up many years ago. The bee colony she remembered feeling behind the bricks, was still there. Streams of bees shuttled in and out of the chimneystack. Zoe laid her palms against the wall and felt their comforting vibrations and heard their gentle buzzing. Zoe camped in the cleanest room and collected fallen limbs from the plentiful gum trees to light cosy fires. The fragrant smoke and hypnotic flames provided a warm and comforting presence.

The small bathroom attached to the back of the cottage had been renovated. The kitchen, smaller than her childhood memory, waited to beat again as the heart of this house. She sat at the long pine table and prepared paltry cheese sandwiches, while the capacious wood stove and broad bench called for a family and more generous fare.

Brad Woods, a local contractor, managed Zoe's vines. Brad paid Zoe a fee, dependant on the quality and quantity of the grapes he harvested. The climate and soils suited shiraz vines and the grapes made deep ruby wine with complex flavours. Retaining the vineyard when she moved to London meant she had not betrayed her parents' dream. When Zoe decided to come back, she emailed Brad to say she would be using the empty house for an indefinite period.

Weeks morphed into a month, overshadowed by gloom. She would wake in the middle of the night, shaking, switch the light on and read until dawn. Self-doubt haunted her nights. The brightness of morning offered the illusion of hope.

Gradually Zoe remembered her mother and began to understand the strength it must have taken to continue when her father disappeared. The cruel tongues of gossip had been relentless. Her mother had transformed that horror into a positive legacy and Zoe did not have to work as hard as her mother to keep a roof over her head. Each day Zoe ate a little more yet was still surprised how little she needed to exist. She neither wrote nor painted. After several weeks she ventured outside and walked. The exercise warmed her body and began to dispel the gloom.

Chapter 13

Aging Cells

Yves felt the excitement rising from the Alston team. The analysis from the first set of test results using Cheng's innovative idea was promising. The work was demanding, daring and utterly absorbing. Inspired by new equipment, the team worked long hours in the new laboratories. Challenges flew between them like fireworks, and then had to be tested, refined, and explained.

'There's no doubt Cheng's hypothesis is promising,' Nathan said as the team gathered to discuss updating Yves over morning coffee. 'How much do we tell him?'

'And you all thought it was over-imaginative. It took me days to convince you it was even worthy of testing,' Cheng shook her head. 'Sceptics.'

'Well, without my statistical design, which meant we could do the tests in only about 10,000 replications, we wouldn't have saved the weeks of work necessary for the next trial,' James added. 'Now we can do micro samples and aggregate the treatments in cross-matched testing regimes. It's brilliant having access to the equipment we need. Simply brilliant.'

'I must admit I'm enjoying the freedom from the dreaded money man,' said James 'I even bought new discs.'

'Sorry, but the salaries are the best bit,' said Nick.

'I like the fume cabinets – my clothes and hair no longer smell of acid.'

'And the staff lunchroom has clean bench tops, fresh fruit and proper coffee. I sure don't miss the university's old wooden benches impregnated with generations of instant coffee powder, and the air, hazy with burned toast,' said Cheng.

'I'm pleased we haven't seen any signs of intellectual interference,' Nathan said after Yves left. 'He's a bit pushy though.'

'That's true,' James responded. 'The company shows interest in our work yet gives us plenty of freedom. I'd be pushy too if I was funding us. We're expensive.'

Nathan suspected the company staff didn't understand the research. He was happy with that, as long as they kept their distance.

'We're amassing data by the truckload. Might need some additional help. We've got two terabytes of data already. At least 500 variations on the cellular stuff will be necessary before we can design trials to prove this new mechanism idea. If we're to be sure, we need to scale up, prove non-toxicity then do whole body testing. Our testing on mice seems safe so it's time to move up, fast,' said Nathan.

'Don't forget – we'll need human trials to see if it really works, but everyone else will too. It's not sufficient to know that our product is non-toxic,' Cheng added. 'That's the easy bit.'

'Yves has committed to help – says he's secured the budget.'

Privately the team knew that human trials couldn't be anywhere in the developed world if they wanted fast results. That's where it got sticky. They simply didn't have enough data yet to satisfy the ethics committees that controlled human testing in most European and first world countries.

Yves had been busy planning the next steps. Alston Pharmaceuticals had operations across the globe. In countries wracked by war or famine a little unauthorised testing would always slip below the radar. He predicted the research team would leave those decisions to the locals and not get their hands dirty.

'We will advance the trials as fast as possible,' Yves said at the next meeting. 'I'll organise the access needed.'

'We need quite a lot of testing if we are to to satisfy both the scientists and the regulators in Europe,' said Nathan.

'I can get things organised as we move from test tubes to people,' said Yves, silently planning to contact African connections.

'We'll leave that side of the business to you. We'll specify the conditions we need, define the dosages and sampling regimes. You can organise the subjects, we'll analyse the results,' said Nathan.

Nathan looked around the lab. The team had worked forty-eight hours straight and the room was littered with coffee cups, pizza boxes and caffeine drink cans. All of them had crumpled clothes and stringy hair and were slumped in chairs in various stages of exhaustion.

'Look at you, sacrificing youth on the altar of research for anti-aging. Go home everyone. Get some sleep – and don't come back for three days.'

The lab slipped into silence as they trooped out, a motley bunch of kids with a ton of brains but not enough wisdom to eat well.

In his office, Yves called an old colleague in Africa to confirm that he could source test subjects.

'I have a job for you Jerome,' Yves began. 'Simple testing, we don't expect problems. When you receive the samples, there will be full instructions and you can engage the people necessary to monitor the trials.'

'Happy to help Yves. There are plenty of people around here who are focussed on finding their next meal. They're not inclined to ask inconvenient questions.'

'This work should be low risk. You'll need to make some careful measurements though. Organise this well and you'll have plenty of money for another big fishing trip.'

Yves and Jerome put the plan into place. The game had begun. For that was how Yves saw it. It was a game, and games were rarely played among equals. Despite all the soft social policy he saw around him, Yves knew life was fiercely competitive. He learned that at age six in the backstreets of Marseilles, fight, hide, and remember. Then you might live to fight again. Without question, people were not born equal; life was governed by the survival of the fittest and Yves was committed to being the fittest. More money, more power, these were the spoils of the victor, his definition of success. He expected to enjoy the results of this gamble soon. But, he was interested beyond the financial potential. His interest in these results was personal. He spied the 'Fountain of Youth', and if anyone had access to that prize, it would be him.

Chapter 14

Breakthrough

'These latest cell replication trials are brilliant,' said Nathan. 'Even after thousands of replications, the cells are not senescing. Exactly what we wanted – cells that can reproduce without error or loss of vigour for many, many generations. The golden key to anti-ageing.'

'Our challenge is to extend these effects. We need more than skin. The treatment must influence the whole organism,' said Cheng.

'I'm glad Yves organised the preliminary testing,' said Nathan. 'Our designs should sort out any problems. Then after we establish non-toxicity, the next phase will give us comfort provided we get the reassurance the experiments in Africa will be conducted according to our protocols.'

'Remember only 100 people. Not statistically significant,' cautioned James.

'No, but an important transition to whole people rather than individual cells,' Nathan added as the researchers poured over the data from every angle.

'100 subjects is not enough. We'll need extensive tests before we can be confident. Yves will want updates and information about trends and interpretations every day if we're not careful. Thank God the initial toxicity screening didn't unearth problems,' said James.

'I agree the first results show promise, but let's wait till next month's figures before jumping to conclusions. If nothing causes concern then I think we'll be ready to apply for testing and registration approval in Europe,' said Nathan. 'I assume we can leave those details to Alston. Or at least Yves.'

'If the African tests are replicated in stage 2, major trials could be completed in a year,' said Cheng.

Nathan remembered the commercial terms in their contracts: bonuses on successful delivery of defined milestones; salaries were good. He had a reliable car and for the first time ever, didn't scrabble to find rent money at the end of the month.

'I think we need to plan the last stage as soon as possible. Glad I can put my brain to that problem rather than writing grant applications.' Cheng smirked. 'And there's been no interference. Mind you, I'd bet none of those suits understand the complexity of the experimental design.'

'Yes, we'll need massive data sets to identify potential dangers. The company calls them side effects. Bloody political correctness. People might experience problems, and they might be dramatic. I want numbers – probability and severity. Lots of stats,' James replied.

Silence crept across the benches. Equipment stretched gleaming along the corridor; the lunchroom was immaculate. But as Nathan glanced around the room, he thought how little had changed since they started working together. New clothes and sinks didn't resolve the scientific and ethical challenges.

'People experiments are tough. Complex and variable metabolism. Plenty of genetic variation. We can't control lifestyles. I wish mice or rabbits would do. Simpler to buy genetically identical clones and keep them in cages, eating standard diets in the same environments. People are maddeningly diverse,' Cheng said.

'And no data sets are absolute. That's always the problem. All the experiments must be able to be replicated. Let's hope unexpected outcomes don't ambush us,' said Nick. 'Tough news for most companies to swallow. At least we can take some comfort from knowing the drug isn't lethal. Even in massive doses over many months, the rats showed no ill effects. But we can still only offer probabilities.'

'As we've agreed, the complexities of aging in people make this tough. Reliable experimental design is always difficult to achieve,' said Cheng.

'Well, even knowing that cells, tissues and organs function together, I've restricted the number of measured variables to make a result possible. Skin thickness is the easiest attribute amenable to measurement. Also, for cosmetic effect, skin thickness is important,' said James

'Getting wrinkles is always unpopular and, if nothing else, this treatment would generate a market for wrinkle reduction. I am convinced skin changes are enough for the first stage. If all goes well, we can add more factors later,' said Cheng.

Yves instructed the Alston product development team and the marketers to schedule trials in Europe to get the right permissions and clearances to sell. Preliminary testing without much scrutiny had great appeal. Fast and cheap. Marketing words could be selected with care, and outrageous claims avoided. Ageing was not considered a disease, so no cures were promised. The lawyers assured them that this would allow them to escape the more stringent tests required under the provisions of the pharmaceutical law. The product might be on the shelves within the year in Europe. First to market always won the biggest rewards. The company was hungry for a strong return on their major investment.

Chapter 15

Richard Branches Out

On the last Friday of the month Zoe, Monica, George, and Richard, together with various strays who might be passing through, had a standing arrangement to eat together. This month, George chose Andre's Cuchina. He'd heard the new chef was exciting everyone with his Sicilian inspirations. The friends settled in and perused the menu.

'I miss Zoe. Wonder how she's going? Has anyone heard?' asked George.

'No,' Monica said. 'It's months since she left. She always was too serious about that bloke,' said Richard. 'Interesting menu, George, I've never heard of blackcurrant sorbet.'

'I haven't had blackcurrant since I was a child,' said George.

'I only remember Ribena. Did you know I named my first company RiDina as a play on the words Richard's DNA?' Richard asked as he poured a red wine. 'I wanted to seed the idea that money was encoded into my DNA and I could replicate it at will,' he chuckled.

'Nice try Richard, but your success has been due to your clever mind and active imagination more than your genes,' Monica replied as the friends tucked into a delicious antipasto plate. 'Try these braised artichokes, they are amazing.'

Monica knew that money symbolised freedom and independence to Richard whose father was killed when he was a child of six. His mother had struggled to raise him alone. Richard's financial security and lifestyle was hard-won. He was a master at drawing together young people with innovative ideas.

'Monica helped me gather useful people this month for my new venture,' Richard said to George. 'I am now waiting to see if she has any gold star gossip for me tonight.' He spread his open hands and looked as pleading as a puppy.

'You mean you find useful things among the endless torrent of ideas, gossip and speculation that pours from my mouth every time we meet?' Monica teased as she rummaged in her handbag to recover a few sheets of paper, which she handed to Richard. He scanned them; his eyes gleamed then the pages were folded them away in his pocket.

'Monica you are the best sounding board for new trends. And of course, a magnet for oddball people with curious talents. Order anything you like. This is my treat,' Richard said.

'Yum, braised pork belly for me. And matching wine please,' said George.

'I'll have the veal for main course, and the pasta salad with three sorts of olives,' said Monica.

'Sounds delicious and I'm having the Fiano with my fish,' said Richard.

'Richard, you are a bloodhound when it comes to spotting trends. Just by knowing who is lunching or sleeping with whom, I reckon you can sniff out deals, business mergers, failures or acquisitions,' said George.

'Perhaps, but I put my money on the line. Mainly good profits, but not always. I need to back my judgement – and despite what you think, it's not easy,' he said. 'There are always conundrums. But that's the fun, I relish all sorts of puzzles. Ever since I was a boy, I've enjoyed trick boxes, crosswords, cryptograms and mathematical oddities like the

Fibonacci sequence and the golden mean… Business intelligence is just another sort of puzzle.'

'Yes, and sometimes I think you practice sleight of hand, magic and optical illusions, rather than philosophical paradoxes,' said Monica.

'I used to think there were hidden codes carried by the page around the letters in addition to the letters themselves,' Richard mused, unusually reflective after a couple of wines. 'Then I learned about photography and the difference between positive and negative prints and I realised one was simply the inverse of the other. You know, is dark the absence of light, or a thing itself?

'And to think I played with dolls,' laughed Monica.

'Information is the alchemy of the 21st century,' Richard said. 'I used to dream about letters. They would float around my mind in a multitude of different colours. Then the letters would gather together into words and take on a new level of meaning. Then the words would gather together into different shaped sentences so that there are already three intertwined layers of complexity, each delivering an additional set of connections and level of meaning. I used to imagine that the letters were like threads, which could be spun into yarn, woven into words and then shaped into fabrics to make magic carpets to explore new worlds of meaning. Each aggregation adds new attributes, and each level of complexity generates new forms and new meanings. I just layer information in the same way to form new meanings and build successful businesses.'

'So, you are really are in the fabric business,' Monica joked.

'In a way,' he laughed. 'Same principle. You supply some of the threads Monica,' said Richard with a child-like delight in the fascinating way words and sentences were just words and sentences to some but delivered meaning to others.

'It's like DNA molecules, information can change from being data to becoming a template to build other structures. I then aggregate them up into companies. I enjoy the complexity, the ambiguity, and occasionally I do something meaningful.'

'I think all those years drilling new oil wells gave you decades of experience in risky assessments. If you didn't send the company broke then, this must seem like child's play,' said Monica.

'There was huge expense in drilling new wells. That's how I learned to manipulate massive data sets, complex models and multivariate analyses. It reduced uncertainty, but the risks were still high. That's why I'm always alert to new ideas, and new forms of analysis, which might reduce uncertainty. Managing shares and innovative new ventures is more about people. They're risky in other ways.'

'You can say that again,' said Monica.

'Monica, do you remember the mad computer kids who were trying to sell off their analyses of satellite maps as op art, because they couldn't get anyone in the mining world to look seriously at their ideas? They were flat broke and just trying to get beer money. They were happy to talk to me when you sent them over. Well, I set them up in business, introduced them to the right people and advised them through the initial negotiations. Nobody thought that surface soil anomalies could be successfully used to predict the composition of strata below. They've made me a packet. I wouldn't be surprised if that technology goes on to make millions.'

'Good work Richard. Fancy that. Satellite maps that can look under the ground,' said Monica.

'The fun for me is that those kids also act as magnets for other young innovative thinkers. I love meeting talented kids with wild ideas and nowhere to go. Some of their latest ideas use computer designed and manipulated sample probes, which snake through underground strata to test strength and composition from within an optical fibre. The idea of gathering data with a high-tech micro snake that can bore through rock is exciting stuff. So, I've invested in them too. I can see ready markets – each company could use the specialised technology to solve a different problem. I'm even thinking of companies to test the sludge in tailings dams, food solutions during manufacturing and even the human body could be next. It's exciting.'

'And of course, you receive a percentage,' smiled Monica.

'I'm glad they stayed out of the art business,' said George. 'The colours were far too garish for my taste.'

'Before I knew you Richard, I used to think that the share market was based on facts and finance. Now I know it is about as dependable as the fashion industry. It's heady stuff, ripe for intervention with well-placed gossip in the right ears and some heavy buying to drive stock prices up or down. Disappointing really,' added Monica.

'Yes.' Richard laughed. 'It's informed gambling for high stakes. The one important rule is that there are no rules – just don't get caught manipulating the market with insider information. But, knowing the market, and being able to play it well, keeps me alert. A while ago you asked me about that multi-armed octopus of a business, *Montague Corp* Monica,' Richard said. 'They have had many changes of ownership, and now are concentrated big time in essential services. They started in the eastern bloc. Emerging economies, even one of the ex-Soviet states before graduating to larger economies. As governments struggled to finance new infrastructure to meet skyrocketing expectations and populations, they've offered service contracts to private sector partners to supply water, energy and transport. Some governments naively believe they could rely on private companies to behave with fairness. Either that or they believed they could manage supply contracts with the finesse and ruthlessness of private companies. Before they realised the danger of having profit-based companies manage essential services, these companies established effective monopolies and controlled the infrastructure. It was a perfect set up for tough negotiations and *Montague* played its cards hard.' Richard continued. 'Underpinned by support from the French government, they won contracts all over the world and established a successful formula. They would bid cheap, use variations and 'community service obligations' to ramp up their payments from government, then buy out their competitors and threaten to withdraw if their price was not met in the next round of negotiations. Public opinion still held governments responsible, and they were responsive to public criticism. Your man Montreau bailed out at a very profitable time just as the expansion was starting and its value was highest.'

'Wow that's a lot to take in Richard,' said Monica. 'You're spoiling my appetite.'

'And I only know him as a buyer of fancy art works,' said George.

Richard's interest had been piqued when Monica had asked him about Montague Corp.

'And there's more.'

George and Monica groaned.

'The company's initial success came from several key mergers. The most important one had been between three diverse businesses. The first, EastPac – had major interests in natural resources, including fishing and timber industries in the Asia Pacific rim. The second, a British group, Servicecorp, was formed from ex-armed service personnel looking for a new role after the Falkland's conflict. The third, a Japanese consortium, San specialised in paper. This series of smart acquisitions yielded a powerful company with an impressive reach and capital base.'

'I think I need either another bottle or another day with no wine if I am to absorb all of that,' complained Monica.

'Your man Montreau was responsible for the profit generated from the Asia Pacific ventures years ago. I suspect disorganised and vulnerable Pacific governments were no match for sophisticated and cash-rich European companies alert to opportunities and hungry for profits. Much of Montague's initial wealth was generated from high value tropical timbers,' Richard continued.

'I know Europe has used most of its hardwood forests. Only tropical hardwoods are available for specialised art framing these days,' added

George. 'If the company is a throwback to colonial days, there'll be slaves and everything.'

'I haven't found any slaves, but there is a suspicious lack of detail about the business and consistently high returns. It is tempting to believe that the pyramid of mysterious deals delivered massive profits from hidden activities. The wood chip business for paper was based on eucalypt pulp from Tasmania. The insatiable need for quality chopsticks from fine timbers came from rainforest timbers around the Pacific Rim. These two contrasting uses of wood added value by using the same shipping, refuelling and supply chains – it was smart business. And it grew quickly.'

'Stop! That's enough for me, for the moment,' Monica said as their main course arrived.

But Richard continued, 'Maybe Montague and their early companies could be worth investigating. There is something not quite right about the company. We might just discover some skeletons in the closet.'

Spicy aromas wafted from the food before them, but Richard kept talking. 'I've already searched the company registers to identify the major partners. But they are adept at establishing networks of trusts and holding companies to split incomes and hold assets in arrangements that minimise investigation and liability. It might be easier to track the movement of funds. I'm surprised there are so many references to New Caledonia in one arm of the business. It's not a usual headquarters for such a large operation.'

'OK so let's call our project the *Pacific Connection*,' said George. 'Probably less than pacific, if all that stuff you said is true.'

'Beautiful food,' Monica said. 'All that talk about the Pacific makes me think of seafood and luscious fruit.'

'My veal was divine. I'm not sure I will have room for dessert,' George said.

'Well, I'm adding another resource to our arsenal,' Monica said accepting a dessert menu with delight. 'I think I need to rescue Zoe from Langhorne Creek. She's been alone long enough. If I make a quick trip back to Australia, perhaps I could add New Caledonia to my itinerary. Have a snoop. Either way I'll draw Zoe out of her misery and into the hunt. You know, I don't think of Adelaide as home anymore. My life is so centred in London and home has become where I hang my hat. I've got plenty of leave owing. I think I'll fly to Australia as soon as possible. A family visit is long overdue. Then I can check on Zoe.

I might even convince her to share a holiday in New Caledonia for some sun. And a snoop around Montreau's Pacific connections. It could be therapeutic for us both.'

Chapter 16

Birds Again

Zoe recognised she was healing when she noticed bird songs in the morning. October was her favourite month in southern Australia; warm enough to have overcome the uncertainty of spring and not yet hot enough to have blanched the landscape. In London, the evenings would be drawing in and the days chilling. She felt like a migrating bird that had followed the sun.

In Langhorne Creek, fresh dewy mornings and warm days encouraged the birds to breed. Among the birdcalls she began to recognise individual species. The ubiquitous melodic warbling of the magpies was unmistakable, as was the chittering of the willy wagtails. She scrubbed the old birdbath, filled it with water and sat watching, as quiet as a statue for hours. Instead of obsessively thinking about David, following the birds became the focus of her days.

Five hectares of vines; then fruit trees and a scattering of native trees and shrubs surrounded the house. Along one side of the property, a tall shelterbelt of dense melaleucas, wattles and eucalypts provided homes and food for dozens of native birds. Her neighbour grazed his sheep a few times a year on the rough grass, to keep it short enough to minimise the chance of bushfire. In wet years, wheat, barley or triticale clothed the surrounding paddocks then sheep or cattle grazed the stubble.

Of the fruit trees that her parents had planted, some had died while others had grown tall. Zoe recognised apple and pear trees, apricots, figs and plums. She heard her father's voice. *Pome fruits the apples, pears and quinces, are called pome because they come from Pommy land. Cherries make you cheery because they are the first to ripen in summer. Don't eat too many stone fruits at once; they'll race through you like a speeding train.* The happy memories brought a tentative smile to her hollow cheeks.

Brad kept an old car on the property and offered to let her use it. One day, during her trip for basic supplies, she passed a chalked sign on a rough board saying HENS. She continued home and thought it might be pleasant to have a few chooks scrabbling around the yard. Fresh eggs would be a welcome change to her meagre diet. Later that week, she looked at the old chook run. It seemed robust enough. She remembered her father burying the base of the corrugated iron sheets deep below the ground to prevent foxes digging under the wall. The chicken wire was still intact, and the perches looked solid. The chickens could roost high at night to stay safe from the foxes. The old building had begun life as a horse stable back in the days when ploughing was done with draught-horses. As a child she would find huge horseshoes when digging in the garden. Clydesdales, her father had said, 'Tall, strong horses to do the work and pull the heavy loads, just like me.'

The hen house still felt cosy even though the old straw smelt mousey. Zoe saw bales of straw in one of the sheds, so dragged in the best ones to freshen it up a bit. She remembered that chickens liked to lay their eggs in a nest with a cover; the instinct to hide their eggs was strong. She arranged an old box on its side and pressed some fresh straw into it. As a child, Zoe was frightened by the blustering chickens which would rush up expecting a treat. But the excitement of touching the eggs over-whelmed her fear and she would force herself into the shed. She would put out the food, drawing the chickens away, and then sit on the straw with the eggs in her lap as her fingers traced the smooth, asymmetrical shells, delighting in the contrast between their strength and fragility and marvelling at their warmth.

Zoe drove the twenty kilometres to Mount Barker for supplies because there was less chance of seeing anyone she might know. She dreaded the thought of answering questions. By the next month when she made the necessary shopping trip, she steeled herself and drove up the driveway with the sign that promised HENS. True to the sign, hundreds of hens roamed in broad open paddocks. She couldn't decide if this was untidy and they should all be enclosed in cages, or whether this was chicken heaven. She decided on nirvana as she saw the owner emerging from the house.

'Hello, hello,' said Ginny as she introduced herself with a warm handshake and a wonderful, welcoming smile. She was about as wide as she was tall, and her wispy nest of hair was pinned to her head by a multitude of clips. As the pair walked from the house toward the paddocks, the chickens flocked toward them, necks stretched and wings flailing. The house, property and Ginny herself looked frayed around the edges as if they might unravel and blow away in a strong breeze like the cast-off feathers that fluttered around the yard.

'Yes,' Ginny said in response to Zoe's question. 'I have hens available for sale, and yes of course they will lay eggs.'

'I was hoping for a few eggs each day. I don't know much about chickens,' Zoe said, feeling ill-equipped to become a hen owner.

Ginny talked to the birds, and, as she reached into her vast apron pocket and scattered a handful of grain, the chickens became even friendlier. Zoe had not met anyone who actually wore an apron. In the ensuing feeding scrabble Ginny bent down, grabbed a few legs and soon had hoisted several chickens upside down. Talking all the time, she folded their wings with care and then placed them in a cardboard carton. In the dark, they settled with soft murmurings. Ginny explained their needs.

'Always make sure they have water dear, and you must lock them up at night otherwise the foxes will kill 'em. Feed them every night in the chook house and they will always come home to roost. Don't worry about them running away – leave them inside for the first few days and they won't wander further than they feel comfortable. They're home lovers like me.'

Ginny assured Zoe that they would lay well and sold her a bag of feed. Zoe loaded the cartons in the boot of her car.

'*What have I done?*' she thought in a panic as she drove down the road. *'I'm struggling to look after myself, let alone animals. Idiot!* She drove home, parked in front of the rejuvenated chicken house and opened the boot with trepidation.

Overcoming her fear, and hoping the birds would not flap, Zoe carted the boxes into the chook house and shut the door. Then she lifted the chickens out; surprised how light and warm they felt. As she placed them on the ground, the hens shook themselves and looked bemused as they rearranged their feathers and eyed each other. Zoe put out some food, filled the water container and left them to adjust.

She returned to the house with a sense of achievement and found herself smiling for the first time in months. *Small things* her mother used to say – *Everything grows from small things.* And it seemed from that small thing Zoe started to grow again. She walked around the vineyard each morning. She noticed trees beginning to flower, the fruit form and ripen. The calls of the chickens in the morning were insistent. They wanted the door open, and to wander around the vineyard. She was amused by their curiosity and tameness. They always followed her hoping for earwigs or juicy worms and Zoe obliged by turning over logs and stones.

These gentle, warm feather dusters gave her fresh eggs and provided calmness and warmth that had been missing for many months. Zoe was healing.

Chapter 17

Harry Hacks

Harry lived in a cavernous flat, re-purposed from a storeroom in the basement of a noisy Hammersmith apartment block.

'It's cold,' he said to his sister Annette who was sitting, as she did every day, in an old floral armchair on the other side of the room.

'I've got more work from Richard,' he said and pulled his jacket closer. 'Probably not enough to heat this big old room, but computers don't like heat. When I get into the work, I don't notice it. Are you warm enough?' he asked, not expecting an answer.

The door behind Harry opened, and his Mum, Maureen called.

'Mealtime you two. Come and get it.' Harry walked over to Annette, gently pulled her arm and together they walked into the kitchen where food was on the table.

'There you go. Eat up. Always plenty now Harry's looking after us,' she said as she did every mealtime.

"Richard's got a new project for me,' Harry said between the sausages and beans.

'Is it a real job?' asked his Mum.

'Real enough Mum. I can do it from here so don't worry. But I've got to meet Richard tomorrow, so I'll be out for a while. He's good to us you know. It's regular work and he likes what I do. I just want you to be comfortable.'

'Don't know how you do it. Tapping away at all hours. It doesn't seem like a proper job to me. Too much for me to understand.'

'That's OK. It's about computers Mum. The one thing I'm good at.'

'Sorry to drag you out this way,' Harry said to Richard when they met in the Café Bean in Hammersmith.

'Well, I suppose it gets me out of the office,' Richard replied. 'I know you don't like moving around much, but you're a good explorer in the digital wilderness,' said Richard. 'I'm as lost there as I would be among the hieroglyphics of a Mayan temple. I'll never know how you can follow those trails through cyberspace. But I love the way you unlock coded doors and find hidden passageways to information.'

'Coffee? Cake?'

'Tea and one of them ham samwiches thanks,' said Harry.

'Your explorations are like archaeology. You strip back layers of information that bury stories as effectively as sand buried Troy.'

'Well, you just gotta follow the clues. Find 'em and piece 'em together to see the stories,' said Harry.

'In earlier generations you might have discovered Pharaohs' tombs, but together we weave together stories of past lives, businesses and relationships,' said Richard. 'I want to know about a Frenchman Harry, Yves Montreau. I know a bit about his current business, but I'm interested in how he got his start; how he made his money. As usual, I won't ask how you achieve your miracles. In fact, I think it's better not to know. But I will say that he seems to have a missing past. I suspect he skates on the edge of the law, and in a few different countries. Documentation may be sparse,' Richard said.

'Is it the Montreau from Alston Pharmaceuticals?' Harry asked in a low voice.

'Yes,' replied Richard with surprise. Harry usually took instructions without comment or questions. 'But it's his earlier life and business dealings outside Alston that particularly interest me.'

'I'll need good money,' Harry said. 'It's me sister see. She's having trouble. That's how I know a bit about Alston. Done some work on Provarin, that Alston make. I think Annette's hooked on it. She's all blank, never talked since the hospital.'

'Just do what you usually do Harry, and we'll see if something useful emerges,' replied Richard. 'I know you'll deliver value for money.'

'I'd like to have a crack at Alston pharmaceuticals. They put up new encryptions all the time,' Harry said.

'Call if you need additional details Harry. Once you've got some material, we'll talk about Alston,' Richard said as he tactfully handed Harry a bundle of cash.

Harry called Richard the next week.

'Current stuff is easy. Alston looks clean enough. Powerful investors on the Board. Montreau is the most recent. That Montreau's empty. Got a lot of money, not much history. Looks suspicious. Messy web of investments and a heap of heavy financial commitments. That wife's a fancy one. Spends up big. All a bit arty. She's got plenty of investments too. Looks like he might have set them up but they're all in her name and she's spending them fast. Montreau's Corporations in the early days are hard to piece together. I hate all this pre-computer stuff. So primitive.'

'Hard or impossible?' Richard asked.

'Well, I decided to follow the money. Financial transactions are the hardest to hack but most reliable. He's hiding lots of assets besides currency.'

'I hope it's not art,' said Richard.

'No, that's easy. Because they need provenance, and art dealers are rubbish with computers, valuable works of art are easy to follow. Even with fake valuations and ridiculous commissions, you can always track the money. Montreau's good at the artwork switch.'

'So, what then,' asked Richard.

'Heaps, I'll make a list for you. But the early stuff's tricky,' said Harry. 'Not there yet. I reckon he's a trickster. Seems lots of his investors have lost money, but he never does. I've given him a handle, Teflon man – nothing sticks.'

Over Friday drinks, Monica asked Richard about progress with Montreau.

'Good, once I got Harry investigating.'

'Harry who?'

'Harry Allthrop, my IT man. We've been working together for almost five years now. He's the geekiest of geeks – a skinny little runt with stringy brown hair and an ordinary face. Practically incapable of holding a general conversation, but the longer I work with him, the more I respect his skills.'

'He must be good to impress you.' Monica laughed.

'I think he must raid charity bins for his clothes. It would be impossible to be so badly dressed any other way. He's a scarecrow.'

'Not exactly your style.'

'All that IT stuff's beyond me. But Harry's the best. About as outgoing as an autistic clam. But he senses beyond the initial brief. He answers the questions, which I would have asked if I knew more. I pay him well. I think he's earning for three people. I knew he supported his Mum but, the other day, he told me about a sister who can't even talk.'

The next day, Harry called Richard at 1 o'clock in the morning.

'I need more power.'

'Harry, do you know what time it is?'

'No. I'm working.

'I need more grunt. Everything's taking too long to crunch. I'll send you a list of what I need.'

'OK OK, I'll look at it in the morning.'

'If you do it now, it'll go faster. I'm going crazy.'

'I can hear that. How much?'

'About €30k will make it quicker. €50k would be better. I'll get you the information, but it's deep. I've started to see his webs. He's secretive and careful.'

'OK,' said Richard. 'I suppose it's an investment, but I'm not happy.'

'Maybe the doctors who prescribe that Alston stuff they give my sister are happy – but they've taken my sister away. It's not illegal, but it's shit and I think there's more.'

'I hear you Harry. I just hope we're on the same horse.'

'Sure. This is big. I never let you down.'

'Make sure you get some sleep Harry. You sound a bit strung out. Eat something.'

'I'll be all right. I'll order the gear and sleep till it comes. You'll need to authorise the payment on your account. I'll send the list in a minute.'

'Done,' Richard said.

'I've been tracking him. It's big money, big research teams, big profits. They've bought a whole new research team and are pouring money into some anti-ageing stuff.'

'This is the work I asked for isn't it Harry?'

'Sure.'

'I never let them know I'm watching you know. I just reroute his emails and have a look through them before I send them on. You'll see how it works soon.'

Chapter 18

Following the Threads

'Monica, I think you should look at this stuff Harry's uncovered,' Richard said over drinks on Friday night. 'He's a strange one. He's got these on-line collaborators all over the place. It's like they're in monastic cells speaking strange languages like scholars using Latin in the Middle Ages. Harry says he never expects to meet any of his contacts, most of them he only knows by handles, not even their real names, but that doesn't stop them communicating with lightning speed all around the world. I wonder what all those brilliant introverts did before computers. They can't all have been train spotters.'

'More efficient than flying,' said Monica.

'Harry's taught himself about anti-aging and follows all Yves' emails. Apparently, the researchers have been testing legitimately and under the radar for nearly a year. According to Harry, they've got a well-developed formula even though they're still arguing between themselves about how it works.

'Hell, anti-aging would be a huge market. Not that I need it myself,' Monica replied with a smile.

'Harry reckons the Alston Board have established a subsidiary to manage the anti-aging team and bring the product to market. Making it cosmetic rather than therapeutic, means less testing, less cost.

'If their advertising only claimed to improve appearance, and that's no more than every beauty product on the market – and they'd still make millions, if it actually worked,' said George.

'Harry thinks the Alston Board members don't trust Montreau and have left him out on a bit of a limb. Apparently, he's even arranged toxicity testing in Africa with some old mate, and they don't know about it.'

'Sounds dodgy,' said Monica.

'Yes, but apparently the outcomes are already really positive – so maybe it really works.'

'A large pharmaceutical company like Alston is not exactly in the foreign aid game. I'll bet they are scared about side-effects,' said George.

'Maybe but for Alston to market a successful product and maximise their profits they'd want it tested in Europe,' said Richard.

'Apparently the research team are pretty keen on more testing, but Yves isn't.'

'Sounds just like my business. Never let the facts stand in the way of a good story.' Monica snorted.

'Harry said Yves isn't planning long-term. He wants immediate returns. He's a man in a hurry. I'll bet most of his profits, would come from share trading then a quick lucrative sale of the company. That way he won't be around if anything goes wrong.'

'The trial results are really good. It works on skin thickness. Ageing makes skin thin, so it goes wrinkled. This works the other way.'

'Well let me know when I can buy some,' said Monica as their meals arrived.

Chapter 19

Setting the Rules

At the Alston board meeting, voices were raised, and Directors interjected.

'I'm pleased you have endorsed the marketing strategy,' said Yves raising his voice. 'In summary, this project promises excellent results, and our legal advice confirms that we cannot be held accountable for failure. After all, women's cosmetics have been selling optimism in jars for years,' Yves said. 'You can all see the profit projections.'

'It is enough to deliver hope and that's always a saleable commodity,' said the Chair whose strained face looked like he needed a whole jar.

'We're on a winner,' said Yves, *provided there are no outrageous side effects*, he thought.

To the research team, Yves was charming, interested and he always deferred to their requests. He had convinced them he understood the importance of their work and didn't want to upset them or interfere with the planned testing schedule. The research team members were young and driven by a heady mix of youth, self-belief and trust, with little world experience of the cutthroat corporate environment. Their optimism and belief that the world was good was transparently obvious to all in the company.

Later that night, Yves called Jerome, his man in Africa.

'The Board and the researchers agree the treatment is slowing and reversing the ageing process,' Yves said with excitement.

'Sure looks like that from here. So, do you need more trials?' Jerome asked.

'After looking at the latest results, speed is what we need. Speed and certainty. Let's quadruple the doses with your lot. See if that flushes out any problems,' said Yves. 'I'm impressed with those before and after photographs you sent.'

'Yep, even the haggard old blokes look better,' said Jerome.

'Wrinkles have been smoothed; faces look fuller and younger looking, it's marketing bliss,' said Yves. *Just what I need thought Yves.*

Yves and Jerome had done a lot of business in the past and Yves trusted him to keep his mouth shut.

'Find subjects, tell them nothing, pay them as little as possible and be quick about it,' Yves directed. Jerome had arranged the test subjects for the initial trial without telling them much. Both he and Jerome didn't want trouble but shared a view about the dispensability of the locals. When no problems appeared, Yves pressed on with greater zeal.

'Yes, I understand that is not what the research team recommend, but when has that stopped us? Get back to me each week with the results from increased doses,' Yves said.

'Send the instructions and get the research team to dispatch however much they need tested,' said Jerome, little knowing that Harry was reporting every exchange to Richard.

'And don't forget ONLY send the test results to me,' said Yves. This is big Jerome. Don't go weak on me.'

'He hasn't told them anything,' Harry said to Annette. 'Not about the trial or the risks.' Annette sat, arms folded tightly around her body, silent.

'Well, I think I might reduce his information. Shield the Frenchy from a few of the team's results. Why should he have all the information? He never gave his investors all the information in his past schemes.

In Africa, those people don't think there are risks. But look at these results. For this poor bloke the thickening process is accelerating. Looks nasty.

What a bastard. Look at this. Rather than stopping the trial, he has instructed the local team to increase the dose. Then observe the changes. The skin thickening is continuing. No bloody respect. The testing team in Africa will just measure and photograph while these test rats suffer. Wonder if this is what the trials for your drug were like,' Harry said as he turned to Annette.

In the ensuing silence, Harry deleted the negative results from the email before forwarding it to Yves.

Back in Paris, Yves waited impatiently for news. Never a good patient, he had been confined to bed with a cold for the second day. After he had showered and shaved, he was horrified to see how old and haggard he looked in the harsh white light of his bathroom mirror. He had been pleased about losing a little weight, but it all seemed to have dissolved from his face, making his cheeks sink and accentuating the lines around his eyes. There wasn't any time to waste.

Chapter 20

The Ides of March

Zoe watched the sun rise. Brightness spilled over the rim of the horizon and streaked the air. Dove-coloured storm clouds roofed the sky, then, for a few moments blushed pink, as if caught unaware by morning. Summer had lost its grip, and in these first days of autumn, flocks of starlings gathered and wheeled screeching across the paddocks. They sounded brash and looked impressive, but most of these juveniles would die of starvation by mid-winter.

The inevitability of it all weighed heavily. Seasons would come and go – relentless, implacable. Not cruel but utterly indifferent. The sun would rise whether or not she was there. The earth would dance with the sun and moon, entranced by gravity as it had done for millions of years and would do for millions to come. Even the planets and stars would pass in their time. But, like the starlings Zoe was a fleeting visitor. Her energy would soon take another form.

March – it would have been her father's birthday. She remembered he used to say, 'Beware the Ides of March – if there is no cake there will be trouble.' As a child she never understood the Ides and thought he was saying 'Beware the eyes of March' and imagined secret watchers. With a quick calculation from her 31 years, her father would be 55. Zoe wondered what her father would have looked like. Her memories were fragmentary. Flashes of a giant of a man with a face made real by photos. Warm feelings of walking hand-in-hand through the vines. Odd sayings, dizzying swings on the lawn and conversations about birds were all she had left.

March and the flocks of starlings were the memory trigger. Her father used to say the autumn flocks were like her class at school – all the kids running together, making a lot of noise and eating anything in sight. How different things might have been if he had been here. He would have revelled in this blustery day when the energy of the sky sent birds skimming, tossed trees and flattened grass.

Feeling at one with the land had helped Zoe heal. The wide sky gave her peace even in storms. The silence was non-judgemental. Zoe gathered wood for a fire to cheer the cool night. As her arms filled with wood, she felt spongy yellow lichen on the almond wood, the soft peeling paperbark of the melaleuca and the cool smoothness of red gum against her arm and felt a flash of joy, a match flare in the darkness sparked by the colours and textures. Across the broken surfaces, subtle colour changes, which marked the tree's growth rings, were magnified. In her mind's eye, the filo layers of cells that marked the seasons filled her consciousness. Life lived on without cause, but it was her skill to witness and interpret the patterns, colours, and the textures.

Scurrying slaters and earwigs scuttled for cover faster than the lumbering wood beetles as her gathering lifted the bark roofs off their worlds. A smile crept across her face as she observed these creatures. They all used wood to shape their houses and provide warmth to keep out the winter cold. From columns of racing ants and clockwork beetles, multi-coloured green ushered curiosity back into her days.

That night, hypnotised by the flames, her mind raced. Being alive was a powerful gift. Like the flames, she was only a temporary blip in the cosmos, but this was her one chance. Zoe resolved not be passive and suffer what the world delivered to her door. Her mother closed the door on life even as she worked hard to build a secure home. In one way her mother had succeeded, but that was not enough for Zoe. Her mother's death nearly seven years ago still filled Zoe with sadness. Mostly sadness at what could have been if they had talked more, spent time together, or known that her time was to be short. Time, time, time; time wasted– too much or too little. Zoe wanted more, much more. The sun might have a fixed path and an eternity to practice rising, but Zoe did not. With a jolt, she recognised that there was no time to waste. She would forge her own destiny. She would not take what was given. She would succeed. She had allowed herself to be made miserable by her own vulnerability and by the weakness of others. It was time she took responsibility for herself. Her father may have disappeared, but he left his genes and a memory of love. Her mother had worked hard, provided well for her in a material way, and showed that passion could build a vineyard. Zoe was free and hard work was no stranger. The devastation caused by David's betrayal, made her vulnerability clear, but it was her vulnerability – hers to control. Zoe's resolve hardened and she would take control of her future.

When the next dawn arrived in Langhorne Creek, Zoe started painting. Sketching the chickens on the back of the shed door was a childhood dream. With charcoal from last night's fire, she sketched chickens stretching their necks to see around the doorway. One white fluffy chicken, conjured from leftover house paint, settled over chalky painted eggs. Another was airborne as her legs grappled for balance chasing a moth. Zoe hoped the chickens liked their portraits on the door of their house. Smiling was starting to feel normal again.

After lunch, Zoe walked the three kilometres into Langhorne Creek revelling in her new confidence and curious to see what had changed. She was delighted to see Postman Pat through the window. That wasn't his name of course, but that was what all the kids called him. He was older and the post office was smaller than the one in her memory. The front wall of the old house was studded with letterboxes so people could use keys to get their mail after office hours. Most of the old people liked going when Postman Pat was there to have a chat and find out what was happening. To her surprise, he called through the window.

'Hello Zoe.'

Stepping around the boxes of wine and soil samples waiting to be posted out and the parcels of every shape and size – from machine parts to clothes, dry cleaning and packages from the pharmacy that waited for collection – Zoe moved inside. Pat knew everyone and everything. His office overflowed with envelopes, packaging and string, calendars, books and toys. The community notice board by the door advertised local cars for sale, a puppy, some furniture and the date of the next working bee at the park, the football club and the next meeting of history buffs at the soldier's memorial hall.

'How are you Zoe?' he called from inside the crowded room. 'I heard you were back in the old house. You're looking good.'

After living in Adelaide and then London for so long Zoe had forgotten that small regional communities seemed sparsely populated, but in reality, they had eyes and ears tuned to sense changes in the district. Of course, he knew she was back – the entire region did. How could she have thought otherwise? Postman Pat asked if she wanted to rent a mailbox. Zoe knew this post office did both delivery and content analysis, and laughingly refused.

'Don't think I will stay long enough to need that, but I'll leave an address in case I win the lottery.'

As Zoe turned to leave, old Ben opened the door. He was an institution in Langhorne Creek, which had a generous share of legends. The district's history was remembered through floods and picnics, good vintages and not so good, sporting successes and hunting, growing and dying. Living that story was furrowed into Ben's face. He had always looked grizzled, like the sun-dried raisins he loved. Now, he looked more like a troll. Frizzled grey hair and full beard left little room for sun and age wrinkled cheeks. He was a bit more stooped and not as quick on his feet, but essentially unchanged.

'Hello Ben, still writing your diary?' asked Zoe.

'Well, well, it's little Zoe Macintosh all grown up. Haven't seen you for a while,' he said as he stretched out his hands. 'I'm still writing, but it's not so easy these days.' Zoe wondered how those ropey veins and thick wrists could pressure the gnarled fingers to write at all. Ben was famous in the district for writing a diary every day since he was a child. He recorded the weather and all the events in the natural environment. He wrote about the grapes his family had grown in this district for the last eight generations, the days of harvest, and the weight of the grapes. He wrote about the rabbits and the birds and the swamp rats, which he said were a huge problem this year after the good rains last year. He worried their tunnels had honeycombed the riverbanks which would collapse when the river flowed again.

I should paint him, Zoe thought. I'd need a large canvas to do it justice. Now that was a positive thought to build on. Why not set herself the ultimate portrait painter's challenge and try for the Archibald?

'Ben, could I do a sketch of you while I'm back here?' Zoe asked.

'This old face's not worth a picture, Zoe. But if you want to waste your time it's no skin off my nose. Come around one day next week. I'm happy to talk.'

Chapter 21

Beached

From the bright light sensed through tightly closed eyelids and the sickening pain that pulsed inside his skull like a giant metronome, Mac assumed he was alive. The groan he heard could have been his own, but he had been silent for so long he wasn't sure what speech felt like anymore. His chest rose and fell. He didn't need to fight against the sea for every breath. With a lurch, he realised he was on land and alive. Relief suffused the pain. Then darkness engulfed him again.

Waking once more, he forced one eye open with a mighty effort. The other was a pool of pain. Bright light, vivid colours, and confusing shapes appeared at odd angles as if through dirty, distorting glass. Mac saw that he was part of a long line of wreckage, strewn along a beach. Broken plants, logs and crushed timbers formed a chaotic tide line as far as he could see. Mac willed his fingers to move and was pleased when one hand responded. He sensed five fingers. He tried to move, and every part of his body protested. Wreckage and sand cased his legs. His limbs were non-responsive, heavy and weak.

One arm was tangled in a jumble of cloth, palm fronds, rope and sand. The other moved reluctantly to his insistent instructions, and he heaved aside wood that pinned his legs, levered his torso upright and struggled to stand. His body, only partly covered in shredded pants and

T-shirt, showed cuts and abrasions, but was essentially intact. Fierce pain racked one shoulder. Dislocated not broken he decided as he prodded the bone. His left arm hung limp and twisted. He was dizzy and sore.

His thirst raged. He looked around for water to drink. From the swathe of damage, he saw that waves had surged far inland before retreating. The sea was now flat calm. It was difficult to imagine the roiling turbulence of his wild ride and the destructive energy it had poured onto the land. Fresh water, even if he could see a source, would be drenched by the salt. Palm trees had been stripped and trees undermined by the inrushing water. Then as the water receded, the uprooted ones had been piled together. He spied a young green coconut and searched for a flattish rock, and a rounder one to use as a hammer. It would be hard to manipulate with his damaged shoulder, but he wedged its fibrous husk in the fork of a fallen branch and angled the rock under. He brushed off the sand and bashed it with the rounded rock until he'd crushed the shell enough to scoop some juicy jelly into his parched mouth. The clean fresh vegetable flavour and smooth gelatinous texture felt like heaven. There was barely enough milk to wet his tongue, but he sucked the delicious white flesh. Exhausted by the heat and humidity he rested in the shade until the sun dropped lower in the sky.

In the cooler evening, he walked along the beach and saw several bodies, caught, as he had been, in the tangle of wreckage. He hurried towards them, hoping for life, wishing they could be saved as he had been saved. Two men were dead, crushed, broken beyond repair. None of the wreckage or the men looked like they came from the ship. Mac thought it must have powered safely through the waves.

He wondered where he was. Then he saw a tiny body. She was whole and looked serene but had no pulse, no breath. His eyes filled with sadness and regret as he covered her face. That could so easily have been him. Perhaps it should be him. His little girl was home alone. He hoped she was safe. Mac struggled further along the beach. Where there were some people, there must surely be others. In the dusky evening, the high humidity sapped his energy. Hungry and thirsty, his damaged body ached as he struggled to support his arm and lessen the agony in his shoulder. Resting in the shade, he wondered what would happen next. He didn't want to die alone.

He must have fallen asleep, then jerked awake as he heard snippets of a foreign language. Had the crew discovered him? He opened his eyes to see trees and three people peering at him looking bewildered. They spoke and pointed at him clutching each other's arms for reassurance. Mac had never seen people like these before and from their reaction, he judged they had never seen anyone like him. Suddenly relieved, tears started in his eyes as he remembered he was alive and knew the people looking at him were not the fishing boat crew. For the first time in a long time, he thought that perhaps he might not die. He collapsed back on the sand with a strangled sob.

'Hello,' he said with gentleness as he recovered his composure and struggled to sit. He stretched out his hands, palms up.

'My name is Mac,' he said, pointing to his own chest. He hoped he looked reassuring and could convince them he offered no threat. 'Perhaps we can help each other.' They looked amazed as his body unfolded, and he towered above them but quickly sank to the ground again sick and dizzy. They looked as puzzled by the tall white man the sea had delivered as if he were a stranded whale.

The massive tidal wave may have delivered Mac onto the sand like a miracle, but it had delivered nothing but destruction to these people. Mac presumed they would be looking for survivors and he gestured to them to follow him back along the beach to where he had seen the bodies.

'Come,' he said. 'I have seen more people.' He pointed to them and moved his good arm as if to hold a child. As they glimpsed the broken bodies, their wailing filled the air and tears streamed down their faces. Their sadness and despair crushed him anew. Together they freed the bodies and trudged along the sand with their sad burdens. Mac followed. Perhaps the tragedy and confusion would draw them together and they may not drive him away. Mac was a stranger who did not know the land, the people, the language or even what country he was in, but they gave him water baled from a spring in a coconut shell and let him rest. It was enough for now.

Several hours later as Mac sat, exhausted and in pain in the shade, a little away from the chattering group, one of the women with kind dark eyes, walked toward him holding a cloth. She, like all the people was short and slender with polished brown limbs and long black hair tied and plaited in many pieces. Talking and gesturing, she tied a rough sling to hold Mac's damaged arm. Mac looked in admiration as she skilfully opened a fresh green coconut with a machete.

'Thank you,' he said doing his best to smile through cracked lips. 'I never knew this could taste so good.' The people welcomed the bounty of fallen coconuts. It was much easier than climbing to retrieve the nuts. The raggedy band ranged along the beach collecting anything useful from among the wreckage.

The next days were occupied with burials as more bodies were discovered and hope for further survivors abandoned. Mac welcomed the feeling of earth under his feet. During the days he helped to scavenge building materials or fallen tree limbs that could be used for building. At night he slept troubled by dreams, drained by exhaustion. The small lithe people often looked askance at Mac's strangeness. Their homes and village were little more than wreckage. All the buildings had been flattened or destroyed. Many people had died. Yet the survivors shared food with him, and he laboured to repay them. Their suspicion diminished as helped to move logs, built shelters He shared their pain and grief for lives lost and struggled to learn their language.

As his body recovered, Mac's strength returned. His dislocated arm healed, and his height made him popular when new huts were built. The village men would choose and chop down saplings for the frames and Mac would haul them into position. The women and girls wove fibre into rope, and men lashed beams together. Mac lifted the panels high and laced thinner bamboos together to support the thatch. In the relentless heat and humidity, a hut thatched with nipa palm provided welcome shelter from both sun and torrential rain. Mac learned to cut and haul piles of nipa fronds, which grew along the mangroves near the re-built village.

Before long, a line of new huts fringed the shore under the brow of the regrowth forest. Plant material, leaves, fibrous roots, branches and many types of bamboo were gathered then shaped, tied or woven into tables, beds, cups and plates. Mac admired their skills in using dozens of different plants to craft a more comfortable life.

Days stretched into weeks and months. He grew to look forward to rice at every meal, enjoyed fish when the fish gods were kind, purple yams, guavas and plantains grilled on sticks. The villagers who initially laughed at his strange swimming grew familiar with his exercise every day. He never tired of the warm clear sea and soon taught many of the children to freestyle and back-stroke. His injured shoulder no longer had the flexibility for butterfly, but, with exercise, the strength in his limbs returned.

Mac knew fish and learned which local ones tasted best. As his language improved, the villagers never tired of telling him about their fear of the strange white sea creature that had been washed ashore by the giant waves. Mac became Mo, close enough. He was in their country, but still did not know its name in his language. Their names held no meaning for him.

For months he took pleasure in the fresh air, eating new foods, knowing he was free, and getting stronger. At the end of each day, as he settled for sleep on his bamboo mat, Mac's thoughts returned to the people he loved and the family he had left behind. But, for now, he crafted a living and tried to discover where he was. When he solved that mystery, he could fashion a plan to try to repair the damage he had caused.

Mac took over a year to fully recover his strength, mend his bones and learn sufficient local language to communicate outside the village. After talking to the occasional trader, he deduced that he was living on one of the remote islands off the east coast of Mindanao in the southern Philippines. Even if he had wanted to contact someone he couldn't. The people with whom he now lived were subsistence fishers. There were no phones, the few roads were poor, and he had no money. He was without identity, without resources and felt shame beyond hope.

The survivors were philosophical; natural and manmade disasters came and went with the seasons. They endured raiders every few years, and, when desperate, could be pirates themselves. They fished, farmed a little and grew bananas of more types than Mac had ever imagined. They had children and buried most of them. Life and death hovered close every day. Survival was success. These were people who believed in fate if not god, lived for the present and knew they had little or no control of the future.

Over time Mac supressed his guilt and accustomed himself to the silence and the natural rhythm of the days. He shared his life with Ni, the woman with kind eyes who'd bandaged his arm. Her partner had died in the flood and as Mac became a villager, the union seemed natural. The sea took with one hand and gave with the other. Grateful for his life, unable to imagine a way to return, years passed. Only when Ni died, he yearned for his former life but Australia was a dream, a dream that was impossibly far away.

Chapter 22

The Sailor Returns

After weeks of island hopping, Mac reached the Solomon Islands to be confronted with the desperate conditions in that failed state. He despaired. Nothing worked; no trade was happening, and gangs of desperate men wandered the streets looking for trouble. He hung around the docks, looking and feeling hopeless as he struggled to keep himself out of fights. He approached all the boats looking for work without success. After a week, his heart leapt as a new boat arrived and he heard the unfamiliar but sought-after twang of an Australian accent. He splashed some water on his face, smoothed down his grizzled beard, and shoved his tangled mop of curls under a scruffy baseball cap. Nothing he could do would improve the worn shorts and faded shirt.

'Hi, Mate, looking for an extra hand?' he called from the pier hoping the hat's brim hid the desperation in his eyes.

'Maybe. Depends. We're heading for a little fishing in Papua New Guinean waters,' said the crewmember sizing up Mac's strength and tatty clothes. 'You look a handy sort. And ya look hard up.'

'I've got plenty of experience. Been on fishing boats for years and can work hard if you're headed south. I'm looking to get back to Darwin,' Mac replied.

'I'll get the Captain. Wait there,' said the crewmember who looked as down on his luck as Mac.

'Not much money,' the untidy Captain cackled through broken teeth as he stood on the deck appraising Mac.

'I'll work for my passage.'

'Can you keep your bloody mouth shut?'

'As long as I can arrive quietly in Darwin,' Mac replied looking the evasive captain deep in the eyes hoping for a deal.

'Tomorrow, 6am we leave. No questions, no answers, but work hard otherwise you're shark bait.'

After speaking bisaya in the southern Philippines, and struggling with all the languages in between, the English words felt uncomfortable rocks in Mac's mouth. His tongue stumbled over the harsh sounds, but his heart leapt. This opportunity was too good to miss. Mac just hoped they weren't carrying too many drugs. He didn't want to be caught in another disaster.

Within the week, he could speak, think and mix with the crew almost as if he had never left Australia almost 20 years ago. Between scrubbing decks, stowing crates and washing greasy dishes, the journey unfolded. Dangerous weather, island-sized container ships, and pirates all sailed these tropical waters. Mac wondered why the boat was so short-handed but kept his mouth shut and his eyes averted. Papua New Guinea appeared on the horizon and was bypassed without a word. Mac kept out of the captain's way. He was happy the boat was headed south so he worked like the slave he was, asked no questions and assumed the less he knew the better.

A week later, his heart leapt as they entered Darwin harbour. The closer Mac got to re-entering Australia, the more he feared discovery. Each night he tossed and turned. He imagined every signal on the radio to be trouble. With the crew's agreement he hid in the heads as the boat docked. In the cramped space with fear pounding in his heart, memories of hiding on a much bigger boat filled his thoughts.

As the captain went ashore, Mac feared betrayal. During the months he had island hopped through the myriad of Pacific islands getting closer to Australia, he only dared focus on one step at a time. Now Darwin was a reality, he could only hope this crew feared scrutiny from the authorities even more than he did. He kept out of sight. Later that night, heart pounding, he strolled ashore with another member of the crew. As he cleared the port, he resisted the urge to run and shout. He kept his steps steady.

He was in Darwin and alive. Relief surged through his veins, more powerful than the strongest drug. With every breath Mac felt like shouting with joy. He couldn't believe his luck. He'd achieved the impossible. Being in Australia was like winning the lottery. Now he could think about finding his family.

With only a handful of dollars from the taciturn captain in his pocket, Mac needed a change of clothes, and a way to eat. In the Philippines and all the way through the islands, he worked for barter, eating rice at every meal, vegetables and fish from the sea. While there were fast food stores on every Darwin corner; bread, meat and pizza looked and smelled like greasy whale. Australian people loomed, loud, fat and pale. He wavered between exhilaration; crushing certainty that neither family nor friends would want to see him, and fear that the police would arrest him. Even without having much hope for a solution, he burned to know what had happened in Langhorne Creek since he left. If he knew, he could plan.

A truck seemed the answer, but even to hitch he needed to smarten himself up for the long, hot trip from Darwin to Alice Springs. Mac walked the streets until he found a Salvation Army Op Shop and threw himself on their mercy.

'I've lost everything M'am,' he said. 'But not to drink, I'm a sober man.'

'Well let's see what we might have to fit that big body,' the dowdy woman with warm eyes replied as she imagined another sad story. Together, they scoured the shelves.

'This is much appreciated. I need some good luck,' said Mac as he tried on almost new checked shirts, some King Gee work trousers, a pair of footy shorts and a khaki jumper. Work socks were found but no boots were big enough for his feet, which had spread wide after many barefoot years. She even found a nylon sleeping bag and stuffed it in a backpack. Mac left feeling well equipped except for the thongs. He walked the streets, looking for ways to earn some cash; and searched for big boots. Even window-shopping felt strange. If he was to get a job with trucks, he needed boots.

Dozens of trucking companies worked the routes in and out of Darwin. Every day, haulage rigs and road trains filled with cattle, headed south. They looked massive, shiny and well maintained compared to the jeepnies, motor scooters and smelly black-fuming trucks that criss-crossed the Philippines and the Pacific. He could still load and tie, so trucks would be his best option. He fidgeted like a homing pigeon anxious to fly. First, the 3000-kilometre journey south along the Stuart Highway to Alice Springs, then down to the city of Adelaide that he once knew so well.

After two weeks in Darwin, surviving by doing a few odd jobs cleaning up at a trucking depot, he felt acclimatised. He was eating and had a spare set of clothes. One night on the beach a travelling hairdresser put up a sign offering haircuts for a few dollars. The seat on the sand suited his budget and after being shorn of his curls and his beard he felt lighter and cleaner.

Looking at his reflection, he was shocked to see how old he looked. His skin was leathery, and his dark hair streaked with grey. His body, clothed in almost new denims and a serviceable work shirt, was lean and fitter than most men in town who used beer to cope with Darwin's heat. Mac might look like many a tanned and weather-beaten man who had spent a lifetime labouring in the bush, but he was no longer a young man full of bravado. His back and strong legs may ache every morning from a lifetime of hard use, but he stood tall without a stoop. He felt as ready as he would ever be to head south and discover what had happened to his family. For much of his life he had run from the shame of his actions; now he ached for the place he used to call home.

During his exploration of Darwin, he learned that the cross-continent railway, started in 1901, now linked Darwin through Alice Springs all the way to Adelaide. Past experience had removed his appetite for being a stowaway. Hiding may have saved his life once but Mac was older, less flexible and not confident he could get away with it. He didn't have enough money for even the cheapest fare. The last thing he needed was attention from the police. He had no means of support, no identification, no address and no credible story. It would be too hard to claim amnesia. He began a cover story so he could pretend that he had never left the country. Without that, if he were questioned, it would obvious that he had not been in Australia for years. He wouldn't risk jumping the train.

As in other tough times, he fell back on the skills he knew – lifting and loading. Tying loads was essential for truckies and fishermen, so he hung around the busiest depots watching how the trucks operated. He was given odd jobs cleaning, moving cargo, security at night, which made him a few dollars. He loaded trucks at one of the numerous break-point depots, but couldn't drive without a licence, so no one would take him on. With a bit of practice, he might pass a driving test, but he needed identification and cash. He waited, gathered his courage and walked in to the 'Great OutDoors Trucking Depot' and asked for a lift south. He was overjoyed to hear welcome words.

'Sure Mate, I'm off to the Alice. You can ride south with me as long as you have some good stories and can keep me awake over the next 1,500km.'

At dawn, clutching a small blue backpack that wasn't even bulging, he climbed into the cab of the truck. Pedro, the third Peter in the depot, took the name to reduce confusion, but there was no confusion with the red Kenworth prime mover. It was massive and the trailers were loaded to the hilt. Pedro cleared the town and headed onto the highway, the truck gathering speed at an alarming pace. Mac stifled his anxiety as the truck rocketed across the hot dry country. The massive juggernaut had comfortable seats, a fridge and air conditioning and, as the hours rolled by, Mac appreciated Pedro's skill. The sky was impossibly blue, and the horizon a hundred kilometres away. Pedro kept the truck cabin filled with country music, truckies jargon from the CB radio and endless chat. Mac learned to ride with the bumps that used to be kangaroos and emus.

After ten hours, Pedro slept for a couple of hours in his comfortable cab as Mac froze in his thin sleeping bag on the sand as he watched a million stars wheel across the clear sky. The desert landscapes: fine clay and bright sands with grey and khaki trees looked harsh after the softer green jungles of Mindanao, but the magnificent desert country painted stunning colours at dawn and dusk. This land was ancient; it had seen a lot of mistakes, but it endured. Like me Mac thought. Old and worn.

Back on the road, Pedro continued his favourite topics.

'Well, what do you think mate; our politicians haven't got a clue have they? Bloody parasites. Pity they don't work for a living like us.'

Could complain for Australia, Mac thought. *He should try scavenging for a living.*

'Whole country's a mess. The nanny state, that's what – always telling us what to do. One minute the cattle trade is booming, the next minute they ban live exports. A bloke doesn't know what's coming next. And the mongrel media, they're always ready to sink the boot in. Even the boss – and he's a hard man, thinks they're off the rails.'

'Yeah' said Mac, and the driver continued.

'Can't trust anyone. The churches have been kiddy-fiddling for years, the tax blood suckers want all our money and there's too many people sitting back sipping their fancy lattes.'

After twenty hours driving on the road, Mac helped Pedro unload at Alice Springs. He was amazed that one man could talk so long. 'Thanks mate, and good luck,' said Pedro as he handed Mac a few dollars for a meal. 'It was great to chat.'

Mac was obsessed with thoughts of people he once knew. Perhaps some had died. What about his family? What did they think when he disappeared? How could he have abandoned them? Would they still be in Langhorne Creek? He hoped they were safe and had managed without him. He worried about Costas and the boat.

After a meal at Alice's Diner: a schnitzel that hung over the edge of the plate, a mound of golden chips, thick mushroom gravy and a token lettuce leaf, Mac hitched another ride down to Adelaide. He pumped Nick, his next driver, who was not such a talker, for information about Adelaide.

'I've been away for about twenty years,' Mac said.

'Well from the look on your face, it's not a welcome you expect,' Nick replied.

'Family trouble,' Mac replied with a shrug. 'What's happening to the footy?'

'Usual rivalries between Port and the Crows. Battlers versus the toffs. I'm originally from Sydney so I prefer rugby myself, but not much of that in Adelaide. Latest thing there're getting girls to play. Most ridiculous thing I've ever heard.'

'And how's business,' Mac asked. 'What's my chances of getting a job?'

'Well, I'm working two. One to pay off the first wife, and one to live with the next one. Can't wait till the kids grow up and leave home. They just hang around forever these days. Not like my old man. He gave me fifty bucks, an umbrella and a suitcase when I turned fifteen, then said good luck boy and showed me the door.'

Better than me, Mac thought. *I just disappeared.*

'If you can drive, you'll always pick up something. Taxis if you're desperate, trucks are better. The hours are long but OK if you can keep awake.

Mac mused that nothing had changed. The trucks may be bigger and the times tougher but underpinning it all were battlers who worked hard and had a lot of time to complain. But they have hospitals and schools he thought, not like the people in my village.

As they reached Port Wakefield, Mac felt uncertain about his next step in this old/new world. A rush of nostalgia poured through him as they neared Gepps Cross and he knew Adelaide was close. Mac helped unload at the depot, then hitched a ride to town.

Mac recognised the clean straight roads of the city grid, and the city squares that were unmistakable Adelaide. Buildings had changed and much looked new, but Colonel Light's signature was clear.

'Anywhere will do. Thanks mate,' he said to the driver who dropped him on King William Street. After an hour wandering around, gawking like a tourist, Mac queued with the down and out for a helping hand at the Salvo's on Pirie Street. The volunteers offered him a bed in the hostel on Whitmore Square, which seemed better than a wooden bench in the park. Despite bright spring days, the air felt cold and dry on his skin after twenty years in the tropics. He was pleased he had a jumper as he talked to other homeless men.

'Why'd you want to find out what's happened since you went away – nothing useful,' one offered. 'But you can read all newspapers, for free at the library, if that's what you want.'

'Comfy chairs there,' said another.

'But they kick you out if you don't look like you're reading'.

Next morning, Mac walked to the State Library on North Terrace. It was nothing like he remembered. The location was the same, but it had an imposing glass foyer and was full of computers. Overwhelmed, he sat outside on the bench under the trees and watched. Each day, when he wasn't knocking on doors for a job, any job, he ventured back to the library. Mac wasn't the only patron who looked down on his luck. Among the students and pensioners, were people who looked in need of shelter rather than enlightenment. Just walking in and out of the big building was intimidating, but each day he walked in unchallenged, his confidence grew. Within the week he asked for help from the older librarian with the kind face.

'You mean I can use the computer, for free' he said.

'Yes absolutely. As long as you book the terminal,' she replied. 'I'll show you if you like.'

'Thanks. I'd like to search for local news about the Fleurieu Peninsula.'

I'll be able to find her, Mac thought.

He was pleased when an issue of the Fleurieu's *Southern Argus*, flashed up on the screen.

'I'm looking for material about the Strathalbyn district, from about twenty years ago,' he said to the sympathetic librarian. 'You know the people and things that happened.'

'Certainly,' she said. 'Type in the year first, and if you can be more specific about dates and names, this search function should work,' she said, passing him a set of basic instructions.

'That's excellent, thank you. I'm happy to browse,' he said as memories of Catherine and Zoe flooded back. Mac was apprehensive. He needed privacy in case a wanted poster with his face was plastered over a front page. There were a lot of reports about sport. If he had not been so stupid, that would be where he would be now, a happy tennis player among friends rather than an outcast who was too ashamed to show his face in his hometown.

Wanting home and familiar things was one of the problems of getting older. All the years he was in the Philippines, he'd suppressed thoughts of home. Now the pull of what used to be home surged strong in his veins. He'd escaped the boat and survived the tsunami, then worked for years and years with his hands and his back to stay alive and earn his keep. He had the scars, a ropey physique and painful back to prove it, but his mind was scarred by the memory of his stupidity. Then, as a new issue opened on the screen, pain exploded in another form.

'Oh no,' he gasped as he read the article reporting Catherine's death. People at the other desks looked up in surprise and disapproval. Oblivious of the attention, Mac wailed, 'She was too young to die. My poor Catherine.' He buried his head in his hands, jammed his elbows into the desktop as tears clouded his eyes. It took minutes for him to recover enough to read again. An aneurism, whatever that was, had suddenly killed Catherine almost ten years ago.

Conflicting, powerful emotions flooded through Mac as he remembered his early days with Catherine. The grainy newspaper photograph showed her beauty had not faded. The report listed her as a Langhorne Creek vigneron, and he felt proud that she had made their vineyard dream a reality. No tributes from a partner suggested Catherine hadn't found another love. There was touching sadness from Zoe. Friends and neighbours were generous. Mac was consumed by guilt again. He burned to know what Catherine had thought and done. As the library closed, he left in misery and sadness, vowing to continue his quest to find out what had happened to his daughter.

It wasn't until two days later Mac found a small article headed *Local Artist Makes Good in London* that reported an exhibition of her paintings. His girl was all grown up and living in London. He wished he could see more of her face behind the long blonde hair. His heart lurched with a powerful blend of loss and pride. Mac was pleased that her love of drawing had developed into a career. She must be good to have an exhibition in London.

With Catherine's death, Zoe was alone. It was time to confess but he didn't want to go to Zoe as a beggar. The trucking company he had hitched with offered support if he took a heavy vehicle licence test and worked for them for at least a month. But he needed identification. Perhaps, Donald Macintosh was legally dead.

'Excuse me,' he said to the sympathetic library helper. 'I'm trying to find if a friend of mine is still alive.'

'Let's check, the Register of Births Marriages and Deaths,' she said. 'You will need to pay a small fee.'

'I have some cash but not a credit card,' said Mac recognising yet another problem. This world had changed a lot in fifteen years, and he was slow catching up.

Chapter 23

New Caledonia, 2013

Monica wanted Zoe back working in London, the city they both loved. She believed a challenge would help Zoe shake off her depression, so she decided to make one of her increasingly rare trips back to Adelaide and drag her back if necessary. There would be plenty of time on the long flight to catch up on some sleep and plan a strategy.

Monica knew Zoe had emotional skeletons in her closet, fears and uncertainties that came from a troubled childhood. There had been education, plenty of books and a strong work ethic instilled in her by her single super mum. The father event was never discussed. Managing a career as well as a small vineyard and raising a child on her own would have been tough. It was time Zoe's fears were shaken out in the sunshine and blown away. After admiring the artwork that had been installed as part of the rebuilt Adelaide Airport, Monica gathered a bag of pate, cheese and other basic necessities from the gourmet shops in the airport, collected her luggage, her duty-free alcohol and negotiated a taxi to take her on the 75-kilometre journey to Langhorne Creek.

Driving away from the Airport, they passed through the city on the way to the hills, and Monica was swamped by memories. She was born in Adelaide and always admired the neat streets and the way the city sprawled along the plain with long white beaches to the west and green hills to the east. Her journey took her through the western suburbs where she went to school and toward the city where she went to university. While changes were everywhere, there were plenty of familiar sights. After she had majored in politics, she knew Adelaide could never contain her galloping ambition. Now, after years in London, it seemed impossibly small. In London, Monica had bounced from job to job with frightening speed and a voracious capacity for work, which made her popular with all her employers. Now she was one of the most successful investigative writers in her field.

Her friend Zoe had yearned to see the galleries of Europe and dreamed of making a successful career, rather than just a living from painting. While London had been difficult for them both in the beginning, Monica knew it suited them both – as Samuel Johnston said, *London, the city of which any lover of life cannot tire.*

Monica chatted to her friendly driver. Taxi drivers were a part of her web of contacts across London. Her network was often useful to her investigative work and she knew that the best information often came from those with ears and eyes close to the ground. The so-called little people went un-noticed by important people who too often presumed taxi drivers, cleaners and waiters to be blind, deaf or too stupid to understand the significance of what they said on telephones, while eating or driving.

As the driver sped along the South East Freeway, the easy drive lulled Monica to sleep and when the driver spoke again, she was startled to realise they were almost at Langhorne Creek. She gave directions to the driver who was unfamiliar with the regional roads. As they negotiated the driveway, she was pleased to see Zoe sitting in the garden.

'I thought I would find you here,' she said as she burst out of the taxi and gathered Zoe in an affectionate hug. 'I knew you wouldn't respond to my mail – so I just had to come and find you.' she said.

After a moment of shock, Zoe was delighted to see her old friend. It was impossible not to like this bold Rubenesque woman. Her voice seemed louder than ever in the quiet vineyard.

Monica tried not to look shocked at Zoe's appearance. Little did she know that Zoe believed she was in good shape now, both in body and mind. It was almost a year since she had left London. Monica was even more worried when Zoe told her she had hardly painted since leaving London and had little inclination. It was only then that Monica knew the depth of her friend's despair. Never solid, Zoe had lost both a lot of weight and the curious look with which she challenged the world – and that fuelled her best paintings.

Talking non-stop, Monica asked the taxi driver to unload her supplies, as she wheeled in her case and two bags of duty free which clinked with a familiar glassy sound.

'Come, I have loads to tell,' said Monica paying the taxi driver and steering Zoe inside. 'George sends his love. I need a rest and some food. That flight doesn't get any better. Looking around your kitchen, I am glad I brought supplies. Have you eaten at all since you left London?'

'You haven't changed Monica,' Zoe said as she went to the cupboard for glasses. 'Not much in the way of bedding, but we'll manage.'

'Wine, I need wine,' answered Monica as she dived into her supplies and pulled out cheeses, packets of biscuits, pate and her favourite ham, scattering little plates of treats across the table.

'It's quite a while since I've had a party,' said Zoe.

'It's freezing,' said Monica, fossicking in her bag for a jumper.

'True, but you should be acclimatised. When I first went to London, I hardly noticed the cold. I sucked up the concerts, the museums and the gorgeous buildings,' Zoe reminisced. 'My list of favourites grew and grew. What about the Museum of Natural History? Remember those columns of minerals that hold up the building? Art, science and engineering all in one package.'

'Those gentlemen explorers plundered the world to build those collections. Thieves or vandals we'd call them now,' Monica mused.

'I love that striped brick facade and the gargoyles and carvings of animals. And what about the fossils? Weird. I remember wandering for hours, saturating myself with all the shapes and the stories about how they were collected. And, Charles Darwin, my hero, overlooking the entrance all grave and reflective, the weight of his knowledge bowing his shoulders.'

'For goodness sake, he's a statue, Zoe! I prefer the kids shrieking through the doorway, terrified by the huge dinosaur skeletons. Then seeing their teachers screaming. Much more fun than stone fossils.'

'Collecting is such a British obsession. Lucky for us it was combined with a commitment to scientific research and education.'

'Much more interesting than the crown jewels,' added Monica. 'That's not about gems. It's all money and power. Symbols of subjugation displayed by the victors. Although my editor didn't appreciate my views on that topic,' Monica said.

'I even miss the tiny Physic Garden in Chelsea,' Zoe admitted. A living encyclopaedia and pharmacopeia of the days when plants were the drug stores. Even the stones that bordered the garden beds had been on their own voyages of discovery as ballast. And I liked seeing the Chelsea Pensioners resplendent in their red uniforms, on my way there.'

'I can't imagine a pharmaceutical company building and sharing a garden like that these days. Their profits would be spent on toys like Ferraris for their executives,' said Monica. 'Do you want to talk?'

'Not yet. I remember feeling that it was England that was topsy-turvy, not Australia. All the buildings and people history are old, and all the geology is young. Everything here is the other way around. Old landscapes, ancient fossils, only the lightest touch from people. The cities and land clearance have wrecked it of course, but out in the bush, it's so clean. In England, signs of people are everywhere. You just can't get away from them. Barrows and ditches, old roads and castle ruins, even the planted forests are like scars. Marks of people dominate. Buildings have been raised, reshaped or razed and then it is all done again. People are so hard on the land.'

'Mmm,' said Monica. 'I'm too tired for philosophy.'

'It's good to see you Monica. You make me feel normal again. No more paralysis. No more staring blankly ahead for hours.'

As Zoe showed Monica to the bedroom, she knew she would never fully trust a man again. Monica was there like a rock, and Zoe would anchor herself for a while.

'I've got a job for you. We'll talk about it in the morning. I'm dead,' said Monica, flopping into bed.

The next morning dawned crisp and cold. As Monica described her latest quest, Zoe was pleased at the possibility of a painting. She could earn some money while helping Monica.

'Come away with me Zoe,' Monica implored as she grabbed her friend's hands and danced around.

'It's freezing here, and I need some serious sunshine and a few days to relax in a place with tropical flowers and crazy drinks with little umbrellas. We both have a holiday due. I've been thinking New Caledonia would be perfect, a total change of scenery.'

'Well, I am sick of this unpredictable autumn. A bit of warmth and brightness wouldn't go astray.'

'When I first went to London, I learned to pile on layers of clothing – and had to buy hats and gloves and scarves.'

'I just hated the darkness that shortened the days,' said Zoe. Even in October, you could go into a shop in what seemed the middle of the day, and the dark night would sneak up and smother the sun while you were inside.'

'True, the bright days are good here.'

'But the summers. Ahh they were wonderful. After months shut inside, we luxuriated in warm days and long, soft twilights. I thought cricket on village greens, cottage gardens and summer pudding were only in the movies.'

'Yes,' said Zoe. 'I even asked how flowers and window boxes could grow in those big baskets on street poles and without needing dripper hoses. People just smiled. Anything seemed possible on English summer afternoons. The gentle temperatures and moist air are kinder to plants than the searing heat and desiccating dryness of my childhood summers here.'

'Yes, let's get warm,' Monica said.

Within a few days they were at Adelaide Airport queuing to board the flight to Noumea on a cheap and cheerful holiday package.

'It's been a long time since I felt like such a tourist,' Monica laughed.

'Lucky to be women in the 21st century. We can travel across the world alone, and do things not even dreamed about by women in earlier times.'

'I need to get back to work,' said Zoe. 'Freedom needs money.'

'New Caledonia is not random. So, tell me about your latest project,' said Zoe.

'You know me too well. Of course, I have a project in mind. New Caledonia seemed too good an opportunity to miss when I'd already decided to come back to Australia to see you. First, I need to get warm and relax, and then I need to do some snooping.'

As the plane touched down, a wall of warm moist air rushed up to meet them and wrapped around them like a fragrant blanket.

'Smell that! A tropical cocktail – land and sea, moist earth and rich vegetation. It's like plum pudding,' said Monica.

'Can you see our ride? There it is – Paradise Waters,' they laughed at the flashy neon pink sign.'

'I feel like a uni student again,' said Zoe as they sweated in the tropical heat. 'I'm looking forward to photogenic beaches and waving coconut palm trees – my own tropical postcard.'

'Ooo look. Generous size is clearly a virtue in Polynesia,' Monica smiled with enthusiasm as a large islander man walked past. 'Just my style. 'Monica gathered a colourful lei of flowers and her bright clothes looked almost subdued against the backdrop of lavish hibiscus.

The small yellow bus rattled as if it might fall apart on the way to their resort, but the driver had a bright, infectious smile and the trip was short. Bamboo furniture, copra matting and lush vegetation were as cheerful as the cotton throws on the beds.

'This fruit looks too good eat,' Zoe said, then laughed as she discovered it was artificial. 'The note on the tray does promise a tray of fresh fruit will be delivered at eight o'clock every morning.'

The warm, blue sea beckoned.

'We need to swim. Let's check out the local shop.'

'Ooh look,' said Monica waving a vast, lurid red and hot pink print number she pulled from the rack in the hotel shop.

'Wild purple and yellow passionflowers for me,' said Zoe.

Soft wrap around sarongs and shady hats completed the hasty ensembles and dressed for the part, they strolled to the beach.

'The sand is so warm. Race you in,' said Monica.

'It's like a bath.'

After floating and paddling around for a while, they lay on the beach in the shade of some trees – toasted to the core.

'This is so utterly different to the landscape I've lived in for months,' observed Zoe.

'Palm fringed beaches are not in my neighbourhood either.'

'I love Australian trees, said Zoe. The English climate is so gentle, no heat and glaring light and no shortage of water. I guess here in the tropics the challenges are wind borne salt and fierce cyclones. I think I love my Australian trees, because they are survivors like us Monica.'

'They're just trees Zoe.'

'No, they're not! Each has a different palette of greens. Around home in Langhorne Creek, it's khaki, blue-green, waxy silver and gold. A huge contrast to the soft fresh limes in England and these deep greens here.' Zoe realised she was thinking about colours again.

'I'm on the hunt, Zoe. And, not for new colours. I'm keen to find out as much as I can about a French businessman who started operating here maybe twenty years ago. Since then, he's ranged around the world. Dozens of his companies are registered here and I can't figure out why. His name is Yves Montreau. He'll be the subject of my next exposé and your next portrait. New Caledonia might be good for a relaxing holiday but doesn't seem a natural centre for any multinational business. I want to know why Montreau set up businesses here. I've talked to the staff of the resort. They are young and beautiful and convinced that tourism is their future. Their idea of business is a dive boat or a tour bus if not a large hotel. None of them look older then twenty.'

'Then why don't we go into the town and see if we can find some art supplies? That way I can do a few sketches and that will give us both opportunities to quiz some local people,' Zoe said warming to the task.

The town had a pioneering, outpost feel. The architecture was functional; dominated by the need to keep cool. Windows were wide enough to catch the slightest breeze yet able to be boarded over when fierce tropical storms threatened. Many of the people walking down the street were Polynesian with an overlay of French. For years, Noumea had been named Port of France and to Zoe's ear the French had a local twist.

'Looks like Gauguin country,' Zoe said. 'The street and building names are a bit eclectic. I feel as if I am on a set for *South Pacific* where all the players have lost the script and are making up another story.'

'Businesses here would need good planning. Cyclones, language differences. The distance would be less limiting each year as air travel became cheaper and email ubiquitous. Was it a tax haven? The sea was rich and provided the natural resources, which was the basis of a wide range of businesses. Monica began to sense how a French speaking company, which did not wish to attract attention, might feel comfortable anchoring a business here while their activities ranged across the Asia Pacific. There was an active Chinese community evident in the large number of busy shops. The Japanese interests were less obvious but hinted at in sedate offices with muted colours and clean lines.

While shopping, the duo made a reservation for dinner at the smartest French restaurant in town and prepared for an interesting night. Three days would pass in a flash. After their first day of relaxation, they needed to work fast and didn't have much to go on. Monica had shared the information compiled by Harry. He had done his best, but the trails were fragmentary. She hoped that here in New Caledonia, there might be people who remembered.

'You look beautiful,' Monica said with a gentle sigh, as they waited for the hotel taxi to take them into the town for dinner. Monica was thrilled to see Zoe recovering and keen to focus on something diverting.

'But you look alive and interesting,' replied Zoe. 'I still feel like a ghost.'

The holiday atmosphere enlivened by the combination of Zoe's good looks and Monica's bubbly personality created a devil-may-care feeling. They had nothing to lose and no time to waste. Their boldness sparked some interesting conversations. Monica's ability to talk to anyone was heightened by the excellent French champagne. They cruised around the banquet tables that night and chatted to dozens of people.

After the meal was finished, Monica spoke to the headwaiter. He looked one of the few staff old enough to remember 15 years ago.

'I wonder if you remember a Frenchman called Yves Montreau who did business here about 20 years ago?' Monica asked

'Never forget a face, especially the good tippers. But names? Not so good.' He peered at the photograph Monica offered.

'Maybe – maybe – maybe, he looks an important man, perhaps one who had big business here. Not seen him for a dozen or so years maybe more. Not sure.'

Harry had tracked Yves Montreau's name on the business register of several companies in New Caledonia. Exotic products had been sold for high profits years ago, and those funds had given him enough money to start investing back in France. The girls didn't have much more to go on.

The next morning, they gobbled an entire tray of fresh fruit on the beach. Surrounded by the salty tang, the pineapple was sweet, the mango sumptuous and the pawpaw deep and musty.

'Looks like anything may be possible in this town,' Monica summarised.

'Apart from the usual propositions, we've been offered pearls and investment proposals at high rates of return for beautiful women with a spirit of adventure,' Zoe chuckled.

'My impression is that non-conformity with the law could be managed, and it must have been easier 20 years ago,' agreed Monica. 'Influential foreigners, known throughout the region, were all described by nicknames. There were no details, just nods and knowing winks. This feels like a place shady business could be done.'

'There's an art shop in the main street, I'll buy supplies and ask some questions,' offered Zoe.

'I'll search out the addresses of the registered offices Harry found,' replied Monica.

When they met for lunch back at the hotel, Zoe was excited.

'When I asked the man at the art supply shop about a French busi-nessman, he looked uncomfortable. He wouldn't say anything directly but suggested I look at the registered business nameplates on the build-ing next door. I don't know about these things, but I made a list for you Monica,' Zoe said pulling a sheet of company names from her purse.

Monica had discovered that an old Chinese trader remembered his face, but she had drawn a blank with every name and address. It was as if Montreau was a shadow.

'It was still a good idea to come here,' Monica said. 'I've found a few potential leads. Nothing concrete. I suppose any clue is better than none.'

Monica's notebook was full of names and dates that she managed to scribble furtively under the table the night before. Her nose was twitch-ing like a hound on the scent. She could smell a good story, and this one felt juicy.

On their last night, Monica and Zoe booked for the feast at the resort. Under festive lights on the beach, happy staff unwrapped fish and vegetables from banana leaf parcels cooked on the coals in a fire pit and loaded the steaming morsels onto leafy plates. Tasty food and plenty of cold beer in the soft darkness was a perfect end to their trop-ical retreat. Laying on the sand, they listened to the rhythmic susurra-tion of the waves.

'So – any love in your life Monica,' Zoe asked. 'You used to have lovers at uni. I was a bit shocked at first. Then I was jealous. Wished I had your guts. Have you given up on the male species?'

'I'd need a special bloke to take me on. Like mating with a dragon, most would say. Maybe if I lived here, one of these warriors would relish the challenge but not too many in London go for my style.' said Monica. 'Besides I usually pick wrong-uns and then get hurt.'

'I've sworn off men,' said Zoe. 'Once bitten, now very shy.'

'You'll miss the sex too much.'

'Didn't say I'd give up sex. Might sow the seed and then throw away the packet.' said Zoe. 'Anyway, I have a new challenge. I'm going to find out what happened to Dad. I missed him so much in Langhorne Creek. I would have given anything to see him there. You know my mother never believed he was dead. Just got himself snared up in something he couldn't get out of. Maybe she was right. Reckon I'd rather investigate than chance another bloke.'

'Well, we'll be busy either way.'

Chapter 24

The Waterhouse, 2012

After Monica left Langhorne Creek with all the drama of a storm front, Zoe knew it was time to get back to work. A week later, she answered an unexpected knock on the door.

'Don't usually do deliveries, but I was passing, and this looked important,' said Postman Pat with a vaguely embarrassed smile.

'Thanks,' said Zoe who ripped open the big envelope to reveal an elegant formal invitation to the opening of the Waterhouse Exhibition at the South Australian Museum.

'I love the Museum. Wow, it's an invitation to the opening of the best natural history art competition in Australia,' said Zoe. 'I might just go.'

'Why not,' said the Postman. 'My kids always loved going to North Terrace. The museum, art gallery and library all in one strip.'

Memories of the Museum flooded back. During school holidays when she was a child, Zoe would pester her mother to let her spend the mornings in the Museum while she worked, and then they would meet for lunch. Those were her favourite days. The Museum was packed with treasures that invited exploration and imagination. She planned exotic feasts in the Egypt room with golden cups accompanied by music from the strange instruments. Zoe became the worshipped queen who dripped with jewels and saw all through kohl-painted eyes. The insect rooms, heavy drawers laden with butterflies and beetles in every shape, size and colour, were also favourites. She pictured old men in fusty suits aligning the samples and writing the tiny labels with spidery copperplate letters. In the Antarctic rooms, her imagined husky team would pull Mawson's sled and arrive with spare supplies just before the blizzard.

On the first day of each holiday, she would fly through each gallery to check that all her favourites were in order and check out any new displays. Then she chose a theme for each day. After Egypt, it would be the mammals with the monkeys swinging dangerously close to big cats, fat peccaries and the worn lion with the tail that twitched.

Zoe would always leave the Pacific Gallery till last. She would wonder how long it would take to chop a huge canoe like that from a tree and imagine ferocious battles with the daggers, clubs and fierce masks. The penis sheaths always caused a shiver of guilt. The pictures of children, eyes bulging under tight bindings to elongate their skulls made her feel slightly sick no matter how many times she looked at them.

Monica's fingerprints were all over this invitation. She would know that Zoe could be jolted back to serious work by seeing some new and beautiful art. Monica must have convinced the organisers to issue a special invitation to the London artist who was now a hermit in their midst. And, of course, it worked. She could hardly wait. Her resolve set like steel. After the exhibition, she would end her self-imposed isolation. She would return to London. She would be successful with her painting. She would investigate her father's disappearance. She would paint Ben and why not add entering the Archibald, Australia's most prestigious portrait prize.

Her passion and energy soared as she searched among her clothes for something elegant to wear. It was an important night for the Museum; she had better frock up and play her part.

Chapter 25

South Australian Museum, 2013

The shadows lengthened and skeins of beautiful people streamed along the leafy avenue into the museum. Whimsical mermaids, fancy-dress sailors and balloons drifted like bubbles around the whale skeleton in the foyer. Golden light, music and chatter floated around the door, drawing in guests and tempting the curious crowd that gathered on the pavement. Zoe's upswept blond hair and slim figure drew admiring glances. Her cream tooled-leather stilettos with double ankle straps tapped out a story from a more adventurous city.

'Smile Miss,' the official photographer by the door called, as he angled the camera to ensure the impressive doors framed each guest.

'Group shot please,' asked photographer. 'Come, Miss MacIntosh, here in the centre with the Director. That will suit the newsletter.'

Zoe was guided to the front, shook the Director's hand and smiled at the camera. Her eyes swept across the crowd outside, knowing there would be no one she knew. The tall shape of an old man in the crowd caught her attention. He stood near the entrance, aloof from the crowd. Behind the camera, he moved back under the trees and when Zoe glanced again, he was gone. The photographer, notebook in hand, asked Zoe her name and checked the spelling.

'Thank you, Miss Macintosh. Have a good night,' he said moving to the new arrivals. The old man had scurried back behind the granite fountain and watched from under the trees. The pale silk of her dress shimmered in the evening light. Her delicate pashmina would have fitted through a finger ring but warmed her shoulders in the cool air.

Passing the massive meteorite on display in the foyer, Zoe moved into the museum. The invited guests basked with the calm assurance of sleek well-fed cats. Those in the crowd who gazed wistfully at her beauty might have been surprised by her thoughts. For a brief moment, the old man had reminded her of her father. But art prize night at the museum was not the time for uncomfortable thoughts, old shadows.

'We are so delighted you could join us,' gushed the Director.

'Zoe, please. Thanks for the invitation.' She smiled with genuine warmth. 'I always love seeing new work, especially here. This museum was very special to me when I was a child.'

'It is a pleasure to welcome you back here. Our Board members particularly like to celebrate home grown successes. Especially budding artists who are making good abroad.'

'Thank you. You have an enthusiastic crowd.'

'Yes. The South Australian Museum's Waterhouse is now the richest cash prize in Australia for artists who draw inspiration from the natural world. Perhaps we might expect an entry from you in future years,' the Director continued. He guided her to the drinks and excused himself to greet another guest.

'A Langhorne Creek red?' she asked the drinks waiter.

'Yes M'am,' came the welcome reply.

Sipping her wine, Zoe wandered among the exhibits amazed that while artists have drawn plants and animals for millennia, there was always a new style. The variety was dazzling. Some sketches captured the essence of an animal in a few lines; other paintings seemed shaped by the wildness of dreams.

'Nice wine,' she smiled as she stood next to a young woman trying to look invisible against the wall. After a knot of people squeezed past, Zoe asked 'Do you have work in the exhibition?' The young woman studied her own scuffed shoes intently.

'Yes,' she gulped. 'I'm so nervous.' She shot Zoe a fleeting glance. Zoe noted that her layers of op-shop vintage clothing had style.

'I do like your top. Don't worry. It gets easier. I was really scared at my first exhibition. I hope you do well tonight,' Zoe offered as she moved to the next exhibit.

An older man, immaculate in a dark three-piece suit, flamboyant bow tie and matching pocket square, bustled over to Zoe.

'Good evening. So, you are the famous Miss Macintosh. I'm Thomas I'Anson,' he said as he offered his hand and drew her towards a chatty circle. His impeccable dress suggested an eye for detail. Zoe wondered if he had produced the dramatic pencil drawing on display behind them.

'Is this your work?' she asked gesturing to the charming portrait of a penguin. She suddenly noticed an uncanny resemblance between man and subject; broad white chest, sleek black hair and pursed lips looking more penguin-like with every moment. She suppressed a smile.

'Yes, yes,' he responded, and puffed with pride.

The group welcomed Zoe, peppering her with questions about her work. The chatter swelled with genuine preferences and stage-managed conversations. Professional and amateur critics voiced their views. Artists and groupies jostled for proximity to those with influence – and those with money.

Enjoying her wine, Zoe drifted, feeling alone, but not uncomfortable. She did not need attention. It had been a long time since she had been to a party and heard the babble of a crowd. She watched as some artists preened, keen to be noticed; others shuffled with impatience, anxious for the cheques to be presented so they could bolt for the door. In a dash of over-exuberance, a mixed media exponent gestured wildly, and his drink crashed to the floor. There were buyers, art lovers, bargain hunters, some with partners to be indulged or denied. Guests juggled positions, drinks and opinions. Some of the patrons boasted of yet another possession, others hugged their pleasure silent and close. As Zoe moved through the crowd, a friendly, mellow voice was directed at her.

'Good evening. Our esteemed Director is in fine form tonight. If he talks any faster, I think he will explode.'

'Or perhaps wind down like a clockwork toy?' Zoe said as she turned, a smile creeping on to her face, and almost bumped into an outstretched hand.

'Michael Elston. I'm pleased to meet you Miss Macintosh.'

'Good evening. Zoe will do,' she responded, noting his hand was warm and dry, pleasant to the touch. The handshake lingered, but not too long. She decided nature had been generous in constructing that face and body with the mellifluous voice.

'Our dear Director was so delighted you could come. He loves trophies,' Michael said his lips curving in a mischievous grin. 'But seriously, these works are beautiful don't you think?' He turned to the next painting, a realistic whale. 'Mmmm it's good, but tonight I'm in the mood for some fanciful abstracts and wild colours. We all need occasional relief from reality don't you think?'

'Definitely,' responded Zoe. They moved along the length of the gallery, side-by-side but not together. They admired the skill and imagination that transformed a few charcoal lines into the essence of lyrebird; layers of clay which became banksia cones; glass and metal butterflies that looked ready to fly, even a koala shaped from chicken wire and a driftwood pelican. Past a mask of bones, and a magnificent mandala of eucalyptus leaves there was a cone composed of varnished animal droppings.

'That proves there is art in all things,' said Zoe.

'Perhaps, but I'm not having one of those in my house, however many layers of varnish it might have,' Michael laughed.

Among the watercolours and oils, Zoe wondered about her unexpected companion. Nice voice, warm eyes. Among the sculptures, she was distracted by the incongruity of some works. Hard glass depicted delicate grass heads: indestructible plastics represented the fragile tentacles of jellyfish, and robust metals became the evanescent quicksilver of sparkling fishes. Things were never exactly what they seemed.

'These bronze frogs are particularly fine,' said Zoe.

'Perhaps they will surprise us and leap off the wall,' said Michael moving a little closer.

Zoe edged back. 'I still prefer the plants,' she said as they moved to the botanical studies where buds, fruits, flowers and seeds were drawn side by side in fine detail, providing an identification guide, a lesson in morphology and an object of beauty all at the same time.

'Do you know that this tradition grew from the needs of medieval doctors?' she offered. 'Plants look the same in all languages if they are drawn well enough. As a child I was captivated by the accuracy. My father would buy me copies of proper botanical studies, and we would make it a game to check the level of detail,' she continued. 'I would be tempted to continue that thousand-year-old tradition if I didn't have to earn a living,' Zoe shrugged gazing off into the middle distance.

'We all need to earn a living. I use language myself. Don't worry I'm not a journalist. I'm not going to extract details from you and write an expose´ in tomorrow's paper. I'm a researcher.' He passed Zoe a business card to allay her stricken look. 'Perhaps I use words like you use colours? What about this portrait of a rhinoceros? Now there is a nose. I love the way the artist has painted the body in loving detail then sketched the missing horn in a single line. This painting shouts a story.' Zoe was captivated. She understood loss.

'Look out,' Michael laughed as he reached forward and took her arm to steer her away from a large woman holding three glasses full of wine in front of her like a snow plough. 'Wine is so much better inside than out,' Michael said.

'I agree and as a loyal Langhorne Creek girl I don't believe in wasting good wine. Let's move away from the bar,' Zoe responded.

The crowd circulated, ebbing and flowing around the paintings, the bar, the food and the regular exhibits in the museum. Zoe watched as the crowd stratified into groups like the paintings themselves. Some of the patterns were direct and obvious: Adelaide's landed gentry, the government people, the critics; others were complex with hidden or half-hidden meanings especially those connected by sex. People and paintings, both were complicated.

'These tiny ceramics of dead birds look sad,' said Zoe.

'But look at this,' Michael directed Zoe's attention with his hand cupping the small of her back. The kangaroo portrait had a gleam in its eye and in that tiny shard of reflected light, there was an entire landscape, a telescopic view of another world. 'I wonder if beauty is more universal than language?'

'I think so,' said Zoe. 'Everyone loves beautiful people.'

The Durer-type portrait of the grasshopper impressed them both. It was crafted from delicate portraits of hundreds of other insects; a brilliant concept, masterfully executed in great detail. She turned to Michael.

'This is so clever. Do you think we are what we eat?' she teased.

'Well my portrait would need to be ham and cheese croissants,' he chuckled.

The ceremony to award the prizes was announced and they moved into the Pacific Gallery. Zoe nodded in agreement as the invited speaker acknowledged the artistic struggle behind the creation of every work. The prizes offered the artists both recognition and money. Zoe was pleased when the young artist with the op-shop chic won an award.

All the works were available for sale. The Director spoke next. 'I would like to encourage everyone to purchase a work tonight. The investment will bring you beauty, our thanks and a reminder that art raises us above the struggle to eat or be eaten.'

Zoe took the challenge to heart and purchased a small work. From her first tiny exhibition in Adelaide, she remembered the pain of displaying work without sales. Her acquisition, an intriguing combination of realism and abstraction, was called *Camouflage*. Appropriate she thought. Just like me. Detailed part-portraits of animal parts including eyes, feathers, quills, fur and scales meshed together to form an abstract in dozens of shades of brown. She was pleased to support both a local artist and her treasured museum and looked forward to hanging her new painting when it was delivered after the exhibition closed. As a child, the museum had been a comfortable place to spend time and feel safe. She sighed, worried that her need to feel safe was becoming a recurring theme in her life.

'I must go,' she said looking at her watch. 'Pumpkin hour. Langhorne Creek is a bit of a drive and I've ordered a car.'

Michael escorted her to the door. She was flustered. After so many months of misery her warm response to him was unexpected. His quick kiss was full of promise. She bid him a hasty goodnight, relieved to see the driver of her pre-ordered car holding the door open. It saved further decisions. It seemed her treasured hometown museum was helping her recovery in the same way it had been a companion following her father's disappearance all those years ago.

Chapter 26

Mac's Surprise

Early one Friday evening as Mac emerged from the Library after another long day of searching, he saw a crowd gathering around the entrance to the museum next door to watch beautifully dressed guests enter. Idle curiosity held him there. A photographer bustled; arranging guests in front of the entrance for a publicity shot.

'Miss MacIntosh,' the photographer called 'Could you turn this way and shake the Director's hand please. Yes. Heads up, all smile please, and another.'

Mac turned as he heard the name, rubbed his eyes and stared. Could this be Zoe? Mac had only just got used to the idea that she was in London and doing well. That had given him some comfort and renewed his pledge to stay anonymous. He had certainly not expected her to be in South Australia let alone appear like a bolt from the blue right in front of him.

He looked, transfixed. She was just like Catherine, but taller like him. Zoe must be almost thirty now. Just the age when women discovered themselves he thought. She was beautiful. Her long back, wide shoulders and brilliant mouth, echoed Catherine. It was a shock to see her so successful. Elegant dress, exquisite shoes. She had always loved shoes, even as a toddler. And everyone was being almost deferential, her fame must be greater than he imagined.

The tonnes of years weighed on Mac's shoulders. He was so proud a lump rose in his throat while the shame of what he had done wrenched his gut. It was such a shock that his little girl was not little anymore. He felt intimidated by her success. There was so much history and so much distance between them. Even in the Philippines he did not feel so far away from her as he did now. Their story spanned twenty years two continents and all his painful mistakes flooded his mind.

She would think he was dead of course. And in reality, he was. After the statutory nine years, chances were he had been declared dead. If not, the police may still want to charge him. He had been in Adelaide for a few weeks and was living hand to mouth. His original thought was to sniff around and just see if he could find out what had happened to his family. The shock of learning about Catherine's death had made him rethink. Catherine would have worked herself to death he thought. She was always a hard taskmaster, tough on herself, even more than those around her. With Mac gone she would have worked even harder. Mac had no trouble imagining that. Now, Zoe was alone. Mac wondered if she could ever forgive him.

Mac wondered for the millionth time how he could redeem himself. For the first time in twenty years, he had the opportunity to confront his past mistakes head on. But he didn't step forward. He retreated like a coward under the trees and watched Zoe from a distance. Shame flooded his belly. He hated himself and his weakness.

Chapter 27

After the Waterhouse

Despite her late night at the Waterhouse opening, Zoe woke at dawn. Rising early was now her habit on the vineyard at Langhorne Creek. At first it was due to the bright sun flooding through the thin curtains in the old house, but after a while she grew to love the quiet drama of morning unfurling. The exhibition last night was exciting and her meeting with Michael diverting, but Zoe fell back into the routines and exercise that helped her stay sane.

This morning she opted to walk rather than run. As she crossed the paddock, tendrils of mist coiled up spirit-like from the damp grass to spiral in the warming sun. Chains of water droplets beaded the bare branches and sparkled. A rosella parrot landed heavily in the almond tree releasing a diamond shower. Against the early sun, its bright feathers shone grey and shadowy but its shape unmistakable, a solid exclamation mark against the sky. Hidden birds cleared their throats and tested songs. Tiny silvereyes flicked in and out of existence, their flight so fast they manifested in one place then another with nothing in between. The plants, like her, unwound slowly. Leaves trembled and the weighty morning dew slid off as the air warmed. The colours grew strong and painted the landscape.

Filled again with the pleasures of morning, Zoe returned to the house, cast aside her damp togs, and took a long, luxurious shower. She dressed in raw silk trousers and tunic and enjoyed the soft rub of fabric against her skin. As she massaged moisturizer into her face, her lips remembered last night's unexpected soft kiss.

Once, the landscape had been featureless, devoid of depth, even of colour – a flat, blank canvass leached by despair. Uncontrollable pain would gush up, hot like a volcano and fill her with searing blackness. Depression consumed every ounce of her energy. The predictable world she once valued had evaporated, and she was forced to understand the painful truth that trust and honesty, which she valued, simply did not exist in the man she once loved.

After months, the weight on her chest lessened enough for her to breathe without effort, she developed routines and exercise to help control her moods. After almost a year she dragged herself to her current oasis of calm. Colour seeped back into her world. When despair pressed close on dark days, her will to survive shaped a new worldview. She adjusted; she grew. Chaos invaded less often. She would not be so vulnerable in the future.

On good days, Zoe listed the positives. Reluctantly, painfully, she now understood at a visceral level, how different people, or even the same people at a different time, did not see the same things when viewing the same scene. Vision depended on an inner sense, not eyes.

She would survive.

Chapter 28

Yves and the Portrait

Yves leafed his way through the few pieces of correspondence on the antique walnut roll top desk. He hoped for an interesting invitation in a heavy envelope of good quality paper, addressed with a skilful hand. He preferred not to commit business matters to paper, but if text was needed it should be in well-presented script preferably in black ink from a Mont Blanc. He opened a chunky envelope to face disappointment. It was an invitation to yet another modern art exhibition opening. No entertaining dinner, the recreation of a medieval banquet perhaps, or the release of a new fashion collection. He did so admire all those beautiful young models.

The last art exhibition he attended without sufficient research resulted from a moment of extreme boredom and his desire to find a young fresh artist to impress. Disaster ensued. The exhibition was filled with ghastly sculptures crafted from recycled objects that all looked like garbage. It had been grotesque. Balls and shapes of wire and plastic crouched around the walls mocking consumer society. Most of the attendees wore shapeless grunge clothes and spoke like cartoon characters, all expletives and exclamation marks. Many guests considered him old or old-fashioned at best and the manifestation of all that they opposed. Except his money of course, they were transparent in wanting him to buy. It was crass and unpleasant, and he would not chance it again. He would seek references before accepting any unsolicited invitations. Revolutionaries and recycling were off his list.

The last item was a neat but bulky package. It contained a letter, several reproductions of paintings and a crisp photograph from the British journalist, Monica Wilson. He had already agreed to an interview with her, and the letter proposed a painted portrait to accompany her article.

Yves was attracted to having his portrait painted. It felt simultaneously classical and modern. Rich people, mining magnates, movie stars even sportsmen were the nobility of the current age. They patronised the arts and the public imagination. Yves contemplated where to hang the painting. He might find a prominent position in the office in Paris if it was flattering. He recalled portraits in recent editions of *Forbes Magazine*, in which the subjects looked distinguished and magisterial. *Yes*, thought Yves as he imagined himself there – with gravitas, the next evolutionary stage of a successful career. From a humble beginning he had morphed into a man of undeniable substance and importance. Success and status felt good. He could position himself well to capitalise on this latest project and gain greater public recognition.

It was clear that the artist, Zoe Macintosh, could paint. He knew the subject of one of her portraits and the work was fair but flattering. The style was modern, and the skill was undeniable. This might just be sufficient to divert him; life had become too predictable.

Yves thumbed further through the sheaf of pages. Her painted faces looked intently from the page. The settings were imaginative, reflecting the coded messages of portraiture from the past. One sitter, a media magnate had newspapers, shadowy racehorses and beautiful women in a delicate collage, drifting around him like a cloud. Subtle, almost ethereal, or perhaps like a fog descending, symptomatic of yesterday's news, Yes, Yves thought, shadowy, and fading fast. It was clever.

Yves was interested in how he would be presented and what people would think. He wanted to appear rich, desirable and in control. He was not opposed to spending the money, but he just wanted to be sure of the outcome. Then, he realised it would cost no more than a couple of Adriana's statues. The photograph in the envelope carried a likeness of Zoe and his interest soared. He liked slim blondes; unconsciously he licked his lips.

Yves telephoned Monica.

'Good afternoon, Miss Wilson. Yves Montreau here. I have called to discuss your proposal. Interesting idea. But I was thinking that your magazine would pay for this work?'

'Sadly, Monsieur, my magazine is not in a position to do that. Also as Miss McIntosh's representative, I can assure you that a work from this aspiring artist would be a valuable investment.' Monica knew the price was high, but she would not reduce it. She was going to extract every last possible dollar of commission from him. They both knew he could afford it and would claim it as a tax deduction.

'I admit I am open to the idea,' he said, thinking that if Zoe's photo reflected the reality, he would be even more interested. 'As for the artist, I would need some time with her before I could agree. I will consider the terms you provided only after I speak to Miss MacIntosh and find her satisfactory.'

The worst thing about Australians was those loud voices and flat vowels, he thought. I couldn't bear it if she had one of those ugly voices. He sniffed. With any luck she might not speak too much and he could just enjoy the view.

He thought of Australians he knew a long time ago. They were tough and gutsy, big, wild, and raw. He wondered what the country was like now. There would be plenty of riches still there. Bartering and getting a good deal were always his first thoughts.

As he thought about a portrait, about being captured in time, about looking even better than he did now, he was open to a deal. Nothing could go wrong. He held all the cards.

Chapter 29

Zoe Returns

During the night Zoe received a text from Monica flagging a commission for a new painting in France. The timing was welcome. Zoe's night at the museum convinced her she was well enough to work. Returning to London would be a convenient excuse not to see Michael again. It was too soon for entanglements. When he called later in the day, she was tempted to accept his offer for lunch but said she had plane flights to book and arrangements to be made.

Zoe knew London was where she could earn well from doing what she loved. A visit to the rolling fields of northern France would also be a delight. Apart from the scenery, French men could be sophisticated and complex. Successful French men dressed well, and she appreciated sartorial elegance. Clothes may not make the man, but they improved the scenery.

Zoe's portraits, sketches and paintings for *Your Business* magazine fitted a specialised niche. They generated a steady income and professional accolades. Both had built her confidence and self-esteem. She learned much about faces by observing and painting. Working with business people gave her an elegant circle of acquaintances, but her old friend Monica, and George, her favourite gallery owner, remained her only true and enduring friends.

In her major portraits, Zoe worked hard to capture the personality of her subjects in a modern and innovative style. She avoided the harshness of caricatures and the staidness of classic portraiture. Endless conversations with George had convinced her that, to make a comfortable living, she needed a recognisable style and something different to take her work beyond image making. Good paintings took time and provided opportunities for conversation, even a little intimacy.

Most of her subjects were accustomed to controlling their public image and interactions with the press. These men, yes, all men so far, often reached positions of power by skillful negotiation. They were well practiced at masking their emotions. But, because they were not accustomed to portrait painters, they were unsure which rules applied. Zoe encouraged a flow of words. Useful snippets of information would emerge during the days of sitting. Successful men enjoyed talking about their activities to attractive younger women. Then like seed falling on prepared ground, Zoe could feed Monica with unpredictable acquaintances, or discover information about ill-gotten wealth. A sophisticated French businessman might need careful handling if she were to find the truth behind the image.

Monica's lengthy follow-up email later in the day outlined the basics. Montreau was the man Monica asked about during their quick trip to New Caledonia. Studying the images, which Monica emailed, Zoe admired the clean lines of his face, his strongly masculine presence and powerful nose. A little gaunt for her taste, but she imagined he used his face well in social and business situations. He would make a good subject. He looked as comfortable in suits as on the yacht or at the races. With a different woman in each of the casual poses, it was clear he enjoyed the company of glamorous women. Zoe did not consider her natural dark blonde hair, fair freckled skin and blue-green eyes showed the symmetry or visual impact necessary to meet her definition of beauty. Beautiful people like Montreau and these women in the photographs faced an easier road.

Monica's email identified offices in Paris and London. His home was a chateau in Rouen. Zoe imagined a labyrinth of formal and informal rooms to entertain and amuse guests, elegant balconies and plenty of staff. There would always be fresh flowers and no need for chores like washing dishes or taking out the rubbish. It was a far cry from her simple cottage at Langhorne Creek. Yves was clearly wealthy and apparently enjoyed acquiring art including paintings. She started to see possibilities for this assignment.

Yves Montreau, aged 53 first came to prominence in Britain when Montague Corporation bought into steel manufacturing. Now pharmaceuticals appeared to supply his wealth. Monica's briefing showed a long list of moneymaking ventures over the past 20 years. Power, influence and money were a sexy combination – no wonder he looked relaxed and confident. She imagined his position of wealth and influence had been gained by money and charm as well as business acumen.

Monica did not indicate the angle for her article. She usually covered good attributes and bad; innovation, ruthlessness, benevolence, unusual skill, rare generosity. Zoe began to think about her approach. A focus perhaps on those clever eyes – no, too trite; too obvious. Perhaps an exploration of his patronage of the arts – boring. There was no hint of 'a poor boy made good' in the material before her. She'd need a story line to plan the image. The portrait and Monica's story must resonate. No point in painting an angel if the article told a devil's story.

Zoe would be the bait to fill in the blanks which Monica, the reporter, could not discover through the usual information channels. George was fond of Balzac's quote, 'Behind every great fortune is a great crime.' Zoe suspected this was what Monica wanted to discover – the great crime behind Yves wealth.

Reading completed, Zoe decided to walk. Open green landscapes gave her a sense of peace. Walking helped her think. A commission offered a clear objective and a rigid timeline. She needed the money. Which personality would be most successful in eliciting information about Yves' character? Sometimes she played the airhead artist who would ask endless dumb questions. But, this man looked urbane, sophisticated and smart. Knowing too much or seeming too interested might arouse his suspicion. A hint of romance and some gentle flattery might be more successful. Admiration worked, especially on those getting a little older.

Monica had bagged the deal, perhaps it was better that Zoe had no time to stew. Zoe pulled out her phone and booked a ticket to London on Friday. Three days to get organized. She would call Brad to make the necessary arrangements to leave the Langhorne Creek house in safe hands yet again. She would send Michael a card and include her email address. Maybe there would be an opportunity to see him again. Perhaps he would visit London. Remembering the kiss and the good conversation, she wanted to keep the option open.

Having made the big decision, she itched to get into back into action. Packing her few belongings would take a short hour. Her life moved from inaction and indecision to an urgent desire to get moving again. Her passion for painting had been rekindled by seeing the Waterhouse Exhibition and starting the commission. But more than this, Zoe's time at Langhorne Creek rekindled her desire to unravel the mystery around her Dad's disappearance. His warm memory was still strong in the house. She was ashamed it took her so long to pick up this challenge. London beckoned, but first she would make a lightening trip to Robe. She would visit the location where the disaster happened and if she was lucky, perhaps she could meet someone who remembered him or harboured a theory about what happened.

'Do you think the old car would make it to Robe and back?' Zoe asked as Brad arrived to organize the house keys.

'Probably not. Why Robe?'

'My father disappeared from there. I always wondered what happened. I thought I'd go and see if I could talk to some of the old fishermen before I fly back to London.'

'That's a pretty good reason. I'll tell you what. You take my twin cab and I'll take the old car home after I'm finished here. At least the Emergency Services won't need to scrape you off the road.'

'Are you sure? That would be brilliant. I'll be back tomorrow night because my plane leaves first thing Friday morning.'

'No problem. It's only about three hours. If you leave now, you'll be there in time for a beer. Bars are always a good place to pick up some gossip.'

Zoe, threw a change of clothes in a bag, grabbed her phone and credit card and set off in a rush. Passing the green vines of Langhorne Creek, she reached the flat grazing country where flocks of pale grey Cape Barren geese grazed. Gleaming mounds of sparkling white salt stood ready for export from Mulgundawa. The salt lakes and soaks became more frequent as the landscape dried. She crossed the cable ferry over the River Murray at Wellington thinking – just add water … it would make such a difference to this land. Only a few hundred meters away from the green ribbon of the river, her eyes were drawn to the pale pink of the drying lakes and the deep purple of the succulent, salt-tolerant samphyre. Soon the rosy colours gave way to the fecund Coorong, a tangle of brackish water, sand dunes and underground water channels crisscrossing a maze of aquatic life, plants and birds.

As the odometer ticked over, she wondered what to do when she arrived. It was twenty years since her father had disappeared. Would anyone remember him? She decided she didn't care. At least she would have tried. Her days of passive acceptance were over. Her reflections came to a screaming halt as a kangaroo burst out of the roadside bushes and bounded across the road in front of her. She braked heavily, wheels locking and smearing rubber across the road, as the huge dark beast, taller than the car, leapt between the Melaleucas without a backward glance. She was lucky, another two seconds and the car would have been a mess, and the roo no better. Shaken, she cut her speed.

After the Coorong, where the traditional owners still went swan egging and everyone enjoyed the Coorong mullet, it was dune and swale country where ancient sand dunes lined the landscape like a collection of softly mounded breasts. Further south, dark brooding pines became more common; and the colours morphed from drought-tolerant pale blue greens and khaki to bright and deep greens.

Robe unfolded against the blue of the ocean in just the way she remembered as the car beeped to remind her that fuel was low. Perfect timing, she thought as she drove into the petrol station. Lining up to pay for fuel, she admired the pin board with dozens of curling photographs of men proudly holding large fish – snapper, whiting, massive mulloway.

'Big fish,' she commented to the man at the till.

'We do good fish around here, lady.'

'So where would I go to talk to the fishermen and learn their secrets?' she asked.

'Down to the breakwater to talk to the line fishermen, the pier for the big boats,' he said, moving to the next customer. Zoe scrabbled in her bag for a pen and scribbled the names of some of the men with big fish on the back of a tourist brochure.

She'd visited Robe many times as a child. It was a friendly town. Fish-packing factory, well cared-for houses, clean streets and docks – a town made wealthy by prosperous farms and the bounty of the sea. Parking in the main street, she strolled along, enjoying the late afternoon light glowing on the old stone buildings. Perhaps she might stay the night, enjoy some fresh fish and walk along the beach in the morning. A few old limestone cottages displayed Bed & Breakfast signs. An outside dunny decorated with a skillfully painted tree had a sign above it – 'lav-a-tree'. It made her laugh.

From the esplanade, Zoe gazed across the harbor to the crescent of white sand and line of dark green Norfolk Island pines standing tall and sharp like a row of sharpened pencils. Her image of a perfect beach.

Boats nestled in the curve of the bay. Odd, she thought, how fishing is so dangerous, but the boats look peaceful bobbing in the limpid bay. Only a few people wandered about. She drove on to the new commercial marina, and then wandered along the dock, moving the reluctant seagulls from their sleep on the pier. The sea was ultramarine, turquoise; lambent, vivid green-blue glowing as clouds moved, changing the angle of the sun on the water.

About thirty boats were moored in the Lake Marina, all well protected from the southern gales. Her eyes flicked across their names. Bombay Sapphire suggested gin and tonics. Jennifer's Pride was straightforward enough. Coast Runner paid tribute to the importance of wind and tide. Challenger, Bushranger and Boss told a bolder story. As she finally crossed the ramp on her way out, she spied a faded and weather-beaten old boat anchored out away from the pier. Its name, the Aphrodite was just legible among the peeling paint. Could this be true? Could this be the boat involved in her father's story? Zoe's heart skipped a beat. She called across the water, but no answer returned to her 'Ahoy Aphrodite'.

Zoe hurried back along Victoria Street looking for the pub most likely to appeal to old fishermen. A beer in the front bar might be the best way to find the owner of The Aphrodite. *The Caledonian* sounded promising but was full of tourists. The front bar of the *Robe Hotel* was scattered with tall, broad men in scuffed work boots who reminded her of her father – long and strong, with work-callused hands and large feet that offered a solid grip on the earth. She hesitated, uncomfortable, and then pulled her cap low, screwed up her courage and moved to an empty seat at the bar. She waited until the older barman with the checkered work shirt approached.

'Pale Ale, thanks.'

'Schooner or Pint?'

'Schooner. Is there anyone here who might remember a fisherman from 20 years ago?'

'Have a word to old Phil over there in the corner,' he said, pointing with his chin as he poured beers. 'He's been around forever. And don't look so scared. He won't bite.'

'Thanks.' She sidled over and pulled up a chair.

'Donald MacIntosh. Now that's a name I've not heard for a long time. Mac, we called him,' the old bloke said.

'That's right, everyone called him Mac.'

'He was too ugly to have a pretty daughter like you,' Phil said in answer to her introduction.

'Never knew what happened to him. He was a good boy. A bit rash. Eaten up by the Chinese, I always reckoned. They were sniffing around like dogs on heat in them days.'

'Was it *The Aphrodite* I saw anchored in the marina,' she said.

'Yep. She was the pride of the harbour once. Not so fine after the salvage. Old Costas is no good now. Past it. He was real sad when Mac disappeared. Never thought he was dead tho'. Said he'd feel it. He was always a bit of a weird one. Said he could smell there'd been Chinese on board. Reckoned they'd taken your Dad.' Phil's old eyes were rheumy. Zoe couldn't work out whether this was an allergy, old age or sadness. 'Said, he wouldn't just vanish or go off by himself. There was no proof of anything though. Stumped the coppers and them insurance vultures. They gave Costas a hard time for years. But he finally got his boat back from the salvagers and fished plenty more years.'

'Mum and I were pretty upset when he vanished,' Zoe said in a masterpiece of understatement.

'Well, that's all I can tell you Missy. Costas is still around in the town, but not at the pub. Some rellie of his runs the B&B down in Acacia Street. I've got to go now. Getting late. Me Missus'll have me guts for garters if I'm not home for tea.'

Zoe walked back along the road rejoicing in this small victory. What did he mean, 'Costas was no good?' At least he wasn't dead. Zoe left the pub and walked down the street to collect a map and some brochures from the tourist office. The town map was easy to follow. A short walk down Victoria Street, around a couple of corners and she was at Acacia Avenue. Costa's Bed &Breakfast was sketched on a faded sign that swung on the veranda of a tiny cottage with a narrow sliver of view to the sea. Zoe pushed the bell.

'Hi, I was hoping there might be a room for tonight?' she asked the young dark-haired woman who came to the door, tea towel in hand, children clinging to her skirt.

'It's small but yes. $50 for the bed, $60 if you want breakfast too. Come in, I'll show you.' she said as children surged around her legs.

'Thank you. That will be fine,' Zoe said as the woman opened the door to show her a small room made smaller by the heavy dark furniture and patchwork bed cover.

'Can I ask you about the name of your place?'

'It belonged to my Uncle Costas. He still lives here when he's not fishing. Why he bothers puzzles me. Hardly ever catches anything these days. I'm trying to make a go of it but its not easy with the kids,' she said as another emerged crying from the kitchen.

'Would he be fishing now?' Zoe asked, her heart pounding.

'No, gone to his room by now. But he'll be up before dawn and down on the breakwater again, just like every morning. We're lucky if we see him much these days,' she said as she rushed outside to prevent one of her small boys from clouting the other with a cricket bat.

Buoyed by the news, Zoe went out to buy something to eat and escape the noise of the boys fighting. Allowing enough time for the children to be in bed, she returned and lay on the bed thinking about her discoveries. She was startled to wake several hours later, shivering and disorientated. She crawled under the covers and snuggled down, cosy and hopeful that the trail may not be empty. She set her alarm for 5am planning to catch Costas as he left to fish.

The morning was chilly and calm. In the silence, Zoe showered and dressed hoping to hear or see the old man leaving. After about half an hour when there was still no sign of him, she walked to the breakwater. An old man sat at the far end of the jumbled rocks, which jutted like an accusing finger into the ocean. She imagined he might sit there even in the rough weather and dare the sea to take him. Hunched in his oilskin coat, he was as still and brown as the rocks, which surrounded him.

'Costas Theodorakis, I presume,' she said as she approached. 'I'm Zoe MacIntosh.'

'Mac's girl? I thought someone would come eventually. You're a bit young,' he said squinting against the glare from the rising sun.

'I'm Mac's daughter, not his wife,' she said as she sat down beside him.

'Can't keep track of the years these days. Often think about him when I sit quietly here. I miss fishing and all those old boys.'

'You're not going to catch many fish without a line in the water.'

'I fish for peace these days,' he said with a crooked smile. 'Not much of that in the house.'

'I'm trying to find out what happened to my Dad, Costas.'

'If I knew, my days would be more peaceful. I'm so old and tired now. I've thought about it a thousand times, but I just can't get it straight. I don't think he's dead. No good reason. Just feel it in my bones.'

Zoe's heart surged. Could it be possible?

'The sea is a big place. It hides more secrets than you could ever imagine. Secrets swept away into the depths.'

'I'm tired of secrets.'

'Don't give up,' said Costas his eyes drawn hypnotically to the horizon. 'Mac's girl. Fancy that,' he said as his focus faded.

Costas seemed unaccustomed to talking. His breath was labored and there were long spaces between words. Zoe left, promising to keep in touch, meaning well but with little conviction. Costas stuffed the note Zoe scribbled with her contact details into the big pocket of his oilskin jacket. She liked talking to someone who cared about her father, but she learned little. She was unreasonably pleased by the thought that

Costas sensed Mac wasn't dead. But, it couldn't be, nothing had happened for twenty years. After an entire year at Langhorne Creek, Zoe cursed that she had left this visit to her last day. She couldn't stay any longer. She needed to get Brad's car back before 3 o'clock so he could pick up his kids.

Back at the B&B Zoe enjoyed a home-cooked breakfast despite the swirl of children. Then she visited the Visitor Centre in the Library. A comprehensive historical display showed someone was interested in things past. She pinned a notice on the board asking anyone with information about Mac MacIntosh, fisherman who disappeared in October 1990 to contact her. She wrote her phone and email and Monica's address on the card and hit the road.

Suppressing a little surge of hope, Zoe thought about getting back to London, picking up the threads of her life and seeing her friends again. Now she was on her father's case, there would be no stopping her.

Chapter 30

London, 2013

During the long flight from Adelaide to London, almost eight hours to Singapore then another thirteen to Heathrow, Zoe watched movie after movie. Diversion was the best way to cope as the pod-like seat encased her more tightly with every passing hour. She was Alice sliding down a jumbo jet trail to the Wonderland of London hoping she could sip from the right bottle to fit her new/old world. The Qantas jet speared through the morning mist and after being sorted and drafted, she gathered her luggage, boarded the Heathrow Express and moved between tube lines with easy familiarity.

Wrapped in a fog of jet lag, and still tasting the stale aeroplane air, she pressed the buzzer to Monica's flat.

'Monica it's me it's me, open sesame.' she shouted jumping up and down to warm her frozen toes. The door flung open.

'Oh My God how can you always look so gorgeous?' Monica said as she grabbed Zoe in a hug that could have smothered a bear. 'I think you're even skinnier. I've put on another 20 kilos,' said Monica holding her at arm's length. 'And you could be in a shampoo ad. How can you look so good after that flight? If you weren't my best friend, I'd hate you.' She laughed as she dragged Zoe into the flat. Zoe beamed; the world felt right again.

'It's SO good to see you Monica,' Zoe said as the hugging girls half fell into the tiny living room of the crowded flat. 'And hello George,' she said with an even wider smile as he struggled to get up from Monica's sagging sofa.

'The three Musketeers are back together,' George laughed as he joined the hug. 'I wonder what mischief we can get up to now. You're too thin. I've missed your colonial candour,' he said as he shoved the morning newspaper aside. 'Political correctness and triple speak are ruling the airwaves. Nothing worth reading these days.' He made space for Zoe among the piles of papers and magazines.

'I'll make tea,' Monica said disappearing into the kitchen. 'It's too early for alcohol even though I feel like celebrating. Mmmm,' she said looking at the wine in the fridge. 'Yes, a little early even for me.'

'I was sorry to hear about your father's death George. How are you feeling?' Zoe asked as she parked her case against the wall.

'You know we were never close, but I was surprised how much it shocked me,' George confessed. 'I'm OK, but these things bring back floods of memories. Death is so final.'

'You know I've had a rotten time too, so I'm in touch with all the inner truth things at the moment. Talking might help,' Zoe said, curling up with a cushion.

'Just what you need after a long flight.'

'No, I mean it. We all had painful times when we were kids. It's taken me a year to learn that bottling it up doesn't help at all. And sometimes you can't pick your times.'

'Everything I remember about my father was grey, grey hair, grey clothes, grey mind. Everyone where I grew up seemed thin and grey. He and my mother always seemed exhausted – it was more than hard times. No imagination, no spark, no search for anything beautiful. Even my schools were dull as the grey skies. Mean architecture and meaner teachers. And you two would have hated the class stuff.' George sighed as Monica returned with tea.

'Dead right,' Monica chuckled. They all settled down, passing cups and sugar, pleased to be together.

'My family's demise was the story of Sheffield. Steel modernised Britain but steel didn't modernise itself. Plenty of pride and nostalgia. No one even knows what a cutler is now even though everyone uses cutlery.' George reflected. 'My father saw his life as a failure. Disappointment is a poisonous thing if you let it eat you away.'

'That's true George. I guess that's why I'm back. My dream may have had a serious hiccough, but I'm committed,' Zoe responded. 'Go on, I want to hear the whole story.'

'When new owners closed the steel works, my Dad drank even more, and his temper shortened. He was a pig at home. All the workers seemed lost and bitter.'

'It is hard to lose something you love,' Zoe winced.

'Yes, but love can also save you. My love of art saved me as a kid. Among the rough and tumble of wild brothers and a neighbourhood of football fanatics, my tastes were peculiar and suspicious. I learned to think fast and run faster. I thought I'd die if I didn't get out. Most nights I had the same recurring dream. I'd have to swim the sluggish, stained waters of the canal near our house. It had dirty weed-choked banks and in my dream, there was always a dark and threatening sky full of smoke from fires in buried coal seams. I would flail around and wake gasping for air, terrified of drowning under the dark sucking waters and slimy plants which were pulling me under.'

'Nasty. I don't think we need a psychologist to work that one out,' Monica added.

'I was lucky we had a great local library. I won a scholarship. Then, as soon as I could, I escaped to university.'

'I remember escaping to university too,' said Zoe. 'It gave us all a chance to reinvent ourselves.' The friends muttered agreement, lost in private memories.

'I loved uni, too,' said Monica. 'Somehow it gave everyone permission to explore. You could find out things that you didn't even know you were looking for.'

'I was a good mimic. I could copy anyone. That always got a few laughs. Then I got pretty wild and stupid until I met Ross. Finally, I grew up.' George reflected. 'Ross helped me live the life I'd always wanted. He helped me believe in myself,' he said with a note of triumph. 'My father's death made me relive Ross's death. I think that's why it was so painful,' said George with a catch in his throat.

'He was a good man. Don't discount the brilliant way he taught you to run the gallery,' Monica called from the kitchen over the sound of clattering cups.

'He was good at buying with a client already in mind, so he could on-sell quickly to minimise expensive holding costs.'

'Well, I'm back and I need to work,' Zoe said with enthusiasm, wanting to drag them all away from sad memories. 'I need to stay awake until dark to reset my body clock, so divert me. Plan my career for me George.'

'I'll use your work to build my business,' replied George picking up on her change of pace and rubbing his hands together. 'Its dog eat dog in the art business, and I'm hungry,' he said growling and making what he hoped was a leering doggy face. 'You need to be pragmatic. Tailor your work to clients who can pay the sort of money you need for a comfortable London life. Happiness is all about positive cash flow.'

'I don't mind – old money or new – both pay the bills,' said Zoe.

'We can work as a team. George you can find the clients. Zoe, you can work on commission painting portraits for your daily bread, and I can write incisive articles which will make me famous,' Monica said. 'Money is the best way to be insulated from the cold wind of poverty that nips around our ankles.'

'Here's what I reckon. Everyone has a digital camera and loads of happy snaps stored somewhere on the Internet, but wealthy people are also vain,' George said looking pensive. 'Choose other subjects for your pleasure if you wish Zoe. But, if you get a good reputation for portraits, you'll get enough clients to make a steady income. Under my brilliant guidance, we'll make money together,' said George.

'Shall I make more tea Monica? I can't get the taste of stale aeroplane out of my mouth.'

'OK George. Portraits it will be. Drawing people is tough. But I'm up for it.'

'Well, my lovely, let's hope you can develop the same skills in interpreting relationships. I'm not going to stay silent this time if you hook up with another suspicious character,' Monica said. 'We orphans need to look after each other.'

'I often wish my father was around, so I could show him my work,' Zoe said. 'I went to Robe to see where he disappeared from before I came back.'

'We're your friends, so no disappearing from us,' Monica said waggling her finger and frowning. 'Are you ready to talk about what happened with David?' Monica asked.

'I really believed in my relationship with David. Our first year together was a dream. You'll remember, George, I worked so hard on my second exhibition and then had that Porter commission. I was producing good work. I felt strong.'

'I always worried that you depended too heavily on David's approval,' said Monica.

'Then one day I got a phone call. She actually called me. I got all the gory details. It hit me like a 10-tonne truck. I remember literally falling on the ground. I couldn't breathe. When I challenged him, he didn't even bother to deny it. It left me so devastated I couldn't even speak.'

'Bastard,' said Monica. 'I always knew he was no good.'

'The worst part was that I didn't see it coming. I couldn't believe my inability to read his behaviour.'

'You were always too trusting Zoe,' said George.

'The problem was that it destroyed my trust, not just in him, but in myself. His behaviour was irrefutable evidence of my total inability to judge other people. So, when I found out that the lies and betrayal had been going on for months, I decided I was useless, hopeless, pathetic. Strangely I didn't resent him leaving. I just knew I couldn't trust my own perceptions. The sky seemed to close over me like a cold grey blanket. I couldn't work. I couldn't see. I couldn't paint. I just wanted to feel warm and see blue sky. So, I ran back to the vineyard. I wanted to shut him and London out.'

'I think you copied your mother,' said Monica. 'I remember you telling me she shut the blinds and closed off the world when your father disappeared.'

'Perhaps, but not consciously. I distanced myself from the pain. I was utterly lost. When I rang you, I couldn't even talk to you in a way that made me feel better. Like a wounded animal I crawled away. Langhorne Creek was the only place I could go. It had some sad memories, but it was once home.'

'Well, it's good to have you back,' said Monica. 'We all have horrible setbacks from time to time. But if we support one another, we'll endure. Come on, let's go out to lunch.'

Chapter 31

The Portrait

Yves had been flattered by Monica's approach – but wary. He was not drawn to the candour or drama of the British press but his investment in pharmaceuticals was safe. He felt secure and at the top of his game, but he didn't want to seem eager.

'*Your Business* magazine is one of the most prestigious in London. Our decision to feature you will showcase your achievements to Britain and provide valuable promotion for your new company,' Monica cajoled over the phone appealing to his sense of vanity. Yves knew that positive exposure would align perfectly with his future plans for the new product. He'd millions invested in Alston and looked to the future, confident in the new product.

'Can I confirm that you alone will do the interview?' he asked believing he would have no trouble charming Monica.

'Yes, I'll be the only one to interview you,' Monica said. She smiled as she sensed Yves struggling to preserve his reputation as a tough negotiator.

'And the portrait?'

'Zoe Macintosh is our portrait specialist. I have sent you details of her work. You may recall she has already done two very successful portraits for our magazine. I believe we have already agreed yours will be the first in our new prestigious series'.

Yves eyes lit up with the promise of a double challenge. There was no doubt the girl could paint, so at worst he would have a fine portrait to hang in one of his houses. He could always pull out of the interview if things started going wrong. Monica may be a top journalist but he could charm her to produce a favourable article. Her vigour and broad Australian accent grated on him, but she enjoyed the confidence of many influential people in London. He couldn't afford to ignore her.

'Very well, I submit,' he said with feigned reluctance.

'Good, I'll liaise with Ms MacIntosh to find a time convenient to you both to start the portrait. Then, as it nears completion, I will interview you. The theme will be the future, your plans, your ideas and perhaps your views on the state of business in Europe today, if we can fit all of that in. Do you agree?'

Yves basked; he would look powerful and influential, a role that he relished as his growing wealth insulated him from day-to-day business. He started to practice his most elegant stance.

'I think you've talked me into an expensive deal Monica,' Yves said softly.

'Thank you. I think it will serve us both well. Zoe is available to schedule the sittings from the beginning of next month. I will look forward to meeting you three weeks after that,' said Monica.

Yves returned to the Alston headquarters feeling very pleased. Even the weather was fine. He entered the modern building, admiring the imposing façade and new signage. His appointment with the marketing team was on the third floor, where the team of eight was assembled ready to discuss their plans for a major campaign for the new product.

'I'm sure I don't need to tell you that this new project is make or break. The Board is looking for a high-end, saturation media strategy which will reap maximum benefit for the company in the first months,' Yves stressed.

'I'm on the case,' said Damien, the marketing executive whose eyes gleamed at the thought of the bonuses. 'We've planned max exposure via mobile, news and editorial. Social media on steroids, YouTube and Internet chat to generate interest, plus the usual paid avenues. Third party reports will give it credibility,' he outlined. 'Massive promise – no detail – it's a marketer's wet dream. We've already got twenty angles for the social – we'll go viral.'

'To make money we needed to convert interest into sales. Position and price are crucial,' said Yves. 'I need an inspired distribution network, and fabulous design of all the packaging and promotions to generate sales at this high price point to generate maximum returns. We also need all the disclaimers double-checked and correctly placed to meet all the legal requirements. The last thing we want is a lawsuit on our hands.'

'We're hoping you will front some of the media Yves. Right image and being so important in the company gives great credibility.'

'Of course,' Yves preened and told them about the portrait and the articles with the magazine. They all understood the value of key advocates to place the new product in the right price bracket. The plan was to sell very small amounts at very high prices to create status, demand and, of course, profits. Yves hoped the slick team could exploit this opportunity to maximum advantage.

That night, safely back in his apartment in Paris, Yves dreamt of a network of private clinics and a waiting list of super-rich clients. The company would restrict supply quickly of course. Scarcity was part of the plan. No supermarket shelves. Yves was excited in a way he hadn't been for years. Money, cornering the market, and the prospect of a fine elixir from which he could personally and financially benefit were exhilarating. His star was in the ascendency as up-to-date results flowed from the research team.

When the product was released, Yves would ensure that the research team was entrained in the process to mitigate his risk. He was always a good risk manager. If anything went wrong, he could escape without obligation.

Chapter 32

Yves Decides

Yves decided to take the drug after seeing the latest results from Africa. They were compelling. He'd read and analysed the data more than a dozen times and convinced himself the researchers were being too tentative about the need for long term testing. Timid never succeeded in business. Scientists always erred on the side of caution. Yves didn't have time to waste; each year made him look older.

He dialled the number of his old colleague Jerome at the African station in Sierra Leone.

'I need one of the three-month samples returned to me,' Yves said.

'You're the boss,' said Jerome, a loyal employee of long standing who always did whatever he was asked.

Very handy having Jerome, Yves reflected. He'd 'gone native' many years ago after appreciating the benefits of a big shady house on the banks of the mighty river where he loved to fish and a house full of servants he could never afford in France.

'How's the fishing,' said Yves.

'Fabulous,' said Jerome. 'The fish in Africa are like the land itself, wild, big and dangerous. Tiger fishing last month was great.'

'Good thing we pay you well. Don't forget among the odd jobs, we expect and pay for discretion. This work is not just sourcing subjects, make sure you store products well and dispose of any inconvenient things.'

'I've explained the villagers in the region are poor and they welcome the small payments, we make to *volunteers*. Life is often short and uncertain here. The subjects don't ask questions. I make sure I pay the right people. I know how things work here.'

'Good,' said Yves.

'So, you want a sample back. Should I ask why?' said Jerome.

'No. I don't pay you to ask questions.'

'Happy to oblige,' Jerome said. 'No skin off my nose to send a parcel back.'

Jerome's got it easy this time Yves thought. Nobody liked deaths, even Jerome. It strained his relationship with the village.

Yves had instructed that after the initial trials, high doses were tested before the research teams controlled longer term and lower dose trials. Yves ensured that Jerome never knew the full details but would receive products and instructions about the way they should be administered and what should be measured.

'So, you've trained the locals and they're doing all the reporting now?' said Yves.

'Yes, all the measurements are done by the staff. They're convinced that western medical knowledge will pave their way to a better future,' said Jerome.

'So apart from photographs, they are taking detailed measurements of height, weight, skin thickness, the location of subcutaneous fat deposits and any symptoms like nausea or irritation,' said Yves.

'Yes, that's what the research team specified. I supervised the first sets. After the initial measurements and photographs are recorded, readings are taken for comparison each week for three months. The first results showed no negative effects; the subjects looked well and have reported no ill effects. Even I can see an improvement.'

'Well, the before and after photographs suggest that too,' said Yves.

'Medical tests are always a bit of a gamble. I guess,' said Jerome. 'It was a relief to do these rather than some others I remember with, shall we say, inconvenient side effects.'

'I look forward to the next set of results. Don't forget, results to me as well as the research team.' Yves said.

Yves started taking the drug as soon as the samples arrived from Africa. He monitored his reflection with great attention, anticipating improvements like those he saw in the photographs.

Yves followed each set of experimental results carefully, analysed the trend graphs and studied the photographs. Even though the majority of the test subjects were not beautiful and often not young, there was no doubt that beneficial effects could be seen after the first three months of treatment. Of all his deals and all his successes, this one was giving him the biggest thrill.

At one of the regular bi-monthly briefings with Yves, Nathan announced the team's breakthroughs in identifying the mechanisms of action.

'We hope to expand our results to other aspects of ageing beyond skin thinning. We're now convinced that the drug turns on genes that are active in childhood but become quiescent in adulthood. When our initial hypothesis failed to support that theory, we discarded it, but we now can say with confidence that the extract is insulating the ends of the telomeres and stopping them unravelling,' Nathan continued with enthusiasm.

'You know I find the technical language difficult, Nathan,' Yves said. 'Can I summarise by saying that turning genes back on results in skin thickening?'

'Yes, yes,' replied Nathan shaking his head with impatience.

Yves shrugged off the criticism. It was working. He saw dollar signs and his wrinkles vanishing. He was a happy man.

The company's Directors and shareholders would be happy too. It would be premature to share the good news with them. Yves wanted to benefit from the drug and his investment.

He prepared his arguments for a bigger a share offer to increase the company's working capital at the next board meeting. Nathan's team was good but they, and the extensive testing that was needed in Europe, would be expensive. The new share offer and options would raise the necessary capital. The other Directors would not know that Yves had arranged to purchase most of the shares and thousands of share options, through a series of subsidiary companies that he controlled, but kept well hidden.

'You're looking good,' Bettina said as she massaged Yves face. 'What new products are you using?' He smiled. It was working.

During the board meeting later in the day, the figures outlining the performance of the company for the previous year were released. The company results were solid, even without the new formulation. Although preliminary test results were available, Yves convinced the research team to delay the latest reports until after the AGM. Careful timing of these announcements was necessary to maximise his profits. Yves was confident, and in control. The board granted him the requested additional share options. The research results were more promising than those he shared. Yves relished being in control and the attention and free promotion that he, and the company, would get from the positive media exposure. He imagined the share prices soaring.

Chapter 33

The Art of Living

Zoe decided to stay with Monica in her already crowded two-bedroom flat until after Yves' portrait was complete. Money was short and she could paint at George's gallery. There would be time to find a new flat when she received her first big payment. She trusted the isolation and happy memories of Langhorne Creek to help her heal. It had worked. Now, back in London, Monica's company was welcome, and the commission gave her purpose and a timeline.

Strangely, the damp air and threat of rain from the steely sky felt as familiar as the wide blue skies of South Australia. Zoe realised with relief that she could block out painful memories of David most of the time, even though this location had been so filled with his presence. Much to her surprise she even welcomed the steady thrum of traffic noise. It was good to see and hear bustling people and businesses thriving among the historic architecture.

London was always vibrant. People and opportunities jostled. Zoe was captivated anew by the dream, the dream that lured many with ambition to live and work in big cities around the world. She would reinvent herself; build her reputation and connect with a broader range of wealthy buyers. She'd work hard and mix with the right people.

Zoe savoured the frisson of excitement and the adrenalin rush, which starting a new painting created. The feeling was almost sexual, a quickening of the pulse, an unsettling buzz deep in the gut. Sometimes she imagined sufficient wealth to pursue her art free of the market, but there was no doubt that staring poverty square in the face helped her focus. She could live simply in Langhorne Creek, but money made the world go around in London. And apart from the money, this commission was a welcome challenge.

Monica's flat in Wandsworth near Putney High Street was just two streets back from the Thames. As Zoe stepped outside, she heard the boats, which still carried freight and people across the slick, surly water, which had served as grave and sewer for this great city for centuries. It carried stories in every inch of its sediment. The river may be cleaner than it had been for centuries and the fish might be back, but Zoe still imagined dark deeds, clandestine deliveries and secret disposals occurring under the cover of darkness.

To celebrate her first day back, she indulged in a favourite treat – coffee, and luscious pastry at *Giuliano's* on the banks of the river near Putney, before heading off to see George. Zoe sniffed the heady scent of aromatic coffee. The smell was almost enough. While coffee houses were hotbeds of politics, sex and sedition earlier in London's history, now the ritual of mid-morning coffee was shared over no greater plots than office politics and weekend amusements. Zoe wondered how many of the morning crowd knew the chequered history of coffee, its links with rebellion and prostitution. She scraped the remnants of mille feuille from her plate and watched the hypnotic river stream.

Well-fortified, she walked on to the bus stop heading to her usual art supplier near George's studio. Wrapped in her thoughts, she marvelled at the strange feeling of privacy that came from being anonymous in a big city. People may surround her, but they hurried past without curiosity or impact despite close proximity.

Public transport was so easy in London. Bus, train or tubes went everywhere at high frequency following routes, which even Zoe, map-challenged as she was, could decipher. From Monica's apartment, the buses crossed Putney Bridge, providing easy access to most parts of the city with one swipe of her oyster card. She had made the trip so many times that she slipped into the routine as easily as an old pair of ugg boots. The number 14 bus was her regular. Then she followed the roll call of stops, off at Onslow Square through Sydney Place around Walton Street near Brompton Road then around the corner. Zoe instantly recognised the maze of narrow curving streets near George's gallery. Among the eclectic, ever-changing window displays of the dozen nearby galleries, George's passion, *The Gem* stood out. The display was fresh, energetic, marking his style in a world jostling for attention.

'Hello George, only me' she called as she walked through the door.

'Welcome back my lovely,' he gushed, warmly hugging Zoe as she came through the gilded doorway to his office.

'Wow, you must be doing well,' Zoe said, seeing the recent refurbishments and walls crowded with new works.

'Come and meet my new major exhibitor, Salvatore. He brings Brazilian jungle colours and exuberance to the grey landscapes of London.'

As Salvatore joined them, Zoe sensed that there might be more behind George's enthusiasm than professional artistic merit. Usually, George segregated business and private life, otherwise, it was too easy to lose money.

'I love your bold colours, Salvatore,' said Zoe. 'They should sell well. Commercial acumen is George's major strength in this cutthroat world.'

'You know as well as I do that paintings need an edge; a voice greater than artistic merit,' gushed George. 'Haven't I already convinced you that your painting will be a mere hobby unless you can sell your works in the same decade that you paint them? Better to sell them even before you have finished them, and for a good price.'

'Stop, stop, George, I surrender,' Zoe laughed. 'I have returned focussed. I'm committed to being financially successful with these portraits. Your single job after that is to help me sell other brilliant works that I will create.'

As they continued the tour of his gallery, Zoe hoped she could capture the essence of her subject. That elusive quality was essential to avoid being a purveyor of mere representation. She and George had talked for hours about the coded messages implicit in the objects used in historical portraits. They told the hidden stories of the subject's life and times. Erudition, interests, fidelity, even fertility and hence desirability for marriage in times gone by, was conveyed by the choice of fabrics, flowers and objects chosen to accompany the subject. Nothing was random, nothing without meaning. It was decoration to the untutored, yet rich with embedded meaning to those who could read the clues.

'Money, money, money, it all comes to money to live the high life in London,' said George as he steered Zoe back to his office and Salvatore left.

'You know me George, I'm not seeking too much of the high life, but I do need good food and good wine and plenty of space to paint.' At Langhorne Creek, Zoe had been frugal, eating little, spending less, and there was no need to pay rent. That sort of life was not possible in London where the prices were high. 'Remember no starving in the garret,' George reminded her.

'Apart from the delight of seeing you George, I need to prepare my canvas for Rouen. I've some ideas, and he's got a brilliant face.'

'Be careful, my love. It might be a little too soon for an entanglement. I bet he'll fancy you though. That'll make you feel good.'

Zoe smiled as she left George's. He always made her feel better. She hoped that Salvatore was not a sponge. George needed love in his life too.

Back at Monica's, Zoe prepared for the visit to Rouen and the handsome Yves. She turned up the heating, and reflected that Monica's flat, like so many in London was testament to competition for land and heating. The rooms were small, and the walls were thick. She wished the fixed radiators that circulated hot water or hot oil – Zoe never remembered which – could do more than take the chill off the air. Through the solid wooden entrance door, which looked heavy enough to withstand a siege, Monica's flat was one of four on the second floor. The communal hallway and stairwell always smelt musty from lifetimes of wet umbrellas, damp shoes and too little sunshine. The steps had worn treads and bald patches on the carpet from generations of steps. Inside the flat was all Monica. Cheerful Moroccan rugs covered the dun carpet, colourful throws brightened the stolid furniture and bright prints lined the walls. It was a tropical bowerbird's nest crammed with books, papers and memorabilia.

As she mechanically washed dishes, Zoe looked forward to the sensual delight of blending colours, the fresh smells of the oils and the pull of paint on canvas. It gave her great satisfaction to transform ideas into a tangible object. But, to create a portrait of quality, she needed to capture the essence of her subject. That was why her first meeting was so important She would need to look deeply and understand the nuances in his face and the movement of his body. She sighed. Birds were not so demanding, but then they didn't pay so well either.

'I must paint you one day Monica,' she said as the friends met for dinner.'On one level you'd be easy. Hard hair though. Beautiful black but the wildness! Besides you couldn't sit still long enough!'

Zoe loved Monica's mobile face for the way she reached out and embraced or challenged and never stood back aloof. A generous mouth dominated her beautiful face. It was always active, eating, drinking, laughing, and talking, without pause. This stream of sound was her umbilical cord to the world, a two-way exchange which sustained her and provided data and drama which she grabbed and shook like a terrier. Anger, intrigue, frustration, joy, could flick across her face with lightning speed. Even Monica's clothes were mobile. Her flowing styles, which she described with self-deprecation as camouflage for the war zone below was dominated by clothes that always included generous pockets with zips, buttons or tabs that were often awry; her handbags with multiple compartments housed an astonishing range of objects. She would joke that her pockets could sustain her for days if there was a revolution. She moved with grace and restless action. It would be a challenge to portray her strength and restless energy. She would also need to convey the loyal, sensitive woman fuelled by a sense of justice who hid beneath the tornado.

'Back to work: Yves. I'm on the case. I've been wandering around the National Portrait Gallery in my usual quest to study the devices used to convey the lives and interests of their subjects in times gone by. I saw some wonderful scenes, often tiny, reflected with subtlety and skill through windows or mirrors. It's a clever way to tell a story behind a story. Any ideas about devices for Yves yet?'

'No, only what I've already shared. His picture's your bag. I've got too much on my plate getting the story right,' Monica said and downed her beer.

Over the past few days, Monica had prattled on with of snippets of information, but Zoe kept drifting off, preoccupied with planning the painting. From the stories of his Pacific connections, extensive travel and his ability to clinch deals, an idea was forming in Zoe's mind. A faux frame inside the frame, with tiny miniatures representing those deals. Could she imbue these images with hints of deals within deals? Zoe would ask Yves for the symbols he thought best represented his businesses. It might help Monica identify further companies.

'Pharmaceuticals seem flavour of the month for him,' Monica said. 'Before that – steel, the usual financial management weasel words, timber, wood chips, chop sticks and a host of paper products, lots of things from the Pacific.'

'Those will make a brilliant border,' said Zoe.

'Fish too Zoe. You know about seafood. Perhaps bright red snapper or even a lobster. You can make Yves look like Dali with a lobster telephone on his desk.' They collapsed into gales of laughter. 'He might even look good with a Dali moustache.'

Zoe liked working with Monica again. It felt good to laugh.

She envisaged a contemporary portrait inside a classical frame painted with symbols demonstrating his interests and the sources of his wealth. Stories within stories.

That night, Zoe's head swam with ideas and shapes. As she drifted off to sleep, surreal visions of lobsters swam Dali-like in and out of her portrait. Zoe fell asleep wondering for the millionth time what had happened to her father, her idea to search for clues was being crowded out again.

She woke with her father's disappearance close to the surface of her consciousness. She remembered laughing, screaming and running away as he chased her. Her father loved shellfish and would tease her in the kitchen by wriggling their claws as he prepared them for the pot. Zoe didn't know she retained that memory. It was uncanny. Zoe's father worked with lobster, Yves worked in the Pacific, but from what Zoe remembered, lobster only grew in very cold waters, so that connection didn't work. She needed tropical fish.

Zoe had three days to prepare for Rouen. She had pre-ordered the canvas through George; conventional cotton canvas. It painted well, lasted well and provided a reassuring link to admirable painters from the past. It even smelt healthy. Paint technology had moved faster and further than the cotton and linen canvases. The masters of old would have been jealous of the wide range and low cost of the durable paints that Zoe had available; no need to grind expensive lapis lazuli to make her blues, or risk lead poisoning from the black and white pigments. As she gathered sketching paper, pencils, charcoal and pigments she reflected that, tubes of easy colour did not reduce the challenge of producing a quality painting.

Zoe packed and repacked, then brushed her hair again. She wanted to do a good job. Not just a solid, workman-like job. While not tormented by a vision to create, she craved a portrait that would attract attention and admiration – one that satisfied her need to paint well and lead to future commissions. Fear and excitement crowed for attention raising goose bumps and making her fingers clumsy as she prepared her canvas.

Her mother's praise had been rare, so Zoe was accustomed to working hard for approval. When, at twenty, against her mother's wishes, she boldly described herself as an artist, the bravado masked deep doubt. Voicing her dream helped shape the reality. Determination and hard work began the journey, but a good dose of terror at the thought of failure could be relied on to increase her motivation. The more she feared failure, the harder she would work to avoid it.

As she checked and crosschecked her lists, Zoe relaxed. She was sufficiently prepared to avoid embarrassment. Canvas, paints and art supplies had been packed and dispatched. Then she needed to look the part. An aspiring artist, positioning herself as painter of the rich and famous could not arrive looking ordinary or gauche. She bought and packed new clothes, which she had chosen to blend with the elegant surroundings in which she would spend the next days. Denim jeans and comfortable shirts might be OK for Langhorne Creek, but it was time to slip back into a London skin and dress for the occasion.

Chanel perfume, her favourite, was essential. Two toothbrushes and two sorts of toothpaste; she was keen on sparkling teeth. Two new dresses and tailored trousers with matching shirt would give her options for dinners, which were likely to be more formal than a British pub or Langhorne Creek barbeque style. A stylish haircut ensured her hair behaved. New white trousers, a shirt for painting and reliable strappy sandals. She liked shoes. All fitted neatly into her small case.

Lunch with Monica was scheduled for noon before she caught the Eurostar to Paris. From there she would drive to Rouen through some of her favourite French countryside.

'You look suitably gorgeous,' said Monica as she met Zoe at The Ship Inn. 'You'll have him eating out of your hands.'

'Sure. You know my brilliant track record with men,' Zoe laughed, completely unaware that she looked exquisite. 'I did get a nice email from Michael. He wants to keep in touch. That made me feel good. Nice place,' she said as they ducked under the low lintel. 'Perfect for lunch. A comfortable blend of old and new.' The thick walls seemed to grow from the landscape and the name reflected trade of an older sort.

'Oh yum, plenty of choices on the menu,' said Zoe. Eating helped the nervous flutters in her stomach. Traditional favourites like roast beef and beer battered fish and chips vied for attention among curries and Asian stir-fries. The waiting staff, young people of many nationalities offered friendly service and the pub's location on the riverbank provided relaxing views and a quiet place to talk. Monica and Zoe ordered and settled back to talk business.

'I'll take care of the article,' said Monica. 'Any information you can glean about Yves' background would help. Richard and I are still puzzled by a complete lack of information about how he made his early money.' Fragrant fish and speckled hen beer arrived.

'I think the key will be to gain Yves' trust and flatter him into feeling comfortable and superior. Just encourage him to talk about himself. Most men like that.'

'My first priority is painting,' said Zoe. 'We know he's a ladies' man, so getting him to talk should be easy enough.'

'The best bet is probably to keep yourself at a distance. He is reputed to be extremely persuasive and very sexy,' Monica warned.

'Don't worry. Remoteness may be my most alluring attribute. You know I am naturally good at that,' Zoe smiled. 'I've had a lot of practice.'

'After the first sittings at Rouen are completed, I might have additional information. Then we can regroup and identify anything else we might need. The second sitting in London is not for another month. Then my article is not due for another month after that, so there's time to gather our thoughts and plan the next steps,' Monica said.

Monica's research suggested Montreau had left a trail of destruction – shattered dreams, wasted investment, and empty wallets – across the globe for the last twenty years, but she did not want to prejudice Zoe's ability to gather information or influence the painting. There would be plenty of time to expand on her theories later.

'OK I'm ready,' said Zoe.

'Good luck, and don't forget to reply to the South Australian Michael,' Monica said.

'He sounds delicious. I need a picture.'

'Google him then,' Zoe said as she set off full of expectation and excitement to catch the Eurostar. Monica stayed to meet Richard. His cryptic message hinted that he had made an interesting discovery. Half an hour later, as his tall lean frame appeared in the doorway, Monica could see from the lurking smile on his face that he had news.

Chapter 34

A Glimpse of Rouen

Battling through the crowds at St Pancras station in London, Zoe was relieved she had couriered her canvas, paper and supplies ahead. They were not heavy but would have been awkward to manage in the crowd. She checked her E-ticket against the flashing information boards, confirmed the correct loading platform and wheeled her small case to the Eurostar platform. After finding her carriage she boarded, pleased to be on time and out of the hustle and bustle of the crowds.

Settling into the comfortable seat, Zoe was conscious of two sensations she had not felt for over a year. She was eagerly anticipating her work and she thought she looked good. Yves had a reputation for being charming, very much the ladies' man. That could be entertaining. His face imagined from the photos she had been sent, and the Internet of course, was appealing. Her portrait must offer significantly more than an identification shot or a family snap to justify all the extra time and effort. Acknowledging this difference had been key to convincing the magazine editors to have the series of portraits rather than standard photographs.

The targets Monica selected had money as well as big egos. George's idea to ask the subjects to pay for the portrait helped. Magazines were a cutthroat business. Getting the subjects to pay was often easier than convincing them to commit the time necessary to do the interviews and get the portrait painted. But Zoe worked at putting the subjects at ease, and once the work started, it was usually enjoyable.

Monica had negotiated a ten-part series. One feature each month except for the madness of Christmas and holiday January. It would be a big year. The editor had already endorsed Monica's choice of subjects and left the negotiations about the portrait payments to her. The magazine would also sponsor the portrait launch and the subject would pay for, and keep, the painting with the magazine holding publishing rights. Everyone knew the portrait would be written off as a legitimate business expense. A good portrait could build status and reputation for both the subject and the painter.

As the train effortlessly pulled away from London, Zoe hoped she had recovered from David's betrayal. She told herself she was only one year older but a great deal wiser; her wounds had been serious but not fatal. A successful painting would be the key to re-establishing discipline and purpose in her life. Painting allowed her to escape from her demons, lose herself in work and re-establish a productive life. That was why she had turned to drawing in her childhood. Since she had resumed painting, she felt alive again.

In Rouen, Yves was keenly anticipating Zoe's arrival. He was accustomed to surrounding himself with the good things money could buy. He enjoyed houses, fine food and wine, the right clothes, and attractive or powerful people. It was all a game. He played it well and relished his success. It gave him an endless selection of playthings and provided opportunities for seduction, which was always on his mind.

Feeling proud about having a portrait painted, he felt it an elegant throwback to earlier times. Lately though, he caught himself looking in the mirror more often. He had a flutter of nervousness realising that a good portrait showed character. What would Zoe see? He wanted her to see an attractive man of taste and elegance, at the peak of his powers. As he caught a reflection of himself in a harsh light, he feared that she might see an aging man, a man beyond his prime, or horror of horrors, an ugly man. He cringed. He would rouse himself from this morbid thought and make another appointment for a massage, manicure or haircut. His team of personal carers were always flattering and banished negative thoughts.

Yves selected the country house at Rouen to meet Zoe and have the initial sittings. He looked forward to impressing her with his delightfully decorated mansion. Several rooms with tall windows should be suitable to channel the natural light. Staff members of the Rouen house were discreet; he had often used the house for assignations. He wanted the portrait, but he also wanted to have a good time.

His wife, Adriana was conveniently far away on one of her endless shopping trips somewhere in Italy. He vaguely remembered it was sculpture this time, or was she moving to mosaics? She would return soon enough with boxes of statues and a marble limb or two, all of which he would have to admire. Still, that was a small price to pay for a month of peace, quiet and the opportunity for amusement, without her.

The house was a short leafy walk from the village, across the narrow bridge and along the grassy bank of the river, which formed a natural edge to the north side of the property. As the time approached for Zoe's arrival, Yves mentally reviewed the arrangements. All was in order. Staff members would deliver excellent catering at the house. That would be more discrete than eating in one of the restaurants in the town. Yves did not want to encourage local gossip. If Zoe was amenable, and Yves was confident she would be, he did not want intrusions. The house was big enough to keep secrets.

The first sitting would occupy most of the scheduled three days, and Zoe had accepted his invitation to stay. That should give him plenty of time. He had studied photographs of Zoe and was looking forward to another challenge. It was a long time since he had seen an Australian woman who looked so elegant and attractive. Distant memories of that year so long ago in Australia were vague but most of the women he recalled had been far too hearty and robust for his taste. They had been strong and independent, but too often the sun turned young skins old and leathery before their time. He had been pleased to move to New Caledonia where the musical French language and the soft coffee-coloured skins wove a gentler and more pleasing feminine tableau against the tropical lushness.

After a smooth rail journey, Zoe collected a sleek black Peugeot 308CC from the car hire depot at Paris Gare Du Nord and began to drive on the bright, dry morning. While she enjoyed the convenience of public transport in London, it was a joy to drive a good car on the open roads of the impeccably neat French countryside. Satellite navigation had transformed her experience of driving. She relaxed remembering that maps and French road signs were no match for a contemporary GPS. After typing in her destination, she chose a scenic route rather than all motorways and felt her spirits lift as she cleared the suburbs and was soon enveloped by green fields and neat forests.

Perhaps coming from the Mediterranean climate of Australia, she might have been attracted to the south with its warmer weather and casual atmosphere, but she loved the order and slightly restrained landscape of Northern Normandy that was a scant two-hour drive from Paris. The area had been immortalised through the works of the impressionist painters who travelled cheaply into the countryside on the railways built in the nineteenth century.

Zoe relished feeling part of the rich and successful tradition of painters who had made their names if not their fortunes here. Monet, Matisse many of the impressionists had painted the landscapes and people of this land. As she passed Giverny, she remembered Monet's work. Huge paintings of his gardens and especially the waterlily pond were recognised around the world. Waterlilies had never been the same. His house and gardens had been preserved and prints from his paintings abounded. Such was the power of art. Zoe resolved to come back again soon to visit Honfleur and explore the cider and calvados producing areas of Normandy.

As the landscape reeled by, Zoe admired the earthy harmonious colours and traditional stone and tile fabric of the villages. Even the ruins of castles and fortifications had lost their association with violent times and represented peace and picnics in the bucolic countryside.

To Zoe, Monet's painting of the Gothic cathedral symbolised Rouen. During its long history, the cathedral had suffered the ravages of time, wars, lightening, and bombs. All had taken their toll. Zoe was pleased to see scaffolding in place signalling major restoration. Driving past the modern monument that marked the location where Jeanne D'Arc had been burned in the town at the tender age of 19, Zoe reflected that the church never appreciated strong women. Ironically, Joan was now a Saint, but it came too late for her to enjoy. Aware of the distance remaining to make the planned lunch appointment with Yves, she pressed on, making a mental note to explore the town later.

The car's navigation system directed her flawlessly to Rue du Bel Event, which was only a few kilometres north of the city centre, in a green and pleasant part of the city fringe. Yves' chateau rather tritely named *BienVue* was first visible down a long double avenue of plane trees. Forests in this region had probably supplied timber for every purpose from housing to war ships for hundreds of years. There were gardens on a grand scale, rather than the untidy forests of her native South Australia. The tall strong trunks and uniformity of form were so European. While Zoe missed the familiar smell of eucalypts, the artist in her was drawn to the lush woods of northern France

She admired the setting and the balanced proportions of the house. The size and shape of doors, windows and balconies combined to create an overall impression of effortless harmony, and the honey-coloured stone toned into the landscape. Zoe arrived as scheduled, relishing her challenge, exhilarated by the drive and delighted by the countryside. It was a heady mix.

Yves was immediately captivated as she unfolded long legs and stepped from the car. He saw a face that was radiant. It shone with health and excitement. Her hair was long and free, and her tall, slim figure full of controlled energy. As Yves welcomed her to the house, he felt more than his spirits rise.

'Welcome,' he said holding her hand. 'Do come inside. I will get one of the staff to manage your luggage.'

As Zoe met Yves in the flesh, she thought he was far more attractive than his photos.

The housekeeper showed Zoe to a spacious, light filled room. Her case had been neatly placed in an antique armoire. Vases of dusty pink roses scented the air and matched the wallpaper and the bedspread, which also featured rosebuds and girls in 19th century costumes on swings. Around the half-closed shutters that kept the room deliciously cool, fragrant climbing roses framed the windows. Zoe, almost overwhelmed by roses, freshened up in the small bathroom, which was only slightly less floral, and prepared to meet Yves for lunch.

She walked back down the wide staircase, admiring the high ceilings and rooms, which unfolded in every direction. Everything was large, the tables, the urns of flowers, even the massive fireplaces. The housekeeper directed her to a small table that had been set on the balcony overlooking the garden at the rear of the house. Herb borders perfumed the warm air with the zesty scents of thyme and marjoram as she walked over the massive flagstones crushing the herbs that grew in the cracks.

'This is a beautiful house in a marvellous setting,' said Zoe gesturing vaguely at the manicured gardens.

'Thank you,' said Yves. 'It is delightful in this warm weather.'

The starched white cloth and gleaming cutlery made the simple meal exotic. Chevre salad and fresh fruits were perfect for the warm day. Rich red juice sparkled, jewel-like in the crystal decanter.

'Juice?' he asked. 'It's pomegranate. Did you know the Moors brought pomegranates to France?' Yves said as Zoe admired the taste and subtle efficiency of the household.

'Together with many other foods, beautiful architecture and mathematics, but perhaps not the wine,' Zoe replied.

'No more thank you,' said Zoe who was enjoying the lightly chilled Chablis. She laughingly covered her glass as Yves moved to refill it. 'I want to work this afternoon, and if I drink a second glass, I won't be able to concentrate.'

Lunch was a promising beginning for them both. The food, the wine and the setting created the perfect ambience. The conversation was light as they both felt their way. After lunch, they walked back down the wide stone staircase and Yves showed Zoe the main rooms on the ground floor, so she could consider the best setting for the painting. High ceilings and tall windows gave all the rooms a generous, airy feeling which was amplified by the afternoon light streaming from the west.

'This will be a beautiful room to paint in,' she said as they reached the salon Yves had privately chosen but left until last. Zoe practically skipped around the room, delighted by the pale, non-distracting cream colours and the floor to ceiling mainly glass doors, which opened on to the terrace and then the garden. 'This is perfect.'

Yves thought how perfect Zoe looked in his house.

As she stepped outside to admire the view from the balcony, she wondered how much this garden revealed about its owner. The formal design made the front garden almost a living extension of the house. Yves may be a classicist, or more likely he had bought the house after the garden had been established. Huge urns and dark sculpted cypress trees planted in long clean lines with neat edges framed the geometric forms of the carefully chosen trees. A garden for display, she thought. Not a garden for living in or for dogs to play. I'll bet I couldn't find a vegetable anywhere, she thought. Or there might be a kitchen garden placed neatly out of sight. This was a garden for the rich and idle to display themselves and their wealth. Beautiful though, just like Yves.

Reluctantly they left the sunny balcony with the calming green view and fragrant breeze.

'To work,' she said and paced around the chosen room.

'Do you have a preference for a pose?' she asked.

'No, that is your speciality.'

Zoe selected a place near the window for Yves to sit, for she had already decided on a seated pose. She was glad she didn't have to waste time talking him into it. As she moved his body and adjusted the position of his arms, Yves' nostrils twitched a little. Zoe felt that he would have a poker face in business negotiations but as her body moved close she sensed his slight intake of breath.

Zoe studied him closely with the permission of her art and thought *I bet he used man creams long before the marketers even thought of calling them that.* She admired his skin and, as she moved to position his head, was very aware of the dusky scent of his woody aftershave. His skin contrasted the sun-scarred faces of people who lived in the harsh sun of Australia and the beautiful young girls with "peaches and cream" complexions in England. Here in France, Yves had found a central path between English porcelain and the harsh "le tan" leather of French sun worshippers. His face was tanned without excess, groomed to perfection, and as he gestured toward the window, she realised even his fingers were beautifully manicured.

'I need to know which way the shadows will fall,' she explained. 'I suggest we spend the rest of this afternoon finding the right chair, choosing your clothes and experimenting with angles,' she said. 'I have a general concept in mind and would like to be sure that you are comfortable with it. After all, you may have to look at it on your walls for many years.'

'I'm relying on you to make me look good Zoe,' Yves smiled back.

Zoe selected a carved mahogany chair, which shone with years of gentle polish. Its wide back curved protectively and would frame his torso well. The deep purple velvet upholstery was so dark as to be almost black. It avoided crass comparisons of pseudo-royalty, Zoe thought with relief. He may think he is the king but that would be too much. She would also leave out the royalist allusions of fleur-de-lis pattern around the table.

As Yves took Zoe to the dressing room to consider the clothes that he was suggesting, she felt the frisson of excitement arc between them.

'Grey eyes, grey tie, grey suit – but you are anything but a grey man.' He smiled warmly in response. 'I think you have chosen well. Grey wool suit, white shirt, the pale lavender touches in the tie and single deep violet chair will fit well in this room. The cool colours will contrast well with your striking dark hair. It's an interesting choice.'

Zoe set up her easel and paper and began some sketches. From his seated position Zoe could feel Yves studying her closely, but while she worked, he was a subject, not an amusement.

Zoe occasionally dived forward, repositioned his arm, tilted his head and moved back to her sketching. Twice, three, four times she asked him the change the angle of the chair or his body. She prowled around the room and adjusted the curtains. She vigorously tore three initial sketches from her easel and threw them crumpled, to the ground. She sketched swiftly. Finally, she paused. Then she was very specific.

'Now before you get up, without moving the chair, I want you to remember exactly how you are sitting. You need to remember your arms, the tilt of your head, the angle of your back. Everything. Do you think you can do that?'

Yves smiled, concentrated, and stepped away. Then to her amazement he sat again and repositioned himself. He was good, very good. Not perfect but definitely good. This was a man aware of, and in control of his body. Zoe was impressed.

'It must be cocktail hour,' he said.

Zoe had her preliminary sketches, and the work was taking shape in her head. As they walked through the house, Zoe noticed a small, mirrored cabinet with an exquisite collection of delicate white porcelain.

'This is beautiful Yves. Will you tell me about it?'

'Just an old hobby of mine. Chinese work. About 300 years old.' Yves reached in a selected a milky white piece and held it up to the light. To her amazement, she could see a multi-coloured ship figured within the clay.

'It is exquisite.'

'Not easy to find these days, but I was lucky to collect this many years ago.'

Drinks on the balcony, were elegantly presented on a tray with extra ice. A tiny crystal vase held a single white freesia and its spicy fragrance coiled around them in the warm afternoon sun. It was tasteful, peaceful. A tractor mowed in the fields away beyond the garden, scenting the air with fresh green fragrance. A few birds sang and sounds from the roads were faint and far away.

Yves had chosen anisette, possibly the one French drink that Zoe had never warmed to, and Zoe, partly to test this French household chose Pimms. When prepared well, it was her English summer drink of choice, and somehow, she thought it would be prepared well. She was not disappointed. The proportions of Pimms and soda were correct, the cucumber crisp and the citrus juice and mint sharpened the taste to make it deeply refreshing. As they sat on the terrace, the warmth of the day mellowed, the shadows deepened, and the world seemed perfectly ordered.

'Tell me your story, Yves. It will help me understand your face.'

'My current fascination is with pharmaceuticals and the promise they offer to make us live longer, healthier lives. It's an exciting field. The astonishing capacity of new drugs and medicines is growing fast, and I'm pleased to be part of it.'

Zoe smiled to encourage him to elaborate.

'For many years I was involved with making products like steel and selling goods, often wonderful ones but selling is not as amusing as creating new products.' His face glowed in the evening light.

'And are you interested in the art world?' she asked after ten minutes of the inner working of his new product which she did not understand.

'Not really, I tend to remember people, galleries and places I have visited more than the works themselves. I know what I don't like.'

'I'd better be careful then.'

As he left briefly Zoe admired the symmetry of his face combined with his cool approach and immaculate grooming. Like a snake she thought, mesmerising. But was he a parody of perfection? As he had talked, Zoe sensed that his remoteness was contrived, and he practiced careful mastery of his emotions. His exquisite face came to life as he relaxed in this comfortable setting.

'Mmmm Krug champagne, one of my favourites,' Zoe crooned as Yves poured. 'I first tried it in London. I've lived there over seven years now. How long have you been here?'

'Well, the house has been here about 200 years. I can only claim about 10 of those.'

'I wonder how many people I can paint in 10 years?' she mused. 'It's interesting looking back. 10 years passes so quickly.'

'Sometimes that's true, it passes in a flash. I hope we will get to know each other better,' Yves said looking seductive through lowered lids.

Zoe blushed and wished she had learned some of Monica's clever interview techniques.

Changing tack to deflect Yves' romantic intensity, Zoe spoke about people she had painted years ago who seemed to retain their good looks. This interested Yves, especially after she spoke at length about the way she observed the differences in the rate of the ageing process in various people.

'Australians are acutely aware these days of the danger of skin cancer and the rapid aging which sun exposure brings.' Zoe was careful to keep the conversation neutral, not of course about Yves.

That night, as he returned to his room, Yves realised the conversation had been toxic to his libido. He was very attracted to Zoe and was mortified to be talking about the inevitability of ageing. What was happening to him? Clearly, he was losing his touch. Instead of seduction he was discussing vitamins and dietary supplements. But it certainly got him thinking even if the thoughts were not comfortable ones.

Doubting his virility for the first time, he was particularly interested in his emails from the research team. Nathan's results from the laboratory were encouraging, and the fourth set of results from the trials in Africa was very exciting. Yves read the emails with mounting enthusiasm. The test subjects had been given significant doses of the new compounds, and this was now the fifth month of the trials. The indications of success were captured by physical measurements, which included metabolic rate, skin density samples as well as the subjects' responses to a suite of questions about general health. The skin density was important because of its involvement in wrinkling and the thinning of skin which first showed as ageing on the back of hands and around the eyes. Metabolic rate influenced energy levels and resistance to disease. It was the unanticipated reports of increased libido that also interested Yves. It was important to him to keep looking good, but he also wanted to continue to feel that edge.

The research team reported that, as the results from Africa had been so positive, they recommended starting trials in Europe as quickly as possible to meet the registration requirements. Yves revelled in his earlier decision to start taking the drug; he might even become famous as the earliest recipient of the treatment in Europe. He refused to think of himself as a test subject, he was simply an early adopter, the initial beneficiary of this cutting-edge research. How lucky that he was in the right place at the right time. He carried the thought forward in his imagination. He had visions of himself in twenty years' time, still looking as handsome as ever and richer, much richer. This treatment would earn him record profits. His confidence restored, he eagerly anticipated the next few days.

In the quiet moments during the sitting the next day, Yves thought about his childhood and what he might say if the need arose. He could invent something when necessary, but the truth would never see the light of day. Still, the afternoon passed easily, with him doing almost all the talking. Yves was surprised how much he enjoyed her interest. Zoe's detachment was not false or hollow; it made her infinitely more desirable than any woman he had pursued for years.

By dinner on the second day, they were warm and comfortable with each other. They had developed a pleasant intimacy from being together companionably for many hours. Zoe talked about Monica and her determination. Yves laughed as he recounted how she had been very successful in negotiating for the portrait. Zoe shared with Yves that she had been to university with Monica and that even so many years ago, Monica had been brash and forthright.

'My mother always said that Monica had *more front than John Martins*,' Zoe said. Yves smiled as if he recognised the slang, and the conversation continued.

On this second night, they enjoyed another beautifully prepared dinner and excellently matched wines. A crisp riesling with the cold cucumber soup. Then seared scallops on a pea puree, followed by a pinot noir with the duck. Each course was skilfully conceived, cooked and served with care and attention to detail.

'You seem to appreciate seafood. Do you have a favourite?' Zoe asked.

'You Australians are lucky having such long white beaches surrounding Australia, I think it is you who have a particular fondness for seafood.'

'We also have the Pacific on our doorstep,' Zoe offered.

With every conversation lead, Zoe became aware that Yves was happy to talk about Europe but skilfully deflected questions about other places in the world. As they walked around the garden in the bright moonlight, they both relaxed. It had been a delightful day. Yves was very keen, very attentive. Zoe seemed attracted, but much to Yves' disappointment maintained her distance.

As Zoe slept, she dreamed. She was digging cockles out of the sand with her toes as her father held her hands. They were on her beloved Goolwa beach where the white sand stretched in a long curve that she used to believe went on forever. Her father was laughing. She felt so happy. On Goolwa beach you could find lunch by twisting your feet in the sand as the tide came in and the sand and the water combined to make a slurry. Then, with hands or feet, you could feel the smooth cockle shells hidden in the sand and just pick them out.

In her dream, Zoe felt her father tall above her. His strong hands held her against the waves as the sand and water swirled around her legs. Then his big body blocked out the sun and the sunny world went dark. There was a man and a ship crawling with lobster. The darkness increased, and the noise of the storm and the rushing water thundered in her ears. She woke with a start and realised the sound of the wind was real.

After two beautiful sunny days, a cold change had arrived with strong winds. The leaves rattled angrily, and loose shutters slammed in the wind. Zoe's dream lingered as she looked outside to see that the racing clouds had changed the morning sky from blue to grey. She felt cold and alone. If only she knew. If only her father had stayed. Zoe felt the loss like stones on her chest.

The sunny terrace, which they had enjoyed yesterday morning, swirled with dust and leaves. They ate breakfast indoors. Zoe was subdued; she was a little frightened of the quiet intimacy and attraction that had developed so quickly between them. She was unsettled by her dream and perhaps too many glasses of wine last night. In contrast, Yves was alert. Zoe excited him. The next sitting meant he would be in London soon where he would catch up with the research team.

Zoe worked diligently for the next two hours, burying herself in her work. Yves was patient, thoughtful and charming. Zoe had to resist the desire to fall into his arms. She wanted the warmth and excitement that he offered. All too soon, she was scheduled to leave, drive back to Paris and catch her train to London. Zoe was puzzled. Yves seemed wonderful. She had discovered nothing useful to Monica, nothing suspicious.

Zoe received a text offering her a meeting about another commission and she would need to discuss it quickly if she was to secure it. The welcome prospect of more work distracted Zoe from Yves as she prepared to leave. She couldn't wait to see Monica. Could Monica be wrong about Yves? She hoped so.

Chapter 35

Action

Zoe arrived in London tired, but pleased with her work. The first stage of Yves' portrait had gone well. She was relieved her technical competence was intact – it had kicked in when she needed it, smooth as a well-maintained engine.

'Tell all,' Monica said as she bustled through the door unbundling her coat and scarf.

'I had no trouble establishing a rapport with Yves,' Zoe said smiling. 'He's gorgeous and utterly charming. If he weren't on your wanted list, I could have fallen for him in a flash. He's keen.'

'Careful,' said Monica.

'Strong feelings can be useful. One of my best portraits was of a man I disliked intensely. It allowed me to show the sharpness behind his eyes and hint at his roughness. Even his wife agreed that I portrayed him well.'

'I don't want to stop you having fun if you want Zoe, but I suspect he's a rat,' Monica warned.

'I was also surprised that Yves' English was so perfect. He wasn't even confused by some of my Australian slang,' Zoe said. 'He has a reserve about him, which makes me uneasy. Perhaps it is a cultural difference. All the people I grew up with were like open books. Europeans in big cities are different. They learn to be more circumspect, more subtle. Perhaps it's because he's French, a question of style. But his French-ness, especially the delightful accent, only adds to his allure.'

'Snails are French too. That doesn't mean I like them.'

Monica's flat was chaotic.

'My editor is being demanding. I'm preparing a new story. You know housework has never been high on my agenda, but this is worse than usual,' Monica said as Zoe moved a tumbling pile of magazines.

The next morning, Zoe decided to step up to the task. Staying rent-free, it was the least she could do. As Zoe cleaned, she thought about her love of order, her neatness. She liked everything in place; clothes, shoes, living arrangements, her life. She liked clarity, purpose, and routine. Perhaps that was what haunted her most about her father's disappearance – the pain of not knowing. In a strange way it would have been easier if his body had been found. He must be dead, mustn't he?

Zoe tidied, putting items where she hoped they could be found again. She washed and scrubbed. Monica's flat would never be neat but at least it was possible to sit on the chairs without crushing something. She piled clean mugs in the cupboard. The simple work was calming.

As Zoe worked through the morning, she thought about her vivid dream, her painting, and Monica's determination to bring Yves to justice. Monica had been keen to succeed at uni but was now a crusader for the underdog. Zoe wondered what had triggered this passion. Journalists often grew cynical rather than sympathetic. Over a cup of tea Zoe admired her cleaning. Good results came with focus and hard work. No wonder she hadn't found anything about her father, she'd been disorganised and half-hearted. Later that night, when Monica returned to a clean flat, Zoe said,

'I'm going to get serious about Dad. You're a good sleuth. Teach me your technique.'

'Well, sometimes my investigations don't amount to a hill of beans, but I'll try. Things and people just don't disappear without trace; there are usually footprints, a trail, something. You just need to find the key. Which reminds me, did you find my spare keys during the blitz?'

'Yes, down the back of the sofa, with a dozen other things.'

'I'm hungry, but don't feel like cooking,' said Monica.

'You're not messing up that kitchen' said Zoe. So the friends set off, arm in arm, to the local pub. Monica's flat was close to the Bricklayers Arms, and the surrounding streets offered a rich choice of eating places, pubs, newer wine bars and small restaurants. *The Brick* was a firm favourite. The low ceilings, leather lounges and dim walls cluttered with old photographs created a cosy atmosphere that was quintessentially British. Some nights Zoe and her friends would sprawl over the sinking leather seats drinking beer and inventing imagined lives and exploits for the moustachioed men who peered down from the sepia prints. They joked about the huge horses and carts that delivered beer and coal and how different the city would have smelt knee deep in horse manure.

'Now tell me what is happening with Richard,' Zoe said. 'You two are such good plotters, I am sure you have at least one tricky plan on the boil.' Fortified by hot and spicy curry, Monica brought Zoe up to date. In return, Monica wanted to know all about Yves.

'He is very luscious – very smooth,' Zoe said. 'Smooth like a snake I think, and maybe as slippery.'

'I think he is a big snake with a very big appetite. Poisonous too, I suspect,' Monica said. 'He's been involved with plenty. Richard's got a wad of reports thick enough to choke a horse. You remember those snippets we discovered in New Caledonia? Well Richard has set his bloodhound, Harry, on the trail and our French connection was up to his neck in multiple deals that went wrong. His trick is to set up limited liability companies, attract investors, then step back and manage the business for big fees. No risks and no losses for him.'

Monica went on and on, but Zoe's mind was on a different track. 'If Harry is so good at tracking things down, perhaps he could help me. The most viable theory, hinges on lobster. Their disappearance seems the best clue for my father's disappearance. I thought it would be useful to track down potential buyers and see if there was anything dodgy going on back then. A boatload of lobster was worth stealing. But it was a tight industry. I'll bet all the fishermen were taking more than their quotas and didn't want anyone sniffing around. I've spoken to the major buyers who were active in the region at that time. They don't have any new thoughts and seem genuine enough. They were nice about my Dad, so I don't think any of them bumped him off.'

The night was cold, and they were both tired as they walked back to the flat sharing Monica's umbrella.

'We've come a long way from uni,' Zoe mused.

'And we have a much longer way to go yet,' said Monica as she fumbled for the key. The rain changed to a steady downpour as Monica fitted the slippery key into the lock. This is the sort of rain we need in Langhorne Creek, Zoe thought. If only we could make things happen as we want them.

'Tomorrow I'll get back to the portrait. I've only got two weeks before Yves is due in London for the final sitting. At least I've got the composition decided in my head. He will emerge from a skewed frame, a trompe d'oeil piece of trickery. I'll wrap the frame with symbols of his business like coiling vines.'

Zoe drifted off to sleep listening to the rain. There was wild music playing and the storm got louder and louder until it turned into knocking on her door and she awoke with a start, her arms locked around the pillow. She groaned, groggy with sleep as Monica shouted, 'See you tonight. Time is ticking. Don't forget to ask Richard about using Harry. Yves will be back before you know it.'

Chapter 36

Reasons for Action

Zoe crawled out of bed and the familiar ache to solve her father's disappearance re-surfaced. Under a hot shower she decided to copy the way Monica researched. She would gather as many facts as possible and see if any patterns emerged. The police investigation at the time was inconclusive – Mac was a missing person. His disappearance and the loss of the lobsters seemed more than coincidence but there was no concrete evidence linking those facts. While her mother was alive, questions had been forbidden. Zoe couldn't bear to see the pain on her mother's face if the subject was mentioned. While no new facts had been identified in the past twenty years, it was also true that no one had been looking, so no surprises there. Perhaps she would see something different looking with fresh eyes through the rear vision mirror.

Giving thanks for the ease and reach of the Internet, Zoe opened her computer and accessed Trove, the National Library of Australia's web site. Dozens of newspaper articles were cited. Images of her father caused a fresh wave of sadness, but beneath the sadness there was purpose. She had nothing to lose. The hours slipped by.

Zoe was still engrossed by the time Monica returned home.

'This Trove site from the Australian National Library is great,' Zoe called into the kitchen where Monica was making coffee. 'I'm on a mission to hunt out everything I can find. Then I'll look back with the insight of an adult. Be objective. Then, even if I don't discover any answers, I'll feel I've done my best.'

Monica brought in coffee and Zoe showed her some of the old newspaper articles.

'Everyone looks so young and that time feels so far away. I don't even remember that photo of Dad. Mum made sure I didn't see any of these newspaper reports when I was a kid.' Mac's disappearance had been a hot topic for weeks. First, he was missing. Then Costa's boat was also missing, and then lobsters reported stolen. Mac's disappearance was soon linked to the loss of the boat. The *Aphrodite* wasn't salvaged for weeks. 'Mum would never discuss his disappearance; she just clammed up – I guess she was too upset to talk. Even though she would never say what she thought happened, I think she must have had a theory.'

'But look Zoe, there's plenty of speculation from others. Here are interviews with the Harbourmaster, fishermen he knew, local shop-keepers and farmers, an overwrought Costas, other boat owners, the owners of the lobster, and the police – all of them sprouting their own ideas,' said Monica.

'But all their ideas came to nothing. The public discussions faltered then faded away and it was assumed Mac stole the lobsters and died,' Zoe replied. 'Well, I've already talked to Costas. He's unconvinced about Dad's death but no clues about what happened. I'm going to contact some of these people who gave evidence at the hearing and see if they have heard anything since or had any other thoughts.'

Zoe gathered contact numbers and over the next days, made dozens of calls in the middle of the night to speak with people in South Australia during their daytime. Zoe gathered addresses and contact numbers. But time is cruel. The Harbourmaster was now aged over eighty and when she tracked him down in an old folk's home, he was deaf and forgetful. The local shopkeeper had passed away. Of the registered fishermen in the region at the time, most had retired or moved away, some were dead or didn't return her calls. One by one her leads evaporated. Doing what she would have done if her father had disappeared in Langhorne Creek, she even called the Robe Post Office to see if they remembered anything unusual. Another dead end. the postmaster had only been in the district for five years. The previous postmaster was travelling around the outback in a camper van – a grey nomad, and out of contact.

Zoe ordered a copy of the transcript of the enquiry from the Coroner's Court and it took 10 days and $100 to arrive by email. After reading every word, she understood little more. The facts were still sparse; in essence – boat missing then found, man missing, lobsters gone – no conclusions. Zoe tried to sense what people might have thought happened. His bank accounts had not been accessed so he had not run away. Zoe was furious with herself for not discussing it with her mother during her teenage years.

Over the next days, Zoe's anger grew. She was angry with her father for disappearing, angry with her mother for not talking about it, angry with herself for not asking.

'I'm still keen for Harry to find out about the business side of things,' Zoe said.

'Good idea, he's a whizz at finding things.' replied Monica trying to look sympathetic.

While the resolve was strong, Zoe phoned, and Richard agreed that Harry could help Zoe as long as he could do it without interfering with Richard's investigations of Yves. He offered to set up a meeting with Harry, knowing that the almost autistic nerd was very fussy about where he would go. Within the hour, Richard had arranged for Zoe to meet Harry the next morning at the Coffee Cat, a dingy little coffee shop in one of the back streets near the Hammersmith interchange.

The meeting was awkward. Harry's introversion made Zoe nervous. They both took refuge in the business to hand.

'I am trying to find out what happened to my father over 20 years ago,' she began. As she sketched what she knew about her father's disappearance, Zoe couldn't decide if Harry was happy with this arrangement. It was like trying to decide if a turtle was happy. There just didn't seem to be facial muscles available to convey meaningful expressions. Zoe was sensitive to eyes and loved their ability to show expressions, but Harry was so introverted that he could not, or would not, engage in direct eye contact. That, combined with his limited conversation, made it difficult for her to judge his reactions. Forewarned about this by Richard, Zoe ploughed on, setting out the information she knew and the steps she had taken. She was struggling to imagine how Harry could help so many years after the event, but Richard said this young man was a wiz and could find anything.

'My father was a wonderful man,' Zoe said with a tremble in her voice. 'I don't believe he would run off leaving Mum and me alone. I think there was something peculiar going on around the lobsters.'

Harry's silence made Zoe even more nervous. For years she feared that her father had abandoned them. Was that the reason for fights between her parents in the last few days before he disappeared? Had her mother locked herself away because she believed she drove her father away? Twenty years later, faced with Harry's non-threatening, non-judgemental silence, Zoe confronted the shape of the fear she never articulated. Her life was a series of abandonments. First it was her father, then her mother, then David. Was that why David's betrayal had devastated her? All her uncertainties and childhood fears coalesced together and engulfed her in the fear that she was not worthy. Zoe then understood her burning need to resolve her father's disappearance. She wanted to believe that someone else was involved; she wanted someone else to blame. Zoe was conscious that Harry waited in silence for Zoe to finish talking. She grappled with her emotions. Tears welled and she dashed them angrily away with the back of her hand.

'I just need to know,' she squeaked, hating her own weakness. 'Perhaps you can track someone or a company buying lobster and fish in South Australia which yielded huge profits at the time. I really have no idea,' she said shrugging her shoulders in dejection.

Harry's quiet response surprised her.

'You might be worried that your father didn't love you but trust me that's a whole lot better than having a bastard of a father who hates your guts. I'll have a look – no promises mind but it's surprising how long a bad smell lingers, even in the ether.'

Later that night, as Zoe concentrated on memories of her father and their lives together, she remembered fragments and impressions that she did not know she possessed. She wondered if children ever understand their parents. The memory of her father Mac remained as a strong and wonderful man, even if a little impatient. Her mother Catherine was loving, but cautious. Zoe remembered love but she also remembered friction between them before Mac disappeared. Zoe felt the tension – every child knows when parents argue. Doors might be shut and voices lowered, the temperature in the house is cooler. Zoe knew her father worked hard, perhaps too hard. He was often away and looked tired. He wore different clothes for different jobs. Waterproofs and a big yellow leather belt with pouches for secateurs for pruning vines in the cold weather, blue protective overalls for spraying, normal khaki king gees for driving trucks and the harvester. She hated the warm fishing jumpers most because, when he crewed for the lobster boats at Robe, he would be away all weekend.

With research and hindsight, Zoe understood her parents had heavy debts. They would have been nervous about interest rates rising. Her Dad increased his workload and took on extra jobs – Zoe remembered they fought about money but couldn't recall any other fights.

The next day, when Monica returned from the office and they cleaned up dishes and mess, Zoe brought her up to date.

'I've struggled to remember every snippet of information I can. I believe there was something stronger than usual about those last dis-agreements between my parents. I have this feeling that my father had a plan but my mother feared he was doing something stupid. Perhaps that's why Mum never wanted to discuss it.

When I started this quest, it was uncertainty that drove me. I convinced myself that I would be happy just to know what happened. This mystery has haunted me. As a child, I was devastated. How could the father I loved, leave me? I just wanted him back. I wanted security, the warm, enveloping feeling of love, of safety. I wanted my mother to be happy again. I wanted the aura of fun-filled chaos that surrounded my father to enclose us like a magic cloak. As I got older, I wanted answers. Why did this happen to me? I resented my father's disappearance. For years I buried my memories. It wasn't till David left and I collapsed, that I recognised the depth of my own feelings.'

Monica hugged Zoe, pleased but surprised at Zoe's self-awareness and her preparedness to discuss her inner feelings. As they settled into the sagging settee and its overstuffed cushions, Zoe continued.

'My father's disappearance seeded doubt in my heart. I guess I felt abandoned because I was unworthy. This latest depression was fuelled by my belief that all those from whom I expected the greatest love, left me. My father was the first. Then, when my mother died without warning, I was deserted again. So, when David, the man I trusted with my happiness, betrayed me and disappeared with another woman, my world collapsed. I was alone because I was unlovable. It was all my fault.'

As they stretched out on the big sofa, deep in this cathartic heart-to-heart, Monica was unusually subdued. They were enclosed in a rare bubble of trust and candid reflection.

'Then I looked for someone to blame. If my father was taken away, then perhaps I could forgive his desertion – if I found someone else to blame.'

'I understand,' said Monica. 'Maybe if you knew that someone else was responsible, then you could reassure yourself that he loved you. After all, we all seek love and sometimes reassurance is what we crave the most.'

'If there was a lobster deal that ensnared my father and caused his disappearance, I wanted to know who organised it. But most of all I wanted to know if perpetrators planned to defraud my father, or did they kill him? Harry is now on the job, but I doubt I'll never know.'

The next day, as Zoe shared coffee with Richard, her quest took another turn.

'Think about it,' he said. 'Do you want the truth? Or do you want comfort? At what point could you convince yourself you know enough to put this all behind you?'

'Don't know.'

'Watch, wait and think of a plan,' Richard said as Zoe started to look cross. 'Don't get angry, get even,' he continued. 'Anger might be useful fuel, but if you're to get the truth, you are going to have to work even harder.' Richard uncharacteristically reached forward and clasped Zoe's hands from across the table. He was not one for casual touching. He looked deep into her face.

'If I were you, I'd want revenge, not just truth.'

Zoe's eyes widened as she was shocked by her own naivety. How pathetic was she? In her schoolgirl dream to find the truth, she had reverted to a child's way of thinking. What was the truth anyway? Someone may have stolen Mac's life, and hence a very important part of Zoe's life. At the very least, her father's trust may have been stolen. Should she let someone get away with that? Thoughts flooded through Zoe's mind. Did she want revenge? Did she want justice? Did she simply want the truth? Richard was right. Up until now she'd framed her quest as one for truth, but it was more than that. Zoe wanted someone to pay. She wanted the perpetrator to suffer the sort of losses she suffered. She wanted them to acknowledge the pain that was caused by their actions.

'I need to walk. I do my best thinking in motion. See you later.' Zoe grabbed her bag and strode from the shop, leaving the puzzled, but delighted Richard to pay the bill.

'I always knew that girl had spirit under all that niceness. I'll be interested to see the plan that results from that walk,' he said under his breath.

As Zoe walked along the path by the river, she was blind to the trees and the sky that usually demanded her attention. She knew the path well and the day was dry so she could walk without splashing through the usual puddles. Her mind was consumed by the sudden, urgent need for action. After years of failure to engage, she saw a way to exorcise the demons that had mocked and threatened from the shadowy edges of her consciousness ever since her father's disappearance.

Holes in hearts were like a vacuum in nature. They didn't stay empty. Zoe's had been filled with doubt. She now recognised her doubt was caused by fear; – fear of her weakness, fear of fault, and fear of failure.

'What do I really want?' Zoe asked out loud. Justice sounded noble, but what would it mean after all these years? If she found the person responsible, what would be accomplished by dragging the perpetrator before a court of law? Was it recognition of the crime, or recognition of the consequences that she sought? A trial with hollow statements of fact and rebuttal twenty years after the event could be cold and empty unless it was murder. Zoe wanted the perpetrator to acknowledge the crime. She wanted her pain to be acknowledged, then she wanted an apology. Formal justice, as offered by the application of the law, didn't seem enough.

Was it compensation she wanted? The idea of surrendering a thing of value in return for a wrong had merit. But she lived in a society when compensation was expressed in monetary terms. Dollars couldn't replace loss she felt.

The pain caused to a child by the loss of a father was beyond measure. Her father had gone. She was alive. She would seize the opportunity to hold the perpetrators to account before it was too late.

As her feet pounded the pavement getting faster and faster, her resolve hardened. When she finally stumbled and almost fell on the roughening path it was like waking from a dream. Instead of the dream receding away as consciousness asserted itself, Zoe was full of purpose, clear in intent and primed for action.

Her surroundings came back into focus. The path ran beside deserted industrial yards; she'd walked a long way. She wheeled around and smiled as she retraced her steps back along the path until, almost an hour later, she re-joined the busy streets leading toward Monica's flat. She saw the people around her with a new clarity. She wondered about their lives, their hopes, and their dreams. She wanted to take them by the hand and look them in the face and say – you too can take action to solve the problems in your life. Don't be passive and accept what is given, give voice to your darkest fears and just doing that will make it more bearable. Zoe was energised and felt strong. This was her life; she would do and not be done to. She'd take control. She would solve the mystery behind her father's disappearance.

Chapter 37

A New Face

As Yves sat in the picture-perfect room of the picture-perfect flat in the most elegant part of Paris, he was aware of an unusual feeling. He wanted Zoe to like him. All his life he had pursued women. He had enjoyed female trophies on his arm to feed his ego, reinforce his confidence and excite the envy of other men. As other men may have practiced golf or tennis, he practiced seduction for the thrill of the chase and the glory of victory. Some women were amusing but his conquests were often as self-absorbed as he was with his own needs, his own image. Intent on making a good impression Yves and his partner of the moment spent significant time attending to the needs of fashion and grooming and being seen in the right places by the right people. After many years of successful preening and positioning, he was surprised by his dissatisfaction.

After meeting Zoe and the enforced stillness required by the sitting for his portrait, Yves wondered if he was missing something in his life. Did he need a sense of vocation? Perhaps his life and the lives of many in his social circle were no more meaningful than a well-crafted film set, a thin façade, a two-dimensional snapshot of life. Could it be time for a change? Should he focus on art with Zoe, and gain a new level of meaning in his life by understanding the making of art. Was there more to it than price? Could Zoe and her work become his entree card to a more meaningful life?

Now rich and respectable, the excitement of making more money had paled. Becoming rich had been the central goal of his existence. Money was power, freedom and independence. It proved he was the winner; he was the best. This had been the guiding principle of his life for over two decades.

His feelings for Zoe were unexpected and uncharacteristic. He saw this portrait as the pinnacle of a long and successful life of money making. He was flattered. Then, Zoe arrived into this world of control and contentment. She was beautiful. Above this she had inner strength, a calm reserve and sense of self-reliance. Yves found this independence unusual and attractive. He had always surrounded himself with women who wanted to attract his attention. Zoe did not. Her behaviour wasn't a ploy, a studied position to pique his interest. She loved to paint and seemed unaware of the effect she was having on him. Remoteness made her desirable.

Throughout the days he spent with Zoe in Rouen, Zoe had resisted his advances with tact and grace. Yves had been his most charming and flirtatious. He showed his strengths, talked about his successes, tried to impress her with his wealth, his power and influence by talking about his houses and all the accoutrements of his success. She had been charming but aloof and apparently unimpressed. Zoe fascinated Yves by being focussed and professional about her work. She was alluringly feminine yet independent. For Zoe, painting was more than a hobby, more than a job. When she painted, Zoe was passionate.

After the intense days of the first sittings, Yves, who could have resented the time commitment, was sorry their time together ended. In the face of his failure to seduce her, Yves was surprised how much he wanted to see Zoe again. She had invaded his thoughts and made him wonder. It was disconcerting. It made him preoccupied and distracted. He was pleased he could look forward to the next scheduled sittings in London. They had also committed to attend the magazine launch together when the portrait would be unveiled. Quite simply he did not want their association to end. In addition to a powerful sexual attraction, he admired her and, he wanted her to like him.

Even when concentrating on business, his thoughts drifted to Zoe. That was very unusual. It was an important time for the company. He had invested many millions in additional shares and exercised his numerous share options. Logically, Yves had over committed. He might be a very wealthy man but Adriana, his houses and his lifestyle were high maintenance. He needed to feed his capital and deliver greater income. Always a gambler, he had taken a significant loan to negatively gear the new Alston shares, gambling on the rising value of the shares to deliver both his profits and his repayment potential. He was positive it was a safe investment; after all he had seen the research results and knew he was on a winner.

In two weeks, he was due back in London for the final sitting. Then a fortnight later they would attend the launch. He had not seen the portrait or her for a week even though they had kept in touch by phone and email. He felt proud and excited. It was a high moment, one that they could celebrate together in public. He was in good spirits, riding high.

Chapter 38

London Plan

Yves arrived in London and booked into his favourite hotel in Sloan Square. Number 10 Cadogan Gardens was everything a London hotel should be: solid stone steps flanked by formal topiary that led up to an old oak panelled foyer lit by warm golden lights and brimming with helpful staff. The library, which branched off the entrance hall, had the right mix of leather-bound books, paintings and a well-stocked drinks cabinet.

'Hello Zoe. Yes, thank you. I have arrived safely,' he said on the phone.

'Great. I'm working very hard. I can't believe we're on the final countdown to the launch,' Zoe continued. 'But I'm having terrible trouble with your hands,' she groaned.

'I am sorry to think I am troubling you without even being there.' Yves laughed.

'You know what I mean. I am pleased with your face, which is the most crucial part of any portrait – that is almost complete. I am delighted with the setting. I have included a trace of shadowy vegetation through the window to hint at your beautiful garden. It amplifies the greys and lilacs in the room setting,' said Zoe, remembering the way the light from the garden of the Rouen house filtered through the huge window to suffuse that beautiful sitting room. 'Yves, I need some more time to get your hands right,' Zoe said. 'I wondered if I could come to your office with my sketch pad to give me a new perspective?'

'Of course. Come to the Montague office in Harrington Street next Tuesday. It is so much quieter than the Alston office. Now I understand to your interest in light, I think the mellow light of the timbered office there will be more appropriate than the bright lights of the modern Alston office. And, Zoe, I'm pleased that you are happy with my face. I like the idea that it kept you company.'

Zoe smiled. She wanted to see the Montague office in London. With Yves' record for disappearing offices, it was an opportunity too good to miss. It was the perfect chance for some snooping.

She had been pleased with her idea of the frame within the frame, although it still had room for a few more elements in the decoration. Just how many business ventures had Yves been involved with? Perhaps she would learn something new during her visit.

Zoe arrived as scheduled and was met by his secretary.

'Good morning Miss MacIntosh. Mr Montreau is expecting you but has been unavoidably delayed. He will only be about 10 minutes. Traffic, I believe. He sends his apologies. Please take a seat. My name is Jennifer. Can I get you tea, coffee, a drink of water, perhaps?' Jennifer, in her mid-fifties, was well polished in this role. Her neat navy suit and smoothly combed brown hair matched her manner and well-ordered office.

'No, nothing thank you,' Zoe said as she wandered around the warm old oak panelled foyer and glanced at the ornately decorated ceiling. 'But you could tell me about this wonderful old building. My friend George is interested in architecture and this seems a gem. Perhaps we could have a quick look around.'

'I love it too. I have been here for almost twenty years. Well before Mr Montreau took over. It is a very traditional building. It suited the old law firms and family businesses which had offices here for almost a century.'

'You are not that old, Jennifer,' Zoe joked.

'No, no, of course not. But I meant firms with old traditional values. They go back long before my time.'

'I love this old style. Those black and chequerboard white tiles in the entrance hall always seem very nineteenth century to me, but I think they will always be in fashion,' Zoe replied.

'That's true. My son Kenny used to love them when he was small. He used to spend hours stepping from tile to tile. This was such a happy place when old Mr Ashenden was here. He was even happy when Kenny lay on the floor, so he could look at all the pretty colours on the ceiling. Now several companies share the offices. It's different having new people come and go.'

'It certainly would be easier to see the colours looking up from the floor,' said Zoe craning her neck as she admired the detailed blue, gold and white painting and complex patterns.

'This is my favourite room,' said Jennifer opening a pair of heavy wooden doors. 'This is the main meeting room. Mr Montreau has scheduled to meet you in his smaller office.'

'How gorgeous. And more of those lovely ceilings,' said Zoe admiring the intricate red and gold decoration and warm wood panelling.

'It would be easy to get attached to this gorgeous old furniture,' said Zoe wriggling back on a large bench seat in the foyer. 'I'm tall, but I think this was made for very tall people.'

'Oh yes.' Jennifer laughed. All the Ashenden family were very tall. All gone now. The whole family has died out. It was sad to lose that history and atmosphere.'

'Hello Zoe,' Yves beamed as he walked through the door. 'Sorry I'm late.'

'Not a problem. I was admiring the architecture.'

'Of course. Through here,' he said putting his hand discretely but intimately on the small of her back and guided her toward his office door. 'Jameson, deal with these,' he said brusquely, handing her a pile of files.

'Zoe, you look even lovelier than I remember,' said Yves as he shut the door, gently held her arms and kissed her cheeks, one and then the other.

'Good to see you too, Yves. I need some time with your hands. The sketches I did in Rouen were far too rough,' she laughed. 'Besides I have changed the angle of your arm to fit the frame and they need some more work.'

'Happy to make my hands available Zoe,' Yves said with suggestive smile. 'I'm delighted to see you again. It's been too long.'

'Yes, and I'm struggling to meet the deadline,' said Zoe. 'I have been inundated with work, sketches and paintings. It's great to be in demand but I have been flat out. So, I might seem distracted. I'm sorry but I won't be much good for a sensible conversation until this work is finished,' she apologised. 'But please talk to me while I work. I can't guarantee to reply. You know how I work by now.'

The hour they had allocated passed in a flash as Zoe sketched and Yves chatted. Zoe worked with the intensity. She was pleased to have her sketchbook between them, it was the perfect excuse to keep him at arm's length.

'There, I think that is enough for now' she said with a sigh. 'Hands are always difficult. I had an uncle whose hands were so huge they looked out of proportion. But that was how they were. My father had big hands too. Functional, but not fine and symmetrical like yours.' Yves recognised the compliment. 'I remember our discussions about symmetry at Rouen.'

As Zoe packed her things to leave, she glanced around the office and noted several porcelain vases on the mantelpiece over the large fireplace, which were utterly different to the other furniture. Their pale colours, one rose pink, one with pale blue tracery like veins under delicate white skin and the third milky alabaster, contrasted strongly with the dark old grandfather clock in the corner that looked as if it had been there for a hundred years. 'That porcelain reminds me of the fine cups in your Rouen house. I'd like to meet again for a short time in a week if you can spare me a few minutes Yves. Just for some final touches,' she said, glad to have the excuse of time pressure to deflect Yves' offer of dinner.

'Of course, please find a mutually convenient time with Jameson as you leave. I'm sorry but I need to take this call,' Yves said apologetically as he checked the incoming number on his mobile.

'Until next week then,' said Zoe as she bustled out the door throwing him a kiss.

At the appointed time the following week when Zoe entered the office, she noticed that Jennifer, the efficient secretary, was not there to greet her. Yves came out of the office at the sound of her footsteps and ushered her into his office.

'I am so excited Yves. I'm now confident the painting is good. A few more details to finish the frame and then I'm done. I won't take much of your time. Then if we agree on the launch details, we're ready to go.'

'Happy for you to take my time, Zoe. It's becoming one of my favourite London experiences.'

'I promise I won't be so rushed after this is finished Yves,' Zoe said with a rueful smile. 'You have probably realised by now, I'm a bit obsessed by my work.'

'Yes, and it is one of the many things I admire about you.'

'Thank you for being so understanding. I have had a productive and very enjoyable afternoon. I will need to work hard to finish your border on time, but I am so looking forward to seeing you at the launch. It promises to be a big deal. Monica is surprised the magazine is being so generous.'

'I would like to see you before the launch Zoe. Can you spare time for lunch?'

'That sounds delightful, but it will be difficult. Call me next Monday, I'll see how it's going,' she said breezily. 'I'm being very tough on myself. My plans to ramp up my career depend on your face you know. I'm hoping it will bring me critical acclaim as well as additional work. Goodbye, Yves,' she said with unfeigned reluctance as he kissed her gently on the cheek.

Zoe left the office, feeling very attracted to Yves. He was perfect; charming, thoughtful and he smelt delicious. He told interesting stories with humour and seemed to both understand and appreciate her dedication to her work. She liked that in a man.

As she walked along the street from the office toward the tube station, she was surprised to see Jennifer sitting at a table outside a cafe just down the road from the office.

'Hello,' she called brightly. Jennifer looked up, startled and Zoe was shocked to see blotchy eyes and tear-streaked cheeks.

'Oh Jennifer, are you all right?' Zoe said reaching her hand forward instinctively. Seeing Jennifer's distress, she drew out a chair and sat beside her.

'Oh. It's you Miss MacIntosh. I'm sorry. I think I'm in shock. I don't know what I'm doing. It's just that I can't believe it. Twenty years I have been there and never a cross word. Twenty years. Now I'm out on the street. I won't get another job at my age.'

'What ever happened?' Zoe asked.

'That horrible man. I always knew he was trouble. It's my Kenneth you see. He came to see me this morning. He knows he is not supposed to come to the office anymore, but he was all upset. He was crying and everything. Well Mr Frenchman came out looking like thunder. He called to me and said, cold as you like. *Get rid of this nuisance*. Well, my Kenneth doesn't like it when people are nasty to him or me. He's a big man. Not big you see in the brain department. But a very big man now. He always liked coming to the office when he was little. Well, when Mr Montreau saw my boy he wasn't very nice. And, when Kenneth wouldn't move, he called him ugly names and tried to push him out the door. Kenneth doesn't like that. So, he shouted back. Then Kenneth kicked him.'

'You mean he kicked Mr Montreau? Oh dear,' said Zoe as Jennifer nodded. 'I can imagine he didn't like that.'

'Well, I was rushing about, and they were both shouting. I said it wasn't Kenneth's fault because Mr Montreau was so rude. There was shouting and name-calling. Then Mr Montreau took to me saying I must be embarrassed that Kenneth was my son and couldn't I get him locked away. I was horrified. I said I would need to take him back to the carers because he was so upset. It was terrible.' Jennifer burst into tears.

'Then Mr Montreau said go. Go and don't come back otherwise I will go to the police and charge him with assault.' I've taken Kenneth back, but I am so upset. I don't have the courage to face that beastly man, even to collect my things. I just don't know what I will do.'

'A pot of tea please,' Zoe called to the waitress as she fished in her bag for some tissues. 'And a slice of that nice cake please,' she added when the tea was delivered, steaming hot in a big blue china pot with matching cups and a strainer. 'I hope you like sultana cake, Jennifer. It's my favourite.'

'Oh. Thank you, Miss MacIntosh. You're so very nice. I thought that from the first moment I saw you.'

'Have you seen Mr Montreau like that before?' Zoe asked as the cake arrived, and Jennifer's storm of tears had passed.

'Oh yes. Nice as pie to some people but not nice underneath. You should hear the way he talks to some on the phone. Not that I listen mind. And sometimes he speaks in a foreign language. French I suppose, so I don't know what he is saying. But it's not nice.'

'Oh Jennifer, I'm so sorry.'

'It's not for you to be sorry Miss MacIntosh. Some people just can't deal with people like my Kenneth.'

'But I can see how upset you are. We'll have to see if we can help,' Zoe said with genuine sympathy as Mrs Jameson babbled on in shock.

By the end of the second pot of tea, Jennifer Jameson had retained her composure. The women had exchanged phone numbers and Zoe had promised to help her get another job. Apart from genuinely wanting to help this poor woman who obviously had a difficult time coping with a giant of a son with a very limited IQ and a short fuse, Zoe thought with a little shame that she could be a useful contact for the team. As the afternoon drew in and they parted at the tube station, Zoe thought how complex the world was. Just as you thought you had some answers, other new questions emerged. Perhaps Yves might not be so handsome on the inside.

Chapter 39

Research Success

In the dim, quiet back corner of the Fox and Firkin in Putney the friends sat close, drawn together by the excitement of information and ideas to share. Zoe, Monica and Richard looked like the conspirators they were. This old pub's low ceiling and thick walls looked as if they had been designed for harbouring secrets. Zoe had been twitching like a hound on the scent since her last meeting with Harry. Her quest to try and solve the mystery of her father's disappearance hovered in her mind just below every action. Thoughts of revenge energised her.

'Tense Tommy, my up-tight, tight ass editor, has signed off on my proposal for the next series of articles at last,' Monica announced with a wide smile. '*Your Business* will continue the monthly feature which has been popular, and they've agreed to run a supplementary set on business ethics. My personal by-line will feature key people behind major companies operating in Britain today. They will be high profile, prestigious pieces covering major services – finance, water, electricity and gas, and pharmaceuticals for the National Heath Scheme. Each will profile a strong personality, and each quarter the special feature will be accompanied by a portrait.' She punched the air.

'Congratulations Monica. You've worked hard for that,' said Richard.

'Montreau will be the first in this high-profile new series. Mind you, my editor is a tight-fisted bastard and has only agreed if the subjects pay for the portrait. Ever since I convinced Yves to pay up front, Tommy thinks I am a cash cow.'

'Just make sure you do a few flattering pieces, and perhaps showcase some admirable characters otherwise no one will talk to you Monica,' said Richard. 'The business community is already wary of your tough questions. If you expose too much bad behaviour, they will all think you are out to get them. Be careful.'

'We know your articles will be fantastic Monica. And don't forget you lured me back to London with the promise of rich commissions. I'm relying on you to deliver plenty of work,' said Zoe poking her arm in fun.

'Its OK for you, you just need to paint them.' Monica laughed. 'I have to be clever and find out all about Montreau. He's a tough nut, but I think we are at that exciting moment when all the pieces start fitting together,' Monica said. Richard's tablet and papers were spread across the table. As the discussion progressed, he drew more and more pages from a thick wad that he had crammed into his leather shoulder bag. The friends deliberately chose Tuesday night to meet, knowing it would be quiet enough for them to be able to talk business and spread papers all across the back tables of the old pub without taking up valuable drinking space.

'I won't pretend to understand all of these spread sheets Richard. Are you telling us that as you unveil page after page of ownership transfers and money flows, they are all linked to Yves?' Zoe asked.

'I will definitely need food before I can take all this in,' Zoe said beckoning to the waiter for menus. Despite its name, *The Fox* served good pub food, which pleased them all. Richard valued the great selection of good red wines. Over the past months, Zoe had chivvied Reg, the proprietor to stock her favourite Langhorne Creek reds from South Australia. Having grown up in a land that specialised in luscious fruity shiraz, Zoe and Monica both discovered they were perfect to ward off the bone-chilling British winters. After Reg stocked them her choices proved popular with the locals. It was always useful to keep a publican happy. The trio ordered dinner, chicken for Zoe, steak and kidney pie for Monica, curry for Richard and another bottle of Langhorne Creek red to share.

'You must admit, I have good instincts as well as a good wine palate. I'm not infallible spotting cheats but I think dishonesty must be an addiction, like drinking or smoking. Once someone crosses the line between right and wrong, they do it again and again,' Monica said.

'I think you can smell crooks at twenty paces Monica. You can be our official sniffer dog.' Zoe chuckled. 'Perhaps we can station you at the airport to check out the arrivals. I have decided that I hate deception the most. It seems the worst thing that one person can do to another. I get so cross when people like Yves get away with making money by deceit year after year.'

'Well, that's the most satisfying part of my job,' Monica sighed. 'All of the people I have selected for the feature articles are smart; a few have a few minor shadows. If I am right Yves has a very dark past. He might make an explosive start to the series.'

'Can you give me a simple summary of what you've discovered Richard?' Zoe asked feeling overwhelmed by the mountain of paper that covered the table. It was good to be back in London, but she felt like she had stepped into a fast-flowing river. Richard sat back.

'We believe Yves is the driver of a business operation which started over twenty years ago. A private company would be established, often registered in New Caledonia. There would be a business plan, investments from several parties and a surfeit of optimism. Each company had a minimum of three core members, of which Yves was one. Yves and at least one other collaborator would gain majority voting rights. They controlled all sorts of business structures, a plan, a partnership, a prospectus or a company. Most often they chose a raw material, like fish or the copra in New Caledonia. Some of the ventures involved high value products like jade or tropical timbers. Others promoted manufactured products using, for example, botanical extracts from exotic places in Africa or the French Pacific. The deals were all romantic and tax deductable. The entities floated on the edge of legality and provided enough detail to lure investors with the offer of excellent returns. All the companies gave the appearance of financial solidity and were operated through various office addresses in Europe,' Richard explained.

'So, if we are going to talk about what pushes our buttons, I'll tell you mine. After decades producing things in mining and extraction, my pet beef is with people or businesses which don't produce anything – just take from others,' Richard said.

'True. I'm no businessperson but I don't understand how Yves made money while others lost. Are you sure Yves is the crooked one?' said Zoe.

'Well, to run the businesses, the partners engaged a management company, which earned big returns until the subsidiary company faced trading difficulties. The reasons were many and varied, however each time the investors lost their money. Yves made a lot of money through management fees and selling off products and assets below value. By the time the company needed to be tracked, all the evidence had disappeared from the elegant European address. The management group stripped companies of assets. Yves and his people disappeared, the entity dissolved, and any remaining funds vanished like snowflakes on a bright morning. Very slick,' Richard said.

'I think we should start a list of disgruntled investors, and track them down,' Monica said starting to write.

Richard continued, 'I think Yves was the smooth one. His role was to convince investors of the value of the project. It might be new business in a town, a promise of jobs, or access to markets through his contacts – something like that. One by one the investors lost money, products, cargoes or all of the above.'

'So his greatest skill is deception.' Zoe said. 'I bet that's what happened to my father.'

'Got it in a nutshell,' said Richard. 'Harry worked it out from money transfers. The other things, names, addresses, products, people changed every time,' said Richard. 'It was only when Harry linked the money trails through the lawyer, we found the connections. Harry, the on-line bloodhound came up trumps. By the way, how are you getting on with him, Zoe?'

'Well, he is a strange one. But we are starting to talk,' Zoe said.

'He reminds me of a ferret, like the ones my strange old uncle used to keep. 'He's single minded, quick, and able to dive down dark tunnels.'

'You've done a great job Richard,' said Monica leaning back on the couch. 'It makes me wonder if anything is private. It's a good thing I'm honest!' Before anyone could contradict her, the door opened, and George ducked under the low lintel. They waved him over.

'Hello all. I'm not sure what you troublemakers are up to, but I smell conspiracy. Do tell why you're looking so pleased,' he chuckled.

Richard refilled glasses. They often met here, happy to soak in the ambiance and history of the old pubs. Although smoking was banned, an old pub smell remained, a strangely comforting combination of beer and wine, new and old food, furniture polish and wood fires.

'We are continuing a long-standing British tradition of solving problems over a drink,' said Richard.

'And Monica likes to imagine that these walls bear witness to the hopes and dreams of many generations,' said Zoe.

'Stop teasing, you know I love all these photos of earlier days. The Toby jugs and horse trappings, beer medals, even the darts all make it very cosy.'

'I think the atmosphere here is due to generations of spilt beer,' George joked as he sniffed.

'You're so boring George. I think I can feel a link with the plotters and planners of the past. Just imagine the explorers and adventurers who may have sat here. I can see them mapping out expeditions and hoping for discoveries. And there is evidence that political intrigues were hatched right here and played out in these streets.'

'Must have been hard among all the horse manure.'

'Yes, knee deep.' Zoe laughed. The sense of close human history in these old pubs on narrow winding streets contrasted starkly with the wide-open vistas of Australia.

'I love that when you want something – you go for it,' said George. 'Your plotting is more complex than chopping someone's head off.'

'Australia gave us optimism. Monica and I can do anything.' Zoe grinned. 'We're not weighed down with all that class stuff like you lot. White Australian culture may not have long history but it's big on personal freedom. Our ancestors had the guts to spend four months crossing the globe in horrible cramped ships. Those who survived bred independent larrikins like us with little respect for authority,' Zoe added.

'Well, I believe that everyone deserves a fair go and, if we are right, this bloke we have been looking at doesn't,' Richard said.

'True, and justice is possible. I enjoy sticking up for people who have been wronged,' Monica added.

'I feel like we are playing three-dimensional *Monopoly* on steroids,' said Zoe. 'I see big money, wheeling and dealing, penalties for landing on the wrong spot, random chance cards, the threat of going to gaol, and "Get out of gaol free" cards masquerading as company charters.'

'You're right Zoe. Harry's uncovered a web of deals which have been played like a complex game, plenty of luck and rolls of the dice,' Richard said.

'Richard's been a genius working this out,' Monica said. 'I think he enjoys piecing all this together. Too many company names and legalities for me.'

'Well I'm out of my depth,' said George, as he refilled their glasses.

'But I've met Yves Montreau. Definite eye candy for those who like an older man – handsome. Sadly straight. Charming.'

'That sounds like our man,' laughed Zoe.

'He seems to have made evasion a pattern in business,' Richard said.

'Maybe I'll add a slippery eel to his portrait,' Zoe said with a smile.

'I'll ask around and see what else I can discover about him,' offered George.

'I'll check the research. Yves has been involved in pharmaceuticals for the past few years. I know a bit about Alston and think its above board. It's powerful. Maybe he's operating within the law these days. Buying into an established business is a good way to launder money.'

'Or you could buy some art,' said George.

'Maybe, but Alston's piqued Harry's interest. I've never known him to offer an opinion, but apparently he's got a beef about undisclosed side effects in pharmaceuticals,' said Richard.

'I'm amazed at the stuff Harry's unearthed. I'm glad you can understand it Richard,' said Zoe.

'Well, there's no doubt Yves has poked his fingers into a lot of pies. He's grown very rich while many deals have lost money. He must be good, no one's taken a successful legal action against him in 20 years,' Richard said.

'We only found him through the company nameplates on the building that you found in New Caledonia, Zoe. Harry was able to track Yves through the lawyer connection,' Richard said.

'His partner's legal creativity has given Yves the imprimatur to spread his hands and shrug his shoulders in that Gallic way and claim unknown legal loopholes as investor's money disappeared into offshore banking havens,' Richard said.

'I wonder if he's doing something shady with Alston,' said Monica.

'Harry says he's dramatically increased his shares by withdrawing investments from other companies. Apparently, he's recruited a bright group of promising young medical researchers to join Alston for some secret project. He might be a snake in the grass, to change Zoe's analogy from slippery eels,' said Richard.

'Can you help me plan some clever questions for Yves when I see him next? I haven't got long, we're close to the final sittings,' said Zoe.

Food and wine finished, they agreed to gather additional data and meet again, same time, same place in two days.

Chapter 40

Failed

M onica was bone tired. After deciding to write a powerful article about Yves and his shady deals, she didn't have sufficient documents to convince the magazine's legal team to publish; plenty of circumstantial evidence, but little hard proof. She worked hard on other pieces during the day and trawled through documents about Yves every night. Meeting Richard at the pub, she threw her bag on the ground next to her chair and ordered a beer.

'I'm making stuff-all progress,' she complained as she delved down, wrenched a sheath of papers out of her bag and slapped it on the table. 'Look at this pile, I reckon he's conned hundreds of people over the past decades.'

'I'm frustrated too,' said Richard. 'I've never spent so much time investigating for so few results,' he said.

'We need fresh ideas and I need comfort food.' Monica sighed as they sipped their beers. 'Let's call Zoe and George.'

'Good idea,' Richard said.

They arranged to meet at an old favourite Indian restaurant, *The Mogul* on Putney High Street, which specialised in Britain's most popular cuisine. Hot curries were perfect to steam off bad feelings and they made beer taste even better.

Zoe caught the tube and noted new Spanish and Indonesian restaurants as she walked along the main street.

'Hello you two. Why so miserable?' Zoe said. 'There's a great looking Spanish Tapas Bar and a new wine bar just around the corner, Monica. We might try a glass or two after the curry. You look like you need perking up.'

The bead curtains, which separated the softly lit foyer from the tables clinked, George appeared and was shown to their table.

'Hi George. You're looking fabulous. You remind me of the pin-up my mother had of Gorgeous George, the wrestler. He had long blond curls wore glittering gold lamé. That might look a little obvious in Putney,' said Monica as she hugged him warmly and kissed both cheeks.

'Hello my favourite conspirators. I'm starving. Let's eat first, talk later.'

George was one sort of gorgeous. He was witty, charming and a font of knowledge. A good friend.

Soon little dishes full of taste sensations surrounded them. As they dipped between chicken tikka, basil beef and red duck curry with mango chutney, the table was transformed from a beautiful tableau to chaos. They shared dishes, broke naan breads and drained the beer.

'Looks just like my desk,' Monica sighed. 'A short time ago it was neat and full of promise, now it's a mess.' They talked and talked and drank more beer.

'I got a lengthy e-mail from Michael today,' said Zoe.

'Michael from Adelaide?' asked Monica. 'Oooh, how long's this been going on?'

'A while. He's nice. His emails are fun. He's planning a wine tour.'

'Surely there's enough wine in South Australia. They produce about a billion dollars' worth,' said Monica.

'True but there's always more to learn. He writes the most interesting things. Did you know some of the oldest cabernet vines in the world are in South Australia?'

'How can that be?' asked Monica.

'Phylloxera killed practically all the vines in France, and plenty had been planted in Australia by the 1880's,' said Zoe.

'I didn't know that,' said Monica. 'Is he coming to Europe perhaps?' asked Monica.

'Stop plotting Monica, let's decamp down to the Duke's Head,' said Zoe. They trooped out into the cold night and headed down the road. The small crowd at the pub were well settled over their drinks and as the friends settled on the deep couch in a corner to share a good bottle of red. Monica brought George up to date.

'You know I'm working on Yves Montreau,' said Monica. 'You said you'd met him. Well, I've learned that many British companies have plenty of history to hide, but his dealings look like the pirates of old.'

'I don't know about his business life but Montreau is an occasional buyer on the arts scene,' George said. 'And Monica, you know that plenty of rich people are only a generation away from dirty money. Many of our famous family names were involved in tea, sugar or rubber and all these are based on slavery. Companies like Hudson's Bay and the Dutch East Indies Company didn't get wealthy without dastardly deeds. Why would this surprise you?'

'It doesn't. Except that everyone pretends slavery only happened a long time ago. It's depressingly common – 40 million slaves around the world! I love uncovering these stories of exploitation. All that talk of bringing civilisation to the colonies was a pathetic excuse for seizing their wealth and treating the locals with contempt. You can see the heavy colonial chip on my shoulder.' Monica smiled. 'But the lawyers will be on to me if I can't prove the facts. My research skills might be legendary, but I'm finding Montague hard to pin down.'

'The Montague Corporation made my father's life a misery. They're ruthless. People in Sheffield were gutted when they closed the steel works,' said George.

'I like that my forebears were convicts shipped in chains to Australia and now I'm back in the motherland holding rich people to account for dishonest businesses. I've even found links between Montreau and rain forest timber being illegally harvested in the Papua New Guinea. It's big money,' Monica continued.

'The trouble is that many Pacific nations are dirt poor and their governments can't match the wealth and sophistication of traders with hundreds of years of cunning,' Richard added.

'Stealing to eat is one thing but I take great exception to big companies prancing around Europe pretending to behave ethically while fleecing people in faraway countries.'

'Maybe you're wrong,' said George.

'I don't think so. But I'm getting bogged down. I need help,' she said. 'We've collected and sifted through tons of data. All the documentation is fragmentary and the only thing we can conclusively prove beyond doubt, is that Yves was part of many deals.'

'We do know most of them failed their investors. The contentious ones have the least compelling documentation about why. It's no crime to make bad investment decisions,' said Richard.

'I'll call my old copper friend Stan and see if he can help. He deals with the financial regulators all the time. I hope we have enough to convince someone with teeth to get involved. With the complexity of the law and the international reach of the transactions, it may be difficult,' said Monica.

Chapter 41

Call the Police

On Friday night the friends gathered to discuss the evidence, this time at Richard's rather grand house in Church Road around the corner from the Wimbledon tennis courts.

'Richard, meet Detective Inspector Stan Evans,' said Monica. 'He's been a member of the Fraud squad for a decade and I've known him ever since I came to London. He's a good bloke with good connections.'

After shaking Richard's hand, Stan whistled as he saw the heaps of files and spreadsheets piled across the desk.

'Look at all this we've gathered Stan,' said Monica handing him a summary and leafing through a pile of reports. 'I told you he's a crook. How much do we need to convince the law to take action?' Monica said.

'Take a breath Monica. We've collaborated on enough of these investigations for you to know I respect your work. While I accept you've decided this bloke's a crook, the evidence needs to be clear and compelling. I need to be able to get someone to prove it in court,' said the detective. 'Do you think your data does that? Will it stand scrutiny? How did you get it?'

'You're infuriating,' said Monica. 'You sound just like the legal eagles at work.'

'Give me a break. I haven't even had a chance to look at it all yet. Even if the evidence stands up to detailed analysis, most of it may be inadmissible in a court of law, if, shall I say it may not have been sourced with the proper permissions. Besides, the regulator would need to decide on the appropriate jurisdiction. Could he be prosecuted in New Caledonia, France or England? The laws are all different. Often to prove fraud, the law requires the intent to defraud,' said Stan as they riffled through the papers.

'Losing money happens all the time,' Richard concurred. 'You wouldn't believe how many small businesses and even a number of large businesses fail every year. I agree it's hard to believe that everyone lost money except Yves. That's still circumstantial.'

'I agree that it looks suspicious and you could be right. I'd have to see something compelling to be able to convince my bosses to spend years and the hundreds of thousands of dollars necessary to bring a case like this to trial let alone achieve a successful prosecution.'

Monica was exhausted. Her face was haggard, her hair a mess; and she had been drinking to excess. It was a dangerous combination. Obsession with a cause generated high motivation – but it did not aid clear thinking.

'We believe Yves has defrauded hundreds of people, and I'm committed to seeing him suffer like the people he's fleeced,' said Monica.

'You know I'll help where I can,' said Stan. 'We need civvies like you to help us put away some of these clever white-collar bastards. Give me your best evidence and I'll get it checked out. I really hope I can help. But, for God's sake don't tell me about your collection methods.'

'Well, I have to admit I'm disappointed. But, not surprised,' said Richard as they waved the burly detective farewell from the doorway. 'I know the way the corporations' law works, and I understand Stan's hesitation.' Richard said.

'It's going to be tough,' said Monica. 'I think you almost admire this bloke Richard.'

'Some people work hard and save, others sell great ideas, but people like Yves convince someone else to them give money in get rich quick schemes. If people are greedy or gullible, they leave themselves open to abuse. All that rubbish about the meek inheriting the earth. Like the song says, there's a sucker born every minute. They make it easy for people like Yves.'

'Don't pretend you think this is OK Richard,' said Monica.

'I don't but there's more here than we're seeing,' Richard said. 'It is almost as if he popped into existence rich – no family, no story. You know I like patterns, and this one doesn't feel right.'

Angry, disappointed and tired, Monica stewed as she hailed a taxi. She was too exhausted to grapple with the tube and then walk home from the station. Monica had to remind herself that she was not so poor these days. She gazed out of the taxi window and took small comfort from the busy streets. She loved London, more with every passing year. It retained the capacity to absorb wave after wave of people, ideas, innovations, technology and even scandals and still remain quintessentially British; absolutely London.

As the driver negotiated the narrow streets, Monica watched the open shops, people walking and talking and buses running despite the late hour. It was a living city. Her taxi stopped to allow trucks to manoeuvre around road works near a new excavation. A large hole had been excavated, deep enough for the foundations and basement of a new multi-story building. There was always something new being constructed or rebuilt in this old city. Buildings were made to last and renewal was always underway. The hole was huge, slicing deep down into the ground.

Monica admired the builders who worked like keyhole surgeons, inserting huge new buildings into modest-sized blocks. Constant repairs were needed to keep a city in working order, and land was too valuable to be left idle. As Monica and her driver waited, a crane manoeuvred giant steel formwork into place with great delicacy. Monica's eyes were drawn to the wall of earth forming the back of the hole. It was tens of meters deep and, as she scanned down the earth, she was conscious of layer on layer of previous buildings, scrambled earth, rubble, clay and strata stained dark from fires. It was a layer cake of history, laid bare before her, and flood lit in the dark night. She imagined the dozens; perhaps hundreds of buildings and thousands of years of loving and hating, violence and joy, sadness, death, disease and destruction on that single spot. She felt weighed down by the history and distressed by the futility of it all.

'What does it matter?' she muttered out loud as she thought to herself. 'We are all food for worms, our brief lives will be over soon, and nothing will matter.'

'Have you been in there?' the taxi driver said, jutting his chin at the building next door. 'The Museum of London. Great place – shows all the things that have happened here – right here on this spot.'

'No' Monica said with more sharpness than she intended. She usually chatted to drivers, but tonight, exhausted, she did not have the energy for a late-night conversation that could go anywhere.

'It's really brilliant; full of ancient history fossils, geology, and all the people stuff. I take my kids there heaps. They love the Roman relics,' the driver continued.

Monica was transformed. Here I am, exhausted in the middle of the night with a taxi driver who loves taking his kids to the museum. That's what the struggles are for, she thought. Damn Malthus with his – *life is nasty, brutish and short.* Having the majority of the population able to read, work in relative safety (although sometimes safety for a taxi driver in London could not be taken from granted) and bring up their kids and take them to the museum – that's exactly why it's worth struggling. This is democracy in action. Not voting, but the democratisation of opportunity, the decoupling of people from endless backbreaking labour and giving them the chance of improvement. That was worth hundreds of years of struggle. It is about a legacy of wealth she thought.

It's about each generation leaving something that the next generation didn't have to relearn. Not wealth in the narrow meaning of money but literacy, hope, clean buildings and public institutions like museums. She found the idea comforting. That is why I like fighting these injustices. What, she asked herself am I going to leave?

It was too late at night to be having this conversation, even inside her head. But it inspired her to look at the problem in a new way. 'Be dammed, if I'm going to let Yves get away with it,' she mumbled to herself. 'I might not have any kids, or be a great artist, but I'm good at my job. One less bastard in a position of power would be good. That'll be my legacy,' she thought. She felt her energy returning. 'I just need to think with more creativity. If Stan can't help me, I need to think of a new angle.'

'Here's your address m'am,' the driver said, shaking her back into the present.

'Thanks mate,' she said with warmth as she left a generous tip. 'Take your kids on another visit to the museum.'

Monica vowed to talk to Richard again in the morning. One form of retribution, or was it justice, started to glimmer in her mind. After a night's sleep it might have a little more substance, a little more credibility.

Richard couldn't sleep either. He received her early morning text message proposing another meeting as he stewed over the frustrating discussion with the detective. He was used to getting what he wanted. He had an unmistakable feeling that he was missing something – it niggled like a sore tooth. He too began to formulate another plan. Perhaps, if they were lucky it might even work.

Chapter 42

All in a Name

Zoe had been giving interviews all day, TV, radio and the papers. She was exhausted. Sliding into bed alone, she wished for good company. Comfort, companionship. No – a hard male body. She had no doubt that she could enjoy good sex with Yves, but she also craved warmth and closeness. Her thoughts strayed to Michael. She hardly knew him, but that didn't stop the fantasy. Nice wide shoulders. Warm eyes. Looked like he knew what a good time was. Giving Yves what he wanted was not part of her plan. Her head whirled, emotions on a high. She hoped her painting would be critically well received, and good money would follow.

Richard and Monica had been full of news and information about Montague Corporation, Yves and Alston. Progress about her father was glacially slow. After their first awkward meeting, Zoe and Harry found surprising satisfaction in working together. There were few words but pleasure in small things; a shared commitment to putting things right.

This morning after weeks of no progress, she'd received a postcard from Jack Robinson, an old fisherman from Robe. He had heard from Costas that Zoe was asking about exporters her father may have dealt with. He decided to write to her because he had liked Mac and always wondered about what happened. When Zoe had spoken to the other old men, Jack had been travelling around Australia in his caravan. Returning home and talking to his old friends, he'd remembered that there was an aggressive buyer called Tang in Hong Kong and hoped that the information may help. Jack wished her luck and it gave her hope.

In her half sleep, information from the two investigations swirled in her thoughts. Yves seemed reluctant to answer her questions directly, which made her suspicious. After Rouen she remembered his response to the colloquial expressions she had deliberately chosen to test him. Yves had understood; none of them had fazed him, even when she had said that Monica had more front than John Martins. His smile meant that he had been to South Australia, not just Australia. The big department store and the Christmas pageant had become an institution and its name had crept into the vernacular. It was enough to make Zoe believe he had spent time there. Then Harry confirmed Zoe's hunch that Yves had spent time in Australia. Everywhere Yves went he had opportunistic fingers out making money. Zoe wondered if Yves could be involved in her father's mystery.

There was no doubt that Yves knew a lot more about the fishing industry than he readily admitted. He'd talked about cockles rather than pipis so Zoe was convinced he'd been to Goolwa where these delicacies were famous. The world was a strange place and with all the shady dealings the team had uncovered, she should keep alert to new possibilities.

Harry discovered Yves often used other names in his business dealings when he was young, and these were yielding valuable clues. Maybe Stan would be able to prosecute him under one of those names. As Zoe's mind drifted on the edge of sleep, a half memory niggled at the back of her mind. Then, through the drowsiness of half sleep, she heard her father's voice from the depths of her memory.

Good Aussie bush boy that he was, he often called people *mate* and explained that this guy did this or that. Before his disappearance, Zoe could hear his frustrated pleas with her mother. 'It will be all right. No one will lose from this. The guy promised – or no ...was it Guy promised?' She vividly remembered the anguish in her father's voice. Could pronunciation be the key to the riddle?

Pronounced the French way, Guy was *Gee*. Harry discovered that when he was young, Yves had used his first name Guy. French pronunciation or not, was this the clue she had been missing? Could a Frenchman called Guy have led her father astray? Zoe sat bolt upright in her bed, wide-awake. Could they be hunting the same man?

Zoe waited impatiently until morning, anxious to share her theory.

'Monica, wake up. I think I've come up with something,' Zoe blurted out as soon as she heard Monica stirring.

She explained her theory. They decided to contact Richard and Harry.

'Let's meet for lunch, Monica and I have a new idea,' Zoe said to Richard. They'd all been busy and had progress to report. Zoe sent a text to Harry hoping he might have some additional snippets of information.

As soon as the friends had gathered, Zoe spilled her story.

'As I traced back through the newspapers from those days, some fragmentary memories surfaced. I've tried to match my memories to the facts. Last night, half asleep; I recalled that when I was a kid, one of the last things I remembered about my Dad was excitement about talking to a French guy.

You all know my father was involved in seafood when he disappeared. I've identified several Chinese buyers who were actively buying lobster all that time ago. The Tang buying group out of Hong Kong was the most aggressive. Initially as we tried to track down Yves' early businesses, there were no connections. You persuaded me that he was worth investigating. He's been involved in a lot of dodgy deals, especially when he was younger. When I met him, I found him very charming. He showed he could be very persuasive. There is no doubt in my mind that he could probably convince anyone to do anything,' Zoe said.

'Yes, he is very compelling,' agreed Monica.

'Then Richard, you discovered that Yves used the name Guy. Harry and I have confirmed that Yves was in Australia around the same time my father disappeared, even though he seems to evade that question.

From some of the older fishermen, I confirmed that Tang was buying lobster in South Australia at that time. Harry's identified payments to Yves from a large seafood consortium involving Tang that sourced products from Australia.

I sort of remembered my father talking about a French Guy. But what if he was talking about a Frenchman who would pronounce his name Gee but to Australians like my father he would be called Guy.

So if I put 2 and 2 together to make 5 or even 6, I propose that Yves, who called himself Guy at that time, was probably the man who struck some sort of deal with my father to buy lobster to go to China. Whatever happened next, perhaps we will never know, but I am starting to think that Yves, alias Guy was implicated in, if not responsible for my father's disappearance.'

Everyone was riveted. It seemed plausible. It fitted the pattern. Zoe had plenty of circumstantial evidence.

'The more I think about it, the more I believe it's true.'

There were nods all around the table. Richard said, 'You could be on to something Zoe.' He waved another Harry report. 'Could Shakespeare be right? Is it all in a name?'

'Yves Montreau has received income from many businesses over the years, most of now defunct, with only shadows, and hints remaining in the graveyards of trading accounts and convoluted transactions. He seems to be a master of camouflage and deception.

'I thought about the way people use their names too. Using the company and owners' names in various combinations Harry and I changed our search criteria. We believe Yves operated under several different names when he was younger. His full name is Guy Yves Montreau de Ville. We believe he has used various combinations of those names, and others at different times. In the same way that people use predictable repetitions of their pets or children's names for computer passwords, Yves combined and recombined his names and the names of his companies in many configurations. That's why it was so confusing. This was not sufficient difference to need a legal change in identity. It was almost as if when he was young, he decided to practice using a name which he could later discard. So the man we know and have been following as Yves Montreau used to be called Guy de Ville.'

'You mean our two investigations have converged? God, talk about six degrees of separation,' said Monica her voice spiralling like a skyrocket.

'What are the chances that research for my articles in London about a French business man could show he was responsible for the disappearance of my friend's father from South Australia twenty years ago?' Her voice got strident.

'First I thought it was a bridge too far, even for my imagination,' said Zoe. 'But, the evidence is pointing in that direction. I feel like rushing out, grabbing Yves by his well-tailored lapels and forcing him to tell me what happened,' Zoe said sideswiping the wine bottle so hard it flew off the table.

'Hold it,' said Richard. 'A man with a lifetime of experience in manipulating the truth is hardly likely to go weak at the knees and confess the truth. If you want to know, you are going to have to magic it out of Yves without him suspecting that you are involved. If he knows you are Mac's daughter, you won't see him for dust. Our ability to pin anything solid on that man would be compromised.'

They'd all forgotten Harry, who sat in his usual invisible way at the end of the table gobbling his lunch as if it was the last meal he would ever see. Harry saved his news for Zoe until last. Late last night he'd traced the Tang Group that traded seafood all around Australia, New Zealand, from across the cold Southern waters and throughout the Pacific, for the Asian market.

'Here's what I've found. A consortium operated a fleet of boats, some of which were traders, some of which did their own fishing supplemented by purchases. The consortium, in turn, had a joint venture with a Chinese importer in Hong Kong, which was very active at the time of Mac' s disappearance,' Harry said as he pushed his empty plate to the side of the table. 'You all know that Zoe's father was probably on board a boat which had a missing load of lobsters. Well you might be interested in this photo,' he said shyly as he slid it across the table.

'Bugger me,' said Richard, who was usually much more careful with his language. The photo was old and grainy, taken from the Hong Kong newspaper *The South China Morning Post* in 1990. It showed a group of men in front of a boat in Hong Kong Harbour. The headline read *Huge Shipment of Prime Seafood Reaches Hong Kong*. And, among the happy faces, complete with caption was Guy d'Ville – a very youthful Yves Montreau.

Chapter 43

Payback

The morning started badly for Monica. It was raining even more than usual in London. Grey skies and miserable rain were not unusual this time of the year but the cold wind blew the rain up and under her umbrella, so she arrived at work damp, her cheeks glistening wet despite her waterproof coat and voluminous scarf. The foyer of the office was cluttered with dripping umbrellas and the fusty smell of damp wool hung like a pall as the heating struggled to cope. Monday morning meetings were often tense. It was the worst time of the week in the office. Thomas, the editor, always seemed angry. Accusations and papers had already been thrown as he took some of his frustrations out on reporters who were not in a position to protest.

As they were dismissed and moved back to their offices, Monica mused to a colleague. 'I think poor Tommy is in an impossible financial position. He likes the good things in life and if wife number one got half of his assets, then wife number two got half of the remaining half, then he had to share the last half of a half with wife number three; there's not much left.'

'No wonder he's miserable. It is a good thing that he's the editor and not the financial controller of the magazine otherwise we'd all be in trouble. I'm going out until the storm has passed.'

Monica escaped from the office as soon as possible on the pretext of an interview. *Parliamentos* was an oasis of calm in her frantic world. They served great coffee which she could smell half a block away and they had the best pastry for miles. The wide, comfortable plush seats encouraged a longer visit. Monica was a woman built for comfort not for speed; a generously proportioned woman, Rabelaisian she liked to call it. Perching on a slippery stool or a hard, narrow bench was just not conductive to ordering another cake with your second coffee.

'Good Morning Monica' said the chief waiter Raphael as rushed over to help with the heavy door being buffeted in the wind. 'Come in. Come in, it is a good morning for coffee.' As he took her umbrella, Monica hung her dripping coat and savoured the scent of rich coffee and baking. 'Your friend is already here.'

'Ah the scent of civilisation,' Monica said. 'What treats can you offer me this morning Raphael?' It was a pleasant ritual as he listed his favourite selection from the morning's delicacies, and together they would choose with enthusiasm.

'I love choosing my snacks here,' Monica said with vigour and a wide smile to Zoe across the room. 'You know Zoe, the thin, snotty little girls down in the closer but not-so-warm shop down the street raise their eyebrows at my generous frame. Their lack of enthusiasm might even deter me from ordering a second pastry.'

'Hard to imagine,' Zoe responded warmly.

'Ah, It's good to be here. Testosterone clouded the air of my office like nuclear fallout.' They glanced at the newspapers as Raphael prepared coffee and plated the raisin pastries; it was all very satisfactory.

'It's another frantic week at work – I have three major articles on the go and an editor who has just split up with his third wife and is more fractious than usual.'

'It's often like that after a holiday. Holidays are supposed to be relaxing; a time to spend with the friends and family but all too often they are tense combinations of exhaustion and unrealistic expectations,' replied Zoe.

'I know we were all frustrated when we failed to convince the police to take action against Yves. I understand you want revenge on behalf of the people Yves had defrauded. But after Harry's photo confirmed that Yves was in the seafood game and probably responsible for my father's disappearance, it became much more personal for me.'

'Not just you Zoe, all your friends feel the same way. You may want to challenge him but we all want our pound of flesh,' Monica replied. 'Now even more than before.'

'Yves is being very attentive. He's utterly convincing. It's hard to believe he is not the man he seems. I can see why he is so good at conning people. I need a man who is like he seems, intelligent, charming, attentive, rich and good looking.'

'No you don't. You want one who is honest, regardless of what he looks like. You know it's more important to be true to yourself and your friends rather than put your faith in a handsome rat. I'd tell you to be patient Zoe, but I know patience isn't easy for you.'

'I've been too patient for 20 years. Now I'm learning to take control. Yves is pretty keen. He thinks he is going to add me to his trophy cabinet. Whatever we plan I want to be able to look him in the eye when I show him that photograph,' said Zoe.

'I'm still planning to use bits of what we have discovered when the time is right,' said Monica. 'I've made good expose´s from less.' Monica ordered a second pastry and relished the rush of caffeine coursing through her veins. The pair was ready for action; refuelled, warm and prepared. They agreed to catch up with Richard and Harry on their usual Friday night get-together.

Zoe wandered back to the flat, so preoccupied that she kept jostling against other pedestrians. She collected Monica's mail, climbed the stairs and, with her hands full of the usual bills and advertising flyers, unlocked the door. Tucked among them was a large envelope addressed to Zoe in a childish hand but with Monica's address. She opened the letter, a single sheet torn from what looked like a school exercise book. It was wrapped around a small notebook. The short note began. *Dear Zoe, My Uncle Costas has had to go into an old folks' home and I found this when I cleaned out his stuff. It looks like it belonged to your father and since you were trying to find out about him, I decided to post it to you. Hope it helps. Best wishes, Diana Theodorakis.*

The blue, bent notebook had thin pages, some damaged, mostly empty; others scribbled. Zoe clutched it. It made her feel odd, as if her father's hand had reached through the years and touched her hair. Weird, she thought, this is getting to me as she flicked through the pages, hoping for a clue, a hint, anything.

Chapter 44

Three Pronged Attack

The trio chose the AllBarOne for drinks after work.

'I contemplated making Yves' portrait a caricature with him looking evil, but I've nearly finished. Can't change it now. Besides I can't afford the damage to my career,' said Zoe. 'He is so handsome. It is hard to hint at something rotten beneath such an elegant exterior. I was thinking of a different track. From what you've told me, and from my first-hand experience, he's made seducing women one of his favourite activities for years. I'm in his sights as his next conquest. If I string him along, and trust me that won't be hard, he might get even keener. If I look even remotely interested, I think I can suck him in. I don't think he likes failure. Then I'll tell him he is an ageing rat. That might put a dent in his over-blown ego. It sounds a bit underhanded, but I guess it would give him a taste of his own medicine. It might also give me a chance to make him feel vulnerable while I tackle him about my father.'

'Maybe,' Monica said looking doubtful. After a busy week, Monica had recovered her sense of humour and enthusiasm. Over the second drink she said, 'I think I can contribute a public exposé,' she said rubbing her hands together. 'If we can't get him prosecuted, a public stoning might have to do.'

'We all agree we just can't let him get away with this. We have to do something. If our best legal advice is that we don't have enough information to get him prosecuted, we need to take action ourselves,' said Zoe.

'A pointed media article can be powerful Monica. But how much do you really think your editor, or the libel lawyers will allow?' Richard queried. 'If you can't name and shame publicly, perhaps leaking anonymous information to carefully selected people at the right time might be more effective.'

'I've been looking at Yves' finances,' said Richard. 'His portfolio is very unbalanced.'

'Well how can we hit Yves where it would cause maximum pain – his bank balance?' asked Zoe.

'I think money is Yves' passion. It's the foundation of his lifestyle. If we can't legally hold him to account for past misdeeds, maybe we can get revenge by hurting his bank balance. Losing serious money would be painful. I think the best plan is to try to damage Yves by depriving him of a great deal of money and damaging his reputation,' offered Richard whose long experience as an investor gave him a clear understanding of how rumour and gossip influenced share prices.

'Sure, Richard. But how can we do that?' said George.

'Oh, I've thought of a plan. It might just work if we all pull together. We need to combine the three plans,' said Richard as the three huddled closer. 'It's all about information and timing. Zoe if you are charming and captivate Yves even further, we might be able to isolate him from information at a crucial time when we spring the trap. Monica you can write the articles you want to write but hold off publishing them for the moment. I think the environment for release may change soon. While some of the material we have unearthed may be leaked out, I think we need to intervene more aggressively,' he said, his eyes cold as frosted steel.

'Getting justice for all the people he has deceived is good, but I need more than a court appearance,' Zoe complained. 'I need something personal.'

'Get real Zoe. There is nothing more personal to a rich man than losing money. Besides, it's our best option. Yves' financial exposure is with the pharmaceutical company and share prices in that realm are often volatile. Prices can leap around based on perceptions and hints rather than concrete data. With careful management of information, we might be able to influence the share price, and that could cause Yves plenty of grief. But we'd have to be well prepared and skilful,' Richard said. 'I've got a loose group of investors I work with from time to time. If we agree this is a good idea, I can probably convince them when to buy then when to sell. Together we might just be able to change the share price. The way Yves has concentrated his portfolio is risky.' Richard said.

'I've made money from companies associated with leading edge research in fields like this before. Even before a product comes to market, it can make or lose investors a great deal of money. There's serious investor interest in all sorts of medical inventions at the moment. Things such as heart replacement valves or innovations like the bionic ear. The next big money will come from rejection-free implants. But with the aging population, cosmetic treatments are also popular, and if this anti-aging treatment works Alston would be a great investment. I've asked Harry to focus on what the current research team is up to in Alston. I think Yves is positioning himself to make a killing. He seems very sure of himself. Fortunately for us, that overexposure makes him vulnerable.'

'Do you seriously think that manipulating the share price could work?' said George. 'I can see that anti-aging is the Holy Grail. From ground-up monkey organs to gold leaf, people have been captivated by the idea of the elixir of life forever. Probably ever since they became aware of the inevitability of death. It is the perfect set-up for a scam,' said George.

'But I don't think it's a scam George. Scanning through Harry's summaries of the research from the new team at Alston, I think they're on to something big. Their research is delivering positive results, and there's a cashed-up aging population desperate to look younger for longer. I want to buy some shares,' said Richard smiling.

'I agree. Drugs are used in higher quantity and variety than ever before in history. The opiate of the masses. Doctors have become a powerful priesthood since the success of antibiotics,' said George. 'The holders of arcane and sought-after knowledge. If this has potential, I don't see how he can lose.'

'At this stage of the research, information and confidence are the keys,' said Richard.

'But what could we do to ensure Yves loses money this time instead of everyone else?' asked Zoe.

'I think we'd need a careful plan for both share buying and selling together with a very well-orchestrated release of some crucial information. I'll meet some friends tomorrow and see if we can rustle sufficient money to swing this,' said Richard.

'OK. In the meantime, Zoe, I think your idea to get closer to Yves is a good one,' said Monica.

'Absolutely. If we manipulate the share price, we need you to distract him at a crucial time, so his shares lose value. Harry will also be important. If we are to succeed, we might need to be able to track and perhaps even control Yves' access to information and availability at certain times. That way we may be able to delay him trading his shares at a crucial time. I'll give Harry a call now,' said Richard.

'I think my man is coming out of his shell a little,' Richard confided. 'Harry was almost enthusiastic. He's always been good at discovering things. Very focused on this job. I even think he's enjoyed working with you Zoe. He says he started down this path some time ago – seems to have his own agenda.'

Zoe said, 'I'll find out whatever I can while finishing the portrait. I'll play it cool, flutter my eyelashes and capture Yves' attention even more. If he has a heart, I'll engage it. Any additional information I discover will be a bonus.'

'I'm going to continue with the article for my magazine. I'll take a business ethics slant. Then I can raise public attention about unequal contracts and the abuse of power. The idea that companies behave with altruism or even ethically is already suspect with the public. Initially I won't refer to Yves, but if we release information about his deals, public pressure will be quick to judge his bad behaviour. I think it will be easy to convince my editor to do another feature on Yves – he's photogenic, wealthy and a little exotic. We've already lobbied for a special feature each month and I will use my good reputation for delivering interesting copy to convince him to go with this ethical theme.'

'Not bad,' Zoe agreed.

'I've already made initial contact with Yves and buttered him up. He's bought the personality piece. That will sow the ground with fertile seeds about his looks, his status and of course, his wealth. The next stage will depend on what we can uncover and use without the legal advisors getting too jumpy. I don't want to get caught in the cross-fire,' said Monica.

'Do you really think this could work Richard?' Zoe asked.

'Not in isolation, but maybe everything together.'

Walking home, Zoe smiled. Richard was working on it. Harry was working on it. Monica was already in action. The portrait and the hours necessary to deliver it had provided her with a golden opportunity to get closer to Yves. Perhaps even at the launch, she could discover something useful. Delivering restitution for some of the people Yves wronged, would be worthwhile.

Zoe felt shredded, thin, pulled in too many directions at once.

Monica wanted the story; Richard had big money riding on her performance, Michael kept mailing good wishes. Zoe wasn't suited to bloody revenge; she wanted to put the ghost of her father to rest. Instead of exhilaration, she felt alone and sad, wishing for the impossible; for time to be turned back, for her father to suddenly appear.

Fairy tales, she thought as she willed herself to focus on the plan. Zoe would hold Yves on tenterhooks; he was luscious even if he was a rat. Now she knew he was probably responsible for her father's disappearance Zoe wanted closure. For her, money was only money, but Zoe sensed Yves valued cash much more than she did. Perhaps losing millions would be sufficient punishment.

Chapter 45

Helsinki

'Look what I got this morning,' Nathan said as the team gathered for the morning round up. 'I think we've made somebody's list,' he said as he passed around the elaborate invitation complete with an airline ticket and a hotel voucher from the conference sponsors.

'I've always wanted to go to Helsinki,' said Cheng. 'I'll go.'

'The program looks spot on – "*Contemporary Thoughts on Gene Action*,' said James. 'They've got speakers from everywhere. Be a great place to meet potential collaborators.'

'The invitation depends on me leading a group discussion to share ideas about current research and working with industry,' said Nathan.

'What do you think Yves will say?' said David.

'He doesn't bloody own us,' Nathan snapped. 'I'll be circumspect; talk in general terms and not about applications. That should satisfy him.'

'Well, I reckon he's a bit touchy about us talking outside the company at this stage of the research,' said Cheng.

'Tough. I'm going. I think I deserve it.'

'OK. Sounds like he's not the only touchy one,' said Cheng. 'Good luck.'

At home that night, Nathan waved the letter to his girlfriend Beth.

'If they're paying for me, it will only cost us one airfare. We already have the accommodation.' Beth shrieked and hugged him.

'Brilliant. Do you know we've been together for four years now, and a while ago I was beginning to think we we'd live on beans forever.'

'Yeah, maybe the food will be good too. What on earth do they eat in Finland?' asked Nathan.

'God. It's only three days away! We'll have to find our passports and get organised,' said Beth. 'Reliable hot water, big baths, fluffy towels, heaven. I don't have another gig for two weeks and I can get Karen to cover the restaurant shifts. She needs the money,' said Beth.

'I feel like a kid on a summer holiday,' Nathan said as they headed to the airport. The flight from London to Helsinki was only two hours in the air but a dramatic change in culture and scenery.

'I've never been offered vodka for breakfast before,' Beth said as they watched TV and ate peanuts. 'That movie about the polar bears was scary. Do you think we'd be able to see one from the plane?' Beth asked peering out of the window.

'No, crazy girl, but I think I can see a couple of thousand lakes. I think Finlanders might need fins. There seems far more water than land, and fab scenery.' The plane cruised to a smooth landing; they found their luggage and were soon speeding away from the small airport in a taxi.

'If this is summer, I'm glad we are not here in winter Nathan.' Beth said. 'I can feel ice in the air. Look at all these birch trees. No wonder they make so much furniture. They're so white. Oh, and look at the cool trams. Helsinki looks great. It's so clean, I'm glad we came.'

The deep harbour was bristling with giant ferries and cargo vessels. The shrieking of the gulls and the deep sirens of the ships in the harbour gave the centre of the city an adventurous air. The holiday-makers checked in to their hotel next to a wharf.

'Cute windows,' said Beth. 'They're just like portholes. I've never seen thick little round windows in a hotel before. Look at this,' she shrieked as the tall stacks of a ship funnels slid past the window of their second-floor room. 'There's a market down there. Let's go.' Beth grabbed Nathan's arm.

'OK, OK,' said Nathan as they practically raced down the stairs. The cobblestone market was next to the dock. It was summer, but chunks of ice still floated in the sea. The air might seem cold to Nathan and Beth, but the locals had short sleeves and summer smiles.

'I just have to buy this mug with a reindeer pattern,' said Beth. As the stallholder wrapped her mug, Beth chatted on.

'Do you know what the locals do when the ice starts melting?' she asked Nathan. 'Travel even further north to enjoy the unfrozen lands in the brief summer, swim in the freezing lakes, go fishing. They're a tough lot.'

'Not for me,' said Nathan. 'I need something over 10 degrees.'

'I'm exploring the city while you're at the conference tomorrow. I've bought this city pass from one of the stalls and get free transport and entrance to all the major attractions.

They've got great music here. I think we should go to a Sibelius concert.'

The conference, opened by a local dignitary informed delegates that Finland was so close to the North Pole that six months of every year the country was wrapped in icy darkness. Fins survived the harsh conditions with a unique blend of creativity and stoicism. Dramatic music and fine arts flourished in these people for whom extremes were routine. It was a good introduction. Next to Nathan, a young, and very good-looking journalist applauded loudly.

'Are you a speaker?' she asked. 'Fabulous, I'm Mandy,' she said showing her press pass and extending her hand.

'I'm running a workshop tomorrow,' said Nathan.

'Great. I'll come, and then could you do an interview for me? Something the general punter can understand.'

'Will it help me win the Nobel?' said Nathan.

'Probably.' She laughed as they checked their phones and headed for the next session.

Back in London, Richard received Mandy's text saying *Contact established.*

Nathan's text from Yves was brief. *Share issue going well. Phase 2 research funds now available.*

Nathan walked back to the hotel and met Beth in the bar.

'I feel on top of the world,' he said. 'Literally and metaphorically. But I wish the experiments at home could be fast tracked. There's a lot of smart brains working in this field, they might beat us unless we can isolate the mode of operation soon. We've conclusively proved the compound we isolated suppressed gene replication errors and delivered favourable experimental results,' said Nathan.

Beth groaned. 'Drink please.'

'Sorry, get a bit carried away. More important, I got a text from Yves which gives us the funds to segment the test subjects by age and skin type.'

'I'm sure you'll do great things. I'm not sure I understand it, but it sounds good to me,' Beth said.

'The best thing is we've eliminated the unpleasant side effects caused by the first formulations. Our future will be much rosier if my career takes off,' said Nathan.

'I bet good science isn't sufficient to satisfy Yves though,' Beth said.

'He wants a marketable product that will make him millions or billions even better,' Nathan said. 'It was brilliant to talk about our work with other researchers today. I'd forgotten how much I enjoy that. I've also been looking at the clear complexions of the northerners at the conference. I must get Cheng to test the effects of temperature on the telomere fraying process. If the drug worked well in Africa, it might work even better in cold climates.'

'While you've been talking genes, I've been to this amazing church. It's cut right into the bare rocks of the mountainside,' Beth said. 'The tour of the city was good too. I didn't know that Finland was ruled by Sweden for years. Apart from the weather it would be hard being a tiny country squeezed between powerful Sweden and immense Russia. And, back at the hotel I met this amazingly friendly woman from England who has invited us out to dinner,' Beth said. 'She's great fun and has travelled everywhere. She's even been to Australia, so you can talk about home. She has a Finnish friend who is buying us all dinner and offering to tell us all about the country too.'

'You know me. Never knocked back a free dinner. What time?'

'Eight. Should be fun, the invitation is to a Lapp restaurant.'

'They were talking about that at the conference today. Apparently, it's called Sauri food, from the far north.'

'I always thought it was Lapland, home to reindeer and Father Christmas.'

'A free dinner invitation and seeing you so happy sounds good,' said Nathan as they went back to their room to rug up before walking through the cold clear air to the tram stop.

Scores of young people strolled along the streets, talking and laughing, some played music in the park near the harbour. Armed with a public transport map, the addresses of their hotel, the restaurant and plenty of Euros, which they hoped not to use, they navigated easily.

'Look. They sell Foster's beer,' said Nathan pointing to the billboard. 'The world is a lot smaller than it used to be.'

After a short tram ride, they arrived at Annankatu 22 and found the restaurant. Traditional, it said on the window in curly red letters arced around a reindeer's head.

'I hope this is a good decision,' he said. 'Smells OK, and it's warm.'

The door swung back, and they saw the hundreds of objects that crowded the room. Mandy and her friend rose from their seats and came forward smiling.

'Welcome, welcome,' said Mandy. 'This is my friend Pekka.'

'This is an amazing place Pekka,' said Nathan. 'I can't decide if it is a museum exhibit, nomad tent or a film set.'

'Yes, this place shows many things used by the people from my country. You will see all objects hanging from horns on the ceiling and the walls are made from reindeer. Tools, utensils and decorative objects carved from reindeer bone and horn. Although in English it is better to call antlers. Reindeers shed their antlers every year; that way we can get a set of antlers and the reindeer stays alive. Horns are a more permanent arrangement,' he smiled.

'This restaurant is a shrine to the reindeer –very much liked by the tourist.'

'Come and sit,' said Mandy. 'The reindeer pelts are very soft.'

'This red, black and white embroidery is beautiful,' said Beth.

'First, a drink,' said Pekka pouring them all a yellowish drink which looked like advocaat.'

'Yum. What is it?'

'Cloudberry liqueur,' said Pekka. 'Keeps the cold away.'

'That table looks like a sleigh,' said Beth.

'I'm starving,' said Nathan. 'Look, reindeer, and plenty of fish.'

'I don't get how the reindeer can eat with snow on the ground most of the year,' said Beth as she loaded her plate.

'Reindeer have wide, splayed feet. They scrape snow off the lichen so they can eat it. Tough animals. My people learned to use all the reindeer –the pelts, even the bones and hooves. The variety surprises even me.' Pekka laughed.

The four of them settled into a wide table in the corner. The staff members were welcoming and soon the table was full of food and drinks. As well as craft and music, the Finns were great drinkers, and the restaurant was soon abuzz.

Beth's new friend Mandy was gorgeous as promised, and her handsome friend, Pekka was a well-informed local with a winning smile. The national drink, Cloudberry cocktail was made from small yellow berries, which looked like cranberries if the illustration on the label was to be believed. The liqueur slipped down easily and from that promising beginning, the drinking proceeded at a fierce pace. As they ate through plate after plate of smoked or salted fish and drank plenty, they were instant best friends and drinking buddies.

'We have four talented orchestras here in Helsinki and unless you hear Sibelius in Helsinki you will never understand Finland,' Pekka said moving closer to Beth. 'I'll tell you all the best places to visit here in Helsinki,' he said leaning forward.

'Let's start with Sibelius,' Beth said. 'I'm a violinist too you know.'

Pekka's deep blue eyes shone and for the next two hours, they discussed music and passion. The food was fragrant, the reindeer tender and prepared in several interesting ways. Fine slices of dried carpaccio, stewed or roasted; were delicious. Over yet another bottle of wine, Nathan relaxed.

'Are you sure you are interested in all of this,' Nathan asked. 'I've been rabbiting on about my work for almost an hour.'

'Absolutely,' said Mandy. 'If I understand it, you are really working on the Elixir of Youth,' she cooed. 'You must be so clever. It's like a dream, you must tell me more,' she said as Nathan preened. The wine was finished, and the Cloudberry liqueur circulated again. It was a deceptive drink. Smooth and sweet on the palate it packed a significant punch and by the time they stood to leave the table, Nathan discovered his legs were not as responsive as usual.

The taxi arrived and enclosed them in welcome warmth against the sharp night air. Nathan and Beth made their way unsteadily across the lobby of their hotel.

'She's got amazing eyes,' he said.

'Yes, deep brown, almost as deep as her cleavage,' Beth answered.

'You know me – always been a breast man,' he laughed.

'Well, I enjoyed Pekka, so its tit for tat. But I didn't get to see his tat,' Beth said and they both roared with laughter.

As they staggered into bed, Mandy was furiously typing. Despite appearances she had drunk very little. After an intense hour's work, she called Richard.

'Pekka occupied Beth while I grilled Nathan,' she said. 'You're right Richard, it's a great story. God it's weird here. Night's officially over but the sun is still shining. I've emailed a copy of my article to you. My editor's on board. I hope the headlines will shout something like '*Secret research team makes Major Anti-Aging Discovery*'. With any luck it will be quickly syndicated, and I will earn a fat bonus as well as a giant boost to my reputation.

'Anti-aging is a winner. It will get coverage,' said Richard from London. 'Nice to have the first stage of the plan falling neatly into place. Well done Mandy. Let's talk again tomorrow.

Chapter 46

Portrait Launch

The launch was to be a glittering affair in the style London did so well. Unbeknown to Zoe, Yves had called in some favours and supplemented the entertainment budget to ensure the crowd was large, enthusiastic and supplied with plenty of good quality champagne.

'Good evening to you Miss Macintosh, Queen of the Portrait,' he announced with a flourish as he opened the door of the stretch limo which looked out of place outside Monica's flat.

'Good evening, my subject,' she joked, extending her hand for him to kiss as he lapped up the aura of youth and excitement which surrounded her. 'Tonight, I am the star of the show. I can't wait to see who is there. Monica said over two hundred people accepted the invitation. I hope to get at least another ten commissions from the super-rich who will be bowled over by my brilliant work, and my modesty!'

Yves kissed her glowing cheek while wanting to devour her, piece by luscious piece.

'I am already your greatest fan. The guests will soon be lusting after a MacIntosh rather than a Maserati.'

The car cruised to a standstill and Zoe took a quick breath. The lobby of the hotel, complete with red carpet, overflowed with jewels and furs in front of the eager press. The crowd had been well orchestrated.

Cameras flashed, and the large function room was packed. Waiters circulated dispensing sparkling glasses of champagne between the hum of conversation. Yves, handsome and exuding success in an impeccably tailored tuxedo, circulated Zoe through the crowd, working the room, savouring each moment, and enjoying the envious glances from the men. In his mind they were already the perfect couple.

Zoe beamed with delight. Her dress of startling cobalt blue highlighted her shining eyes. Against the vivid patterns and gold stitched embroideries, that studded the room, her dress might have been seen as stark. The simple cut and high neckline accentuated the perfection of her tall, slim figure. Seen from behind, the plunging cowl back with pearl trim was daring. Zoe thought it epitomised her personality – apparently simple and straightforward, but with boldness and complexity underneath. She was no virgin queen, no simple soul. Her clear skin upswept blonde hair and single pearl earrings completed the image of timeless beauty. She had chosen a classic design; she wanted to treasure the photographs from tonight for years to come. She felt drunk even before sipping the champagne.

At the sound of spoon on crystal glass and the crackle of the microphone, a hush fell, and all eyes turned to the dais at the end of the room. The editor of the magazine, Roland Milligan asked Yves and Zoe to join him on the stage. As they made their way forward, he welcomed the guests, and the formalities began. The head of the business association mumbled dull words about a natural fit between art and business, which no one believed. Roland was the official host, and behind the screen he signalled with enthusiasm to the drinks waiter. Zoe was amused to see him sneak down two more glasses of the excellent champagne before reclaiming the microphone.

'*Your Business* magazine is renowned for its innovation in profiling important business successes and the people behind them. At this exciting launch tonight, we are unveiling the first of our new, exciting 'Portrait Series'. Please welcome our first French subject, Yves

Montreau.' The crowd clapped politely. Yves looked every inch a work of art. He drew approving glances from the women, which increased as he spoke in his mellow, slightly accented voice. His words were few and well chosen.

'Thank you,' he said casting his eyes down with appealing modesty. 'But the main purpose of the evening is to unveil my portrait painted by the talented young Australian artist Zoe MacIntosh. I can't wait to see the final product myself. You might say I have a vested interest in it,' said Yves.

With a dazzling smile he added further warm words about Zoe, her skill and what he hoped was her promising future.

Together, the three threw off the red silk cover to loud applause.

It was a compelling work. It was a fresh, exciting portrayal of Yves. His realistic torso leaned dramatically forward and piercing eyes engaged the watcher. The likeness, all cool greys and shades of purple from the darkest velvet chair to his pale chevron tie, was powerful. This image was framed by an almost surreal painted doorway decorated with an unusual collection of small, brightly coloured tropical objects including trees, fish and coconuts which could only be seen with close scrutiny. The internal frame was skewed from the external frame of the painting. It delivered an arresting impression of depth and complexity. It was a bold combination of classic portraiture in a modern, fresh context. As the applause died down, people smiled, and many moved forward to inspect the work; others were pleased to return to drinking and chatting.

Yves could barely tear his eyes from Zoe. Her face glowed. People surged forward with congratulations and the couple accepted the warm accolades with modesty and grace.

'You are a goddess,' he whispered in her ear as they descended from the podium once the crowd had thinned.

'Even goddesses need to eat.' She laughed batting his attention away. 'I am going to die of starvation if I don't eat soon. I couldn't eat earlier because I was too excited and now, I'm ravenous.' Yves laughed mentally, contrasting her enthusiasm with the many French women he knew who made it their life's work to subsist on lettuce and cigarettes. It was a pleasure to share a meal with someone who enjoyed food with relish.

'I've already booked,' said Yves.

'I'll settle for a pie or a hot dog if necessary, I just need to eat,' said Zoe as the crowd drew them apart. Despite the accolades and the excitement, Yves was pleased the remainder of the event was mercifully short. As soon as the champagne stopped being served, the crowd began to disperse.

'I am taking you to a proper dinner,' Yves said, breathing seductively onto her neck from behind as he circled to take her arm. 'I have arranged everything and have a car waiting.' Zoe's thoughts were racing. George was occupied, Monica away on another job and Zoe had not even seen Richard among the crowd, so she had no backup available to deflect Yves. She needed to be careful. Yves looked luscious. He was keen. She was on a high and the excitement made her sexually alight. She wished she were eighteen again, naïve and without responsibilities. Zoe knew he was dangerous, and she was playing with fire, but she needed to captivate him, string him along, capture him but not be seduced. Most of all she would have to work hard not to give the game away.

Yves had chosen a French restaurant, a response to his national pride. They arrived like royalty and were ushered in with the deference Zoe hated. Service was good but too servile for her taste. It brought her coldly back to the task at hand. As they were shown to their table Zoe's heart raced.

'It's been an exciting night. I couldn't ask for better promotion,' Zoe said as she struggled to stay in control.

Yves was keen to promote both himself and his products. Both would benefit from the success of the portrait. She demolished her plate of fois gras and bolted her first glass of champagne with indecent haste. Then she gathered herself and sighed.

'Enough about me. I'll get a swollen head. Where were your parents from? What did they do? What did they want you to be?' Yves blinked. He had to think. The truth was not an option. He could not share with this beautiful woman he was desperate to impress, that his mother and father had been petty criminals. They were dead to him even if they might be alive. Even as a young man, Yves predicted their risky lives of violence among the shadows would take its toll. When he changed his name for the first time, he left the name and the mean, cruel, penny-pinching ugliness behind. His parent's single enduring legacy was a burning ambition to escape. He worked to craft a life to fit his ambition and not be bound by his grim beginnings. The only traces were rat cunning and a fierce commitment to win. He had no desire to open that can of worms.

'Modest beginnings. No highflyers in my ancestry. My father was a cabinetmaker who taught me about timber and furniture,' he said without a flicker. 'What about you?'

'My father was a fisherman with a great desire to become a grower of excellent grapes,' Zoe responded. 'We sound like a Bible story, the carpenter and the fisherman,' she joked. They chatted on and on, raw sexuality sparking in smouldering looks between them as course followed course of delicious food. Yves was on top of the world. Zoe was elated. She knew this portrait was an important step in fulfilling her ambition to become famous and she now had Yves in the palm of her hand.

'I'm excited about having your money tucked up in my bank account now,' she teased. She made a mental note to check the funds were cleared as soon as possible. She was looking forward to renting a small flat, which she would keep impeccably neat so she could focus on her work. She loved Monica dearly but couldn't think in the chaos of her home. The wine was a delight and as she mellowed, she found it increasingly hard to match the image of the devil they had researched with the attractive man in front of her. She reminded herself to stop drinking. Desperate for diversion, Zoe tried another tack. 'Tell me what you remember about Australia.'

Yves demurred mumbling about the long distance and his memories being lost in the past. 'I prefer to talk about London. My company has an elegant flat just behind Sloan Square, which is rarely used. There are good restaurants and interesting shops nearby. I am finding London very attractive and would like to spend more time here,' he said with a very direct stare.

Zoe recognised a proposition when she saw one. It had been a long time since she had enjoyed such good company. He was rich, it was clear he lusted after her and a liaison could be enjoyable for them both. Her parents had instilled in her a fierce desire for independence, but a fling, with this wealthy man who offered the luxury of high-quality food and wine, could be fun for a while.

'I do love your choice of restaurant,' she said skating past the unanswered question, which lay between them. 'You have great taste.'

'I have a distinct preference for you,' Yves said as he leant forward and cupped her hands. 'I like my life. I would love to be with you. You excite me, amuse me and I admire you. That sounds like a good recipe. Why don't we try it?' Now the offer was on the table, Zoe was nervous. Perhaps she was not as good at the spy game as she would have liked. Was he hooked? Could she pull this off? She was tempted.

'Let's not rush,' she said with a smile, which she hoped conveyed excitement laced with a tinge of hesitancy. 'Some recipes need longer preparation.'

'Zoe, you know I've wanted you ever since we met in Rouen.'

'And what a beautiful house you have there. Who is using all that style while you are in London?' Zoe replied slipping in a tangential reference to his wife in an attempt to cool his ardour. 'Now you have fed me such delicious food. To be honest, I am exhausted. I have interviews and appointments all day tomorrow. Perhaps we can have lunch together on Friday and talk about the future. I've loved getting to know you, and don't want to lose any delights by rushing.' Zoe hurried to more neutral conversation.

Yves put his serviette down knocking the plate. 'I'm not a patient man,' he started but as he looked across the table, he decided she was worth waiting for.

'You Australians. Not always as direct as you'd have us believe,' he said. 'Now let's choose a dessert to round off this delicious meal. I can be very persuasive Zoe. We are made for each other and, I'm already counting the minutes until Friday.'

Chapter 47

Executing the Plan

The stock market opened with a buzz on the big open floor full of traders and media screens at the stockbroker's office. Richard smiled. Then he started making calls from one of the soundproofed rooms.

'Good morning, Zoe. We're ready. I'm looking forward to making big money this week if all goes to plan. Buying first. Mandy's first article will be released tomorrow, and we should see the Alston share price rocket.'

'You sound excited Richard,' she said.

'It's the gamblers rush. You know risk and the chance to make big money. I think we've got enough information and I'm ready. I'm doing a lot of trading to ensure these transactions don't attract undue notice.'

Zoe imagined Richard with his heart pounding and his eyes wide.

'I can't wait,' said Zoe. 'If our plans work, Yves will get a nasty shock. He's delivered plenty of shocks in his time. Let's hope he gets a taste of his own medicine.'

They didn't have to wait long. The stock market opened with Alton shares at €5.70. Just as Richard had predicted, the first upward price movements of the morning were small. He and his collaborators bought small parcels.

'Is everything going as you might expect?' Zoe asked when he called back.

'Sure, but there are plenty of variables. We can't be sure that things will respond as expected.'

'Don't worry I won't dent your cool image by telling people how hard you've worked and worried.'

By the end of the day the price had risen to €6.89 and Richard called Monica.

'The hairs on the back of my neck are starting to prickle,' he said.

'It wouldn't do to feel jaded, Richard. 'I know you've had an exciting and lucrative career – travelled to every corner of the globe, and now you are here fighting for the little guys,' Monica laughed.

'Maslow's hierarchy is true you know. For a while life has been a little too comfortable, a bit too easy. I've worked hard as well as being lucky. My mother used to say, the harder you work, the luckier you got. It's my low threshold of boredom you know. At least when you prick my conscience it brings a little piquancy.'

'Yves is an arrogant bastard,' said Monica. 'I think you'll enjoy bringing him down.' 'It's not been easy. And we aren't there yet.'

'For all his crooked deals, Yves is a cunning and secretive quarry. I'm not surprised the police weren't confident enough to prosecute.

'I think his motto is *Never step in the same river twice.*'

'Well, I'm glad you have girded your financial loins, prepared your weapons and are on the battlefield,' said Monica.

'Ghastly metaphor, think I'll go home now.'

'No – wait. Have a bet with me. How much will the share price rise tomorrow after Mandy's article?'

Richard glanced around his stockbroker's office, all pale grey and brushed steel, lined with walls of computer screens, and full of sharp young men with trendy haircuts, fashionable suits and expensive after shave.

Dozens of phones rang, the screens flickered, and the hubbub of voices started to pick up pace. Richard's eyes stayed on the share price of Alston Pharmaceuticals. To everyone in the office, he was his customary calm and urbane self.

'100% by the close of trade,' he said.

'We'll talk then,' said Mandy.

Alston had foreshadowed a statement 11am. Their optimistic forecast triggered some buying. At noon, Mandy's article hit the airwaves under the headline '*Exciting Young Scientists make Breakthroughs in Anti-Aging*'. The media lit up.

In his Oxford Street office, Yves was annoyed at first, but soon realised the positive coverage was a godsend. Every company wanted third party endorsement for its products, and this coverage came without cost.

'Going well, Monica,' Richard said on the phone. 'Thanks to Harry, we know that Alston's marketing team is planning to announce the breakthroughs soon. The share price is likely to rise again. I'm confident that through Mandy we are in control of the information timetable. I reckon Alston's marketing team will scramble to support the positive reports in the media. It might be a bit earlier than we planned, but still OK.'

'It's looking good Harry. After Mandy's article the price has risen to €10. Let's hope it builds momentum. We need this to be our gold rush. A few big buyers could spark an avalanche. I really hope this plan works,' Richard said.

'There are plenty of rumours circulating,' Harry replied. 'I've seeded extra ones anonymously on social media just to help things along.'

'Well, I'm monitoring the market, Monica is covering the press, I need you to watch the Internet for anything unexpected. But, most of all I need you to keep your electronic eyes on Yves.'

'I win,' Richard said to Monica. 'OK I'll buy you a wine,' she said.

'How good?' she asked.

'True to my predictions. No actually even better. Higher than I expected and even higher than I'd hoped. Demand and prices are still rising. Perhaps the promise offered by this new treatment would be like the Tulip Mania in the 1630s when the price of tulip bulbs became worth a house or two. There is a lot of volatility in several segments of the market. Everyone clamoured to get a slice of the action. At the end of Thursday's trading, Richard called Zoe.

'So far so good. The response is excellent. I've increased my stock value by two hundred per cent at the close of the Stock Exchange. I have a solid holding, but I know Yves has much, much more. The stage is set perfectly for the next stage of our plan.'

'Thank God for Harry,' Monica replied.

'Are we sure that Yves hasn't seen the negative research results?' Zoe asked.

'As sure as we can be,' Richard responded. 'Harry says the instability and negative results from the first trial batches have been a great source of worry to Nathan's research team. The revised drug, which is now being trialled in Europe, is more stable, and apparently there have been no more negative effects. The team has been working to define the characteristics of people who may have a negative response. It might be business as usual in the chancy drug business, but negative reactions are dynamite to the public.'

'Are you sure that your newshound Mandy has enough information?' Zoe asked.

'Yes, I briefed her well using all Harry's information. I might have engineered her meeting with Nathan in Helsinki, but she delivered the goods by getting excellent information directly from him. We can trust her to continue the good work. She's keen to make a big name for herself and has great networks.'

Catching Zoe's nerves, Richard called Mandy to get an update.

'Don't worry Richard. I've got enough material for at least three articles. The positive one I released last week has been taken-up in all the major media services. It's getting traction in the social media space too,' she said.

'I've hinted to my contacts that new revelations are coming. There'll be a huge response when I release the negative article tomorrow. I'm all set to go. The best time for release is in the middle of the day. Plenty of time for them all to get organised for the afternoon news services and then for evening TV.'

'A good deformity story always scares people. And, just as back up I've written the piece on the dodgy trials in Africa and I have another one prepared which casts doubt on Alston's ethics. That ought to send out plenty of shock waves.'

'Great work Mandy. Don't forget to send me copies too. Monica has plenty of contacts. She'll distribute it as well,' said Richard.

'Relax. You know I'm good in the social media space. The first article delivered me thousands of followers. I know that interest will soar with each release. I've already started blogging and tweeting furiously hinting at big announcements to come.'

'Till tomorrow then. Speed is important to keep Yves guessing.'

'Thanks Mandy. It's a pleasure dealing with you. Love the initiative.' Richard said, full of admiration for this smart, gutsy woman who was so keen to get ahead.

'Thank you for the info Richard. We should work together more often,' Mandy countered with a hint of promise in her voice.

'Let's talk again tomorrow to check our timing. We'll only get one shot at this.'

Monica's popular article and the publicity around his portrait had worked together to ensure Yves' likeness had been reproduced widely.

The leaked information about the exciting new research set the scene and the share price rose steadily. Yves would be feeling confident.

The next stage needed to be precise as a surgeon's scalpel. Mandy's story about the negative results in Africa would be released 12.45pm.

'Mandy at work is like a boxing match, fast and dangerous jabs that do a lot of damage,' said Richard. 'The release of the deformation results is the key to the share price plummeting, Monica.'

'Agreed. If we can't use the information in the legal system, social media is even better at spreading public fear. Besides, there is nothing the public likes better than the mighty falling.'

'But, for the plan to work, Yves must not be able to sell his shares. That needs Zoe,' said Richard.

At the end of Thursday's trading, Richard sold a significant parcel of shares at a pleasing profit. He called his confidential share buyer group and they were primed to follow his lead and sell all their shares just before midday on Friday. Richard traded many other shares and signed a contract to buy an expensive property. He knew the insider trading line was fine.

'Yves is a gambler. His confidence in the research results will convince him to hold his shares in the rising market. When Mandy's article about the negative research results hits the news, it will trigger a wave of panic selling.'

'Zoe must keep Yves completely engrossed over a long lunch. Harry will delay his messages as long as possible.'

Over the next weeks, the plan was for Mandy to release additional negative information to ensure the stock price did not recover, at least in the short term. In addition to the data Mandy had collected, she had encouraged her reporter friends to contact people who had lost money in Yves' schemes. With the reach of the Internet, faraway places were not so far away these days. Social media had the power to bring the people Yves had damaged together.

If all went well, Yves would lose his fortune, the value of his options would plummet and when he was unable to service his debt, the bankers would strip his carcass.

Chapter 48

Springing the Trap

While painting Yves' portrait, Zoe had been drawn to him. His wide browed symmetrical face with a slim nose matched her idea of perfection. His tall, spare body exuded masculinity without any hint of the football field.

Zoe had wanted to believe Monica's assessment of Yves character was wrong. She could have had fun with that man. He looked good, had sophisticated tastes, was an excellent conversationalist and was rich. The fact that she was drawn to him so powerfully in such a short time convinced her of his consummate skill in getting people to trust him. Was she was still too gullible? Was she her father's daughter in more ways than she acknowledged? David had fooled her. For a year, she had wrestled with and beaten her demons. She'd come face-to-face with her own weakness and vulnerability and rebuilt her self-esteem from the ground up.

Then, when she discovered that Yves had, at a minimum, been involved in her father's disappearance, desire was replaced by anger. Yves' schemes had been responsible for her father's death. Now she wanted answers. The princess had toughened up. She had left her weakness behind and was determined never be taken for granted or fooled again.

Blissfully unaware of these developments, Yves remained confident he could win Zoe. He was accustomed to success. She had been charming every time they met or communicated, but he wanted more.

'Red roses, on Monday I think, classic symbols of desire,' he said to the florist over the phone. On Wednesday, a beautiful book of eighteenth-century botanical illustrations, which he knew she admired. Yves planned to close the deal sooner than later. He planned a weekend away. He ached for it. More than anything he had wanted for a long time. Zoe agreed and mentioned a specialist art exhibition near Lake Como that looked exciting. Yves sourced a personal invitation and prepared to surprise her. Influence and power was always a winning combination for women.

'Good morning honey trap,' Richard said with a laugh in his voice as the conspirators met for early coffee to review the plan on Friday morning. 'Yves needs to be out of action for at least an hour for our plan to work. Zoe, you need to be utterly entrancing and keep him away from his mobile phone.'

'We all know the success of our plan depends on everyone playing his or her assigned part,' said Zoe. 'I'm channelling my anger into charm. Don't worry; I'll convince him he's irresistible. Men love that.'

'When we have succeeded in parting him from a great deal of money, then and only then you can challenge him,' Richard reminded her.

'This is my quest Richard. You might want to show how clever you are and Monica might want an exposé but I want revenge, and I have bought a fabulous new dress to do it in.'

Zoe looked forward to challenging Yves face-to-face so she could get the satisfaction of seeing his reaction.

'Have you rehearsed your script?' Monica said, aware that Zoe was feeling anxious. 'Hold your fire Zoe. Don't tip him off early.'

'OK, OK, I get the picture. I'll be my most charming even though I want to tear him limb from limb. And Monica, have you convinced your editor to publish?' asked Zoe. 'We need public humiliation as well as financial pain.'

'Yes, yes. The bulldog never sleeps,' Monica said.

'So, Zoe you need to make him forget about his mobile phone, and Harry will delay messages and calls to Yves for as long as possible,' Richard continued.

Monica had always been an avenging angel. Now the four of them were committed to payback. After checking the timetable, Zoe, nice as pie, confirmed the time for her lunch date with Yves and raced home to dress for the occasion.

Yves had booked Regatta's for lunch. The white decor with marine blue trim and the clean angular lines of the Nordic furniture echoed the maritime name. The well-spaced tables were set with heavy silver cutlery, dense linen napery and sparkling glasses. The posies of tiny white roses and delicate gypsophilia on the tables were repeated in cascading arrangements between the wide windows. Subtle cello music played in the background and the appetising aroma of warm bread and delicious cooking spiced the air. Yves sat in the portico his blood warm at the thought of Zoe's arrival. She respected his time and was never late. Yves found that refreshing.

'Hello, Zoe,' Yves' eyes shone. 'You look sensational.'

Zoe had dressed to please him. Her soft cream dress was a mastery of delicate folds and hand-crafted silver buttons, which formed a tracery to draw eyes all around the perfection of her body. Her sleek dark blonde hair epitomised the classic taste he admired. Her ivory cheeks with a sprinkle of tiny freckles across the bridge of her slender nose highlighted her youth. Her dark eyes glowed warm and focussed intently on him. For years he had sought the quickening pulse that the presence of a beautiful woman brought. He could taste the satisfaction her conquest would bring.

'Hello Yves,' said Zoe as her welcome kiss enfolded him in a whisper of expensive perfume.

'I love the flowers,' she said glancing around. As they were seated at a quiet table in a bay window overlooking the garden, Zoe thought to herself, Monica would appreciate these wonderful wide chairs. The thought made her smile as the waiter offered the daily card.

'Hand-made paper, no less. I imagine each of these dishes is delectable. 'Yves, you are a master.' He beamed.

'I think all restaurants should only offer a few special dishes each day. If they specialised in food which was in season, we would savour it more,' she said.

'Then I think we must end with the berries which are most delicious here in the English summer, but there are so many choices before that,' Yves replied appreciating the sentiment.

'What would you recommend?' she asked the waiter with a winning smile. Yves noted the effect Zoe had on the waiter while feeling a powerful combination of lust, pride and ownership. Yves focussed on selecting the wine as Zoe considered the main course. 'I'm starving and there are some wonderful choices. Can we make this a special long lunch?' Zoe asked with promise in her eyes.

'Mm. The wines are excellent. Perhaps a champagne to begin, a crisp pinot gris with the asparagus, scallops and then a boujolais, I think,' Yves said, knowing that, like him, Zoe had a fine palate and enjoyed matching perfect wines to great food.

'Perhaps a Hill of Grace for the red, Zoe interjected, it comes from near my home and I can recommend it without reservation,' she offered. Yves demurred. She always surprises me, he thought. But, already I trust her excellent taste.

'Yes. It is always delightful to try something new,' he replied.

'Only new for you Yves,' Zoe said. 'I always hope to surprise you.'

The champagne arrived draped in white linen and nestled in a large silver ice bucket. The crystal flutes were perfectly chilled, and the waiter filled the angled glasses, respectful of the delicate streams of bubbles, which captured the light.

'You belong in settings like this,' Yves began.

'Cheers,' said Zoe keeping intense eye contact.

'To us,' Yves responded.

'This is delicious. I can taste traces of honey, crisp biscuit and delicate fruits,' Zoe responded trying to hide her nerves, as she sipped more vigorously than usual.

As the asparagus arrived, the pale green spears glistened with hollandaise and were garnished with fine crumbs of crisp prosciutto. Deep down, Zoe wondered how she was going to eat. She knew that their success depended on her performance. She cast her mind back to the portrait and studied him with her artist's eye. Looking across the table at Yves, she was again reminded of a snake, exquisite, smooth, compelling, made more exciting the by the frisson of danger.

Yves was also intoxicated. His rich dark chocolate eyes drew her and tempted her with the hunger of desire, which every woman seeks.

Breaking the spell, Zoe took her mobile out of her bag and Yves' eyes showed a flash of annoyance. Then she turned it off.

'This is the perfect setting for a marvellous lunch, and I think you and I have important things to discuss,' she said. 'It would be a pity if we were interrupted,' and his heart leapt. 'Perhaps, you might do the same.' Yves agreed and reached into his pocket.

'You have my full attention Zoe,' he said as he looked across the rim of his glass.

In the world outside Regatta's, Richard did his part. Yesterday his share-trading group had swung into action and this morning the buying and selling was vigorous. All shareholders benefitted from the rise in Alston's share price on the back of Mandy's positive article last week. Today, they planned that the timing of the negative media releases and the selling by the investor group should create a large enough wave to tip Alston shares into free fall.

Richard needed to hold his nerve. He watched the clock. The minutes flicked over with agonising slowness. Mandy's dynamite article would be issued just before one. Time crawled as his heart raced. The share price needed to crash. Then, and only then, he would tell Zoe that the critical time had passed. Then she could then challenge Yves.

By the time Yves and Zoe had finished the champagne, Yves was feeling confident.

'This asparagus is delicious. I love the contrast of the earthy tips with the rich egg of the hollandaise,' Zoe enthused. She was stalling for time and terrified of looking anxious. She gathered her thoughts and her patter, confident that her sex appeal would distract Yves. Food was always a safe and fertile topic of conversation. By the time the main course arrived their faces were flushed with the exquisite wine, the delicious food and the anticipation of surprises to come. She agreed to the trip to Como, they planned a future.

Chapter 49

Revenge

As Richard watched the flickering screens at his stockbroker's office, Mandy called.

'The article's out. It's being picked up for the news bulletins for one o'clock,' she said unable to keep the excitement from her voice.

'Good work Mandy. Is it syndicated?'

'Of course. When will you learn to trust me, Richard?'

Richard was uncertain how long the information would take to spread. Everyone was on edge. Richard sold enough Alston shares and other stocks yesterday to ward off any suspicion of insider trading. Then he sold another parcel. Ensconced in his stockbroker's office, he heard the BBC promote the story in anticipation of the 1pm news. Mandy had obviously done a great job.

"*Secret Research on Aging Backfires*" led the news. Richard monitored the lightning-fast response. The negative African results rippled through the bank of TV monitors in his share broker's office. The news spread like wildfire and ricocheted around all the media forms. By 2pm, all hell had broken loose on the stock exchange. The selling began in earnest and the share price plummeted.

At Alston headquarters the PR team were caught by surprise. After the positive media attention, the week before, they scrabbled to meet the demands for additional information and were focussed on accelerating the plans for product distribution. Hit head on by this negative release the team was stunned. The detail and authority of the release was way outside their paltry preparations. The team sent frantic messages to Yves, and when they failed to rouse him from the oasis of his private lunch, they sent for the research team. Nathan and Cheng arrived at the company media office flustered but not alarmed.

'Of course there were a few negative results,' Nathan said trying to be calm. 'But only in response to the earliest formulations. We've always reported them,' he said becoming increasingly defensive in response to their panic. The PR team was in meltdown, frightened by their lack of preparation and scrabbling to shape a response.

'Why didn't we know about negative African results? What else don't we know?' the marketing team leader shouted on the verge of panic. Nathan offered them access to all the results – which of course they could not digest in the time available.

At the Stock exchange, brokers received frantic orders to sell Alston stock. Uncertainty and misinformation mushroomed, and the panic escalated.

In the calm of Regatta's, oblivious to the chaos, Yves enjoyed his lunch, the delightful conversation and the anticipation of delights to come.

'This pinot gris is perfect with the scallops. It is a beautiful wine for summer days,' Zoe said feeling more and more like an actor in a play. Yves was feeling more confident with every passing moment. At the beginning of lunch, he sensed an excitement in Zoe, and as the time passed and the wine and testosterone surged through his veins he interpreted her animation as a delightful promise of things to come.

'We will need to call it Pinot grigio at Lake Como,' Yves said as he produced the invitation to the Art Show. Zoe shrieked with excitement.

'I shall have to practice my Italian.'

'You are fabulous Yves,' Zoe said looking at Yves with a smile that made his pulse race.

'You were right Zoe, this red is excellent.'

'The grapes are grown near my original home,' Zoe explained. 'Have I told you my mother grew grapes? Unfortunately, she is no longer with us, but she was passionate about the vineyard. I think it was the main thing that gave her pleasure, after my father was no longer with us. I love Langhorne Creek and all it represents.' Yves sought to divert the conversation.

'Perhaps we could enjoy a little time together in Italy before going to Lake Como?' He wanted Zoe, but didn't need the family tree.

Richard had arranged to signal when the time was right. At the stockbrokers' office he was glued to the screens and saw the share price plummet with grim satisfaction. He quit his last parcel. Everyone was on tenterhooks. The shock of Mandy's revelations in the media was reverberating through the press and the share price dived even lower than Richard had hoped. By 2.00pm he received a message to say his buying group had sold all their shares. He decided that the time had arrived for Zoe to stop the charade.

The waiter, obviously entranced with Zoe, had hovered within sight, keen to meet her every need. At 2.10pm the waiter approached their table, conscious of Yves' disapproval, and said, 'Mademoiselle, a message.' The card simply said, 'Project on track, over to you, Richard.'

Chapter 50

The Unkindest Cut

Zoe took a deep breath, and a large gulp of the magnificent red wine. She had played her role well and it was time for her carefully planned assault.

'Yves, we may have more in common than you think,' she said.

'I would like you to cast your memory back to the 1990s. You were in South Australia.'

'Yes, I was a guest consultant in a large contract for a short time,' he said, a frown forming on his wide brow. His heart skipped a beat.

'And perhaps you did a little trading in seafood,' said Zoe, her eyes narrowing.

Yves' blood pressure increased.

'Not really,' Yves countered, his heart beating faster with apprehension.

'I believe you were trading in seafood, lobster specifically. It was valuable even then,' Zoe continued.

As Yves mumbled indecisively, Zoe continued with surgical precision. 'You may remember organising a delivery of lobster with a fisherman out of Robe. Perhaps you could talk about it with me.'

Yves leaned forward and attempted to grasp her hand while gathering his thoughts.

'That's a long time ago and I don't remember much from those days. I have no desire to spoil a beautiful lunch talking old business with you, my beautiful Zoe.' Yves' brain clicked into gear. Just how much did she know about those clumsy days? Surely she could not know anything important. He was disconcerted at this abrupt change in direction during such a promising lunch. He had been thrilled when Zoe agreed with his plan for a luxurious weekend in Italy. 'I would like to cast my mind forward to Lake Como. Perfect wine, gentle weather, an innovative art exhibition, front row seats at La Scala perhaps?' he said keen to drag the conversation into hopeful territory.

Zoe breathed deeply and gathered herself.

'Yves, we need to discuss this first,' she said with a winning smile.

'Zoe, Zoe, you know I want you. Isn't that enough,' he continued.

'No,' she countered, her eyes flashing like cold steel. Zoe watched carefully as puzzlement, then irritation flickered across his face.

Where had she got this information? Why did she care? Frantically he cast his mind back to those far away days. He began to remember, even though this was not what he wanted.

'Perhaps I can help you remember. She opened her bag and passed him a single sheet of paper with a copy of a newspaper article. Yves hadn't been aware of the article in the *HK Straights Times* welcoming the lobster and the new seafood partner to one of the exclusive Chinese restaurants in Kowloon. It was all so long ago. But there it was, with him looking very young and very pleased with himself. Yves smiled.

'Is that me?' he laughed. 'An early interest that I have almost forgotten. Why would you bring up ancient history?'

'You will notice your name,' Zoe continued. 'Not Yves but Guy, pronounced Ghee in French, but in Australian parlance, just a 'guy' who may be like any other man about town, especially in the regional areas where people are taken at face value and trusted.' She watched his face like a hawk. Years of observation were crowded into that analysis, and in that moment, Zoe knew there was doubt, then guilt. 'I have endured years of uncertainty, but now I know. You convinced a fisherman to deliver lobsters on the promise of high prices.'

'Business is business Zoe, you can't get rich without taking risks,' he countered.

'The success of that shipment of seafood, including the lobster, made you a great deal of quick money. You were the one who filled a young country boy's head with wild dreams of quick profits. You were the one who led a good and gentle man astray. You were the one who pocketed the profits, and you were safely out of the country when it all went horribly wrong,' she continued, her voice rising and her eyes blazing.

She waited for a response, which did not come. His silence made her even more furious.

'I don't understand,' he said.

'Don't bother to deny it.' Zoe practically spat across the table. 'I have proof you were in South Australia at the time. Here's the truth,' she growled shaking the photo.

Zoe's voice had been rising, and as she stood, she knocked the table, rattling the crockery and spilling cutlery to the floor. Her raised voice and flushed face drew startled looks from other diners. From an oasis of calm, their restaurant table had become a maelstrom of fury.

'You have used people, stolen from them, defrauded them and profited from them all your life' she continued without mercy. 'I've seen a great deal of evidence detailing your dirty dealings. Well now it is your turn Yves, or should I say Guy. They say revenge is a dish best served cold – and over the next days, I hope you remember every one of those people whose hopes you ground into the dust. I hope your losses remind you of the people who lost money while you profited. I hope you suffer like they and their children have.'

By now everyone in the restaurant had turned and was looking at them with shock and astonishment. The maître d' sidled over as Zoe threw her serviette across the table knocking a plate onto the floor where it fell loud enough for everyone in the restaurant to hear. She looked toward the door. Then she turned, and in a voice loud enough for all to hear, shouted,

'Today is payment for your actions. Remember this well. That fisherman, that good man you used and abused was my father. Your actions stole him from me and killed him.'

Zoe grabbed her bag, tossed her head and stomped through the restaurant door.

Yves was deeply shocked. Here was the only woman he had ever really cared about. She had turned into an avenging virago before his eyes. He signalled toward the maître d' and shrugged his shoulders as he called for the bill.

'Women,' he said with a dismissive wave, trying to regain some semblance of composure. As he hurried from the restaurant, he knew how rare it was for him to be taken completely by surprise. If she had achieved this, what else had she done?

Chapter 51

Media Frenzy

'Taxi', shouted Yves. He raised his arm after he had stumbled through the door and half-run out of the restaurant onto the pavement. Mac was the fisherman's name, a lamb to the slaughter; far too trusting, he thought. I never knew what happened, but I was pleased when Tang reported that the shipment of lobster had been acquired as planned and the profits were even bigger than expected.

But what about Zoe? She was so perfect. He'd wanted her so much. A brilliant plan and a good lunch gone to waste, he thought. Could she be that fisherman's daughter? Have I been conned? I must be losing it. Blinded by beauty, he thought, I've been a fool. The horrible thought that a woman had duped him crossed his mind. Zoe's furious face taunted him.

As Yves waited for the taxi to pull in, his thoughts raced. He started to count his losses – he had hoped for a different future. Defeat hurt. He liked the portrait. It had been fun and he looked great. A few lunches had been wasted. Now he had some redundant gifts – but they could be recycled. He'd be more careful next time. But there had been genuine fury in Zoe. He wondered what to expect next. He didn't have long to wait. Harry had removed the block on Yves' phone and as he turned his mobile back on, messages and mail flooded in. There were missed calls and text messages from the public relations team, the company, his stockbroker, and members of the Board. To maximize the value from his new public profile and to keep control, he'd nominated himself as the media contact. Now a frenzy of reporters demanded information. What on earth is happening? He wondered.

'Alston Pharmaceuticals, and fast,' he growled as he handed the taxi driver an address.

He skimmed through the PR team's message about the media articles. He tried to get a grip on his tearing thoughts and to understand how this disaster had occurred. Who'd leaked the information? Without any analysis, he was flying blind. As he punched reply on his phone, he felt sick with apprehension. Was Zoe acting alone? Had she orchestrated this? God – the share price of his beloved stocks would fall. His world would crash around him.

'What's happening?' he asked as soon as Justin from the PR team picked up the phone. The taxi was crawling in heavy traffic and Yves twitched with agitation. 'Driver I'm in a hurry. Find an alternate route.' Someone was shouting incoherently over the phone.

'Slow down,' he growled into the phone. 'I can't understand you. I will be there in about ten minutes. Get a grip. Make sure the research team is in your office when I arrive. I need a full briefing. And monitor all the media. I need to see everything. You PR people had better start earning your money.'

Vulnerability raised his blood pressure and his hands twitched. He hated not knowing what was going on. He arrived at the company offices to find people running around in panic. He raced down to the media team's office and arrived just as the afternoon news began.

'*Anti-aging Drug Causes Deformities*' led the bulletin. The headline unnerved them all. It was on several channels and the radio. Yves was stunned for the second time that day. His eyes widened as he started to consider the impact on all his plans.

'What negative results?' he shouted at the research team who stood there looking bemused.

'Well, there have been a couple,' Nathan said with some puzzlement. 'We have always reported them.' Yves was stunned. How could he have missed negative results?

'Who did this report? Where has it gone? Where did it come from?' he shouted.

Yves nurtured his health and valued his good looks. Surely he thought, the treatment was only cosmetic. It may work or it may not, but I'd never have taken a drug with any negative effects. He was enjoying the positive effects. There was no doubt that it worked for many people, he had seen the results. It was working for him. His mind raced.

'How extensive are the problems?' he said with dangerous calm to the research team.

Nathan and the research team looked puzzled that everyone was so angry. They had always sent detailed briefings to Yves. The negative results were few, but dramatic. Yves looked hard at the photographs of faces of the victims in the report that Nathan handed over. He cringed with horror.

'At first the drug worked as expected but the problem was that it continued to act. Skin got thicker and thicker and as the deposits of subcutaneous fat increased it caused distortion of the subjects' faces. Just like a bad case of the mumps. There were less than two per cent side effects in the African trials. True, the disfigurement was severe. We attempted to reverse the effects but it hasn't worked. Fortunately, we isolated the artefact responsible for the problem in the first African serum and have controlled the problem in later batches.' Nathan went on and on.

Around the research team's dispassionate report, the PR team was gathering the media reports. Some were generating drafts of proposed responses. People were running, phones glued to ears. Sheets poured off the printer. Everyone was sweating.

Yves was horrified. The negative effects resulted from the same batch that he had been taking unbeknown to the research team. Yves slumped into a chair in blind panic. Could that happen to him? How disgusting.

But, for the moment, he had more pressing problems to deal with.

He needed to hunt down who had leaked to the media. But before that he needed to restore confidence in the share market and preserve his wealth. He would need to take charge and respond to the media. He would present the best arguments, all the facts and figures and be utterly persuasive. This was his chance to get back in control – to reverse the tide.

'We'll issue a statement immediately. We need to show we are in control. Tell them the problem has been rectified. Set up interviews with all the media immediately. I'll start with the radio, then tomorrow all the morning breakfast shows and the news. We need to contain this,' he ordered. 'Prepare a full briefing. I need facts, figures, and graphics. And, I need ideas to counter every line of questioning which has been raised today. Get moving. We meet again in one hour. I expect results.'

PR and research teams bustled out of the room, focused on controlling the disaster, as a stream of texts pinged through. His stockbroker. Yves face turned ashen. The share price had plummeted and was falling fast. It was too late to sell without crystallising his losses. Millions down the drain.

Zoe's angry face kept flashing before him. So much damage. He could taste the ashes of defeat on his tongue. Yves found it impossible to imagine that she was that fisherman's daughter. Yves never knew what happened to that bloke anyway. He had left that deal long, long ago. But how did Zoe find out? If she knew about that, what else did she know? Questions, relentless and cold as a blizzard, flew through his head.

Across the bottom of a TV monitor in the pressroom, he saw the stock market prices just as the market closed. No wonder the stock market was in uproar. He'd lost millions. Get a grip he thought. He steeled himself. He would bluff this way through, the stock market would recover and he would recoup at least some of his financial losses, even if he had lost Zoe. Nothing was ever achieved by panic.

Adriana had called. He thought she might be concerned but she was oblivious to his problems and left a message to say she wanted to go on safari. Africa was the last place on earth he wanted to go. She felt like a millstone around his neck.

Yves did calming interviews then worked through the night, reading the volumes of material the team provided. Several times he called Nathan to get clarification when he did not understand. He leafed through a sheaf of persuasive scripts prepared by the PR team. Was he being set-up? Perhaps one of them was the mole.

He decided the underlying message would stress that the results were good and while the few bad responses had been worrying, the problem had been fixed.

Yves looked with horror on the distorted faces of those who had reacted negatively to the treatment. The ill effects took three months to manifest. With a sickening lurch he realized that he had been taking the drug for just on three months. The results showed that the negative responses were restricted to facial disfigurement. It caused some dis-comfort but there was no loss of general health. No reversal had been identified, even after the treatment stopped. The people exhibiting these side effects would endure the rest of their lives being ugly and have to suffer the revulsion of others. It would be unspeakable. He would talk to Nathan tomorrow about the problems. He'd already stopped taking the pills, so surely there wouldn't be a problem.

By the morning, Yves had regained his confidence. He took a long shower and had a hard look in the mirror. Well of course he didn't look his best. It had been a horrible evening and a long night, but he would prevail. He prepared his words and dressed with extra care for the TV interviews. He would be calm, well informed, in charge. He would not lose. He even had prepared words about scaremongering by the media.

He was always one of the lucky ones. He had marshalled his arguments and prepared answers for all the angles. He decided to reveal that he had been one of the first adopters if things got heated. Then showing that he was fine would be reassuring. He would steady the panic and explain how the company was responsible and always overcame problems.

Chapter 52

Celebrations at The Shipp

Richard, Monica, George and Zoe met at *The Ship Inn* for Saturday lunch. They wanted to celebrate. The past few days had been exhausting and they looked forward to debriefing and winding down. The day was cool, grey and thick with the promise of rain, but *The Ship* was warm and welcoming. Zoe and Monica arrived first and sat by the cosy fire while staff prepared a table. It was an ideal place to relax, enjoy a drink and watch the news together as they dissected and savoured yesterday's events.

They had shared many evenings, some happy, some sad, but all companionable between these welcoming walls. Today, each person had an individual and collective victory to celebrate. While they had been confident of some success, all their plans had aligned, and the outcome was better than they dared to hope. Zoe took the lead and ordered. Monica was even louder than usual as George joined them by the fire.

'Australian I think. It's our day to celebrate. Arras please. You could have a bigger list Tom. There are some brilliant sparkling wines available these days. Even some innovative reds, like a sparkling duriff. I'll bring some suggestions next time I visit,' she said to the publican. 'Over here Richard,' Zoe called as he ducked under the low lintel.

'What a great day. Stunning result. A champagne outcome,' smiled Richard as he settled next to George on the long settee. The friends sat beaming around the solid table that had witnessed centuries of celebrations.

'To our success and Yves' demise,' said Zoe as they clinked glasses.

'Have you thought about acting for your next career Zoe? I think your lunch with Yves must have been an award-winning performance,' said George.

'Remember for artists, any publicity is good publicity,' offered Richard.

Zoe, famous painter of the formerly rich and now notorious Guy Yves Montreau d' Ville, will gain valuable publicity from that encounter,' said George with a flourish.

'I think it was one of my finer moments,' Zoe admitted. 'I'll take all the positives I can get.'

'The stock market has been kind to me this week. Zoe, I'm commissioning a series of paintings on whatever topic you choose,' Richard announced. 'And your agent has already negotiated a handsome fee,' Richard winked at George.

Zoe was delighted. It would be good to let her creativity rip without having to worry about paying the rent.

'Very well, I might be interested; depending on what other handsome offers I receive. I'll probably be in huge demand. And I'm warning you I might choose birds. I've gone off portraits for the moment,' Zoe said.

'And Monica, your share trading over the past 48 hours has been inspired. You made some wise decisions and they've delivered strong profits. Perhaps you might invest in some bonds. I hear there was unusual volatility in pharmaceutical shares yesterday. You were wise to quit them when you did,' Richard said, cool and calm with a wide smile. Monica shrieked and leant across the low table to hug him.

'And to complete the trifecta, George, I do believe you have chosen some excellent, although expensive paintings from your gallery for me,' Richard continued as he extricated himself from Monica's vigorous embrace.

George was delighted. He always appreciated good customers and he recognised that Richard was keen to share the bounty of his share trading with the team in a way that would not attract tax scrutiny.

'I am always happy to assist genuine collectors,' George said tongue in cheek while making a mental list of his most expensive and difficult to move works.

A shadow passed across Zoe's face.

'I was hoping against any sort of logical hope, there might be a happy ending to my quest to find Dad. I'd convinced myself that he was the victim of foul play. Now I can take some comfort that we have avenged him. But I also learned a great deal about myself in this process. Thank you all for helping me grow stronger and more confident. It's good to have some sort of closure,' she said with sadness in her eyes.

'On a positive note, I've decided to make a memorial for my father. Then I can celebrate him, close the chapter of uncertainty that shrouded his departure, and reshape my life around the strength I have developed through this journey. Thank you all,' she said, raising her glass in a toast to her friends.

'You could do both,' George said, ever the diplomat. 'Perhaps you could dedicate a series of bird paintings to the memory of your father. He liked birds I think.'

'True. I also think he would love this wine. Maybe I should combine both things and paint a splendid series of bird inspired wine labels,' Zoe mused.

So Richard, what's your final estimate of Yves' losses?' George asked, wanting the air of celebration to return.

'Well, at the close of trading yesterday he would have lost up to seventy million in share value alone. I don't know the full extent of his shareholdings and options but such a loss would hurt even the richest people. Through Harry we know that for the past few months, Yves invested thousands each week in Alston. He sold virtually all his stocks in other companies to achieve that. Over the past few years, he's withdrawn from many of his other enterprises to concentrate on pharmaceuticals. Buying a single stock is always risky and, like many wealthy people he was not as well off as he would like everyone to believe.' Richard refilled their glasses and continued, 'Let me summarise by saying that I don't think Yves will be drinking champagne today.'

'We've also parcelled up the best evidence. Stan will try to mount a prosecution. I suspect Yves will find even an investigation distasteful,' said Monica.

'He's been convincing on the media this morning. I hope he can't turn this around,' said Zoe.

At noon the news began. They crowded in front of the television to see if there was a report about Alston. Monica hooted with delight as the reporter headlined the bulletin with 'We have dramatic breaking news on the Alston Anti-Aging Drug Scandal.' As they craned forward and turned up the volume, the quartet catcalled and jeered when they heard that Yves would be interviewed. They hoped to see him squirm.

In his neat grey suit and non-aggressive pink tie Yves looked suave, sympathetic and in control.

'Initially we were excited about the benefits the drug offered and took the fastest path to bringing it to market. In retrospect we may have chosen a different path but our testing in Africa facilitated the process and we are excited about the good results,' Yves said with confidence. Questions were fired fast as lights flashed. 'Yes, yes, there were some initial difficulties, but this is an exciting development,' he said calmly and with confidence.

'And the distortions? What will happen to those people?' asked an angry reporter. Other indignant reporters hurled questions and the brightness of the lights made Yves temperature soar.

'Hmmm, it is clear there were problems with one of the first er.. formulas, I er ..' Yves mumbled, running his finger around his collar. Ghosts of the past rose hot and acrid like bile from the pit of his stomach.

'God, he looks terrible,' Zoe said. 'Years older than in the restaurant yesterday.'

As the cameras zoomed in like sharks in a feeding frenzy to capture his discomfort, they were amazed to see his face swell and flush darker. Yves saw himself reflected in a screen as his face swelled and distorted. The battery of flashes increased.

Yves struggled to his feet, and fled from the room, away from the cameras. The reporter looked puzzled and, deprived of her subject, continued the commentary.

'We anticipate a further announcement from the stock exchange on Monday.'

At the pub, the noisy quartet was unaware that Harry had sidled into the pub and had been watching behind them. As they sat back in their seats and looked puzzled, Harry pulled up a chair to join them.

'Hi,' he said nodding to Richard. 'Yves has been taking the African drug,' he announced to the team without preamble. 'Somehow he didn't see the briefing about the negative results, and decided to help himself to some serum,' Harry said, with a half-smile.

A stunned look passed over Richard's face. Harry continued talking. 'It is my sister Annette you see. She suffered for years from one of Alston's drugs, so I had more than the usual interest in Richard's research this time. Yves has lost a load of money thanks to you, but over the next few days he will also lose his good looks because of decisions he made. I don't think he will be conning too many people again,' said Harry in the longest speech he may have made in his life.

Surprising them all, Harry ordered a beer. He sat down at the table and a shy smile crept out of hiding, transforming his little foxy face with joy. It had been a heady few days. First the plan, then its delivery, all followed by the drama on the stock exchange.

'Let me get this clear,' Richard said. 'Yves looked strange on television because he has been taking his own drug and this will cause disfigurement?'

'Yes,' said Harry delighting in their shocked expressions.

'That may be the unkindest cut of them all,' said Zoe. 'Yves nurtured his good looks. They were central to his ability to charm, convince and persuade people. If he becomes disfigured, his confidence will be destroyed.' Harry just kept smiling.

'That's amazing Harry, tell all,' Richard insisted.

'Yves encouraged shortcuts with the research and pressured people to get products on the market before they were cleared. Now he is suffering some of the side effects he thought irrelevant in other people.'

'I wonder how Yves will like getting a taste of his own medicine,' Monica said.

'Well done Harry,' Zoe said with genuine warmth. 'For everything.'

'Let's remember Yves impatience and self-confidence became his own downfall. He did this to himself,' Richard said. 'Harry just facilitated his decision-making.'

Food arrived; the team drank, talked, laughed and made more and more noise. It was an emotional time. Many hours and bottles of wine later, they had talked themselves empty and drunk themselves silent.

'Time to go home,' said Zoe as she dragged Monica to her feet, and they linked arms for the short walk back to the flat. Lunch had turned to evening and they stepped into the cool night air.

'I think my father would be pleased. We have avenged him. What an amazing conjunction of events. I'm still struggling to believe it worked so well.'

'I wonder how many businesses and women fell victim to Yves persuasion. We know of some, but I suspect there were plenty of romance casualties as well,' mused Zoe. 'I hope my deception hurt Yves in the same way others were hurt from his dishonesty.'

'And who would have thought that Harry was the dark horse here? Our plan to cripple Yves finances worked well. Who could have expected that Harry's information filtering would lead to Yves getting a taste of his own medicine? He's suffered major wounds to heart, his wallet and his future all in one day,' Monica added.

'It couldn't happen to a nastier man,' said Zoe with a sigh. The fresh air cleared their heads and dampened the sense of elation they felt at Yves' demise. There was no doubt Yves deserved his fate. Working together had forged a welcome sense of family between them.

'We combined brilliantly to bring some sort of justice,' Zoe said. 'Perhaps we could form a regular group and call it the Avenging Angels. I've taken my revenge but I'm still sad. Even more than Yves' punishment I wanted my dad back. Damn Yves,' Zoe said. 'He might be heartbroken, poor and disfigured but he's still here, and my father isn't.' She dashed tears from her eyes.

Chapter 53

Back to Earth

After sleeping late, Zoe checked her emails. There were hundreds. Congratulations, offers, and junk mail by the ton. The drama with Yves had left her drained. The pleasure of a plan well executed had evaporated faster than summer mist. Knowing that Yves would lose a fortune and suffer as he had made others suffer felt cold and remote, yet the hole left by her father's disappearance was dark and close. Zoe had been consumed by the plan, but the successful outcome had not healed her wound.

Congratulations from Michael brought a smile. Zoe had warmed to his gentle persistence. He'd sent details of the latest exhibition at the Museum and enough good pictures to make her wish she were there. He looked solid and real – not pin-up material but smart and fun. He talked about his developing plans for a wine tour and she hoped London would be part of it. Memories of the Waterhouse Exhibition warmed her empty heart.

Among the dross, Brad's message took her by surprise. Every three months, he sent a seasonal outlook with his assessment of the vines and the work that was needed. Today's unscheduled mail advised her that he had been approached by a buyer and asked if she was open to offers.

'I feel adrift,' Zoe said to Monica as they sat on the park bench outside Monica's office.

'Hardly surprising,' said Monica. 'We've all been strung out for weeks, and when the quarry is dead, the hounds don't know where to go. I often feel like that when a project ends.'

'I'm glad we did it. At least I know I've done my best. And Yves deserved all he got.'

'So, what's next?' Monica asked.

'I'll be busy with your next businessman story first. Then I've got Richard's offer to think about. But, this morning I got a curved ball from Brad. Someone wants to buy the vineyard.'

'Has that happened before?'

'No. When I was struggling financially, the small income made a big difference, but I've better prospects now. And, my future's here in London. That land has always been a lifeboat for me. Maybe the vineyard's a complication I don't need.'

'What about the memories? Would you really consider selling?'

'I hadn't thought of it in that way, but now there's an offer on the table, I have to consider it. Prices are good and that's not always the case in the wine industry.'

'I'd let it sit for a week or two.'

'Good idea. I don't really feel it's mine to sell. It was destined for a different future.'

'Well Richard's gone sailing, George is in South America with his new man, and who knows what Harry is working on,' said Monica.

'We're on our own. I feel like I need a holiday,' said Zoe.

'I can't even think about a break at the moment,' said Monica. 'I've got a series to finish. The next articles will seem like baby food after Montreau. I never thought I'd say I want a bit less drama in my life.'

A week later, as the friends met for lunch at their old favourite *Ship Inn,* the sun was making a brave show in the winter cold. Zoe was upbeat.

'Guess what I got in the mail today.'

'A pet tiger? Anthrax?' Monica laughed.

'No seriously, the Waterhouse organisers have asked me to open the next exhibition.'

'Great, I told you any publicity was good publicity.'

'I love that competition. But it's a big trip.'

'Have you decided what to do about the vineyard yet?'

'Not really. How can I when I don't really feel it's mine to sell. The offer's good. I've checked the comparisons. I'd feel like I was finally admitting my father's dead.'

'It might be the right time for that Zoe. Why don't you go back, do the Waterhouse and see how you feel? You might find you want to keep a foot in the Langhorne Creek door. Maybe not. Perhaps Brad would be interested in a long-term lease.'

'That's a good thought.'

'It's not for a month, so I'd have enough time to finish the next portrait. It would give me a bit of breathing space.'

'And perhaps Michael might be around?' Monica raised her eyebrows.

'Mm maybe.' Zoe laughed. 'Let's just say he has encouraged me to accept.'

Chapter 54

Homecoming

As Zoe boarded the plane, she recalled the misery of her last flight. She was not running away anymore. *Bastard,* she thought, remembering David's betrayal. I don't care now. Perhaps I should be grateful I was forced to toughen up. She slept, watched *Miss Potter* again, ate too much packaged breakfast, and soon the plane was diving through the early morning mist at Adelaide Airport. Zoe caught a taxi to the city, checked into a city hotel, and rang Michael.

'Well, I'm here,' she said. 'Ready to take up your offer of dinner tonight.'

'Wonderful. It will be good to see you. What do you feel like eating?'

'Vietnamese please. I passed several choices on my ride in from the airport.'

'Not only plenty of choices but the quality is excellent. You'll laugh at the prices compared to London.'

'P'raps, but the pubs are better in London.'

'Maybe. If you stick around a bit longer, I'll show you some good ones here. There are a lot of small craft brewers doing interesting things. But don't buy any in the big liquor chains. Some of them look craft but they're big brands in disguise.'

'If I prepare my speech for tomorrow, will you look over it for me tonight? I'm not used to that sort of thing and don't want to say the wrong thing.'

'Sure.'

'I've got a meeting with Brad to talk about the vineyard later this morning.'

'I'm at work today. Can I meet you at your hotel at 7?'

'Good, plan, see you then.'

Zoe showered and went down to the coffee bar to meet Brad.

'It's a good offer,' he opened. 'I wouldn't have contacted you if I didn't think it was fair.'

'You know more about the current market and I trust you to give me good advice. But it's a conflict for both of us. I really appreciate you doing this for me.' She kissed him on the cheek then looked at him askance. 'It's not your brother or something, is it?'

'No. Wish it was. There's no money in my family. The offer came to me through a broker. I did check it out. Said they couldn't tell me the name of the buyer, but it's Chinese money. They're keener to get to Australia on the business migration program rather than run a vineyard. Don't think there'd be a future for me in that arrangement.'

Zoe was troubled. The offer was generous. Langhorne Creek was proud of its pioneer history and every time land was sold to overseas buyers, it weakened the community. Absentee landlords never had the same commitment to local affairs.

'What will you do?' asked Zoe.

'I've got enough work. We won't starve,' Brad replied.

'I'll come down tomorrow and have a look at the place,' she said. 'I don't want to rush into a decision.'

I'm not responsible for Brad, she thought, but he was very supportive and helped a lot when I was down. It would be callous to cast him aside just when I'm back on track. *Put it on the back burner* for the moment she thought. I don't need to change things. But first I need to focus on my speech tonight.

Zoe had splurged on a new outfit for the opening, several in fact. Too many choices, she thought as the entire contents of her large suit-case were hung, scattered or dropped around the hotel room floor. She tried on one after the other, looked critically in the mirror, then cast each one aside. I must want to make a good impression she thought. I don't remember ever taking this much time to choose a dress.

'You scrub up well,' said Michael with a wry smile as they met in the lobby.

'People in London would think you were being rude,' Zoe said.

His warm eyes shone.

'The silver's good; morning light on eucalyptus bark reflected in a river.'

'I appreciate the compliment. You look OK yourself.' Zoe had for-gotten he was so tall. Probably as tall as my Dad, she thought – even though I don't remember.

'How tall are you?' She asked, her eyes sweeping his lanky frame.

'6 3' he replied. 'Size 11 shoes and my favourite colour is blue. But I'm not telling you any family secrets – yet.' He laughed.

'Well, I don't have any family so I've no secrets to trade,' said Zoe. Another pang, and she wondered. *Am I going to feel like this all my life?*

'My Dad was 6 foot 3, but I seem to remember him being much taller. Everything seems bigger when you're a kid.'

'Are you happy with your speech,' Michael asked they strolled down North Terrace to the Museum.

'I think it's OK, and I've printed it in case I suddenly go blank. I'm not much good at speeches.'

'You'll be fine. Everyone will love you. You know the rules, say it with confidence; loud and strong. Can you believe it's a year since we were here?'

'An odd anniversary then. It's been a jam-packed year.' Zoe said, wondering if she would ever tell Michael about the momentous events in London. She didn't like to reflect on the deception she'd practiced – it wasn't really her style, even if it was in a good cause.

'Great crowd,' Michael said as they arrived. They walked past security, along the carpet toward the entrance. Cameras flashed, people beckoned to friends, the jazz had everyone jiggling.

'Red carpet no less,' said Zoe. 'I feel like royalty.'

'Hello Zoe. Welcome back,' said the Director Steve Zadow, extending his hand and shepherding her through the guests milling around the entrance.

'A couple of quick photos please,' asked the cameraman.

'Thanks for the invitation. I'm delighted to be here. Do you know Michael Elston?' They all turned and smiled for the cameras.

'Yes of course, a welcome patron,' he said. Zoe was surprised; patron meant money. There was much about this man she didn't know.

'We've decided to hold the opening in the foyer this year. There was a clamour for tickets, and if we have it here, the people without tickets can see all the action through the glass windows,' said Steve. 'Please take a quick look around the new works. I'll signal you when the formalities are due to begin.'

'All right for him,' said Zoe. 'That just gives me time to get more nervous.'

'Rubbish,' said Michael. 'You'll be diverted the moment you start looking at the paintings.' He forged a path through the throng and Zoe scurried in his wake knowing he was right. She was keen to see the offerings. Zoe was engrossed in a large canvas depicting a lyrebird as she heard Steve's voice behind her.

'It's time,' he said. 'Please follow me. Have you seen anything you like?'

'Several. It looks even better than last year.'

'Good, maybe you can say that. Don't forget to encourage our guests to buy. We rely on the commissions for next year's prizes.'

Steve surged through the crowd, guests in tow, and in moments the microphone was crackling. The crowd hushed.

Chapter 55

New Openings

Mac saw the ad for The Waterhouse Art and Science Exhibition on the bus shelters along North Terrace on his way to the football at Adelaide Oval. Posters featured a picture of last year's winner, a colourful glass sea creature. Mac's eyes feasted on the two lines at the bottom: Official opening by renowned London artist Zoe MacIntosh June 10 at 7.30pm. Invited guests only. Last year, he had written the letter but never sent it. He decided he needed to get his life in some sort of order. Now this was his chance to see her.

The night of June 10 was sharp with cold. He'd arrived at four to check the details in the Library then sat, sick with apprehension, until closing. He walked the short distance across the garden to the Museum and admired the banners. He watched staff set up trestle tables, polish the glasses, shine door handles and roll out the red carpet. Security staff cordoned off two walkways and posted *Invitation Only* signs around the entrance. By 5.30 p.m., the light was beginning to fade, and the wind rattled dry leaves away from the trees that had abandoned them. Pride and terror coursed through his veins. His resolve faltered. This was an important moment for his daughter, he didn't want to wreck it. It had been so long. This was his only chance. She might return to London tomorrow.

Mac had dressed in neat trousers and a warm jumper with a chunky beanie. For a man who used to fish in cold waters, his years in the tropics had acclimatised him to warmth and he anticipated a long wait in the cold. As the elegantly dressed guests arrived, he knew he couldn't blend in with the crowd. The media looked scruffy, but he didn't have the gift of the gab to bluff his way in. He watched and waited, feeling detached from the cheerful throng.

By six thirty, a large crowd had gathered on the pavement. Security staff inspected each invitation and directed guests along a carpeted pathway to the entrance. It was a bright, festive scene. A small jazz band was playing, and the air was alive with light, music and chatter. Mac positioned himself on the pavement and scanned the arrivals. Then, he saw Zoe behind the shoulder of a tall man already at the entrance. Before he could make a move, Zoe, if it was Zoe, turned and slipped like a silvery garfish, into the building.

Mac snatched a breath. Was it really her? Yes, of course it was. He'd looked at enough pictures on the Internet to be sure. He moved to the window and peered through the glass like a kid outside a lolly shop. Her long hair and silver dress should be easy to spot.

The foyer was full of milling people and silken banners floated from the ceiling. Each wall was crammed with paintings. Permanent display cabinets held delicate sculptures and a few large carvings and clay works stood on plinths. The contrast in temperature between inside and outside fogged the windows. Mac's eyes scanned the guests; silver was a popular colour this year. His heart lurched with every glimpse of dark blonde hair or silver dress, but it was difficult to identify her in the crowded room. Then a bell rang, and all heads swivelled toward the platform raised at one end of the room. The Director called for attention; the crowd quietened as he began his speech.

After the usual welcomes and acknowledgements, Zoe felt embarrassed by the Director's long and flattering introduction. Yes, she was doing well now, but she felt uncomfortable with quite so much fuss. If there was such a thing a prodigal daughter, she was being set up to be one. The crowd, only minutes ago full of laughter and chatter, was silent and the pressure of expectation closed around her like a diving suit as she stepped onto the dais.

'Thank you for your generous welcome, Director. I have discovered in this instant that while I specialise in portrait painting, I would much rather look than be looked at.' The crowd tittered politely. She continued confidently.

'It is a pleasure to be at this event celebrating art and the artists celebrating nature, which is of course the best artist of all.' Talking about things she loved was easy. 'This competition encourages us all to see the world around us with both knowledge and delight. Far from art and science colliding, they reinforce each other.' Then Zoe glanced around the room and saw a hundred faces staring at her with rapt attention. Her eyes widened and her throat constricted. The Director tactfully passed a glass of water. Zoe sipped, swallowed, glanced at her notes then continued to speak. Michael had said, look up toward the back of the room. Lift your head; it stops you mumbling into your notes. If the faces scare you then pick inert objects, a pillar, the corner of the room and look at them as if they matter, it will calm you.

Zoe lifted her chin and looked intently at the window frame. Her speech flowed well. It wasn't a long one, but she wanted to honour the creativity of these wonderful artists and the importance of this competition. As she looked through the fog of the back window, a man, taller than those around him, looked intently at her and slid off his red beanie. She knew that face. Her heart lurched and she couldn't breathe. She studied the shape of his jaw, the eyes, the way his head sat on his shoulders. Every skill she had developed in analysing faces crystallised into that moment. And as his beanie was pulled off, despite the distance between them and the confusion seeded by a wrinkled leathery face, she saw the curling brown locks of the father she would never forget.

Despite streaks of grey, a bolt of recognition shot like an arrow through her chest. She knew. Her face split in the widest possible smile.

Zoe flushed, read her remaining notes as quickly as possible, as her eyes returned each second to the figure standing tight against the glass at the back of the room. The remainder of the formalities dragged in a blur, and the instant the Director said, 'Thank you for your attention, please enjoy the exhibition,' she charged through the crowd and out the door.

Michael, the Director and the security staff all looked surprised as she elbowed through the crowd to stand before the tall man who turned to meet her and stood wringing his beanie between his hands.

'Is it really you? Dad?' she said, as tears filled her eyes.

Mac's face flickered from joy to despair, from a smile to a frown.

'Oh Zoe. Zoe. It's been such a terrible long time.' He half raised his arms in a gesture of welcome, a plea for forgiveness, surrender, despair. He sobbed.

'How can this be,' she cried. 'I've dreamt of this moment for so long.' Zoe moved forward and clutched the forearms of this stranger who was her father.

Michael had followed Zoe out of the door, puzzlement creasing his face.

'Zoe, let's go inside out of the cold,' said Michael.

'No,' said Zoe. 'I need this man all to myself. We've got a lot of catching up to do.'

'I need to explain,' said Mac. Pain etched his face and uncertainty stiffened his shoulders.

'Michael, please convey my apologies to the Director. I've just met my father after twenty years,' Zoe said taking charge with confidence she did not feel.

'Come on Dad, we'll walk over the road to my hotel. Then we'll sit down and talk.'

Zoe grabbed his arm, wrapped it tightly around hers and together they walked into the dark. She leant into his solid frame, grateful for the support as her legs began to buckle and her body shake.

'It's alright Zoe,' Mac said. 'I won't let you fall ever again.' Zoe was suddenly back on the lawn at Langhorne Creek twenty years ago as her father swung her by the arms in wide and dipping circles and she screamed in fear and glee as he held her tight.

Chapter 56

History Unfolds

Mac and Zoe sat close on the broad velvet settee in the foyer of the Strathmore Hotel. Music played, guests mingled, and drinks were served but Zoe and Mac looked only at each other, drinking in every feature, following every flickering emotion.

'I can't believe you're here,' she said, for the sixth time. 'I hoped for this for so long. Then I realised it would never happen.' Zoe held his big work-roughened hands and Mac smiled like a kid whose Christmases had all come at once.

'It really is you. A lot older than I remember.'

'Older and wiser. But it's been tough.'

'Tell me, tell me everything. What happened, where have you been? I want to know right from the beginning.'

'It's a long, sad story Zoe.'

'Yes, but it's got a happy ending. So, I need to know. We've got a lot of years to cover.'

'OK, I'll start. But I want to know about you too. That will be more fun.'

'Not all fun. We've all had our troubles. Come on,' Zoe said. 'Go right back.'

'My intentions were good,' Mac started. 'I always had big ideas. By sixteen, I was desperate to be successful. I'd worked the lobster boats from when I was about 13. It was hard yakka. I could endure the cold winds, heavy pots and long days. I earned good money for a youngster, believed I could manage anything. More brawn than brain my father said. Turns out he was right.'

Zoe's eyes devoured every emotion on his face.

'When I married your mother, I wanted to give her everything. We dreamt about buying land. Then you came along.' Mac smiled. 'I'd grown up with all these stories of my Dad's family being important. They'd arrived rich, been granted land and then bought more. In a series of spectacularly poor decisions, they exchanged good land for more acres in the far north and learned the hard way it was too dry to farm. After the depression my proud grandfather was reduced to working as an itinerant labourer. He was always bitter. I wanted to change that.

Did your mother tell you about them?'

'No. It sounds like tough times,' said Zoe.

'Catherine and I hadn't planned to have children so soon but there was no doubt that you were what we both wanted. Catherine worked in the city at her accounting job as long as she could, but soon found the long drive to Adelaide exhausting. We'd managed to buy the house and land with the help of her parents, Dennis and Lyn. I was fishing to earn extra.

Lobsters were good money, even twenty years ago. There was a thriving trade in legal sales as well and also under the counter sales. I knew I couldn't afford a licence, but good lobster boats had powerful engines – faster than the inspectors. We all got a bit arrogant.

All the blokes would talk about improving their returns by cutting out the middlemen. The prices paid in the restaurants of Hong Kong and China were the stuff of dreams and I wanted that dream. My beautiful Catherine was working her hands to the bone; I had a baby daughter, a hefty mortgage and interest rates were spiralling up. Every time we talked about the debts on the vineyard, I got angry. It's taken me years to learn patience. The licences and paperwork for overseas trade were a nightmare and doing business with the Chinese looked impossible.

Then I met a Frenchman at one of the meetings. He seemed to know the ropes. He'd come to South Australia for some high-flying computer contract, then branched out. He had fingers in a lot of businesses. He asked me out for a drink, and we got on like a house on fire. Drinks led to talks, talks led to drinks and soon we were discussing plans for selling lobster.

I got on well with all the fleet owners. Guy said he'd deal with the buyers. We were all keen to make big profits. It was exciting. We'd meet every couple of weeks and talk about how it would work. We reasoned that the only ones missing out were the Chinese officials and the Australian taxman. That seemed OK and Guy was confident.'

Zoe bit her tongue.

'Just one boat full of lobster and I'd earn enough to get the mortgage under control. The more Guy talked, the easier it seemed. I was impatient and driven to take the risk. That led me to where I am now, old, tired and in disgrace. I so wish I could turn back the clock.'

'So, tell me what happened,' said Zoe.

'I delivered the lobster, they paid me but when I got back to the boat, they'd switched the money. If I couldn't pay the owners for the lobster, I was ruined. So, I jumped off the Aphrodite, swam to the Peking Star and hauled myself on board.'

'What were you thinking?' said Zoe.

'Well, the Chinese boat had to be operating illegally in Australian waters. The ship had my money and my lobsters, and I needed to get them back. It sounds insane, but it seemed the only option at the time.'

'Crazy,' said Zoe.

'I got on-board. Hid. Couldn't get the money but after a few weeks, decided I needed to take my chance in South East Asia rather than be killed or captured when the ship docked in China. One night, near some islands, there was some sort of a tsunami so I went overboard again into one of the big waves. I got washed ashore. I was in pretty bad shape, in both body and mind. Skinny as, sick for a long time but most of all deeply ashamed.'

'Amazing that you survived,' said Zoe. 'Go on.'

'I was befriended by some locals. Half the village where I washed up had died. It took over a year for me to get healthy and learn the language. I still hated myself. Thought of you and Catherine all the time. Took me another couple of years to work out that I was on a remote island off the east coast of Mindanao in the southern Philippines. Even if I wanted to contact someone I couldn't. The people were subsistence fishers and farmers. There were no phones, no roads and I had no money. I lost all hope. Decided that was my fate.

Everyone would believe I was dead. And that's what I felt like. After a while, I helped rebuild the village and cobbled together some form of a life. I started trading to learn the geography. Those villagers are tough. As I recovered, they were kind to me. I was tall, useful when it came to building. So much time passed. I was stuck there. Hopeless. I learned how to fish and tried to forget.

For ten years, I lived with Ni. Her husband and kids had died in the storm too. I could never forget about you. When Ni died, I decided to try to get back to Australia. I went on longer and longer trading journeys. I worked my way across the islands. It was really hard travelling. My height and skin marked me out. Everyone was suspicious. I finally worked my way to the big island – Mindanao where I could work bigger boats. I hoped my language might be useful if the traders got in trouble. It took me two years, but I finally went south to the Solomon Islands. There were plenty of times I thought I'd never make it.'

'Sounds like a novel,' Zoe said. 'What next?'

'I got back into Australia through Darwin. Didn't have any papers. Crewed on a boat with some really dodgy characters – drugs probably but I didn't want to know. They let me hide as they sailed into port.

I was so sure I'd get caught. It was really hard to adjust back to Australian ways. I just couldn't fish and trade anymore. It was so dry compared to the tropics – and cold at night. Then I hitched my way south to Adelaide.'

'Let's get a coffee,' said Zoe. I'm exhausted.

'Me too. Ever since I arrived in South Australia I've been torn. First, I thought I'd be arrested. Called myself MacDonald just in case. Names are important you know.

Zoe smiled.

'Then I worried I'd been declared dead. I felt terrible. Perhaps I should have been. I was sort of home but not. It was awful. I decided to stay anonymous until I knew a bit more.'

'When was that?' Zoe asked.

'Last year, I cut a deal with one of the truck companies. I worked – they promised to help me get a licence. But I needed some ID. I didn't want to say who I was if it meant going to gaol. One of the guys in the shelter showed me how to use the library. I wasn't on the Police wanted list so I could get a copy of my birth certificate and then get a truck licence again.'

'Wow,' Zoe said. She sipped her coffee and ordered whiskey.

'From the old newspapers, I learned you were in London. I wanted to know everything about you. I'd missed so much. Catherine had died. That made me so sad. Then coming out of the library last year, I saw you. I was so stunned. You. My girl in a beautiful green dress. Going into the Museum. You looked just like your mother.'

'It was you I saw last year!' Zoe said. 'I had a fleeting glimpse at someone who reminded me of you. But when I looked, no one was there,' Zoe said.

'Yes. I was so shocked I couldn't cope. I was a mess. I'd only been in Adelaide a few days. I've spent the last year trying to get myself in shape to ask for forgiveness. I wrote the longest and most difficult letter of my life to you but then couldn't send it. When I saw the ad for this year's exhibition, I just wanted to see you and say I'm so sorry.' Mac's eyes filled with tears. 'I know you can't forgive me, but I never stopped loving you.'

Zoe gulped, her eyes brimming. She put her arm across his shoulders.

'We all make bad choices. Some of us are lucky and get away with it. After you disappeared, it was terrible. We missed you so much.'

'Yes, but you've done so well. Look at you, clever girl. Now it's time for you to tell me your story.'

Zoe smiled. 'Well, you remember that bloke called Guy?'

It would be a long night.

Acknowledgements

Sincere thanks to my indefatigable editor Jude Aquilina for constructive criticism and wise counsel. Special thanks to my husband Barry for endless ideas, discussions, and encouragement.

My writing groups, Writers' Café and the discipline of Sand Writers as nurtured by Roger Rees, have morphed my enthusiastic writing into something more professional. Long may they continue.

I acknowledge the privilege of growing up in Australia in this era, especially for the education and opportunities I have been offered which would be unimagined by women in other places and other times. I hope my careers and hard work honour that debt.

About the Author

Heather was born in South Australia and has degrees in science, librarianship, and business. So far, she has enjoyed careers as a science librarian, with Australia's largest research organisation, in politics and as a CEO in government.

She feels connected to the land of Langhorne Creek where she grows fruit, grapes and enjoys fine wine. Extensive travel with eyes wide open and all these experiences enrich her poetry and prose.